THE
Scoundrel
IN HER
Bed

By Lorraine Heath

LORRAINE HEATH

THE Scoundrel IN HER Bed

A SINS FOR ALL SEASONS NOVEL

AVONBOOKS

An Imprint of HarperCollinsPublishers

THE SCOUNDREL IN HER BED. Copyright © 2019 by Jan Nowasky. All rights reserved. Printed in the United States of America. No part of this book may be used or reproduced in any manner whatsoever without written permission except in the case of brief quotations embodied in critical articles and reviews. For information, address HarperCollins Publishers, 195 Broadway, New York, NY 10007.

First Avon Books mass market printing: March 2019
First Avon Books hardcover printing: February 2019

Print Edition ISBN: 978-0-06-289071-9
Digital Edition ISBN: 978-0-06-267603-0

Avon, Avon & logo, and Avon Books & logo are registered trademarks of HarperCollins Publishers in the United States of America and other countries.

HarperCollins is a registered trademark of HarperCollins Publishers in the United States of America and other countries.

FIRST EDITION

19 20 21 22 23   LSC   10 9 8 7 6 5 4 3 2 1

*In loving memory of
my great-niece Carolyn Rae Crutchfield.
Your sweetness brightened the world, and you brought so
much joy to so many. You are deeply missed, precious girl.
With my love always.*

THE
Scoundrel
IN HER
Bed

Prologue

*S*he'd survived.

Breathing heavily, bathed in sweat, after hours of nearly unbearable pain and screaming, the discovery came as somewhat of a surprise. The midwife had warned her that her hips were too narrow for what was to come, terrifying her with the dire possibility of death, and yet the fear, the agony, and the doubts that had plagued her now faded away in direct contrast to the increasing volume of the indignant wails filling her bedchamber. The robust cries were a sign of health and well-being. A gentle smile curled her lips upward as unheralded joy pierced her heart and swept unerringly through her, taking up permanent residence in every nook and cranny of her being. How could a creature so small have such tremendous impact?

"Is it a boy?" she asked, unable to gain a clear view as the midwife quickly swaddled the babe in starched white linen before offering it to her mother, dressed all in mourning black, her face an immutable mask lacking in any emotion whatsoever, very much resembling a ghastly ghoul as she stiffly took the child.

"Mother." She held up her arms imploringly, waving her fingers as a beggar in want of coins might. "Bring it here. Let me see for myself if it's a boy or a girl."

Without even glancing her way, the woman who had brought her into this world spun about smartly—her heels clacking out a steady and foreboding staccato as she headed with purpose for the closed door.

Terror gripped her, threatening to tear her world asunder. Despite her weakened state, she struggled to sit up, to scramble out of the bed, but strong hands, far too many hands, were suddenly there to hold her down as effectively as iron imprisoned the condemned. "Mother, no! Please don't take the babe from me. Please. I'll be a good girl. I'll never sin again. Please! I beg of you! Don't do this!"

A young female servant dutifully opened the door.

Tears stung her eyes, rained down her cheeks. "No! Have mercy! At least let me cradle it once—"

In my arms died on her lips as her mother swept through the doorway like an avenging angel bent on destroying all in her wake, disappearing into the darkened hallway beyond, taking the precious bundle with her. The door closed with a resounding and ominous *snick* that would forever reverberate through her soul. For a few more minutes she fought to free herself, race after her mother, and stop her from doing the unthinkable, from farming the child out to someone who could not possibly love it with all the fervor that she did. But the past several hours had not been kind, leaving her drained, exhausted, and faint.

"There, there, my dear girl," a maid cooed to her. "Calm yourself. Tomorrow all will be as right as rain."

With gut-wrenching sobs racking her body, she sagged down onto the mattress in despair, while all that remained of her young tender heart shattered into tiny shards that would be impossible to ever piece back together.

Chapter 1

*W*ith a shiver, Lady Lavinia Kent brought the hood of her pelisse up over her head. There was a chill in the midnight air that had been lacking on other evenings, and she wasn't altogether convinced it was a result of autumn giving way to winter but had more to do with the possible peril awaiting her. She was a woman with a purpose, had been since August when she'd escaped her aristocratic life to seek something that would bring her more fulfillment than what had previously been mapped out for her without her consult and none of her desires taken into consideration.

Although her current mission brought with it dangers that lurked unseen in shadowy corners, she was beyond being frightened. Rather she was spurred on by a calling she could trace back a decade to a boy on the cusp of manhood she'd met when she'd been but a girl on the threshold of womanhood.

He'd been some unnamed lord's by-blow, considered beneath her in every regard, in spite of his noble—albeit tainted—blood. Although he knew the identity of his father, he never confided that information to her. She still remembered the sadness in his voice when he'd confessed he knew nothing at all about—had no memory of—the woman who'd given birth to him because he'd been immediately taken from her and handed over to a baby farmer. Learning of his experiences had introduced her to a world she hadn't even known existed, a world through which she now traveled, her bare hand tightening around the cold carved wolf's head that decorated the walking stick that was a constant and reassuring companion when she made these late-night sojourns. Through him, she'd learned the truth of baby farming and the horrors that sometimes accompanied the practice. She learned how the women, usually widows, advertised their services. Recently she'd taken to searching out their adverts, writing to them, meeting with them, paying them. Not to take care of a child as her letter initially indicated, but to give the children presently in their keeping over to her. With the blessings of the Sisters of Mercy who sheltered her, she brought the children to their foundling home, regretting she hadn't the means to open her own shelters. Theirs would soon be full, and then what was she to do?

The women with whom she corresponded were only willing to meet at night, in the darkest of alleyways and mews, the latest of hours, when the streets were ominous with the click-clacking of rats' paws, the odd song with words slurred by too much ale, the occasional grunt, the rare screech. And the feeling, always the feeling, of being watched.

The fine hairs on the nape of her neck suddenly stood on end. She abruptly halted and listened. Tightening her hold on the wolf's head, she quickly lifted the walking stick, grabbed it midway with her other hand, and had the rapier partially free of its cleverly disguised scabbard as she swiftly swung around, her eyes scouring the area intently. No one was about save what appeared to be a beggar curled on the stoop of a building across the way. She'd not seen him before because the alcove hid him from view of anyone coming from that direction. He was only visible—and barely—from her current position. She waited, watching, listening, hearing his occasional snuffling snore. Deeming him harmless, she slid the steel back into place and carried on.

She'd been delighted to find the weapon in a pawnshop and equally relieved the pawnbroker had been willing to take the earbobs she'd worn on the day she was to wed in exchange for it. When she was nineteen, she had been tutored in fencing, loved the challenge of it, and become quite skilled. Her brother had only ever engaged her in a duel once. Being a sore loser, he hadn't taken kindly to being bested, although he had confessed to being surprised by her mastery of the sport. But for her, it had always been more than a sport. It had been a way to survive and retain her sanity in a place that catered to madness.

She shook off the unsettling thoughts. All that mattered was the future, moving forward one step at a time. Forgetting what couldn't be forgotten. So she concentrated on her present and her surroundings, aware she must remain ever alert if she was to meet with success during the possible confrontation that awaited her.

Usually revelers were about after finishing their evening at a pub or tavern, but tonight's meeting was occurring a bit later than customary in an area more deserted than that to which she was comfortable. But nothing could deter her from her purpose. It was all she had now, all she wanted. It nurtured, sustained, and gave her cause to crawl out of bed in the morning.

She was nearing the cross streets that had been written in the missive telling her where and when the meeting was to occur. *Carry on to the other side*, she reminded herself, fighting to ignore the sense of foreboding, concentrating instead on following to the letter the words inked in barely decipherable scrawl. *Turn left into the first alleyway you find. Halfway down—*

She stopped where the light from the streetlamp did. To go farther would be to step through a curtain of blackness. Her courage and foolhardiness had limits.

With discreet, barely perceptible movements, she slowly glanced around the narrow confines, hemmed in on two sides by the brick walls of buildings, the windows dark, the rooms beyond probably uninhabited. These assignations usually occurred in desolate areas where no witnesses could observe the transactions.

In the event she was being watched, she fought not to give the impression she was quite suddenly having misgivings regarding this arrangement.

She kept her breathing steady, even though she could feel her palms beginning to sweat and heard the pounding of her own heart. The sisters had warned her more than once that she shouldn't go out alone, but she couldn't accomplish her objectives if she remained hidden away like a frightened child, and she'd spent far too much of the past eight years in hiding, concealing her true wants and desires from not only herself, but from others. She was weary of it. Done with the past. She was starting over, determined to lead her life as she felt it should be led.

It was the very reason that three months earlier she'd left a good man standing at the altar in St. George's. Not that her abandonment of the Duke of Thornley hadn't worked out in his favor as far as she was concerned, because he'd quite recently taken to wife a woman he dearly loved. The last time she'd seen him—secretively and to beg his forgiveness—he'd expounded on the virtues of Gillian Trewlove, and she'd heard in his voice the raw emotion of a man who had well and truly fallen. It hadn't surprised her to learn soon after that he'd taken her to wife. Much better than taking one he couldn't love and who, with time, as he learned the truths about her, he would come to despise, as she so very often despised herself for her past failures and weaknesses.

She heard a scrape, a footstep. Spinning around, she faced a woman of bulk with a hat very much resembling that of a farmer's brought low over her brow, shading a good bit of her face. The *click click click* of additional steps as two more women, one as thin as a matchstick, the other as tall as a tree, entered the alleyway, the three of them hemming her in with only the dark unknown at her back. Her appointment was with only one.

"I'm here to meet with D. B." She was rather pleased she'd managed to keep her voice calm and level.

"Last week ye met with Mags. She were arrested the followin' morn. Word is she's likely to 'ang for the farmin' she done," the bulky one said.

Which meant, in all likelihood, the authorities had somehow managed to already discern that she'd murdered at least one of the children who'd been placed in her care.

"I don't know any Mags." She knew them only by initials. Was Mags the M. K. who'd handed over three little ones to her last week in exchange for the five quid Lavinia offered her? Most farmers were paid in full when the by-blows were dropped off by a parent or someone close to the mother who sought to spare her shame. Oh, a few paid in weekly installments—those who had an interest in the child's welfare—but many simply disbursed the higher one-time fee and walked away expecting—wanting—to never encounter or be bothered with the child again. Since no more money was to be had after that, those infants were often neglected and then perished, buried without ceremony in un-marked graves so no one would suspect those caring for them of nefarious deeds. To many, one babe looked like another. Who bothered to keep tally of the number in a particular household, especially when there was soon another to replace the one lost? "I certainly didn't report her to the authorities. I'm interested only in the babes and their welfare."

"So ye say."

"I'm not one to lie. Am I speaking with D. B.?"

"Even yer small words sound posh. But they ain't gonna save ye. We can't 'ave ye ruinin' our business."

Business. Her stomach roiled with the confirmation these women viewed children as products, produced by women they didn't know, to be sold away to women who had no love for them. "I don't care about you, I don't care what you do." Which wasn't entirely true. She did care; otherwise, she wouldn't be here. "I simply want the children, and I'll pay to take them off your hands."

"We'll take yer coins . . . after we take yer life."

Swiftly she unsheathed the rapier and brandished it so the steel blade reflected off the distant streetlamp and was visible to them. "Stay back."

The bulky woman smiled, revealing dark caverns where teeth should have been. "Ever wielded a sword before, lass? Ever felt the way it slides into skin and muscle, sinkin' deeper and deeper till it 'its bone, the manner in which the quiverin' of the wounded flesh slithers up yer arm as it gives way to steel?"

"Come at me and discover the truth of things." Taking a ready stance, still clutching the wooden scabbard to use as an additional weapon if needed, with the rapier, she sliced a swift X through the air, loving the way the whooshing filled the silence with menace. Although she'd never cut into flesh, she wouldn't hesitate to bring pain to these creatures who fed on the desperation of others. "Only you won't, will you? Because I'm not helpless or vulnerable or afraid. I'm nothing at all like the sort to whom you usually deliver death."

The bulky one looked at her comrades, then unexpectedly rushed forward while they stepped back. She doubted their actions were spurred by a desire for fairness but rather were prompted by spinelessness. She didn't want to deliver a killing blow if it wasn't needed—she wasn't a barbarian after all—so she made an upward swipe across the woman's face where no cloth protected it, cutting into her cheek, knocking off her hat. With a shriek, the noxious trader in misery reeled back, slapped a hand to her wound, and glared. "Come on, gels. We can take 'er if we all strike at once."

"Not without sustaining a few more wounds, I'd wager," a deep voice said from within the blackness that hovered at the edge of the light.

Lavinia stiffened but didn't dare turn around, didn't dare take her eyes off the women before her.

"Who ye be?" the leader asked, narrowing her eyes.

"It doesn't matter. I don't like the odds. And I daresay, the *lady* and I could dispatch the three of you in a thrice. She seems rather skilled."

His emphasis on the word *lady* alerted her that he wasn't using it without purpose, but to refer to her station, to acknowledge the fact she was indeed nobility. His tone also alerted her that he didn't think much of it. How had he discerned who she was? Was he one of the men her brother had hired to find her and escort her home? Something about his voice was familiar, and yet—

"Yer a cocky one," the beefy one said.

"Not without justification. Ask any man who's crossed me. Now then, I have a use for her, so off with you."

The woman sneered. "Then take 'er. Enjoy 'er. But if she continues to put 'er nose where it don't belong, she'll find she ain't got one no more."

As she watched in stunned fascination, the women scattered, neither gracefully nor quietly, unlike the fellow in the shadows who approached on silent feet and relieved her of the rapier as smoothly and easily as she might a spoon from a distracted child.

She swung around. "See—" The remaining words of reprimand died in her suddenly knotted throat as the distant light revealed what shadows had held secret.

As though he were the lord of the underworld, hard and unforgiving, filled with malice, ready to mete out justice, the man stood there decked out in clothing so dark it blended in with the night, the hem of his greatcoat swirling about his calves in the slight breeze that also worked to tangle the strands of his long blond hair, left free as he wore no hat—strands she'd once knotted her fingers around and found joy in so doing.

He was tall, looming. Little wonder they'd run. She remembered how she'd had to stand on the tips of her toes to wind her arms around his neck, how his would come around her and he would lift her with such ease, as though she weighed no more than a billowy cloud in the summer sky. How he had made her believe herself . . . treasured.

She resented it now, the way he had made her feel, that she had ever given him leave to touch her.

While she knew she should be grateful for his arrival, it was his departure from her life—or more specifically, his failure to show—eight years earlier that had her fuming with incensed outrage, shaking with fury, needing to lash out at the injustice of it all, especially the way her long-dead heart at that very moment seemed to come alive with his presence. Damn the thing for being as traitorous as he was.

He tossed the rapier slightly, and she knew he was testing its balance, weight, craftsmanship, and that he'd not find it lacking in any regard. "Not very practical. A sword, knife, pistol—they can all be taken from you, used against you. Better to learn how to wield your fists as weapons."

Oh, the gall of him, speaking to her in the tone one used when addressing a recalcitrant child. "What makes you think I haven't?"

Then she took her tightly balled *fist* and delivered an uppercut blow to that well-defined jaw she'd once peppered with kisses that had him dropping her rapier and reeling back two steps. She was rather certain the punch would have felled any other man, but he was all sinew, muscle, height, and breadth. However, her actions had momentarily stunned him, which provided all the distraction she needed to swiftly snatch up her weapon and close her fingers securely around it. Before he fully recovered, she lunged forward and pressed the tip of the blade between the part of his coat, against the linen of his shirt. She took immense satisfaction in how still he went, how he barely breathed, watching her, waiting. The temptation to skewer him had her fairly trembling with the possibility of gaining retribution against him. He deserved it for proving himself a scoundrel of the first water by stealing her heart and then crushing it beneath his boot heel once he'd gained what he wanted, what she'd willingly surrendered to him because she'd loved him so madly.

Tightening her hold on the weapon, she fought the memories bombarding her, memories of the kind and gentle fellow she'd once known, the one with whom she'd begun falling in love when she was a mere fifteen.

Chapter 2

London
1861
At First Blush

"Send for the slaughterer."

Her father's words had sent a bone-numbing chill through Lavinia, and now she stood near the stall with her forehead pressed to her mare's, the hand of her uninjured arm brushing over Sophie's gorgeous white coat. She'd pleaded with her father not to send for the horrid man who would take Sophie away.

"I'll not keep a horse that throws a lady off its back," he'd said sternly before marching toward the residence.

She'd known it would be fruitless to argue, but still she'd raced after him, trying to explain the truth of what had happened—but he wasn't having it. The horse was a danger, and he'd not risk his only daughter's safety. He would be rid of this one and purchase her another, his tone brooking no further arguments.

It wasn't fair, wasn't fair at all. It hadn't been Sophie's fault. If anyone was to blame it was the Duke of Thornley—known as Thorne to his intimates—for inviting Lavinia to go riding with him along Rotten Row, then inviting her brother as well, paying far more attention to Neville, who was nine years her senior, than to her. At birth, she'd been promised to Thorne, but that didn't mean she didn't require some level of wooing, didn't yearn to be his sole focus. But no, in spite of her presence, the two men had been discussing some new gaming hell that was rumored to be "just the thing" and how they might go in search of it, because in spite of being "just the thing" it was apparently hidden away somewhere.

As always, they were treating her like a child, to be humored, not a girl on the cusp of womanhood, whose body had been changing for some time now in preparation for marriage and childbirth and who had recently acquired a lady's maid. Feeling jealous and petulant, she'd given the usually docile Sophie a stinging slap on the rump with her riding crop, intending to send the horse into a frenzied gallop in order to pretend to have lost control of the beast so her future fiancé would dash after them and rescue her. However, instead of bolting, Sophie had reared up at the abuse and unseated Lavinia, who had then landed hard on her arm, which had landed even harder on a rock. She'd screamed at the pain that had torn through her and then stared stupidly at the shard of white just above her wrist that protruded through her sleeve and the red that was soaking into the lime-colored fabric of her riding habit.

She couldn't remember exactly—being in shock, she supposed—how her brother had lifted her and she had ended up in Thorne's lap as he sat astride his gelding. Holding her close, while urging his horse to canter at a fast clip, he'd escorted her home, leaving Neville to retrieve her mare. In spite of it being the most excruciating journey of her life, she'd welcomed Thorne's arms about her, his nearness. He'd even carried her into the residence, up to her bedchamber, as though her leg and not her arm was broken.

He'd make an exceptional husband, even if he was eleven years her senior, and presently in no rush to marry, apparently. He hadn't officially asked for her hand, but their fathers had signed a contract upon her birth giving Wood's End, a small estate that bordered up against Thorne's much larger one, to the duke upon their marriage. So her future was settled and done, without poetry, flowers, or grand gestures. The entire arrangement was all so dashed boring, lacking in passion, desire, and mad yearning.

Once he'd deposited her on the bed, Thorne had respectfully

taken his leave, turning her care over to the servants who scurried about with words of worry as though she were not long for this world. Although she knew full well a gentleman did not remain in a lady's bedchamber if he was not married to her, she was still so deuced disappointed that he hadn't hovered over her himself. The physician had been sent for, the bone reset—a process that had pained her immensely—and a splint secured about her forearm to prevent the bone from moving again until it was properly healed.

Slightly woozy from the laudanum she'd been given to dilute the pain, she'd made her way to the stable in order to check on Sophie and ensure she was unharmed. She'd arrived just as her father made his proclamation. And now there was no hope for it. Her beautiful Sophie would be led to slaughter.

"I'm sorry, so sorry, sweet girl," she whispered, over and over, with tears welling in her eyes. "I was incredibly stupid, and now you'll pay the price."

If she weren't hampered with a broken arm, she'd saddle Sophie, mount her, and ride away, a fantasy that overlooked the fact she'd never saddled a horse in her life and had no idea how to go about it. The advantage to having servants was that tasks were done, and she didn't have to bother with learning the intricacies regarding how they were done. Except for the slaughtering of horses. Neville, intrigued by the ways in which London rid itself of its numerous aging and ill equines, had visited a slaughter depot. He'd then returned to regale her with the horrors of the slaughter and aftermath. She'd been all of seven, he sixteen, and she'd awoken with nightmares for an entire month. And now a horrible, ugly, hunchbacked man was coming to do the unthinkable to Sophie, and she hadn't the ability to save her.

"M'lady?" Johnny, one of the grooms, said quietly at her back. "The slaughterer's here. We need to retrieve Sophie from her stall."

With anger, frustration, and grief all warring for dominance, she swung around, and her gaze fell on a stranger, no doubt the slaughterer. Only he wasn't hideous and old and looking to have a heart made of stone. He was young. Perhaps half a dozen years older than she, if that. Beneath his brown flat-cap, his dark blond hair curled about the collar of his plain brown jacket. His white shirt and brown waistcoat were clean, but wrinkled, and she suspected his labors prevented them from remaining pristine all day. But it was his brown eyes that drew her, eyes that didn't look to be those of a killer. "How can you do it?" she asked, her voice rough, her throat raw from all the tears that had made their way down it and clogged it. "How can you murder her? She's not old. She's not wicked. She didn't intend to throw me."

"We do what we're paid to do." His voice echoed resignation, as though it wasn't the first time he'd been forced to address the accusations.

"Surely, you can spare her."

He nodded toward her arm. "Did she do that?"

"No, the ground did, when I fell."

"So she tossed you."

"But it wasn't her fault. I goaded her into it. Normally she's a very docile creature."

"She is that," Johnny concurred.

"My father is stubborn. He won't listen." She took a step nearer. "But surely you will see the truth of things. Spare her."

"We risk losing our license if we cheat the customer."

"But you're not cheating my father if he never learns of it. You're cheating death. How marvelous that would be."

"Sorry, m'lady. Now if you'll be so good as to move aside." He made to edge past her.

She balled up her good hand and smacked his shoulder, certain she'd injured herself more than she'd hurt him. He was solid rock, but at least he stopped and looked down on her, lording over her by several inches. Were he to hold her in his strong arms—which she most certainly would not allow—the top of her head would come to rest just beneath his collarbone. "She won't suffer. I've a way with horses, so I can see to that. The end comes quick. She won't even know."

"You're a monster! How can you do this?"

"Have you any idea how many horses are in London? Do you think people want to be stepping over rotten and smelling carcasses everywhere they turn? We provide a much-needed service."

She heard the defensiveness in his tone, which made her feel peevish because she knew the truth of his words, knew something had to be done with the ancient and feeble steeds. "But Sophie is neither rotten, smelly, nor near death."

"You should have thought of that before you goaded her."

His words stung more than her hand did after hitting him. "You're horrid!"

Ignoring her outburst, he strode past her, opened the stall gate, and slipped a noosed rope over Sophie's head and secured it about her neck, affectionately rubbing the area. "Come on, pretty girl."

He led her out. Lavinia rushed forward and wound her arms around her mare's neck. "I'm so sorry, Sophie. So very sorry. I'll never forget you. I'll always love you, sweet girl." Then she looked at the young man. "Please don't let her be frightened."

Sympathy and sorrow wove themselves through his brown eyes. "I'll sing her the sweetest lullaby ever heard."

"She'll like that." After planting a kiss on Sophie's neck, taking one final deep breath of her fragrance, Lavinia stepped back, nearly crying out at the pain tightening her chest.

She watched as he led Sophie toward the wagon with its wooden enclosure, suspecting not all horses were in a position to take themselves where they needed to go, and that traveling in what looked to be a small plain cottage provided them with a bit of dignity. He urged her up the plank and closed the partial door on her. Lavinia's final look at her beloved horse was her rump and the swishing of her tail as she was being carted off to be summarily executed, like one of Henry the Eighth's doomed wives.

As THE WAGON rumbled slowly through the streets toward the slaughter yard, Finn Trewlove shifted his backside over the wooden bench and tightened his hands in frustration on the reins.

It wasn't the first time he'd been called to a posh house to dispose of a horse that appeared perfectly healthy. The nobs didn't like it when a mare tossed off a precious daughter or a gelding took a nip at their valued heir's arse. Still, it irritated the devil out of him when good horseflesh had to be put down for stupid reasons.

But he'd told the lass true. He was paid ten shillings to dispatch the creature to heaven, and if it was discovered he hadn't, his boss could forfeit his license and Finn would lose not only his position but his ability to find employment elsewhere, because who would trust him after not carrying out orders dictated by law? No cheating of the customer was allowed. The taking of a horse that was to be put down was theft. He wasn't going to risk going to prison, no matter how pretty the girl, no matter how green her eyes—the greenest, prettiest he'd ever had the pleasure to look into. Even if they were filled with anger directed at him, when it should have been directed at herself. Silly chit, to hasten a horse's end by goading her and then begging Finn to spare the beast, as though he had a choice in the matter.

He didn't. At the depot, they were expecting the horse and the ten shillings. It would be killed with one swift blow of an axe. Normally he found comfort knowing that the end came swiftly and mercifully.

But the girl, blast her—he could still see the tears glistening in her eyes—made him feel guilty about his current occupation. It paid well, but it wasn't where he planned to spend his entire life. He was one and twenty, had saved a good bit of money, and would soon be moving on to better things. But no amount of moving on was going to stop him from being haunted by the sorrow reflected in those green, green eyes.

THAT NIGHT, NEAR midnight, in the mews outside the Earl of Collinsworth's massive residence, Finn stood with his black burglary bag resting near his feet. In his youth, he'd gotten involved with an unsavory group of lads. He'd been fifteen when his mum had discovered what he was about and had nearly flayed the skin off his backside with her switch—even with his britches still covering the sensitive flesh. She hadn't taken him in when no one else wanted him and kept him alive all those years to see him rotting in prison or dangling from a hangman's noose. To placate her he'd left the trade of burglarizing but kept the tools he'd purchased as well as the skills he'd acquired, never knowing when either or both might come in handy.

He'd been studying the residence for a couple of hours now, striving to determine which bedchamber was hers, but the girl never peered out a window. Based on the glow occasionally coming from between the draperies, he'd been able to narrow the possible windows down to eight, but not knowing the size of the rooms, he couldn't be certain he had the right of it when it came to their number. In a residence as large as this one, some of the chambers were bound to have more than a single window. Hedges lined the walls, but no trees were near enough to the house for him to climb up and take a peek inside.

Hence the tools. He was going to break into the lord's manor.

He'd considered stopping by tomorrow afternoon and asking to talk with the girl about the fate of her horse but had decided he was safer with a clandestine meeting because absolutely no one except the girl could ever know what he'd done. A lord who sent a horse to its doom for tossing his daughter from the saddle might not take too kindly to a commoner asking to speak with said daughter, especially when Finn was hoping their little meeting would result in her traveling with him. The rationale had all made sense when he'd been tossing back beer in his sister's tavern, although he suspected come morning, when a clearer head was to be found, he'd realize he was every manner of fool.

But that was for tomorrow. For now, he wasn't so far into his cups he couldn't sneak stealthily into the house. He'd watched the lights going out one by one until not a speck was visible, so he was rather certain all the inhabitants, including the servants, were finally abed. The larger the residence, the better it was for burglarizing because so much of it was abandoned at night that a thief could easily wander about, lifting goods without ever running into another soul.

Hefting his bag over his shoulder, pulling his cap down low, he crept toward the massive manor that was the sort he planned to live in when he was older, when he'd made something of himself. As much as he hated his current occupation, he loved working with the horses and hoped, with a bit of luck, to own a horse farm someday where he could breed and train the noble beasts. It wasn't a fancy dream, but he'd rather be his own man, work for himself, not have to answer to another. However, dreaming was for another time. At that precise moment he needed to focus on not getting caught.

When he reached the servants' door, he quietly lowered his bag to the ground, opened it, and pulled out a small lantern, enclosed on three sides, with a tiny hole on the fourth that allowed only a minimum of light to escape. After using a match to light the candle within, he held it up to the lock, grateful to see it was one he was quite skilled at unlocking. He had the tools to pry open a window or to cut away glass when prying wouldn't work, but opening a lock was always the better choice, especially in this case. If the unlocked door was discovered, a servant would be taken to task for not securing the home properly, but that was preferable to leaving glaring evidence that someone had indeed entered uninvited. Removing the small satchel containing his picks, he went to work and less than a minute later he was through the door. He left his bag on the stoop because he wouldn't be taking any treasures with him.

Although it was tempting, so damned tempting, to lift a vase here or an ornate box there as he made his way quietly through the residence, holding his lantern aloft to guide him. Now and then the light would shine on some fancy object he knew probably wouldn't be missed. The nobs had so many blasted knickknacks, as though filling their house with useless things would disguise the fact their lives were lacking in some regard. On occasion, after he'd ransacked a residence, no one ever noted the absence of the silver candlesticks, trinkets, or figurines he'd nicked. Coppers had never been sent for. He'd known because he'd taken perverse pleasure in keeping an eye on the house just to see if any frantic activity occurred the following morning. He'd prided himself on getting away with the thievery, had thought eventually he could become the greatest burglar who ever lived—but then his mum had discovered his antics and put a quick stop to them.

If she hadn't, he wouldn't now be creeping through the residence, up the wide swath of stairs. He imagined the earl's daughter descending them in a ball gown of clover green that matched her eyes. He suspected her dance card would be filled within a few minutes of her arriving in the ballroom. He knew all about balls because they were good for a burglar's business, especially when the guests stayed over. More jewelry to rob because it was seldom locked up when people retired late and were too weary to properly see to things. The gang boss had sent him to case out a few balls, then ordered him to rob one of the residences. It had been the most terrifying and exhilarating night of his life. Until now. His heart was thumping hard, not from fear but from anticipation.

At the landing, he turned down a hallway, and when he reached the first door, he paused, pressed his ear to the wood, and listened. Heavy snoring, male snoring. The next door revealed nothing but quiet on the other side. Probably the lady of the manor, but he needed to check. Slowly, ever so slowly, he released the latch and then inch by inch eased open the door. Fancy houses also tended to have silent hinges, the servants keen about keeping them oiled.

He was halfway to the bed when he gained a clear view of the occupant, a lady—her mouth unpleasantly open and folds of skin gathered at her neck—at least as old as his mum. He made a quiet but hasty retreat, closing the door in his wake. Picturing what he now knew of these rooms and the windows through which light had spilled into the darkness, he ignored the next three doors and slowly opened the fourth, knowing immediately he'd found the correct bedchamber, because it smelled of her: flowery but not sickeningly so. Something rare, a scent he'd only ever inhaled once, when he'd walked past her to get to her mare. The fragrance had haunted him ever since, until this moment when he could inhale it and feel a sense of calm.

On feet as light as a cat's, he edged toward the bed, grateful it was summer, and she'd not drawn the heavy draperies around the bedstead. Carefully, he set his lantern on the table beside the bed, turning it just so in order to direct the flickering flame so it illuminated her face. Lost in sleep, she appeared more innocent and kinder than she had when they'd first met, when she'd smacked him with her ineffectual balled fist. Her injured arm was still encased in the splint, would no doubt be for a few weeks if his experience dealing with broken bones was a true indication of how things went. Her hand rested, palm up, on the pillow, her fingers curled. Her other hand was hidden away beneath the blankets. Her hair, a shade reminiscent of the brightest of moons, was plaited, the braid draped over her shoulder, the tail of it curled beneath her small breast, temptingly so.

With a silent curse, he tore his gaze from a spot where it should not be looking and cleared his head of thoughts he shouldn't be thinking. She was a lady, an earl's daughter. It was folly to think there might ever be anything more between them than a casualness brought about because of a need to reassure her. Folding his hand around her slender shoulder, surprised by how dainty it felt, as though it could easily shatter beneath a tighter grip, he shook her. "M'lady?"

Slowly she opened her eyes. They widened. More quickly she opened her mouth. Swiftly, he covered it with his hand before she could cry out. "Shh. I mean you no harm. I bring word of Sophie."

She blinked. Beneath his palm, he felt her mouth relaxing. "Promise not to scream and I'll remove my hand."

She nodded. Cautiously, he lifted his hand slightly, prepared to drop it back into place rapidly if needed.

"You've come to tell me you've killed her," she fairly spat, the sadness in her eyes belying the tartness of her words.

"Not exactly. But she is in heaven, of a sort. I thought you might like to go there yourself." It had cost him a month's wages to have the horse spared, and he wanted to see reflected on her face that it had all been worth it.

Furrowing her brow, she shoved herself into a sitting position and yanked the covers up to her chin. "I don't understand."

"I want to show you something, now, tonight. I have my wagon—"

"You expect me to go with you, a person I don't even know? Someone who sneaks into my bedchamber?"

Fairly certain she was past the point where she might scream, he straightened, disappointed by her stubbornness and reluctance. He hadn't thought this through. Just because he'd felt a connection, had been drawn to the green of her eyes, didn't mean she was intrigued by him in the least. "I just want to show you that she's unharmed."

"Are you striving to trick me?"

"Why would I do that?"

"Because you're a commoner. You might be seeking to take advantage of me. Or, heaven forbid, kidnap me, and then make my father pay you an exorbitant amount in order to get me back."

Nicking a vase was one thing, but nicking a person? Was her opinion of him truly that low? Christ. What the devil was he doing here?

"Never mind. This was a stupid idea." He spun on his heel.

"Wait."

He shouldn't. He'd been a fool to come here, to care what she thought of him, to have a need to show her he wasn't a heartless bastard—just a bastard. He nearly laughed at the final thought. Swinging back around, he wished she didn't look so delectable and earnest, leaning away from the headboard now, leaning toward him.

"Why not come during a normal hour?" she asked.

"Because what I've done has to remain a secret. Are they going to let you come with me? I sincerely doubt it, but even if they do, they won't let you come alone. Chaperones and footmen will be tagging along. If your father catches wind of your horse not being disposed of as he'd paid for, do you think he'll be happy?"

"No, he'll be furious. He'll have your head."

"Precisely. So it has to be now, in the middle of the night. That's when secrets are best made and kept." When there was no one to see.

She hesitated another minute while he stupidly held his breath as though that alone would influence her to make the decision he desired more than anything else. Finally, she gave a quick nod. "Give me a few minutes to ready myself."

"Be quick. I'll be waiting in the hallway, but if I hear anyone moving about, I'll have to make a hasty escape."

"I'll hurry."

Grabbing his lantern, he headed out of the room, closed the door, then leaned against a wall to wait for her. It was madness, total madness, to be so intrigued by her. No good could come of it, and yet he was compelled to see his plans through.

SOPHIE WASN'T DEAD. She could hardly believe it, wanted to see for herself. She was probably a fool to trust someone who had broken into her residence, into her bedchamber, but if he were going to take advantage, he could have done it while she'd been asleep. Could have conked her on the head and made off with her. He was tall, broad, and she'd felt the firmness of his muscles when she'd punched him. He'd have no trouble at all hauling her away.

As she changed quickly into a simple frock that didn't require any assistance from her maid in donning, she felt both a measure of excitement and terror. Never before had she done anything so risky. Not that she hadn't thought about it, but whenever she'd fantasized about going off with a man alone at night, she'd always pictured herself with Thornley—or at least she'd tried to picture herself with him. In truth, in her dreams the man's features had never been very clear, but to imagine her escort being anyone other than the man who would wed her filled her with shame. Guilt pricked at her conscience now, because without a chaperone attending her she would be in the company of a man she'd not marry. But with a great deal of effort, she ignored the nagging doubts. It wasn't as though they were going to get up to no good. He was simply going to prove to her that Sophie was safe.

It wasn't that she didn't believe his words, but she was in the mood for a lark, a bit of adventure. And she was still rather put out with her father, which made her want to do something rebellious, even if he never found out about it. She could sit at the dining table with a cat-that-lapped-up-all-the-cream smile on her face, knowing she had a delicious secret. She'd never had any secrets.

She was the most boring of all her friends, never gleaning any juicy tidbits of gossip to share. She couldn't share tonight's excursion but could wear the very same smile at the balls she'd attend in the future and that would lead people to wonder what sort of mischief she might be up to. It would give her an air of mystique, make her more alluring, perhaps even to the point that Thornley would finally take proper notice of her.

As she opened her door, she realized it didn't hurt that her escort was a handsome devil. He stood there with his lantern in one hand, his cap in the other. His shirt wasn't wrinkled like the one he'd worn that afternoon, and she realized now that when he'd been so close to her earlier in her bedchamber, he hadn't smelled of horses, dirt, and manure. He'd bathed before coming to her, possibly taken a razor to his face. His hair didn't seem quite as long either. Surely a young man who had gone to such bother didn't have any nefarious plans in store for her.

He settled his cap into place. "We need to be very quiet," he whispered.

She nodded her understanding. Then he did a very odd thing indeed. He took her hand, as though by so doing he could transfer his skill at stealth into her. He wore no gloves, but she'd donned black leather ones because a lady did not leave the residence with bare hands exposed. Still, she could feel the warmth from his skin penetrating through the covering to heat hers.

He didn't make a sound. Although she traversed on the tips of her toes, she wasn't quite as accomplished as he at sneaking about, which became evident when they hit the marble staircase. Each of her steps sounded like someone hitting a nail into wood.

After half a dozen clicks, he halted and held the lantern toward her. "Hold this."

She took it, then nearly screeched when he lifted her into his arms. Such strong arms, so powerful. Thornley's holding of her paled in comparison to being cradled by this strapping young man as he hurried down the stairs. The comparison was unfair to Thorne, who had held her as a gentleman would, with a certain amount of distance because it was the proper way to do it, and in their world doing things properly was of the utmost importance.

Once they'd again reached a carpeted hallway, he lowered her feet to the floor, took the lantern from her, grabbed her hand, and led her in a mad dash to the kitchens.

Before she had time to ponder that no servants were about, he opened a door and escorted her outside. After quietly closing the door, he picked up a satchel and headed toward the path that led to the mews.

Glancing over her shoulder, she noted no light coming to life in any windows. They'd done it! They'd made a successful escape. Funny how the realization filled her with such joy that she wanted to leap in the air and kick her heels together, as though she'd accomplished something truly remarkable. She'd never before thought about doing something she shouldn't, and here she was about to make an entire night of it.

In the alleyway was the ugly cart, the one that had taken Sophie from her. After slinging his bag into the back, he blew out the candle in his lantern and placed it inside. Taking her hand again, he led her to the front, placed his hands on her waist, and hefted her with ease onto the hard, wooden bench seat. Then he climbed up the side of the wagon, scrambled over her, took the reins, and urged the pair of horses forward.

"What's your name?" he asked, his voice low and deep in the quiet of the night, calling forth all manner of secrets.

She nearly laughed, only then realizing they'd never been properly introduced. She shouldn't have even spoken to him, much less clambered into a wagon with him. Unexpectedly, she was hit with an unwelcome feeling she wasn't the first girl to do so. "Lady Lavinia."

"Fancy name."

"I'm a fancy lady. What's your name?"

"Finn."

She suspected he was far too complex for so simple a name. "What's your surname?"

"Trewlove."

She furrowed her brow. "I overheard my brother talking with a friend this afternoon about a Trewlove and a gaming hell. Is that yours?"

"My brother's. Aiden."

"He said it's a secret place."

With the occasional streetlamp guiding them, she could make out his shrug.

"It's not exactly a licensed gentlemen's club."

"But if people can't find it—"

"Oh, they find it. It appeals to the swells because it's not quite proper. Makes them feel as though they're bad and mad and living dangerously." He chuckled low. "When they haven't a clue what living dangerously is truly like."

She suspected he knew, suspected he knew very well. She was probably a fool for trusting him, and yet for some reason she'd never felt safer in her life. "Why didn't you kill Sophie?"

He tugged on the brim of his cap, bringing it down lower as though the half-moon in the black velvety sky would blind him. "Dunno. Seemed a waste of good horseflesh. But you can't tell your father, ever. My boss would see me in prison."

"You did it without his permission?"

"Nah, I had his permission, but he'd say I didn't in order to protect his business, his license. Like I told you earlier, if we don't do the job, we get reported. They'd close us down, find someone else more trustworthy."

She studied his profile, limned more by moonlight now than streetlamps, the latter becoming fewer. She didn't want to consider that he might be taking her out of London, out of England entirely. Why wasn't she feeling some unease? What spell had he cast over her? She seldom spoke to servants, much less commoners, and yet here she was, intrigued by a man who'd only recently left boyhood behind. "Why do you do such a cruel thing?"

"I don't see it as cruelty, but mercy to put a beast out of its misery. I have a way with horses, of talking with them, calming them. I send them to horse heaven without them even knowing they're going to take the journey."

"But there are other ways to earn a living."

"Someone has to take on the unpleasant tasks, so folks like you aren't even aware they exist."

She heard a bit of disgust in his voice, knew she might be deserving of it because she was sheltered and protected. If she was honest, she would go so far as to say she was spoiled. Her father had announced at dinner that he'd already managed to purchase another horse for her and it would be delivered by the end of the week. She never went without for long.

"How is your arm?" he asked, the genuine interest in his tone taking her by surprise, and she imagined him whispering to the horses with the same amount of caring.

"It hurts a bit." The jarring of the wagon added to the discomfort, not that she was going to complain to him about it. "I was given a dose of laudanum before retiring. It puts my mind in a fog, no doubt the reason I came out with you tonight."

"You came out with me because you want to see your horse. Did the bone break?"

"Yes, it was ghastly. Pierced the skin. I didn't swoon though. I was quite brave about it." She was rather proud of that fact, even if the truth was that the sight had dulled her senses to the point she'd scarcely been able to believe it was her arm, in spite of the pain throbbing through it reassuring her that it was.

In near total darkness now, he flashed a grin, captured by the moonlight, and she thought it the most magical thing she'd ever seen. The laudanum was having a strange way with her, drawing her toward this young man with his gentle charms. "You're a brave one," he said.

"Not really. I've never been out this late, never been alone with a man, practically a stranger at that. I'm beginning to get a bit anxious that my father is going to find out."

"He won't. I can slip you back into the residence without anyone the wiser."

She thought of his bag, knew the residence had been locked up tight for the night, yet he'd managed to get in. "Are you a thief as well?"

Something she should have thought to ask earlier.

"Once. Until my mum found out. Now I make an honest living." Grinning, he glanced over at her. "It's not as exciting."

"But safer."

"It is that. I'll never end up in prison doing what I do now. As long as you keep our little secret."

"I will. I promise." Besides, his secret was now tied in with one she needed to keep for herself. Although her father had never taken a strap to her as he had her brother, if he found out about tonight's little excursion, he very well might take action that would prevent her from sitting for a week.

"Why'd you goad her?" he asked unexpectedly.

She lifted a shoulder, embarrassed to admit the truth. "Why does any girl do anything unwise? I wanted someone's attention."

"One of your many swains?"

His tone was a bit confusing, as though he was irritated by the notion she might have beaux. For some reason, she was reluctant to confess that Thornley was a suitor, probably because he wasn't really, not yet. Besides, it lessened her guilt about being out and about with this young man if she labeled the duke as merely a friend. "I haven't any admirers. At least not yet. I'm only fifteen. I haven't even had my first Season."

"Fifteen," he muttered beneath his breath. "A child."

That irritated her. "I'm not a child. I'm very nearly fully grown. How old are you?"

"A good deal older than you."

"How much older?"

"I'm one and twenty."

"That's not so old."

"Old enough," he murmured.

He turned the wagon onto a road much narrower than the one they'd been on. Ahead loomed a large building. Across the front, huge white letters that spelled *Trewlove* reflected the moonlight. "What's this?" she asked.

"My brother's brickworks factory."

"Aiden owns a factory *and* a gaming hell?"

The amused grin again. "No. My other brother Mick owns this, fancies himself a builder with plans to take the worst parts of London and make them posh."

"How many brothers have you?"

"Three."

"I can't imagine it. There's only my brother and I. He's nine years older and seldom wants anything to do with me."

"Do you want him to?"

She laughed at his bluntness. "No, not really. When he does find time, he teases me unmercifully."

"It is a law that brothers must tease their sisters."

"Have you sisters?"

"Two."

She assumed his teasing of them wasn't nearly as irritating as Neville's of her. She actually welcomed the occasions when they went months without seeing each other, when he'd either been off at school or was seeing to one of the family's estates in their father's stead, learning all he needed to know in order to be a proper earl when the day came.

"I hope you don't find my saying this offensive, but you don't speak like a laborer." While his diction was far from the haughtiness of an aristocrat, it did reflect a certain amount of education, more than she'd have expected from someone who slaughtered animals for a living.

"That's my sister Gillie's doing. She's obsessed with ensuring none of us sound like we come from the gutter. She firmly believes we have to speak properly if we ever hope to make something of ourselves."

"And what will you make of yourself, Finn Trewlove?"

With a wink, he gave her another flash of a smile. "That remains to be seen, Lady Lavinia."

He brought the wagon to a halt, set the brake, and climbed down. No one seemed to be about as he walked around to her side and held up his arms. She scooted over until he could bracket his large hands on her narrow waist while she placed her small hands on his broad shoulders. Slowly, ever so slowly, as though he were in no hurry, he lifted her down until her feet touched the earth.

For the briefest of moments, he seemed to be studying her, and she wondered if he was ever going to release his hold on her, wasn't certain she wanted him to. No one had ever looked at her as he did—with such intense interest, as though she fascinated him. It was rather thrilling to be the object of such attention. Finally, he dropped his hands and stepped back. "My brother has wagons and horses for hauling the brick. Over here."

She followed him to a large paddock—not a proper stable, although she could see what appeared to be some sort of wooden shelter in the distance. The horses she saw standing around were much bulkier than the ones in her father's stables, but then she supposed they needed the muscles for hauling something as weighty as bricks. Then she spotted the elegant white mare with her silver mane, and her heart leaped with such joy she was surprised it didn't burst through her chest. "Sophie! Here, girl! Here, sweet girl!"

The horse trotted over, and Lavinia petted her, pressing her forehead against Sophie's. "I thought never to see you again. I suppose after tonight that will be true, but at least you've not been taken from me completely. I'll know you're here, frolicking about, having a grand time with your new friends. I'm sorry I treated you poorly, tried to use you to gain another's attention. Oh, sweet girl, I shall forever miss you."

Throwing back her head, Sophie neighed, and Lavinia couldn't help but believe the horse understood every word she'd spoken and was expressing how much she'd miss her mistress. Then the mare scampered away.

With happiness and relief spiraling through her, Lavinia turned to Finn. "Thank you for sparing her."

Then without thought or reasoning, in her gladness, she threw her arms around his neck and kissed him.

Chapter 3

$\mathcal{F}$inn remembered their first kiss as though it had been delivered only minutes before instead of years. It had been as brief as the blink of an eye, and yet he'd felt as though his lips had been branded by hers. He'd been no stranger to kisses, preferring those that went on for ages, slow and sensual, a feast rather than a nibble. Still, the quick brush of her mouth over his had rocked him back on his heels, just as her quick jab to his jaw had done moments earlier.

Apparently, she was no happier to see him than he was to see her. Not that he was going to let on how much it hurt or angered him to be in her presence after all this time.

With that blade positioned perfectly between two ribs, he stood as still as death. There was only meat to be pierced and it would give way easily without bone to provide a barrier to its destination. The steel was vibrating ever so slightly, and he could see the barest of trembling in her hand, wanted to dare her to finish what she'd begun eight years earlier, the complete and utter rending of his heart.

Their breathing was shallow, fraught with tension, as they each took a measure of the other.

He hadn't planned to make his presence known, but neither had he been in a mood to see blood spilled or to wait to intervene until the situation escalated into an altercation that would have required a bit more effort to subdue. Although he'd been tempted to hold off, to see how well she might have defended herself in the face of three opponents. But he'd spoken true. He hadn't liked the odds.

Although she had some power now to her punch that she hadn't when she was younger and had smacked him the day he'd arrived to take away her horse. He wondered who'd taught her to fight— and knew a surge of unwarranted jealousy at the prospect of some faceless man folding his hand over hers and demonstrating how to make a proper fist that was less likely to result in any broken bones.

He wondered if the same person had taught her to wield the rapier. He'd been impressed with her skill and the confident way in which she'd handled the weapon, although being impressed annoyed him as much as the memory of their first kiss. He wasn't going to race through his memories until he remembered their last kiss, the one he'd thought truly made her his—until he'd realized too late that it was a lie, like everything that had passed between them.

"Have you been following me?" she asked, not even attempting to disguise the bitterness in her tone.

He had been, not that he was going to directly admit that to her. He'd learned only six weeks earlier that she was in the area, and it hadn't taken long to find her once he knew to look. Since then, for reasons he'd been unable to explain to himself, he'd been keeping a close watch on her, unaccountably curious regarding her reasons for being in this area of London. If he were honest with himself, he also had an unwarranted desire to ensure no harm came to her. Damn his instincts to protect that had landed him in trouble more than once. "There's a bounty on your head."

"Yes, I've seen the notices posted by someone my brother hired to return me home. Is it your intention to collect on it?"

"Five hundred quid is a lot of blunt."

"I shall fight you tooth and nail the entire way."

He ignored the need to take possession of that mouth that spoke with such determination and authority, making it impossible to doubt the words. There was a fierceness to this woman that hadn't existed in the younger version. Oh, she'd had a temper and had smacked him a time or two, but he suspected she'd now use that blade on him without regret. Strange how she was acting the injured party when she was the one who had tossed him aside. Finn's Folly, his brothers had called her. She'd lived up to the moniker with a betrayal the depths of which he'd have never believed of her.

"I haven't decided what I'm going to do about you. What are you doing here, *Lady Lavinia*?" He'd intended to keep his voice neutral and yet he'd been unable to prevent his last two words from being filled with the disgust he harbored toward her.

Her answer was a digging of the tip of the rapier more pointedly into him. He felt a prick, thought she might have actually drawn blood. Not that he let his surprise show on his face. He moved not a single muscle, at least not visibly, although every part of him tensed, ready to spring into action if need be.

"Stay clear of me," she ordered.

"Or you'll what?"

Another hard press. This time she definitely broke skin.

"Go ahead," he dared. "Run me through."

"Don't think I'm not tempted."

In one swift fluid movement, he brought his arm up, knocked the rapier aside, closed his hand around her wrist, and snagged the other when she brought it forward in defense. He shoved both her arms behind her back, manacled her wrists together with one strong hand, grabbed her shoulder with the other, and jerked her forward until her breasts were pressed to his chest, her head bowing back as far as she could take it.

Bringing her this close had been a hell of a mistake. Her pelisse had flared out on one side and the hardened peak of her nipple poked his chest where his coat had parted with his movements, creating a small expanse where he could feel the warmth of her, triggering memories of when the entire naked length of her had warmed him. His body reacted as though she'd spread herself out over a bed, inviting him to seduce and conquer. He wanted to torment her as she'd tormented him all those many long years ago. "Once you were old enough, neither of us seemed to have any restraint when it came to temptation."

SHE SHOULDN'T HAVE hesitated to take advantage of her earlier position, but it all had been a bluff. She could no more kill him than she could cease to breathe. And not because she'd never killed anyone, but because he was Finn. While he was responsible for so much pain, there was a time when he'd been responsible for her most ultimate joy.

Now she could barely stand to be this near to him, should have despised inhaling the familiar fragrance of him. After what he'd done to her, how could she still take pleasure in the wonderful dark, rich, leathery scent of him?

Questions hovered on the tip of her tongue, questions she'd not give him the satisfaction of asking. What had she done to turn him against her? Why hadn't he come for her as he'd promised? But it no longer mattered why he'd abandoned her. Too much time had passed. She was no longer the girl she'd been. His answers wouldn't change the past, wouldn't change her or her plans for the future. "Release me."

She could see the anger burning low in his eyes, her words a spark to kindling that would soon be ablaze. He somehow managed to snuff out the flames, his grin slow in coming but devastating when it reached completion. Bold, and wicked, teasing, filled with promises of pleasure—if she would but succumb. "I think not. You drew blood. There's a price to be paid for that."

"There's always a price to be paid with you, isn't there?" Eight years ago, they'd made plans to run off together, to leave everything behind—and he hadn't shown. He'd left her languishing, heartsore and devastated, with tears streaming down her face. "I paid it once. I'll not pay it again."

His smile disappeared, his brow furrowed, his eyes narrowed. His hold loosened only a fraction, his hips swayed back slightly, but enough. Unhampered by petticoats as they were no longer a luxury she could afford, she jerked her knee upward with all the force she could muster, felt his soft bollocks giving way to her hard bone, and felled him with one whack. Grunting with pain, gasping for air, he dropped to all fours, his strangling sound giving her a sense of satisfaction that horrified her on one level because she took such pleasure in it.

Snatching up her rapier from where it had fallen, sheathing it back into its scabbard, she was surprised to note her hands had all their feeling. He hadn't been holding her as tightly as she'd thought, hadn't harmed her. Perhaps she'd have taken pity on him now if he hadn't devastated her years ago. "Steer clear of me," she ordered before spinning on her heel and marching toward the entrance to the street.

"Vivi!" he rasped.

She nearly turned back around, nearly went to him to comfort and ensure she hadn't caused any permanent damage. Instead she carried on.

"Don't call me that," she snapped over her shoulder, her voice echoing between the buildings. He'd given her that particular pet name and he alone had ever used it, his quiet, intimate tone always making it sound like a cherished endearment, back when she'd thought she meant everything to him.

Chapter 4

"Once you are presented to the queen," her mother said, "you will find yourself immersed in a whirlwind of a Season. Such wonder, such excitement, such thrills. Ah, to be young again."

Ah, to be in London again, Lavinia thought as their coach, bearing only she and her mother since her father and brother had returned to the city a month earlier, traveled over the rough road, four horses at the helm. She knew she should be anticipating participating in her first Season, but the eagerness that had her fairly bouncing on the plush leather bench had more to do with her impatience to see Sophie—and, if she were honest, her impatience to see Finn as well.

In the two years since he'd carted off her mare, they'd met at the stroke of midnight every Tuesday and he'd taken her to visit with Sophie. She'd become quite adept at not getting caught. She'd learned not to put on her shoes until she was sitting outside on the stoop. She wore the simplest of clothing, no petticoats, so no rustling noises disturbed the quiet when she dashed down the stairs and through the hallways.

Always he was waiting for her, with that horrid old wagon, but she'd even come to appreciate it because it rocked so much that often the movement would cause her to nudge up against him, over and over, as though the groaning wood and creaking bolts wanted them together.

"I daresay, after you've had your coming out, Thornley will press his suit, will officially ask for your hand. You will be married by year's end, my girl."

Any other lady would be on pins and needles waiting for a betrothal she knew was to come, but Lavinia was in no hurry, actually hoped he might not propose this Season. Oh, she liked him well enough and couldn't deny he seemed to grow more handsome with each passing year, and she understood fully he was her unquestioned destiny. It wouldn't do at all for the daughter of an earl to marry a man whose trade was the disposal of horseflesh. Still, that didn't mean that sometimes she didn't dream . . .

Whenever Finn took her to his brother's brickworks factory, he would lead Sophie out of the paddock, place his large hands on either side of Lavinia's waist, and lift her with his strong arms until she was sitting on her mare's back, entwining her fingers into the silver mane. Then he would walk her up the road and back, up and back, and they would talk about his life and hers and how very different they were. She had time for strolls through gardens, could identify all the flowers, while he barely knew the difference between a rose and a carnation. Although in spite of their dissimilarities, they had a good deal in common. They enjoyed reading adventure stories, preferably in exotic locales. They found solace in looking up at the stars. Sometimes after she'd ridden Sophie, she and Finn would stretch out on a blanket and gaze up at the night sky. He knew all the constellations and had pointed them out to her. Her favorite moments were when they had a picnic, but everything was done at night when secrets were best held close.

"We shall, of course, host a ball," her mother said, interrupting her thoughts. "But not for a month or so, I should think. So many will be wanting to show off their daughters, but we've no need to compete with the mad crush."

Two years ago, she hadn't been able to wait to be old enough to attend the balls. Now she merely wished none occurred on Tuesday.

If her mother spoke true, if Thorne was to make good on the contract their fathers had signed, the next few months with Finn would be her last and she wanted to make the most of them.

When they finally arrived at the residence in Mayfair, she didn't bother sending him a missive. He would know she was back in London. Somehow he always knew. She suspected he kept a watch on the house, on her. She probably should have been appalled, but she wasn't. Nothing about him, not even his occupation, appalled her. Not after she'd witnessed the kindness he bestowed on Sophie.

For the next several days, she made morning calls with her mother, received friends for tea, visited various shops, and counted the hours until midnight of Tuesday rolled around. Then, outfitted in her simplest attire, she made her way stealthily down to the servants' entrance, not even in need of a lamp to guide her because during all of her many outings, she'd fairly memorized the path. She knew which planks to avoid because they groaned, which hallways required she walk a narrow path down their center because of protruding tables, chairs, or statuettes. She knew when to hold her arms at her sides in order not to knock vases from their pedestals. She no longer had to worry about passing certain doorways, fearful her brother might catch her as he played billiards or downed more whisky after a late night out with friends. This Season was one of change for him as well. He'd moved into his own lodgings, modest though they were.

She would see less of him, which meant she might see less of Thornley. Although if her mother were correct, he would continue to come by the residence. However, his attention would be directed solely on her, something she should be anticipating with all of her might, instead of finding she rather dreaded it. After years of yearning for his attention, she wouldn't at all mind now if he delayed giving it to her. All of seventeen, she hardly felt ready to take on the responsibility of becoming a duchess and rather hoped he'd feel the same when he looked upon her. That she might be of an age to attend balls but was hardly ready to take on the management of his household.

Having reached the servants' door, she unlocked it, stepped out onto the stoop, and all thoughts of Thornley flew from her mind like dandelion petals caught in a tempest and blown free of their mooring. Finn stood there, and she wished desperately to have a lamp in hand, so she could get a better gander at him. He seemed taller than she remembered, definitely broader, and she didn't want to consider the number of axe swings that might have caused that result.

With tacit agreement, after so very many meetings, neither spoke, and she'd never found the chore so difficult. She wanted to shout out how frightfully glad she was to see him. Instead she dropped down to the top step and began putting on her shoe. He went to one knee beside her and worked to get the other into place. His warm hand closing around her ankle caused her breath to catch. She should object at the informality, the intimacy, but this was Finn, someone who had become her dearest friend, someone with whom she shared secrets and the night and the truth about Sophie. She trusted no one more, knew he wouldn't take advantage, even though her young traitorous heart suddenly wished he might.

She was appalled by the realization. What would Thornley think to know her yearnings had careened toward a commoner, to someone other than him? But the reality was that as much as she had craved his attention, she'd never truly *longed* for him. Based upon the rather neutral friendship they'd developed over the years, she suspected he had yet to view her as a woman to be desired and still considered her a child, not yet capable of returning the unbridled passions a man of his years no doubt experienced. Besides, she very much suspected at this very moment he was showering those passions over a mistress. She was rather certain it was her brother's need to pursue pleasure that had resulted in his gaining his own residence.

A lady, on the other hand, could have passions aplenty but was given neither the freedom nor the opportunity to experience them. And she certainly wasn't given lodgings of her own, so she could do as she pleased. Therefore, Lavinia was not going to feel guilty for sneaking out of her parents' residence in the dead of night or for having a young man she was quite keen to know better being intimately familiar with the shape and feel of her ankle.

Both shoes in place, he stood, reached down, took her bare hand—she'd long ago stopped wearing gloves when seeing him, much preferring the roughness of his palms to the supplest of leather—and pulled her to her feet. Then they were both racing toward the gate and his wagon.

They said not a word until they were well on their way. She no longer found fault with the swaying of the wagon, the way it jostled and made her brush up against him. Although not as much distance separated them now as it had when they'd first met. Now her hip and thigh rested against his.

"I was beginning to think you weren't coming this year." He always spoke calmly, quietly, without irritation, as though she was one of the horses he needed to calm.

"My mother and I went to Paris first, so I could have some proper gowns made for my first Season. Paris is in France, across the Channel—"

"I know where Paris is." His tone was curt, so unlike him.

"I meant no insult. I forget how much you know." He'd told her once that he and his siblings had a membership in a lending library, so he was forever educating himself. Sometimes she wished he could see her family's libraries at the London residence and the estate. Hundreds of books. She wanted him to have the opportunity to read every one of them.

"I wasn't insulted. Just don't see the point in talking about what I already know. Tell me something I don't. What did you do while you were away?"

She sighed with the reality of how absolutely dull her life was. He, and he alone, provided the excitement. "The same as always. A few country parties, a lot of embroidery, some riding." She'd never told him about Thornley or the arrangement their fathers had made. Finn possessed a moral character, and she rather feared if he knew she was promised to someone, he would bring a halt to their clandestine adventures, no matter how innocent they were. Once Thornley asked for her hand, she'd stop seeing Finn, of course. There was no question of that, but for now, where was the harm in their friendship?

Besides, he was only six years older than she compared with Thornley's eleven, and she found him much easier to talk to. He had no expectations of her, didn't look at her knowing a time would come when he would bed her. He didn't treat her as though she were a child, but then he hadn't known her the whole of his life. Thornley had no doubt seen her in nappies. This Season, when he saw her in her Paris gowns, he would realize she'd grown up. She should have been excited by the prospect. Instead she wished Finn would see her in the gowns. Perhaps she'd wear the green silk on one of their outings. She couldn't get into it on her own, however, so she might have to let her maid in on her secrets. Surely, Miriam could be trusted. Although Lavinia knew she should address her lady's maid by her surname, Watkins, the girl was only half a dozen years her senior and they'd become friends of a sort over the years. Miriam had held her as she'd wept when Sophie had been taken away, consoled her when Thorne was too busy for her and made her doubt her appeal, reassured her when her mother's sharp tongue took her to task for not being ladylike enough. Miriam had even confided that she'd fallen for one of the footmen and hadn't objected when he'd given her a kiss beneath the mistletoe last Christmas, so surely she could relate to her young mistress wanting some adventure before she finally settled into married life. She wouldn't confess all the encounters she'd had with Finn but would merely explain the outing to be an innocent lark with someone she knew from long ago. With

Miriam's assistance, she could wear petticoats and have her hair properly styled. Her maid could help her sneak out. She'd probably enjoy that since she'd found glee in kissing a footman when she shouldn't.

"Is that all?" Finn asked.

His words abruptly brought Lavinia from the scheming she'd been doing. "I beg your pardon?"

"Is that all you did these many months you were away?"

"I went on my first fox hunt. I didn't much care for it."

"Your heart is too soft for the killing of animals."

"Yes, I rather think it is." Thornley had been there and had looked disappointed in her when she'd refused to be blooded with the kill. Such an archaic ritual of smearing the prey's blood on an initiate's cheek. "I wanted the fox to get away."

Putting his arm around her shoulders, he gave her a squeeze. "Sorry I asked. Don't think about it."

"What did you do while I was gone?" she asked, striving to throw off the somber thoughts, while her enthusiasm for the answer wasn't feigned. She wanted to know everything he'd done. They didn't write each other while they were separated for fear her parents might get hold of the letters and confront her about their relationship. It was agony going weeks and months without knowing what he was doing.

"Work. Drank. My sister's tavern is doing quite well. If I don't get there early enough I have a hard time finding a chair to sit in. I'd like to take you sometime."

It was a good thing she no longer sat at the very edge of the bench because she'd have fallen off the wagon. For two years, it had only ever been the two of them and Sophie. "What if someone sees us?"

He laughed. "Of course someone is going to see us. But it won't be anyone you know, and the people I know won't know who you are. I've been thinking about it a lot, about how I'd like to do something more with you than this."

She wanted more than this as well, but what could it be? Crossing accidentally at the park would still raise eyebrows and have people asking questions, causing gossip and speculation. She couldn't do anything that would bring embarrassment to her family or Thornley—nothing that would cause him to question the wisdom in following through on the contract. Her father would see her locked in her room for eternity. A ball was out of the question. Perhaps a darkened balcony at the theater . . . as though she would be allowed to attend a performance without a chaperone in tow. "It would be a risk."

"This has been a risk."

She couldn't argue with that. "I don't know, Finn. I'll be so busy this Season with my coming out I'm not certain I'll even be able to meet you every Tuesday."

"Do you want to keep seeing me?" he asked.

"More than anything. You're my dearest friend in all the world."

He chuckled darkly, a sinister sound she'd never before heard emanating from him. She might have even heard him swear beneath his breath. He turned down the road that led to the factory. "I don't want to be your friend, Vivi."

He'd never called her that before. *Vivi.* In retrospect, after that first night, he'd never called her anything at all, not Lady Lavinia or Lavinia or m'lady. But *Vivi* coming off his tongue sounded almost like an endearment. No one had ever shortened her name, had given her any sort of pet name. She liked it, she liked it very much. But the words that had come before it confounded her. "I don't understand, Finn. If you don't want to be my friend, then why have we been doing this? Don't you like me?"

He brought the wagon to a halt, set the brake, looped the reins around its handle so they were out of the way, and twisted around to face her, to cradle her cheek, to stroke his thumb along the corner of her mouth. "I like you far more than is wise for a man in my position."

Abruptly, he released his hold on her and jumped off the

wagon, leaving her wanting for something she couldn't exactly identify. He came around and held his arms up to her. "Come on. Sophie's waiting for you."

Without thought to their earlier row or whatever it had been, she fell into a ritual in which they'd engaged too many times to count, placing her hands on his shoulders while he bracketed her waist, but this time it seemed as though he brought her down much more slowly, as though their eyes were locked while her body tingled. Her breasts came close to skimming over his chest. All she had to do was inhale deeply or push them forward and the nipples that had pearled would have brushed over him. And she imagined it would have felt as tantalizing as his roughened palm sliding over her hand.

Finally, her feet were on firm ground, but she couldn't say the same of her imaginings. She was aware of him in ways she'd never been before. The breadth of his shoulders. She'd noticed them but had never considered how comforting it might be to lay her head in the hollow of one of them. With the nearly full moon, she could see there was a thickness to the stubble on his jaw that hadn't been there before. He was no longer a lad on the cusp of manhood but had stepped over it in a most magnificent way.

Lord, help her. She wanted his hands on more than her waist. She wanted them on places that only her husband should ever have the privilege of touching.

She was grateful, and disappointed, when Sophie's whinny broke the spell and Finn released her. Swinging around and walking toward the paddock, she came up short at the sight of her beloved horse. "She's wearing a saddle."

"You had a birthday while you were away, didn't you?" he asked, coming up to stand beside her, and she could feel his gaze on her.

Turning her face toward him, she smiled, blinking back the tears that stung her eyes. Last year he'd given her a handful of flowers—picked himself from someone's garden, she was rather certain. "It must have cost you a fortune."

"You're seventeen now, too old to be riding her bareback."

"Finn, I'm so deeply touched that I don't know what to say."

He took a step nearer. "I don't want to be your friend," he said in a hushed, rough voice, repeating what he'd told her earlier, but this time there was an urgency to the words, in his tone. "I haven't wanted to be your friend since I met you. But I've waited until you were old enough and now you are."

She furrowed her brow, none of this making sense. "For what?"

"For this."

Tossing aside his flat-cap, he very slowly began lowering his mouth to hers, giving her time to back away, to still his actions with a hand to his broad chest. But instead she merely parted her lips slightly and waited. What was a few more seconds after waiting for two years?

Although until that exact moment, she didn't realize she'd been waiting for this, for him, for him to finally see her as more than a spoiled child who'd made the mistake of abusing her horse and then become petulant because her father wanted to protect her, had become angry at and dismissive of the man who would take the mare away. After taking it away, he'd brought her the gift of its partial return.

She would lose it again when her betrothal was announced in the *Times*, but not tonight, not for weeks yet, perhaps months, maybe even years. As long as nothing was official, she could claim no commitment to another. As long as Thornley didn't look up at her from bended knee, as long as he didn't proclaim her his, there was always a chance he never would and that chance, albeit a slim one, allowed her to consider herself untethered, gave her the permission she needed to simply wait.

With her heart beating erratically as though she'd raced through London streets to get here, with her breath coming shallowly and slowly as though her lungs feared frightening the rest of her with their sudden need for air, she watched him slowly descending the few inches, his blond curls falling across his brow, his dark eyes—a brown she'd only ever once seen in daylight but with a richness to the shade that she would forever remember—intense, holding her captive as easily as the moonbeams that limned him.

Then his lips touched hers and the waiting that seemed to encompass a century suddenly seemed as though it had been no time at all. And the girl she had been suddenly found herself hovering on the cusp of womanhood and toppling off it.

Because what she had expected to be a gentle meeting of the mouths was nothing of the sort. Now that he had reached his destination, it was clear he'd arrived with a purpose, and as he cradled her head between his large hands, roughened by his labors, she could feel two years of yearning quivering through him, insisting, demanding, that the waiting not be in vain. His tongue outlined the rim, before traveling along the seam she'd prepared for him when she'd parted her lips in anticipation of his arrival. The opening gave way as he thrust his tongue inside, not sipping at her mouth, but drinking greedily, their tongues engaged in an ancient dance that sought to claim even as it granted freedom. A thrill shot through her with the knowledge, the evidence, that he desired her this desperately, that he more than wanted her, he needed her.

She recalled how careful he had always been to keep his distance, to not touch her except when necessary to seat her in the wagon or on Sophie. She'd thought his manners were reflecting a deference to her station in Society when compared with his, but as he lowered his hands, gliding them over her back, pressing her more firmly against him, closing his arms around her, she realized he'd been exercising tremendous restraint, had known what awaited them on the other side of his defenses once they were lowered.

He'd been striving to protect her from what he'd desperately wanted to deliver—until she was old enough to want it, accept it, and not be terrified by it. Although it did frighten her to realize that it seemed impossible to ever have enough of this, to know they would only have a short time together, a limited number of kisses, not nearly enough to last a lifetime.

Growling low in his throat, the vibrations in his chest thrumming against her breasts, he held her tighter until it was impossible for any moonlight, any light at all, to pass between their bodies. She wished he wasn't wearing his jacket, considered asking him to take it off so she could experience a more encompassing warmth coming from him. She'd wound her arms around his neck and her fingers toyed with the ends of his silken hair. He smelled of man, not horses, and she knew he'd bathed before coming to her, always bathed before coming to her. His shirt carried the fragrance of fresh starch.

He dragged his mouth from hers, tasting her chin, her throat, and she wished she wore a ball gown that exposed her shoulders, a good bit of décolletage, and the upper swells of her breasts so his lips could travel over that skin as well, marking all of it as his. Even though it could never be, not for more than a brief amount of time.

Breathing as heavily as she, he pressed his forehead to hers. "I thought I would go mad waiting for you to grow up."

A burst of laughter escaped her. "Had I known what awaited me, I'd have grown up more quickly."

He moved back but took her hand as though he still needed the contact. "Come on. I want to see you have a proper ride on Sophie."

HE'D BEEN A fool to kiss her, but he'd felt a need to demonstrate how much he didn't want to be her friend, even though he knew he could never be anything more. No lord was going to give him leave to marry his daughter—not that he was considering marriage, but he certainly wouldn't object to a few more kisses.

The taste of her was still on his tongue as he leaned against the fence, arms crossed over his chest, and watched her trot her mare up and down the road. The saddle had cost him a fortune, but it had been worth it to see the delight mirrored on her face, to know she was pleased with his gift. He'd considered saddling one of the bays in the paddock so he could ride beside her, but the geldings were built for hauling heavy loads, and while they were magnificent in their sturdiness, they weren't made for prancing. He knew everything about all the different types of horses used throughout London. They were each bred for a particular purpose and at one time or another he'd spoken gently to every breed before wrapping a cloth about their heads, covering their eyes, so they wouldn't see what was to come. They all left this earth with as much dignity as he had the power to grant them. After that . . . well, he'd never had much stomach for what came after: the hiding, the slicing off of the meat, the grinding of the bones for fertilizer, and so many other indignities. The one thing he knew for certain was that he'd never have horsehair furniture in his residence.

In the beginning he hadn't put Sophie down because he wanted Vivi to see he wasn't the coldhearted monster she'd claimed him to be. He had wanted to close himself off from the task that awaited him, as he did each time he had to swing the axe. He told himself he was showing mercy, but nothing ever made him feel quite as whole as she did, nothing ever made him believe he was meant for greater things, was capable of moving beyond his humble beginnings to something grander. But Vivi's faith in him did.

Mick believed he could make something of himself, that with wealth and power he could shed the circumstances of his birth and find a place among the aristocracy. Finn had begun to wonder if the same might hold true for him, if with enough work and effort he could forge acceptability—in spite of being a bastard, in spite of knowing who his father was and still being labeled no man's son. That was the lot of those born on the wrong side of the blanket. They weren't even considered persons.

It had never bothered him before Vivi, before the kiss. He never should have taken that liberty, but how could he regret it when it had been the most fulfilling experience in all of his twenty-three years?

Unlike his brothers, he'd never lain with a woman. Once or twice he'd come close, when the urge was so powerful and his body ached for surcease, but always in the back of his mind was the knowledge he could leave behind a bastard, could condemn a woman to a life of shame or a life as his wife, that if she chose the former, he could be responsible for giving a child a life not to be envied—if he even knew about its existence.

His father was an earl who had delivered Aiden to Ettie Trewlove's door one night, not even bothering to hide the crest on his coach. Six weeks later he'd done the same with Finn. His sire was a disgusting man who used women for his own pleasure with no thought to the consequences.

Finn was always aware of the consequences. He knew without doubt if he continued to spend time with Vivi that heartache was in his future because she wouldn't be, not when it came right down to it. She might fancy him now, but a time would come when she'd want more, when she'd realize he didn't fit into her world and she wouldn't be happy in his. But it was difficult to imagine not being with her.

She brought her horse to a halt in front of him and Finn took hold of the bridle.

"Oh, Finn, I've missed so much giving her a proper ride. Even though I have another mare now, Sophie was my first and will always be special. Thank you for the saddle. Thank you for her."

He almost told her he would give her everything if he could, but saw no point in admitting what he couldn't give her. Reaching up, he placed his hands on her waist, such a tiny waist, and lifted her down. Holding her aloft had been his favorite thing to do until he'd kissed her, but it was now eclipsed by something much more powerful between them.

He didn't know where he found the strength to release her after setting her feet on the ground, but he did. The months she was away at the country estate were always the most difficult, the most excruciating—to have no contact with her at all, to not know what she was doing, if she was well and happy. To walk by the London manor every night hoping for a glimpse of light to herald her return—and then to keep vigil until he finally caught a peek at her.

He understood their need for caution, encouraged it. But was growing weary of it.

Taking the halter, he led Sophie back into the paddock, removed the saddle and bridle, and stored them away so they could be used again in a sennight. The time of the year had come when his life would be reduced to waiting out six nights of mediocrity for one of bliss.

When he was done, he placed Vivi back on the wagon and climbed up beside her. With a snap of the reins, he set the horses into motion. "I meant what I said, Vivi. I want more than this."

"I know. I do as well. But my father is a powerful man and he'd not approve of my seeing you. Although I have gotten quite skilled at sneaking out."

"If we were to go to my sister's tavern, you'd have to steal away earlier, perhaps around ten as it closes at midnight."

"I think I could manage that easily enough. My parents retire around that time, around ten. I usually retire at nine. If I were to take my maid into my confidence, she could assist me in leaving undetected." She heaved a heavy sigh. "I'll have to take her into my confidence anyway as I'm not wearing this in public, and I'll require her assistance to wear something proper."

"What's wrong with what you're wearing?"

Her laughter floated on the breeze. "No petticoats for one thing. And it's just a plain frock."

Although he didn't care what she wore, he had to admit to being pleased that she wanted to wear something fancier when going out with him. "Will you do it? Will you let me take you to my sister's tavern next Tuesday?"

"Yes."

He heard a measure of excitement but hesitation in her voice. "We won't get caught," he assured her, even knowing he was tempting fate to prove him wrong.

Chapter 5

$\mathcal{S}$tanding before the cheval glass, Lavinia couldn't be more pleased. She'd chosen a lime frock with a high collar that buttoned up to her chin and long sleeves that buttoned at her wrists. The flounces on the skirt made it a bit more festive than anything else she'd worn around Finn. Her hair, always braided when she was with him, was flowing down her back, the sides plaited and secured at the back of her head with emerald ribbons.

"I know it's not my place to say, but this adventure involving a commoner seems most unwise to me."

"It's only unwise, Miriam, if my parents discover what I'm about." She swung around to face her maid, with her red hair and constellation of freckles, who wasn't many years older than she was. "I'm trusting you to hold your silence on the matter. You're to tell no one, not even the other servants."

"I won't tell anyone, but if something happens, I'll be held to blame."

She squeezed the young woman's arm. "No, you won't. No one will think you knew anything at all about my plans, and I'm certainly not going to betray you. We've become friends of a sort, you and I." Still, Miriam appeared troubled and guilty, in need of more reassurance. "Besides, I've been seeing him for two years with no one the wiser. I've gotten quite skilled at doing what I ought not without getting caught. It's simply that tonight's venture is a bit more complicated." She looked back toward the mirror. "We won't do anything to get discovered." Then she caught Miriam's gaze in the mirror. "You can't tell me that you've never snuck out."

The girl's face blotched to such an extent her freckles were nearly obliterated. "There was a fella once, at my previous post. A couple of times I stepped out with him. It was exciting, but excitement doesn't put food in your belly. So I stopped seeing him."

"Do you still think about him and wonder what if?"

Miriam shook her head. Lavinia couldn't imagine not thinking about Finn and wondering, what if he were a lord? Or, what if she wasn't an earl's daughter?

Silly things to wonder about. She spun around. "Time to be off."

Miriam snatched up Lavinia's pelisse, this particular garment of emerald green made more for cover than warmth, and settled it over her shoulders. Tugging on her gloves, Lavinia stood to the side as her maid walked to the door, opened it, and glanced out into the hallway. Lavinia's nerves were strung so tightly she feared they'd snap as she waited. Then the girl gave a quick nod, and Lavinia followed her from the room and toward the servants' stairs, not realizing until she reached them that she'd held her breath the entire way. She was surprised her father didn't hear the pounding of her heart and come in search of her.

Down the stairs they went and through a labyrinth of corridors, Miriam cautioning her to stop whenever she heard something portentous. Then they were finally at the servants' door. Miriam opened it quickly and ushered her out.

"I'll make certain it's unlocked later," she whispered.

Lavinia nodded, spun around, and nearly ruined the entire evening by screaming her head off when a form stepped out of the shadows. She pressed a hand to her chest, her heart hammering against her splayed fingers with such force they fairly vibrated. "Oh, Finn. You gave me such a fright. I thought you were going to wait in the mews."

He flashed a grin—she did so love his grins—and, without a

word, simply took her hand securely in his, and she couldn't help but believe it was exactly where it belonged. Then they were dashing down the side path where deliveries were made without disturbing the tranquility of the gardens. Finally, they reached the mews, only to discover it empty.

"Where's your wagon?" she asked.

"You deserve better than that rickety old thing tonight." He led her through the alley, into the street. And there, waiting, was a hansom.

The driver opened the door. Finn assisted her as she clambered in and quickly joined her. The vehicle rocked as the driver climbed onto his seat and then they were off. She couldn't help but laugh as the joy spiraled through her. "We did it!"

Finn took her hand, making her wish she hadn't worn gloves, but one didn't go about bare-handed in public. He squeezed her fingers. "I never doubted."

She couldn't help but believe he was referring to something grander than this outing, that he was talking about never doubting them, as a couple, as a whole. She was suddenly as frightened as she was exhilarated because anything more between them was forbidden, no matter how much it might be desired. "Tell me about your sister," she said to calm her heart, to put them back on safer ground.

"Her name's Gillie."

"The one who cares so much about pronunciation. I remember you mentioning her long ago. Is she married?"

"She has no interest in that sort of thing. Her tavern keeps her busy. You'll see." Bringing her hand up to his lips, he pressed a kiss against her knuckles, and the warmth from his mouth seeped through the kidskin into her very being. "I'm glad you're coming with me."

She smiled with joy and pleasure, always happiest when she was in his company. "I am, too."

She liked how cozy it was in the hansom, how it was almost as though they'd retreated from the world, as though beyond them nothing existed. An odd thought occurred to her: how lovely it would be if they could live here—only the two of them—within the confines of the cab. But, of course, they couldn't. They both had responsibilities and duties, families who would miss them. But she didn't want to think about any of that now, especially when she glanced past Finn and saw they were in a part of London with which she was no longer familiar. It seemed darker, more ominous.

"Where is your sister's tavern?"

"Whitechapel."

"That's not one of the finer parts of London."

"No." Releasing her hand, he slid his arm around her shoulders and drew her in more snugly against his side. "I'll keep you safe."

"I know you will. I trust you, Finn. I trust you more than I've ever trusted anyone."

Tucking the fingers of his free hand beneath her chin, he tilted her head up slightly and lowered his mouth to hers, so sweetly, so gently. She wouldn't mind if they did nothing more than travel around London all night doing this. She loved the way his tongue wandered through her mouth, stroking her tongue, exploring the corners, claiming what had remained untouched until him. She couldn't imagine Thornley kissed like this. It was far too improper, untamed, undignified, really. So very intimate, a partial joining, a coming together that spoke of ownership and familiarity. It was impossible to consider doing this with anyone else—of *wanting* to do it with anyone else.

The carriage began to slow, and he drew back. "Tonight you won't be an earl's daughter. We want to take no chances that someone might recognize your name. You're just Vivi." He grinned tenderly. "My Vivi."

She couldn't stop herself from smiling in return or feeling as though tonight was special. So many girls she knew dreamed of becoming a princess, while she longed for nothing more than to be the cinder girl. "If anyone asks what I do, I shall say I'm the scullery maid."

"Do you even know what a scullery maid does?"

She laughed lightly. "No. Perhaps they won't ask for details."

The hansom came to a stop. Finn handed some coins up through an opening in the roof. The doors swung open. He leaped out, then reached back for her. Placing her hand in his, as always appreciating the strength she found there, she alighted.

And there was the brick building he'd talked to her about so many times with its wooden sign hanging over the doorway, swinging in the slight wind, proclaiming the establishment as the Mermaid and Unicorn. Someone had painted a mermaid in the top corner and a unicorn in the opposite bottom corner. Light spilled out through the windows, casting a warm glow over the brick walkway and illuminating the people inside. Voices, laughter, and a din of sounds she couldn't identify wafted out into the night, and she wondered how anyone could walk past and not want to stop in for a few moments to be part of such revelry.

Taking her hand, Finn escorted her to the door, opened it, and ushered her inside, where it was even more marvelous and unlike any place she'd ever before visited. She was accustomed to people speaking in hushed tones at gatherings, but here it was as though everyone was shouting to be heard over someone else. People didn't walk sedately. They rushed about carrying tankards and glasses. The two women doing the most rushing had plump breasts, the upper mounds nearly spilling out of their clothing. The energy and excitement of the place was overwhelming.

Turning to say something to Finn, she came up short, suddenly realizing that it had been two years since she'd seen him in anything other than lantern light. She'd forgotten how very brown his eyes were. His hair, though fair, also had dark shades throughout, creating a mixture of blond, as though the sun had reached down to touch some of it, but not all of it. He appeared much older than his twenty-three years, certainly much older than the young man who'd come to haul Sophie away. His features contained a ruggedness they hadn't possessed then, a toughness that caused her stomach to do an insane sort of quivering that made her very much aware she was of an age where she was leaving childhood behind. He'd taken as much care preparing for their outing as she. His jacket wasn't the one of coarse material he usually wore, but was made of finer fabric, obsidian in color. His white neck cloth was pristine and stylishly knotted. His black brocade waistcoat must have cost him a fortune. For some reason, staring at him made it difficult to swallow, to breathe, to think.

It was always his company that had drawn her to him, but now, seeing him in gaslight, he offered her more than that. He was definitely a man now, incredibly pleasing to the eye. Being with him made her realize how much she herself had matured as well.

Placing his hand on the small of her back, Finn guided her between some tables, possessively protecting her from two rather bulky men who were laughing uproariously and seemed to be on the verge of tipping off their chairs and onto the floor. When they reached a lengthy wooden gleaming counter, he pushed a couple of gents aside, creating an empty pocket that he urged her to step into, then his chest was against her back, his arms coming around her protectively, shielding her in a way that warmed her heart to its core.

"Gillie!" he shouted.

The tallest woman she'd ever seen, one nearly as tall as Finn, who towered over many a man, turned from her task of filling a tankard from a tapped cast, glanced over at him, nodded, and returned to her chore. She had red hair, cut just below her ears. Lavinia knew no woman who wore her hair in such a manner. Leaning over the counter, she got a better look at her. Her clothing was rather simple: a shirt and a skirt. Unlike the serving girls, she apparently had no wish to flash her attributes. She finished filling the tankard, set it on the counter, and walked over to them. "Finn."

"Gillie, this is Vivi."

"Hello," she said politely, but Lavinia could sense his sister was taking her measure, and she had an awful feeling she was going to be found lacking.

"Finn has told me so much about you," Lavinia assured her.

Arching a brow, Gillie shifted her attention to her brother. "Has he now?"

"I didn't even know a lady could own a business. How independent you are."

"I like independence. What can I pour you?"

"Oh, uh." She'd grown up with first her nanny, then her governess, then a footman simply providing her with a drink at meals and she sipped whatever she was given. On occasion she might ask for tea to be brought to her, but she didn't think this place served tea. She certainly didn't want to insult Finn's sister by asking for something she didn't have on hand. "Have you a . . . red wine?"

Gillie grinned. "I have. And you, Finn. Your regular?"

"Aye."

"I'll return in a flash."

After she walked away, Finn leaned in. She could feel his breath tickling the side of her neck, in a delicious and wicked way. "Don't you drink alcohol?"

"Only wine during dinner."

"Maybe you'll try some other things tonight."

"You'll have to guide me."

"I accept the challenge and will guide you in any manner you want." His voice had dropped a notch, gone deep and provocative, and she wasn't certain they were still discussing spirits.

His sister returned with their drinks. "Sorry I can't stay to visit, but we're really busy tonight."

"We can see to ourselves." He picked up both drinks. "Hang on to my jacket."

Knotting her fingers around his jacket sleeve, she followed him through the crowd, aware of gentlemen's gazes washing over her, but no one reached out to touch her. She had the sense that being with Finn marked her as his, under his care, not to be trifled with. She became somewhat giddy with the thought that at such a young age he wielded so much power. Who knew where he might end up? In Parliament perhaps. Maybe as prime minister, himself.

Although either of those achievements were years away, and she'd be long married by then. It saddened her to contemplate how their paths would soon be diverging.

Stopping at a table where two gents were sitting, both coming to their feet, he didn't ask if they objected to his joining them, but merely set his tankard and her glass down. Sliding his arm around her waist, he brought her in against his side. "Vivi, my brothers Aiden and Beast."

She could see some resemblance between Finn and Aiden—in the eyes, the jaw, the chin—but none at all when it came to Beast, whose height and the breadth of his chest made him quite intimidating. Although it might have been difficult to tell if they favored each other because his long, dark hair fell forward, obscuring a portion of his face. "It's a pleasure. I've heard so much about you." Which was a bit of a falsehood. She knew about Aiden's gambling den, but nothing at all regarding Beast's occupation.

"My brother hasn't been quite so revealing about you," Aiden said.

"I didn't want you trying to steal her away," Finn said easily. "Move over. I'm taking your chair." Then he pulled out an empty one for her, and she settled into it.

After the men shifted around to accommodate the new seating arrangements and were lowering themselves, another—this one dark haired and heavily bearded—walked up holding a tumbler of amber liquid, grabbed an empty chair from a nearby table, set it between Aiden and Finn, and dropped into it.

"My brother Mick. Mick, say hello to Vivi."

His gaze wandered over her slowly, not in a licentious way, but he was definitely assessing her as though she were a puzzle box that when opened would reveal a treasure. "You don't live in Whitechapel."

"No," she stated succinctly. "What gave it away?"

His eyes widened slightly, perhaps because she refused to be intimidated by him, his attention jumping to Finn before coming back to her. "Your clothing. They're very fine threads."

"I have a skilled seamstress."

"Who works with expensive cloth."

"Leave off, Mick," Finn said, his tone a warning snarl, and again she was struck by how he was protecting her, not wanting the slightest unpleasantness to ruin her evening.

"Her diction is posh—I'd say aristocratic."

Although Finn had told her not to give away too much about herself, these were his brothers. Surely, they were to be trusted. "My father is the Earl of Collinsworth."

"Is tonight a lark, then?"

"Don't you have someone else you can go irritate?" Finn asked.

"Not a lark," she said. "I've long wanted to meet Finn's family. Although I daresay, with the exception of Aiden and Finn, you don't resemble each other in the least." They also seemed to be rather close in age, which baffled her.

"We've all different mothers and fathers," Mick said.

"But how can that be if you're all in the same family?"

"We're bastards."

FINN WATCHED THOSE green eyes slowly blink, once, twice, three times, in shock and—he feared—disgust. He loved his brothers, but at that moment he had a strong urge to kill Mick, or at the very least rearrange the perfect cut of his nose. Finn's parentage—or lack thereof—never seemed to matter when he was with Vivi.

Mick's words had suddenly made it matter. Very much.

"We're leaving," Beast said, suddenly shoving back his chair and standing.

Confusion furrowing his brow, Aiden looked up. "Why?"

"We're ruining their night."

"But there aren't any other tables."

"We'll stand at the counter." He nodded to Vivi. "It was a pleasure, my lady." Then he strode off, and Aiden had the good sense to grab his mug and follow.

"Did you not tell her?" Mick asked. He'd been the first brought to Ettie Trewlove's door, the first she'd taken in and kept as her own, and he'd always viewed himself as the eldest, even though none of them knew precisely when they were born, didn't know the exact order in which they'd come into the world.

"Finn's parentage matters not one whit to me," Vivi said with all the grandeur of a queen passing down a decree.

"It'll matter a great deal to your father."

"Go to bloody hell, Mick," Finn uttered through clenched teeth, striving to rein in his temper before he sent his balled fist flying toward that chin that few people knew sported a deep dimple much like his father's because his brother kept it hidden beneath his thick beard.

Mick gave a brusque nod before shoving himself to his feet. "Lady Vivi."

"It's Lavinia," she said.

Another nod from his brother as though he'd suspected her name wasn't as simple as the one by which Finn had introduced her. "Enjoy what remains of your evening."

Finn waited until he could no longer hear the tread of his brother's big feet before looking at Vivi. "I'm sorry you had to learn that about me the way you did. Mick has always taken the circumstances of his birth personally."

She placed her warm hand over his balled fist resting beside his tankard, and he wondered when she'd removed her gloves. "I spoke true, Finn. I don't care."

Relaxing his hand, turning his palm up, he unfurled his fingers and threaded them through hers. "I should have told you."

"Why didn't you?"

"I thought you might want nothing more to do with me."

"Silly Finn." Lifting their joined hands, she pressed a kiss to his knuckles. Whenever she went away for the winter, she always returned changed, but this time the differences in her seemed more pronounced, as though she'd shed the cloak of youth.

There was still an innocence to her, but not a childishness. Her purity was a product of her life, her upbringing. She was sheltered and protected; he found no fault with that. He didn't want her to have to experience the harshness of his world.

"Tell me everything," she said softly. "How you came to have your family."

"Not here." The din wasn't made for sharing something so private and personal. If he was honest, he wasn't certain he wanted to look into her eyes as he told her, didn't want to see the sorrow or the shock or the disgust. The darkness would better suit the telling. "Do you like the wine?"

She laughed lightly. Her laughter always managed to reach into his soul, tickle it, warm it. "I haven't even tried it."

He watched as she lifted her glass, sipped, and the delicate muscles of her throat worked. Then her tongue gathered up the lingering drops from her lips as he longed to do. "It's quite tasty."

"Would you like to try beer?"

With a nod, she pressed her teeth into her bottom lip and her eyes twinkled as though he'd asked her to do something truly naughty. He wished he had. He scooted the tankard toward her, again mesmerized by the delicate way in which she drank. Then chuckled low as her face scrunched up, an expression that would have looked ghastly on any other woman but was endearing on her. It made him want to lean over and kiss those puckered lips.

"It's so bitter," she exclaimed.

"I suppose you have to develop a taste for it. Perhaps we'll try the brandy later."

She glanced around. "Do you spend a lot of time here?"

"Most evenings. Not much else to do otherwise."

"I can't imagine it. My evenings are filled with readings, and recitals, and theater. Then this year, of course, there will be balls and dinners. I fear I might not be able to meet you every Tuesday."

"I'll be waiting all the same."

"I hate for you to waste your time. We could have a signal— drapes drawn aside or a candle in the window."

"We don't need a signal, Vivi. Waiting for you brings me pleasure. If you don't come, I missed out on a pint. Where's the harm in that?"

"Oh, Finn." Her fingers tightened around his. "Things are changing between us."

He nodded, acknowledging the changes might be more than she realized. "If you don't want them to, then tell me not to wait for you ever again."

"It just about kills me not to see you when we're at the estate. I think I would die if I didn't see you when I was in London."

He knew with certainty that he would if he couldn't see her, but he feared frightening her away if she knew the depths of his feelings, so he grinned cockily. "Then see me you shall."

"I'm ever so glad you brought me here. Now on the nights when I'm not with you, I can envision you within these walls, arguing with your brothers. Laughing with your sister." Her brow furrowed. "Where's your other sister?"

"Fancy? Probably abed. She's just a child." She was only nine, having come late into their mum's life. She was the only one to whom Ettie Trewlove had given birth, the result of a man taking advantage. While he and his brothers had been only fourteen when she was born, they'd made a vow to protect her, their mum, and any other woman who was treated unfairly by unscrupulous men.

"I do want to know how your family came to be."

It wasn't an uplifting tale, but he owed her the story.

"Years ago, my mum advertised to take in by-blows for a fee," he said quietly, holding Lavinia against his side as they lay on his jacket in her family's gardens, near the corner brightened with the colorful pansies—not that he could see that, of course, because it was dark. But it was her favorite place to sit and ruminate, and now when she was here, she would think of him.

They'd stayed at the tavern until it closed. She'd tried scotch—which burned her throat—and brandy—which made the inside of her nose tickle but had a warmer feel to it as it went down, and she rather liked it. All the while she'd felt his brothers scrutinizing them and thought she might have a notion regarding how someone had felt being left in the stocks all day, back when people were shamed in such a manner. She'd ignored them as much as possible, because she wanted a pleasant evening with Finn. He was all that mattered.

"Mick was brought to her first. Then Aiden, then six weeks later me. The man who brought me was the same one who brought Aiden. Cocky bugger. Didn't even bother to hide the crest on his carriage."

Her heart kicked against her ribs so hard she suspected he felt it. "Your father is an aristocrat? Who?"

"Doesn't matter. I don't want to be associated with him."

"And your mother?"

"I don't know anything about her. Since he had two by-blows delivered within weeks of each other, we assumed he had more than one mistress. Aiden follows him around occasionally, knows he keeps more than one mistress on hand at a time, has even spoken with him. But I have no interest in him whatsoever. He's not the sort with whom I want to associate—a man who treats women abominably, who gets rid of his children without compunction."

She couldn't believe it. "He just . . . he just gave you away?"

"Never looked back. Never checked on us. Paid our mum fifteen pounds for each of us." He chuckled low. "Asked if he could pay a lower fee for me since she already had one of his bastards. Mum made him pay full price."

"That's horrid."

Rolling over until he was facing her, he cradled her cheek, stroked his thumb along the corner of her mouth. "That's one of the reasons I didn't tell you. It's not a happy tale, but my mum—Ettie Trewlove—she's been good to me. She loves us, all of us, and made us into a family. Not all baby farmers care about the babes brought to them. They're just business. She cares, so I've been fortunate in that regard."

"She's the fortunate one. To have you." And Lavinia couldn't help but think she'd be fortunate as well if she could have him—even knowing that she couldn't, that it was an impossibility. But he was hers at this very moment, secluded as they were, with no one to know what they were about. Her heart ached for him, for all the doubts that had to plague him. She couldn't imagine being cast aside, needed to reassure him that his revelations had not changed her feelings for him—

But even as she thought it, she realized they had changed. They'd grown deeper. What a remarkable person he was to rise above such a sordid beginning. Lifting her hand, she curled it around his neck as she leaned in and captured his mouth, declaring it and him as her own.

As his growl reverberated around them, he didn't hesitate to open his mouth to her, and she took advantage, deepening the kiss, striving to communicate with a passionate sweep of her tongue how much she adored him, how his past mattered only to the extent that it had shaped him into someone she loved.

And she did love him. It frightened her to consider how much she did. She couldn't give voice to the words. It wouldn't be fair to either of them. Eventually, she would have to honor a pact her father had made. But not now, not at this moment.

So she kissed him with fervor and joy and heartache, and didn't object when his hand cradled her breast and squeezed. Or when he lowered his mouth to the taut pearl and closed his mouth over it, the heat sending warmth spiraling through her, pooling between her thighs. Clutching the back of his head, she held him where he was, wishing no cloth separated the silkiness of her skin from the velvety roughness of his tongue. She sighed and moaned and knew she was being a wicked girl, but it all felt so marvelous. Where was the harm in luxuriating for only a minute or perhaps two?

Then his lips were back on hers, and she was dragging her fingers through his hair. She almost gave voice to these feelings that wanted to burst forth like the fireworks she'd seen lighting the sky at Cremorne Gardens.

Eventually, he was the one who showed restraint, who drew back, and looked down on her. "Next Tuesday," he whispered, a vow, a benediction.

And she wondered how she could possibly go that long without seeing him and remain sane.

SITTING IN THE Mermaid, downing his third pint of beer, Finn admitted he hated every night of the week except Tuesday. This night was Wednesday, the night after he'd brought Vivi here. He wanted to bring her again, wanted to take her somewhere else. He wanted to experience all manner of adventures with her.

He barely stirred when a chair was pulled out, spun around, and Aiden dropped into his line of vision, crossing his arms over the back of the chair. "What were you thinking last night to bring that lass here? She's an earl's daughter."

"I'm an earl's son."

"You're an earl's bastard. He's never acknowledged you, and he's never going to. Your mother was his mistress—"

"We don't know that. We don't know anything about her. We just assume that to be the case because he had two by-blows to deliver in short order. She could have been a servant or some lord's daughter."

"What? Are you wishing on stars now, thinking if you take a piece of him and a piece of your mother that you can make yourself a whole that's worthy of her? It's folly, Finn. She's folly. Nothing good will come of this."

Chapter 6

*N*othing good would come from his going after her, but damn her to hell, he'd not be bested by the traitorous chit.

Before the pain had fully subsided, he caught his breath and forced himself to his feet. Drawing on vast reserves of determination, he raced after her, not having to go far before spying her. She walked at a brisk clip, but continually glanced around, searching for any dangers. The girl he'd known hadn't been so self-sufficient, so aware. What had transpired in the years since he'd seen her? He fought not to care, not to wonder.

Slowing his pace, quietening his steps, he managed to catch up with her rather sooner than she probably would have liked. The irritation fairly flowed off her in waves. He'd always been able to read her so well. It was the reason her betrayal had come as such a surprise. He'd been caught completely unawares and, in the end, had felt like a lamb led to slaughter—considering his occupation at the time, the comparison seemed more than appropriate.

She quickened her pace. He followed suit. "You can't out-race me."

Stopping abruptly, she swung around and plowed her fist into his shoulder, knocking him back two steps. He furrowed his brow. "Where did you learn to land a punch like that?"

"None of your business. Now leave me be."

"You just happen to be going the same way I am." Since he was planning to go the same way she did. He despised his curiosity, his need to once again know everything about her. Mentally, he shook his head. He hadn't known everything about her before. He'd only thought he had.

"Then cross the street. Walk on the other side."

"What's the matter? Finding it difficult to resist kissing me?"

"It'll be a cold day in hell before I ever kiss you again." Once more, she began marching forward, a soldier on her way into battle—or striving to leave the battle behind. But he was spoiling for a fight, had been from the moment he'd first clapped eyes on her after eight long years.

It irritated the devil out of him that she was more beautiful now than when he'd last seen her and they'd made promises to each other, promises broken mere hours later. The years, maturity, had added a grace to her that she'd not possessed at seventeen when he'd declared his love for her. It further vexed him that his body— his traitorous cock—reacted to her nearness.

Once more he fell into step beside her, heard her harsh sigh, took perverse pleasure in knowing his presence upset her. Good. He began to whistle a tune he'd tried to forget, one he'd heard at a ball when she had waltzed in his arms. He wondered if she remembered the moment with fondness or if it ripped into her heart the way it tore into his. She'd played him for a fool. No memory of her should be pleasing to recall but there were still nights when he lay awake in his bed, staring at the ceiling because when he closed his eyes he saw her.

Five years of his life spent in isolation and the only thing to keep him company, to keep him sane, were memories of her. They'd sustained him. Originally, he'd called them forth to fuel his need for revenge, for retribution, but the loneliness had increased until he transformed the memories into dreams of what his life would be after prison. They gave him hope that love awaited him somewhere, that a woman would again smile at him, laugh with him, fill him with joy.

He hated her because she'd filled him with so much joy and then snatched it away. Spoiled, pampered daughter of an earl. *Not looking so spoiled now though, was she?*

He should leave her to the thieves, drunkards, and miscreants. But the thought of any man laying so much as a finger on her filled him with a fury that shook him to his core. She was no longer his, had never really been his, and yet a foolish part of him couldn't forget that once upon a time she had very nearly been, couldn't forget the girl she'd been.

"How did you know I was here?" she asked.

"Pardon?"

She sighed with irritation, but he didn't know if she was irritated with herself for asking or with him for making her ask it again. "How did you know I was here? Thornley tell you?"

"No. Gillie did." The duke had given his sister a miniature of the woman who'd left him at the altar because Gillie had been striving to help him locate her. All they knew was that she'd come to Whitechapel. Not why or exactly where.

"So why seek me out?"

He hadn't a clue. Perhaps he'd thought if he saw her, just one more time, he could stop thinking about her, would no longer be haunted by memories of her, of what they might have had together.

"Why don't you return home?" He nearly groaned in frustration because he was the one who asked a question, when he wanted her to think he didn't care. Still, he carried on like a dimwit. "Thornley is married. They can't force you to wed him now."

"They'll force me to marry someone else, some other duke. Mother is determined I'll be a duchess."

"I thought that was the dream of all ladies of quality—to land a duke." He couldn't keep the bitterness from his voice. He shouldn't blame her for deciding she wanted someone other than a commoner, a bastard. But he did find fault with her for the way she'd gone about ridding herself of him.

"You of all people should know that a title mattered not one whit to me, and if you think it did, then you didn't know me at all."

"I knew you well enough to get you to welcome me into your bed." His pride spit out the words.

He saw her flinch, but other than that, she reacted not at all, said nothing at all. "What are you doing here?" he demanded.

"Striving to put an end to the practice of farming out children, or at the very least see that it's licensed. You must have a license to kill a horse but not to oversee the care of someone else's child? It's ludicrous. It makes no sense that we strive to protect beasts more than we do humans."

A couple of times he'd followed her to a darkened alleyway and watched her standing around for a couple of hours, sighing heavily now and then. Then last week, a woman had joined her and placed three children into her keeping. He'd been curious regarding her actions but hadn't trusted himself to approach her without giving away how fiercely her betrayal had wounded him to the core. He'd been so cocky regarding her feelings toward him, certain he'd won her over for all eternity.

Unfortunately, the longer he was in her company, the more the anger he tried to hold at bay was beginning to seethe, to seep out of the crevices into which he'd attempted to chase it. He wanted her to believe him unmoved, even as his burgeoning resentment threatened to overtake his good sense. He hadn't gone to her before, because a part of him had feared the answer: she'd turned her back on him because of the circumstances of his birth. He'd fought his entire life to convince himself his illegitimacy didn't matter. But in the end, perhaps it had mattered to the one person who had meant the most to him. Yet she'd taken up the cause of children born into the same circumstance as he. Was she acting out of guilt for turning her back on him? "Why do you care?"

"Again, Finn, it seems you knew me not at all."

They reached the gates of the wrought iron fence that enclosed the foundling home. The barrier was designed to keep children inside, not to keep anyone with ill intentions out. He could scale it in a blink.

Ignoring him, not even having the courtesy to thank him for

his escort, she shoved open the gate, its hinges squealing in protest.

"The next time you go out at night to meet someone, hire a large bloke to accompany you."

"I think I demonstrated I'm perfectly capable of looking after myself." She stepped through the opening she'd created and quickly closed the gate, causing it to rattle and protest with the force of her actions.

"Vivi."

She stopped but didn't turn around, didn't chastise him this time for using the pet name he'd given her. Lady Lavinia had always seemed too complicated a name for the girl she'd been—or perhaps it had simply been too complicated for him, a constant reminder of her place in the world, atop a pedestal, while he was destined to remain in the muck, always looking up at what he shouldn't touch. "I've no doubt you can handle yourself under most circumstances, but you weren't prepared when I unarmed you—either time. There truly are dangers about this time of night that you might not be prepared to face."

She did turn then, but he couldn't make out her features. She was merely a shadowy outline standing in far darker shadows. "Are you one of them?"

"Yes."

"What happened to the boy who shared his dreams with me?"

"He died." *You killed him, you and your father.*

"As did the girl who shared her dreams with you. What a fine pair we are."

She spun on her heel and began walking away. The sorrow reflected in her voice took him off guard, almost had him going after her, but what good would come of it? Merely recriminations, accusations, and a flaring of the bitterness of her betrayal.

Besides, he had an appointment to keep.

COMING IN THROUGH the rear door, Lavinia stepped into the kitchen where a single lamp rested on the large wooden table, where she had left it before departing for her late-night excursion. Drawing comfort from it, she neared, placed her walking stick on the table, wrapped her hands around the back of a chair, dropped her head forward, inhaled deeply, and tried to stop the trembling that had overtaken her from the moment she'd seen Finn standing there. He knew where she was. How long had he known?

Swinging around, she returned to the door, checked the lock, ensured it was secure. Not that it would stop him, but she couldn't imagine him breaking into the home of a religious order. Surely not even he would be so sacrilegious.

Pressing her forehead to the door, she fought back tears. Having him so near, talking with him, had reopened old wounds. She'd thought them healed, only to discover they'd merely been festering. Dear God, what sort of man was he to speak with her without begging forgiveness for nearly destroying her?

"No children tonight?"

Turning at the voice, she smiled sadly at Sister Theresa. She fought off the melancholy that was hovering because the night had not gone as she'd hoped, because she'd not been able to rescue more children. But eventually she would send an article to the *Times* revealing the details of her adventures. The trial and eventual hanging of Charlotte Winsor several years earlier had helped bring to light some of the abuses of baby farming, but still not enough was being done to protect children. Doing so had become her cause, her reason for rising in the morning, for carrying on. Had given her life purpose, so she was no longer existing but was actually living. If she could just make people listen—

Which seemed an insurmountable task when she hadn't even been able to make Finn leave off. Damned irritating man. She should have run him through. If he approached her again, she wouldn't hesitate to do so.

"Not tonight. No one showed." A small lie, but she didn't want the sister to worry. Tonight was the first time she'd been faced with violence. Poor timing to have met with a woman last week who was arrested soon after. She hated to admit that Finn might have the right of it and she would have to hire someone to accompany her in the future. It was quite possible she was becoming known, and if others were arrested she might be seen as a danger.

"I'm glad you returned safely. Sleep well, Miss Kent."

When she'd sought shelter here, she hadn't told them she was the daughter of an earl. She'd wanted to be as anonymous as possible. "Good night, Sister."

Sister Theresa retreated down the hallway to her bedchamber. After picking up the lamp and her walking stick, Lavinia wandered out of the room, along a hallway, and finally up the stairs to where several bedchambers lined one side of a lengthy corridor while the other side boasted only one large room that ran from one end to the other. Three doors led into the single room, each one left open so any troubled cries could be heard. Quietly she entered, taking some satisfaction in the twenty-five beds lining each wall and the sight of the children filling most of them, several here as a result of her endeavors.

She glanced over at the sister who had fallen asleep in a chair while keeping watch over the little ones. Many of them often awoke with nightmares. Few would talk about what their lives had been. But she couldn't look at any of them without wondering how much Finn's life might have mimicked theirs had he been delivered to a different farmer. Based on all the things he'd told her, the woman to whom he'd been given loved him, and he loved her. Not all by-blows were as fortunate.

Slowly, quietly, she walked between the beds, shining the lamp on each occupant, bringing up a blanket here, tucking a stray strand of hair behind an ear there, moving a rag doll into the crook of an elbow. Each child was precious, and she imagined herself as mother to each of them, caring for them, singing them lullabies, holding them close, showering them with love. Rescuing them filled an emptiness inside her that had only grown over time as more weeks passed with no word whatsoever from Finn.

Then tonight when she'd wanted no words from him at all, they'd flowed off his tongue, threatening to drown her.

With a quiet sigh, she retraced her steps and wandered back into the hallway. Although she doubted she'd be able to sleep, she wasn't of a mood to haunt the corridors like some ghoulish wraith either. She made her way to the chamber she shared with Sister Bernadette, not at all surprised to find her asleep, although her snores were in danger of waking the dead.

Quietly she stripped out of the frock she'd found at a local mission, someone else's castoff. It was a bit worn but still serviceable. When she'd run from the church, she'd been wearing her wedding gown and, in fear of having her escape thwarted, hadn't taken the time to return home for other clothes.

Thorne deserved someone who could give him the whole of her heart, and Lavinia's remained a shattered mess. Although she hadn't realized the true extent of the unfairness to Thorne until she caught sight of Finn at his brother's wedding, two weeks before hers was to take place.

She slipped into her nightdress, another castoff, worn but incredibly soft from so many washings. As carefully as possible, because the bed did tend to creak, she made her way beneath the scratchy blankets and stared at the shadows playing over the ceiling.

Seeing him that day at the church had been like having her heart broken all over again. She'd anticipated he might be there. She simply hadn't expected the sight of him to hit her so hard. He was a full-grown man now, with none of the boyishness of his youth remaining to him. More handsome than he'd been when she'd fallen in love with him. She thought he might have gained some height. His shoulders had definitely broadened. He'd worn the finely tailored clothing well, a mark of success.

After whispering to Thorne, who'd accompanied her to the ceremony, that she'd quite suddenly taken ill—something she'd eaten she was rather certain—they'd made a quiet discreet exit from the nave. He'd escorted her home and then made his way to the wedding breakfast to wish the couple well. She didn't know if Mick Trewlove had read the guest list and known her name was on it—she rather doubted it. Her brother hadn't attended because his wife had been truly ill that morning. Which had no doubt worked out to everyone's benefit as she suspected the Trewloves wouldn't have welcomed him with open arms. Wouldn't have welcomed her either, but her curiosity had gotten the better of her. Sometimes when sleep eluded her, she'd wonder what had become of Finn.

And so she'd seen him at the church and wished she hadn't because the guilt and shame she'd managed to tamp down for so many years had not only raised its ugly head but had increased exponentially as her wedding to Thorne neared. In the end, she'd been unable to saddle him with her. The night before she was to wed, she had made the mistake of confessing to her mother that she thought it would be best for all concerned if she cried off. The countess, fearing her only daughter might make a run for freedom, had locked her in her bedchamber.

The following morning, Lavinia had recanted and carried on as though she fully intended to go through with the marriage. But at the church, her unsuspecting brother hadn't hesitated to give her a moment alone, and she'd been able to make her escape. She'd not been completely prepared for running off, but she'd managed.

Until tonight, until she'd seen Finn. She'd not been at all prepared to face him, to be bombarded with so many memories, and against her will, lying there in the dark, she remembered a magical night when she'd truly become his.

Chapter 7

1863
Finding Fulfillment

$\mathcal{S}$itting in front of the mirror, Lavinia watched as Miriam worked to put her hair up in a style reminiscent of Marie Antoinette, which seemed appropriate as her mother would have her head if she knew the true reason Lavinia had pleaded and begged for their affair to be a masquerade ball. But it had been necessary to Lavinia's plan. Every ball she'd attended thus far had been boring and uneventful. It was her first Season and she should be enthralled with the sparkling glamour. Instead she found it all rather dull and attending the affairs extremely wearisome.

She spent a good deal of her time dancing with one partner after another. Her brother's many friends were all willing to ensure she wasn't a wallflower—even on the nights when Thornley didn't attend the affairs, which was most nights. He had no need to spend his time getting to know the various debutantes. He knew who he was destined to marry so was free to spend his evenings engaged in other pursuits. He would be in attendance tonight, of course, as he wouldn't insult his future in-laws by not showing up. She would have her expected two dances with him, and then he'd no doubt head to the card room or sneak off for a bit of whisky with her brother or leave to find other more interesting entertainments.

But the costume ball wasn't for him. It was for Finn.

A young man who could sneak into a residence, into her bedchamber, could most certainly steal into a grand salon filled with people, especially when they were all wearing masks. All he had to do was climb over a wall—surely going through the back gate would be too mundane for him—into the gardens and then simply march up the path and enter through the terrace doors that would no doubt be left ajar in order to ensure cooler air circulated throughout the crowded ballroom.

Once Miriam was finished with her hair, Lavinia went through the tedious task of getting into her costume—a voluminous white gown that revealed her neck, shoulders, and a good bit of her cleavage. She draped a diamond necklace that had once belonged to her grandmother around her neck. Earbobs. Dragging on white gloves that went past her elbows, she felt like a true lady tonight, not a young girl on the cusp of womanhood. The feeling had little to do with the costume itself but with the manner in which she was displaying herself for a particular gentleman. She refused to feel guilty that she'd never gone to quite as much bother for Thornley as she doubted very much that he went to any bother for her. But Finn would. He'd go to the trouble of securing a costume and mask in order to infiltrate her mother's ball. It was a deliciously wicked thing to do. Her mother would have an apoplectic fit if she discovered a commoner in her grand salon.

But Lavinia trusted Finn to be discreet. They'd discussed the particulars numerous times. She'd never anticipated an evening more, not even her very first ball.

With Miriam's assistance, she managed to get her mask tied in place without disturbing a single strand of her hair. The silver half mask glittered with sequins and was adorned with elegant tufts of feathers.

"Quite striking, m'lady," Miriam said.

"I rather agree."

"The duke won't be able to take his eyes off you."

"I'm sure you're quite right." Although in truth she hoped Miriam was dead wrong. She didn't want to garner his attention tonight of all nights, especially when she'd not held it for long on other nights.

"We could be moving into his fine residence by the end of the summer. At least that's what some of the servants are saying. And that you'll take me with you."

Turning to the side, she studied her reflection in the cheval glass. "Well, yes, of course I'll take you with me. But I doubt it'll be this year. We're not even properly engaged yet. The duke is in no hurry to wed."

"But once he sees you tonight, he's going to fall all over himself."

Laughing lightly, she shook her head. "I assure you, Thornley is not one to fall all over himself."

With a final glance in the cheval glass, she headed out of the room and made her way downstairs to the grand salon where everything was in readiness—except for the blasted doors that led onto the terrace. "Please open the terrace doors, James," she said to a passing footman. "It's such a lovely night and our guests will grow warm otherwise."

Picking up a dance card from a small table near the stairs that led down into the ballroom, she placed it around her wrist. She'd been instrumental in the dance selections, choosing six waltzes, planning to leave each blank since she wasn't certain exactly when Finn might make his appearance and she was determined to have an intimate dance with him. No quadrille or cotillion for them.

At the rustling of skirts, she turned and smiled at her mother.

"You look lovely, m'dear."

"Thank you, Mama."

"I daresay, the Duke of Thornley will find himself anxious to bend the knee in short order, although I don't know why you insisted on the masks. You can have a costume ball without going to such extreme."

"I like the mystery of it, the mystique. Perhaps I'll dance with a gentleman and not know who he is."

"I very much doubt that. You know everyone who's been invited. Most you can identify by their form. Others you'll know for certain when they speak."

"Still, it's rather fun to determine who they are before they speak. Or at least I suppose it is." Reaching out, she squeezed her mother's hand. "I think it'll add a bit of excitement, make our ball more memorable."

"I suppose there is that."

Her mother then left to ensure all was as it should be, and an hour later the ballroom was teeming with guests. Exhilaration was rife on the air. She could sense it from the others in attendance, although she doubted anyone's rivaled hers. She was constantly searching through the gentlemen—many of whom had done little more than don their evening clothes and a mask—striving to find the one who had not received a gilded invitation from her mother.

A tall fellow with dark hair approached her. Her mother had the right of it. She didn't need to see beneath his mask to know he was Thornley. He exuded confidence, wearing his rank like a well-tailored cloak. When he smiled, she thought her stomach should have gone all a'jumble. He was devilishly handsome with power and prestige. She liked him well enough, but he didn't create any sparks within her. Could she marry a man who didn't? Duty dictated that she could and would. But would happiness follow? Would it be enough so she didn't lie in bed and think of another?

"Lady Lavinia," he said in his deep rich baritone, taking her gloved hand and pressing a kiss to the back of her knuckles. "Or should I say Queen Marie Antoinette?"

She laughed lightly, truly delighted by his perceptiveness. Although she did hope he wouldn't be paying that much attention throughout the evening. "You discerned who I am. Jolly good for you. As for yourself . . ." He wore his black evening attire and a plain black half mask. She arched a brow in question.

"Wellington, naturally."

She gave him a pointed look. "You could at least have gone to the bother of dressing in his military garb."

"I'm an older version of him, long after his military days were behind him. Dare I hope you saved me a waltz?"

She glanced at her card. A waltz was next with no name beside it, and since the gent for whom she'd been saving it had yet to show, she said, "You're in luck. The next dance is yours."

Reluctantly, she admitted he was a marvelous dancer as he swept her over the polished parquet floor. Respectful. No wickedness glinting in his eyes indicating he had a desire to hold her nearer. Would he once their betrothal became official? "Do you not enjoy masquerade balls?" she asked.

"Not particularly, no."

"Then I appreciate that you came."

"Your mother would have never forgiven me. Would you?"

"Yes, if I understood your reason. Why is it, do you think, we are taught we must do things we don't want to do?"

"I don't know. It does seem an odd way to manage one's life. Are you enjoying your Season?"

"Very much. I don't want it to end." And then for reasons she couldn't quite fathom, she was prompted to add, "I can hardly wait for next Season and another round of balls."

"Are you in no hurry to wed?"

"No, Your Grace, I am not. Are you?"

He chuckled low. "To be honest, Lavinia, I think we're both too young for such a venture."

She laughed at that. He was all of eight and twenty. She wondered when he'd think he was old enough, but then her brother at six and twenty was also taking great pains to avoid marriage. She angled her head haughtily. "As queen, I relieve you of your duty to remain in attendance this evening. And if you'd be so dashed good as to take my brother with you, all the better."

"Do you truly not mind if I take my leave?" he asked.

"Absolutely I do not mind. I have an abundance of dance partners, some who even went to the trouble of having a proper costume."

The music faded away, the dance came to an end. With a tender smile, he took her hand and once again pressed a kiss to the back of it. "You are a generous queen. A pity one day you will lose your head."

She wondered if perhaps she already had—over another. She certainly had no wish for him or Neville to watch her waltzing with Finn, to note she danced with him more closely than she ought, enjoyed his company more than she had that of any of her other partners. Being the perfect gentleman, he escorted her off the dance floor. "Enjoy your night, Your Grace."

"Enjoy yours as well, my lady."

He strode away, purpose reverberating in every step. She suspected he intimidated many, but then he'd been forced to put on the mantle of duke at fifteen, was very much accustomed to his place.

"You seem to like him," a low voice said in a sensual whisper near her ear.

Her heart thundering, she swung around to face a man dressed in common threads. Beneath his greatcoat, he wore a laborer's jacket, waistcoat, shirt, and knotted neck cloth. His boots, however, were buffed to a shine. His wide-brimmed hat, also that of a laborer or a farmer, was brought low over his brow, casting shadows over his face, a face half-hidden behind a black mask. "You came."

"I promised you I would. I'd never lie to you, Vivi."

She smiled. "Your costume . . ." Not nearly as posh as all the others, but then coins were precious to him. She couldn't expect him to spend them on a trivial matter.

"I'm a highwayman," he said.

Her grin grew. "Naturally. Brilliant. How creative you are. I daresay, you're the only one about." Leaning toward him, she whispered, "You appear to be very dangerous."

"Because I am." His lips quirked up sensually. "But only to you."

Why was it he could so easily cause her entire body to melt, her mind to lose its sharpness? "I'm Marie Antoinette, in case you didn't know. She was the queen—"

"I know who she was."

"I'm sorry. I don't mean to always question your education."

"I saw her in Madame Tussaud's exhibit. You're much prettier."

"Than a wax figurine? I daresay, I should hope so."

"Have you saved me a dance?" he asked.

She nodded. "You promised to learn how to waltz. Did you manage to work in some lessons?"

"I watched while you danced with that last bloke. It seems easy enough."

"How long have you been here?"

"Awhile."

"Why didn't you approach me sooner?"

"Because I didn't want to catch anyone's attention, so I took some time blending in. You're quite popular."

His tone implied he might be bothered by that knowledge. "It's my family's ball, so ladies feel obligated to speak with me and men to dance with me. It doesn't mean I enjoy it."

"Do you not?"

"So much is done out of duty. You're here because you want to be, because you wanted to please me." Although it was ill-advised, she reached out, grabbed his gloved hand, and squeezed. "It means the world to me that you came. Did you clamber over the wall?"

He chuckled low. "No, I used the gate. I didn't want to risk messing up my disguise."

"I hadn't thought of that." Looking past him, she saw a gentleman approaching. "I have to dance the quadrille with Lord Dearwood. Your waltz is after that. Wait here for me." Since she hadn't given any thought to how she would introduce him to anyone, she left him there and met Dearwood on his way to her.

The entire time they danced, she was aware of Finn watching her, studying her, his gaze never leaving her. He cared about no one other than her. He was here simply for her. He made her feel special, unique, cherished. When the dance finally ended, she was grateful to be headed back toward him. Dearwood fell into step beside her. "You don't need to see me off the dance floor."

"Of course I do, my lady. I am a gentleman after all."

She tried to detour them around some other couples and arrive at the edge of the dance floor away from Finn, but it seemed both men had caught each other's attention because Dearwood sought to steer her where Finn was, and Finn had left his spot to meet her. She cursed men and their stubborn natures and jealousies even as she couldn't help but secretly gloat that Finn was determined to claim her.

When they were finally off the dance floor, Finn stepped up. Dearwood angled his head in a way that reminded her of a confused dog. "I'm not certain I know who you are, sir."

"Dick Turpin," Finn said smoothly, his diction not straying from the manner in which he usually spoke, and Lavinia knew a moment of panic, fearing he would be discovered.

Dearwood laughed, but the chortling didn't contain any true amusement. "Clever, sir. However, I was referring to your true identity, not your costume."

"I thought the entire purpose behind a masquerade ball was, for one night, to be someone other than who we truly are." Now, with his words perfectly pronounced, he spoke haughtily, as though he were a king addressing a subject with whom he found fault. In his profession, he no doubt frequently dealt with posh people and had learned to mimic them. Dearwood would think his earlier diction merely part of the role he was playing. Finn bowed slightly toward Lavinia. "Marie Antoinette, I believe the next dance is mine."

Ah, yes, he could definitely be mistaken for an aristocrat. Without hesitation, she placed her hand on his offered arm. "Thank you for the dance, Lord Dearwood." And she was ever so grateful to be escorted away from the prying man. "He's a friend of my brother's. A rather curious one, it seems."

"I think he has his eye on you."

"Don't be ridiculous." She almost told him she was spoken for but didn't want to ruin the magic of the night. Separated from others, they waited at the edge of the dance floor for the cotillion to end. "You handled him well. It occurred to me too late we should have given you a moniker—Lord something or other."

"I'm not a lord."

His tone was flat, and she dearly hoped he wasn't feeling as though he were surrounded by better men, because he wasn't. No one she knew was as kind or interesting as he. "No, you're Dick Turpin, an infamous highwayman. Why him?"

"His story always fascinated me."

She shook her head. "The things you know."

"You can learn a good deal spending your evenings in taverns. I once visited one where he supposedly drank on occasion. They still talk about him—legendary hero to some."

"But if he'd really been a hero, he'd have not been hanged, surely."

"Perhaps not, but justice isn't always meted out fairly."

She didn't want to talk about justice or hangings. "We've gotten rather maudlin."

"We're dressed as people who came to a tragic end."

"Then let's pretend tonight they had no tragic end but lived happily ever after."

HE WANTED TO give her that happily ever after, a silly thing to want when she lived in a world such as this. Although he hadn't missed the shine that had lit up her eyes or the brightness of her smile when her gaze had fallen on him and she'd realized he'd come as promised.

He'd been here for a while, getting a measure of the place, the people. One of the reasons he'd been such a skilled thief was because he never rushed into anything, but took his time, cataloging all the varied nuances of a situation, ensuring he took no missteps. He'd done the same tonight, knowing it was crucial he be mistaken for an aristocrat. He had little doubt that if his true origins were suspected, he wouldn't be merely pleasantly escorted off the property, but would be hauled off to jail with a punch or two delivered along the way for his arrogance.

The earl and countess wouldn't like at all that he'd invaded their exclusive ball. But Vivi liked it. She liked it a great deal, which made the risk worth it.

The tune that had been playing finally came to an end, and he led her onto the dance floor. His brother Mick's lover was a duke's widow, and she'd taught him how to waltz and Mick had grudgingly taught Finn. It seemed he believed as Aiden did that Finn was a fool for spending any time in the company of an earl's daughter, but they were the fools for not understanding what it was to feel complete when in someone else's presence. They didn't know what it was to experience unrivaled joy when taking hold of a hand or gazing into green eyes. His world was drab and dark, his days filled with hard, often gut-wrenching tasks—but whenever he saw her, his past, present, and future were more colorful and brighter. His troubles melted away, or at least they scurried into hiding. As long as he was with her, he was filled with hope.

At that precise moment, his arms were filled with her. Perhaps he held her a little nearer than he should have, his legs brushing up against her skirts, but she didn't chastise him for it. Instead she wore a wicked little half smile and watched him through teasing eyes that signaled she knew what he was about. He wished they weren't wearing the damned masks. He wanted to see her face in its entirety, here in a room where half a dozen crystal chandeliers rained gaslight down on them.

While her eyes were more visible than he could ever recall seeing them, the mask did throw shadows around the emerald. Green had become his favorite color but there were so many different shades that he wasn't certain he'd ever seen one that matched her eyes exactly. He was grateful her mask stopped just below her nose, that her mouth remained visible to him. Her pink lips tempted him to lean in and take possession of them. His hand, with his fingers splayed, spanned a good deal of her back. She was such a delicate creature that he feared she wouldn't be able to survive in his world.

He required a lot of coins if he had any hope at all of making her comfortable. The absurdity of contemplating a future with her was not lost on him.

"I'm impressed," she said. "You've not stepped on my toes once."

"I would do nothing to cause you harm."

Her eyes warmed. "You may not be nobility, but you are most certainly a gentleman. There is no one within these walls who I hold in higher esteem."

Her words touched him deeply, and he didn't doubt for a single moment she meant them.

"Will you dance with others?" she asked.

"No. I'm here for only you. You're the only one I care about, Vivi."

For the space of a single breath, he thought she might lean in and kiss him. "There are two more waltzes and I'm going to dance them with you," she said instead. "It'll be scandalous, but I don't care."

"What makes it scandalous? We're dancing now."

She laughed. "A lady isn't supposed to dance more than twice with a gent. Silly rule, isn't it?"

"I don't want another waltz with you. I want to take you someplace where I can kiss you."

She bit into her lower lip. He'd never noticed before but one of her front teeth was slightly crooked, lapping over the other. The sight of it did something funny to his insides, made him want to protect her all the more. "Between those two waltzes are three other dances for which I have no partner. Perhaps we can take a stroll about the garden."

Away from everyone else, where he'd be more in his element, wouldn't feel as though he was under constant observation. "I look forward to it."

DANCING WITH HIM had been a dream come true. He was so light on his feet. Little wonder she hadn't heard him enter her room that first night. And the way he'd held her, respectfully and not. Where her fingers had rested against his, he'd tightened his hold as though he never intended to let her go. At her back, his hand had claimed her, and she'd dearly wished he'd brought her in nearer, had urged her closer. She should have gone anyway, but she suspected somewhere her mother was watching, brow deeply furrowed, striving to determine with whom her daughter was dancing.

It was all so delicious—even if no one knew she was being naughty. She knew. And so did Finn. He liked that about her. Thornley would not. The duke expected her to remain above reproach. How frightfully boring it was to always do what was expected. She could only hope her eventual marriage wouldn't be as unexciting. Yet she'd have memories of Finn to see her through it.

No matter where she was in the grand salon—on the dance floor, standing about with other debutantes and whispering about one gent or another—she felt Finn's gaze on her, had merely to look over and, with unerring accuracy, would find him, always alone, carefully avoiding being drawn into any conversations, into being questioned by someone who wouldn't take Dick Turpin as the answer to his identity. How lonely it must be for him. How selfish she had been to invite him.

Yet when the next waltz arrived, the one that gave them some time to be alone, he didn't seem the least bit put out. Instead his eyes grew warm and his grin welcomed. When she'd first met him, she hadn't realized that eventually he'd become the most important person in her life, the one for whom she got out of bed each morning, the one she carried with her into her dreams.

She really needed to be forthright with Thornley and inform him she had misgivings about their arrangement. Although there was always time for that as neither of them was in any hurry to see it through. Maybe he even had someone special he'd prefer to marry; perhaps that was the reason his time in her company felt compulsory rather than desired. Unlike her time with Finn. She was with him because she wanted to be, because she would cease to breathe if she wasn't.

"So how do we manage this secretive tryst without getting caught?" he asked.

"As discreetly as possible, make your way to the open doors, go through them, and down the steps. Wait for me there. I'll be thirty seconds behind you."

"Done this before, have you?"

"No." She grinned. "But I've watched others slipping out." Thornley had never sought to arrange a tryst with her. She found the notion of having one with Finn exhilarating. Quite honestly, as handsome as Thornley was, she never thought about kissing him, while she thought about kissing Finn all the time. But then most of her day and almost all her night was spent thinking about him.

When the music stopped, he led her off the dance floor, took her hand, and bowed over it, pressing another kiss to her gloved knuckles. "I'll be waiting," he murmured seductively.

She watched as he walked off, wending his way through the gathered throng of guests, suddenly disappearing from her sight. How had he accomplished that? To blend in until he became invisible to her? Perhaps he'd managed breaking into her room because he was still a thief, hadn't given it up as he'd claimed. He'd certainly succeeded in stealing her heart.

Chuckling at the last thought, the silliness of it, the reality of it, she swung around and came up short at the sight of her mother standing there with condemnation and disappointment etched clearly in her face.

"Who was that with whom you were dancing?" she asked sternly.

"Dick Turpin."

Her mother continued to stare, her glower growing sharper as though her eyes were being rubbed over whetstone.

"The infamous highwayman?" The teasing didn't go over nearly as well with her mother as it had with Dearwood, was rather silly, really. She sighed in defeat. "I don't know. We were both pretending to be who we were dressed as and didn't make proper introductions."

"I did not see him descend the stairs. He did not introduce himself to me. I shall alert the footman—"

"No, he had an invitation. I'm rather certain of it. He showed it to me." Her mother's eyes narrowed, and she feared she'd detected the bold lie. "Or perhaps he didn't, but he came with someone, a cousin, he said. He's new to town. I believe this is his first ball. He might be unaware of proper protocol. When next I see him, I'll bring him over to you for a proper introduction. He's really quite fascinating." The last might have been the only truthful thing she'd said to her mother during this horrid inquisition.

"You're not to dance with him again."

"I won't."

Her mother glanced around, and Lavinia feared if she spied Finn she'd toss him out on his ear. "I shall begin making inquiries, have your father keep an eye out. If he's not versed in manners, it's very likely he is an imposter. I should insist everyone remove their masks."

"Don't ruin everyone's fun. He's very gentlemanly . . . oh, and he's the son of a lord. He told me that." The truth was reflected in her voice. Her mother must have heard it, because she jerked her head back in a manner similar to the way a chicken did when strutting around a coop in search of grain.

"Which lord?"

"An earl, I believe, but I can't recall which one. A lesser one. One hardly known."

Her mother pursed her lips, arched a brow. "Bring him over for an introduction but associate with him no more than that until I am satisfied his family is above reproach."

Was any family above reproach? She was fairly certain both her brother and father were keeping women on the side. She thought it possible that even her mother had a lover, as she spent many evenings out. "Yes, Mama."

Watching her mother walk away was not nearly as interesting as watching Finn, but it did bring with it a great deal of relief. Although drat it all! As she casually made her way toward the terrace, she realized she'd have no further waltzes with him. As a matter of fact, it would be reckless for him to even return to the ballroom. She'd have to say goodbye in the gardens.

A few couples were standing on the terrace, chatting and drinking champagne, no doubt seeking to escape the stifling warmth of the ballroom. Lavinia headed down the steps that led into the garden. Her slipper had barely hit the ground before she felt a hand close around her arm and gently pull her against a broad chest.

"I was beginning to think you weren't going to come," Finn said in a hushed whisper.

"My mother stopped me. She is suspicious of you." Bending back her head, she looked up at him, locking her eyes with his. "You can't return to the ballroom."

Beneath his breath, he released a harsh curse—or at least she assumed it was profanity. She wasn't familiar with the word he'd uttered, but it didn't sound like a nice one. At first she'd thought he'd referenced a duck, but then realized the word wasn't referring to a fowl at all, although she wasn't quite certain what it was referring to, wasn't certain a lady of good breeding should know. "We still have time to take a walk around the garden," she assured him.

He didn't offer his arm, but simply took her hand. This portion of the garden was lit with gas lamps. People were strolling about. She couldn't afford for anyone to see her in such an intimate position, so she worked her hand free and wrapped it around the crook of his elbow. "For propriety's sake," she murmured.

He didn't argue, but simply started walking along the cobblestoned path that wound through the various groupings of flowers. "My mother is incredibly single-minded, doesn't like anything mixed together, so over there are the roses, there the lilies, there the daffodils, off to the side are the delphiniums—"

"So she feels about flowers the same way she feels about people. Heaven forbid a commoner should love a noble."

Her breath hitched at his declaration, one he'd never admitted to, even though she'd long suspected it was true. "Do you, Finn? Do you love a noble?"

Putting his arm around her back, closing his hand over the side of her waist, he drew her off the path, darting between hedgerows and past trellises until they were in the darkest part of the garden, away from the lamps, the posts, other wandering couples. Cupping her face between his hands, he whispered low and earnestly, "How can you doubt it, Vivi?"

Then he took her mouth in the sweetest kiss he'd ever given her. If she'd not already fallen in love with him, she would have absolutely done so at that very moment. His lips claimed her as his, not forcefully or arrogantly, but simply with truth, with longing, with desire. He wanted her as desperately as she wanted him. It was there in the thrumming tension of his body as his fingers fluttered over her bared shoulders. In the way his mouth followed suit as he dragged it down her throat along her collarbone.

"God, this gown drives me to madness," he rasped.

He lowered his head to the pliant mounds, her breasts plumped up just for him to savor. And he feasted, kissing, licking, burying his nose in the valley of her cleavage, inhaling deeply. "You witch. You placed perfume there."

She laughed lightly. She had. She'd chosen this gown because it was so risqué, because it gave him access to parts of her that had always been kept hidden from him by a layer of cloth. Taunting him had been her purpose in donning it.

"I could take you right here," he vowed in a throaty voice. "Against the wall, a trellis, on the ground."

"And if we were discovered . . ." She couldn't even begin to imagine the dire consequences that would follow. If he were a nobleman, in spite of being promised to Thornley, she'd find herself marrying Finn. Her father would insist. But he wasn't a nobleman, and what her father might do to him didn't bear thinking about. He'd no doubt toss him out on his ear, and her mother would lock Lavinia in her room—she nearly laughed at that. They weren't the villains in a fairy tale. They'd express their disappointment and displeasure and forbid her from ever seeing him again. Her father wouldn't punch him, but he might ask a footman to do so.

Any discovery at all would mean an end to their time together, to this wonderful and exhilarating feeling that came over her whenever she was with him.

"It wouldn't go well," he finished for her as he reclaimed her mouth.

No, it would not, but how could her family object to him when he brought her so much happiness, when she counted the minutes until she was again in his company, when he'd never taken advantage of her—

And if he did take advantage, well, they couldn't send him away if he'd totally ruined her.

When his mouth once again began a slow and sensual sojourn along her throat, she whispered, "Not against a wall or a trellis or on the ground. But in a bed."

He went still, so still that if he hadn't remained standing, she'd have thought he'd died on the spot. Leaning away from her, he wrapped his hands around her upper arms. "What are you saying, Vivi?"

"I want you, Finn. I love you. With all that is in me, I love you. I have for ages. Make me yours, tonight." Breaking free of his grip, she wound her arms tightly around his neck and nipped at his strong chin. "Ruin me for anyone else." A nip on his jaw. "Sneak into my bedchamber after the ball." She took the soft skin of his neck between her teeth. He growled low. "Make me truly yours."

"Are you mad? Your parents will catch us."

"No, they won't. My room is at the end of the corridor. I won't make a sound." She brushed her lips over his. "I want to be yours and yours alone. I want no other."

His arms came around her, pressing her close, flattening her breasts against his chest as he crushed his mouth against hers with such hunger and urgency that every girlish aspect of her blossomed into womanhood. This was what she craved: the fire and the passion, the I-cannot-live-without. None of this existed with Thornley. All of it burned with Finn.

He would take her innocence, make a woman of her.

In the distance she heard the music that would accompany a waltz drifting on the breeze. Their time together in the garden had come to an end. Regretfully, she broke off the kiss. "There is the start of the last waltz, the one I promised to you. I must return to the ballroom shortly so I'm there for my next dance partner when this tune ends. I'm sorry we didn't get another waltz."

"I can't deny you anything, Vivi." Taking one of her hands, placing his other hand on her back, he swept her over the grass.

She would have laughed aloud in glee if she weren't afraid someone would hear her, would catch her in this compromising situation with him. Once she was no longer a virgin, it wouldn't matter. But for now, it mattered.

They only danced for half the tune, so she would have time to return to the ballroom before her next dance partner noticed her missing. Finn walked her back to the residence, stopping where the shadows were thickest.

"Are you sure, Vivi?"

"I'm sure. Come to me later." Lifting her skirts, she dashed to the terrace steps that would lead her back into the ballroom, where she would begin counting the minutes before she saw him again.

$\mathcal{H}$e crouched in a back corner of the garden, watching the residence, waiting for the music's final note. He was a fool to consider sneaking into her bedchamber and bedding her there—but he didn't want her to see the squalor in which he lived with one of his brothers. His single room was small, the bed cramped, the walls so thin he often heard the couple on the other side snoring, or worse, going at it. They were so blasted noisy, her always using the lord's name in vain, him grunting and growling like a rutting boar. Then afterward their loud sighs and laughter, each of them always proclaiming it had never been so good.

She was right. They could do it quietly, undetected. Hadn't Romeo snuck into Juliet's parents' home? Finn would leave with the first trill of the lark.

The music finally flittered away into constant and complete silence. The few stragglers in the garden made their way inside. It was at least an hour later before the ballroom went black. He watched as the lights in other rooms winked out, one by one, until finally the residence was encased in darkness.

And still he waited until he could discern no sounds, no movements, no stirring.

Slowly, he unfolded his body and removed his boots, stockings, greatcoat, and hat. He was no longer playing the role of highwayman. But was to be only himself. Finn Trewlove—who'd never taken a woman because from the moment he'd met Lady Lavinia

Kent, he'd felt a need to remain loyal to her, even knowing he would probably never have her.

He'd been a lovesick lad for an exceedingly long time. Tonight, at last, he would discover if the wait had been worth it.

LYING IN THE bed, she was floating above where dreams waited, refusing to fall completely into slumber. She'd had Miriam prepare her for sleep because it was one thing to tell her maid she was going on an outing to a tavern and another entirely to confess she was going to travel the path toward becoming a woman.

She'd left a lamp burning on the table beside the bed, not brave enough to leave the gaslights glowing. A bit self-conscious with what was about to happen, she wanted a modicum of privacy, enough light to see him by, but not so much as to illuminate all they'd be doing.

She didn't hear the door to her bedchamber open but was keenly aware of the light dance of fingers over her hair. Miriam had braided it, but after her maid had left, Lavinia had unraveled the tightly plaited strands because she'd thought Finn would like to see it long and loose.

Opening her eyes, she found him standing over her bed, his expression filled with tenderness, his smile uncertain as though he feared she might snatch this moment from him. But she wouldn't do that. She loved him. She had for the longest.

Tossing aside the covers, she scrambled up to her knees, facing him, skimming her fingers over his beloved face. "I can't believe you're here," she whispered.

"I had to wait until I was certain no one remained awake. And if you're as nervous as I am, I thought you might appreciate a bit of this." From behind his back, he brought forth a bottle with a label indicating it was whisky. Only then did she notice two glasses resting on the table beside the bed.

"Where did you get it?"

"Your father's study." He opened the bottle and poured some

of the contents into the glasses. "Had to do a bit of exploring to find it."

"You're awfully sneaky, Finn Trewlove."

He handed her a glass. "Not with you, Vivi. I'm always honest with you."

Holding her gaze, he took a sip. She followed suit. "It burns." She'd had a taste at his sister's but had forgotten the flavor of it.

"As it works its way through, it'll make you warm and lethargic all over."

She took a larger swallow, coughed.

"Don't rush it," he said. "We have all night."

She angled her head thoughtfully. "Why are you nervous?"

"Because I want to make it good for you, and I don't know if I'm up to the task." Finishing off the liquid in his glass, he set it along with her empty tumbler back on the table and shifted his gaze to her side. "Your hair is so long."

She grinned. "Nearly to my bum."

He glided his hand over the strands, following the path of those that fell over her arm. "It's so beautiful." His eyes came back to her. "You're so beautiful."

"So are you. I've always thought so." Leaning forward slightly, she pressed her face against his chest. "I don't know what to do, Finn."

"I'm not so well-versed in making love either," he said quietly, his words taking her by surprise, causing her to draw back.

"Are you telling me you're a virgin?"

"I've never wanted anyone other than you." With one hand, he cradled her jaw, her cheek. "I've a good idea how it's done. I've just never put it into practice, so we'll figure it out together."

She rather liked knowing she would be his first, that he'd touched no other woman as intimately as he would touch her. "Where do we start?"

"With removing our clothes, I should think."

She settled back on her heels. "You first."

He grinned. "All right. Why don't you unfasten the buttons on my shirt?"

Easing back up, she went to work, the billowy cloth soft beneath her fingers, trembling ones that made the task a bit more complicated to complete. Finally, they were all free. Reaching back, he began dragging the shirt over his head, revealing a lovely expanse of skin and broad chest. Her fingers flittered over the few hairs that resided in its center. Then she flattened her palms on either side of his sternum and glided them up, down. So firm, so warm.

The muscles on his arms bulged, no doubt forged by his labors. She doubted any nobleman possessed such a well-defined body. Physicians could use Finn as a tool for teaching how the muscles flowed one into the other, weaving together to create such a magnificent whole.

She lowered her gaze to the fall of his trousers, could make out a bulge there.

"Do you know what a man looks like?" he asked.

She nodded. "I've seen statues."

"Don't be frightened."

A shake of her head. "I won't be."

Slowly, he unfastened his trousers, taking his time as though to taunt her. Her mother, of course, had told her nothing at all regarding what passed between a man and woman. That conversation wouldn't take place until the night before she was to wed, as though having no knowledge would prevent her from doing what ladies were not to do. But she'd caught the hounds at it, as well as horses, so she had an idea of how it went.

Shucking off his trousers, he kicked them aside and stood before her magnificent and proud, his manhood stiff and straight. And so frightfully large, larger than she'd expected it to be. "Aren't you supposed to put that in me?"

"Yes."

She lifted her gaze to his. "It won't fit."

His grin was endearing, filled with warmth and humor. "It'll fit."

"How do you know if you've never done it?"

"Because I've spoken with those who have."

She ran her tongue around her mouth, bit her lower lip. "Can I touch it?"

"Not yet. I'm close to bursting." He jerked his head toward her. "Off with your nightdress."

Suddenly, she was feeling bold. "You'll have to unbutton it."

It delighted her to no end to see that his fingers were shaking as they neared the placket. His hands dwarfed the buttons as he moved from one to the other, his eyes focused on his task, on the cloth that was parting to reveal her skin. When he was finished, she stood up on the bed, reigning over him. Reaching down, she gathered up her hem and brought it up over her knees, her hips, her waist, her breasts, her head, and flung it aside.

"Christ, Vivi," he rasped. She watched the muscles at his throat work as he swallowed. "You're perfection."

She dropped back to her knees, lowered herself to the mattress and pillows, and held out her arms. "Come to me."

The bed dipped with his weight as he stretched out beside her. Reaching across her, he took her left arm and carried it to his mouth, where he pressed a kiss against the ragged scar on the inside of her wrist. "Without this, I'd have never met you."

He shifted his eyes up to hers, released his hold on her arm, and cupped her face. "And I'm ever so glad I did."

Then, as though whatever tether had been holding him back broke, he moved up, covering half her body with his, slipping his knee between her thighs, keeping his weight off her by levering himself on his elbows. He bracketed her face between his large hands. "I love you, Vivi. I'll always love you."

The earnest proclamation humbled her as he claimed her mouth as his own. Claimed all of her, with strokes and caresses.

And she laid claim to him, as though she were an explorer discovering an unchartered land. She tested the firmness of all his muscles, skimming her fingers over them, curving her hands around them. So strong, so magnificent. All of it hers. To feast on with eyes and lips, to appreciate, to touch to her heart's content.

Cradling her breast, he plumped it up and lowered his mouth to it, dotting kisses over it until he neared her nipple. His velvety tongue circled it, causing it to pucker, then he drew it into his mouth and suckled. His actions so decadent, her reaction so wicked, as pleasure coursed through her and she wanted to cry out for more.

Only she couldn't cry out. They had to remain quiet, nearly silent as the ecstasy built, as the secretive spot between her legs began to throb, to demand attention. As though he could sense it, he pressed his hand to her core. Heat swarmed over her.

Working her hand between them, she wrapped her fingers around him. He bucked, growled low. He was hot, so hot, velvet over steel.

He shifted until he was resting between her thighs. She felt him poised at her entrance. Taking hold of himself, he rubbed the tip over her, again and again, driving her to madness. He eased into her. She stiffened.

"Relax," he ordered.

"It hurts."

He began pressing kisses to her throat, until all she was thinking about was his mouth and the trail of dew he was leaving in its wake. Then he pushed harder.

She bit back her cry. Rising above her, he held her gaze. "I don't know how to make it not hurt. Do you want me to stop?"

She shook her head. "I want you to make me yours."

Reaching beneath her, he lifted her hips, changing their angle, and then he plunged, deep and sure, blanketing her mouth, absorbing her shriek. She was his, and in spite of the pain she was glad for it.

Slowly, he rocked against her until her body was more welcoming, until the pain eased, until she was lost in the wonder of them being truly united, two becoming one.

The pleasure she'd experienced earlier began to return, but with more intensity, more purpose. She dug her fingers into his buttocks, guiding him, as his movements quickened. Her nerve endings began to prickle, her breasts grew heavy, and her womanhood came fully awake, bursting with sensations that had her gasping and making little mewling sounds. Once again, he covered her mouth with his, quieting her with a swirl of his tongue, a stroke of hers.

Then everything came apart and something completely unexpected burst through her, as stars shot around her, seemed to explode within her. He pumped into her, groaned throatily, went stiff and still, although she could feel the tiny tremors cascading through him, through her.

Burying his mouth in the curve of her shoulder, he went limp. They both lay there, breathing heavily, and she felt her love for him expand in an all-encompassing emotion.

Laboriously, he lifted himself up, met her gaze, caressed his thumb over her cheek. "Are you all right?"

With a soft smile, she nodded.

"It shouldn't hurt so much next time."

"It doesn't matter if it does."

"Of course it matters. I never want to hurt you. I love you, Vivi. I love you with every part of me."

Chapter 9

I love you. Words that had once been so easily given, words he doubted he'd ever utter again.

Sitting in the darkened bedchamber, he waited, striving to ignore the stink of some perfume that was overly sweet. Why would a man wear something that made him smell like a rose in bloom? Or maybe the Earl of Dearwood kept it on hand for his paramours.

In spite of the fact that the man's name was familiar, Finn couldn't quite recall where he'd encountered it before. He should focus on puzzling it out, but thoughts of Lady Lavinia Kent kept intruding, demanding attention. Vivi. He recalled a time when merely murmuring her name had been a balm to his soul.

Why was it that after all these years and all the pain she'd caused him, he still found himself drawn to her? He'd wanted to press his lips to hers, caress his hands over every inch of her silken flesh, tangle his fingers in her hair, push his cock into the tight cove of her womanhood, where once she'd held him so snugly he'd had no desire to ever leave.

He had to wonder: if he'd never known her, if they'd had no past, if he'd only met her for the first time tonight—would he have been as intrigued, would he have wanted to learn all he could about her? That was the hell of it. He'd have been more intrigued because there would have been nothing to cloud his thinking, his judgment.

What had happened to shape her into a woman who would risk so much to ensure the safety of children? Although he couldn't forget how comforting she'd been when she'd learned the truth of his parentage. She hadn't turned away from him as he'd expected. Why had she later?

In retrospect, what he'd known about her, what he'd felt for her, had been little more than the passions of youth. He knew little about her politics, her religion, upon what she placed value, how much she might be willing to sacrifice to achieve her dreams. He couldn't even claim to know precisely what her dreams were—or had been.

He'd thought she'd been willing to give up her aristocratic life for him, but she hadn't been waiting for him. Instead it had been her father who had informed him she wouldn't be coming. Had she changed her mind about the life he'd been offering?

If so, then why was she now living what appeared to be a much harsher life, one with fewer niceties, one without him? What had taken so long for her to choose this path? What had prompted her to do so now? The questions, so many questions, swirled through his mind with such speed and ferocity that he thought he might run mad if he didn't obtain the answers. She was the only one who could give them to him.

Better to be done with her, to forget he'd ever found her. Even better to take her to her brother and claim the five hundred quid. The irony of that path wasn't lost on him. They'd sent him to prison because he'd wanted her. Now they'd pay him a reward because he no longer wanted her and would return her to the place she belonged. Although he wasn't quite certain she did belong there any longer, and the thought of returning her didn't sit well with him.

He missed her, damn it all to hell. She'd been his first, but not his last. He'd had other women since her, but none of them had managed to work their way into his soul. The coupling was always perfunctory, just an act, skin touching, hips thrusting until the release came—always unsatisfactory and disappointing. Only with her had he ever caught a glimpse of something that closely resembled heaven.

Hearing the echo of distant footsteps on the stairs, he shoved aside all the unsettling thoughts and questions about Vivi. Inhaling a deep breath, he brought forth a mien he didn't particularly like, but it served a purpose, albeit one he didn't especially care for, but it was all for a greater good. The door opened, and a gentleman staggered in, carrying a lamp. Finn was surprised the bloke hadn't set fire to his residence on his journey up. He waited until the lamp was safely set on the bedside table and the gent had turned away from it. Patience was one of the virtues that made him so good at what he did. "My lord."

The Earl of Dearwood yelped like a kicked dog, staggered back, and grabbed one of the bedposts. "Good God! How did you get in here?"

"That's my little secret. You've been avoiding my brother's establishment of late."

"I've been playing elsewhere."

"Be that as it may, my brother has grown weary of waiting on you to bring what you owe him. Five thousand pounds is a lot of blunt."

"I'm well aware. Unfortunately, my luck has yet to improve, as *he* is no doubt well aware. I don't have the means to pay what I owe at this time." He released his hold on the poster and straightened his back, although he did weave a bit as though the room was continuing to spin. "I'm good for it."

"He'll need some collateral."

"See here—"

"Your watch, ring, and neck cloth pin should do it."

"I'm not parting with anything at all—except for your company. See yourself out."

Finn slowly unfolded his body. He had a couple of inches and a couple of stones on the dandified lord. He cracked his knuckles, the ominous echo filling the room. Even in the dim light, he could see the lord pale.

"Let's not be hasty here." As Dearwood spoke, he was unhooking his watch chain from his waistcoat button.

On silent feet that had the lord looking even more unnerved, Finn approached and held out his hand, suddenly recalling where their paths had crossed before. A ballroom. Finn hadn't liked him then; he liked him even less now. Avoiding his gaze, Dearwood dropped the watch, ring with the diamond in its center, and the diamond stickpin onto his palm. "Which arm do you favor, right or left?"

The earl jerked his head back as though he'd been punched, no doubt a result of the threatening manner in which Finn had delivered his question. "What does it matter?"

"Which arm?" Finn asked in a tone that would brook no disobedience.

"Right," the earl said hesitantly.

"Wear a splint on it for the next six weeks."

"But it's not broken."

"It will be if I see it without a splint. I was to deliver some pain as a reminder not to run afoul of the owner of the Cerberus Club. I wouldn't like for him to discover I'd not followed through on his orders." A lie. As long as Aiden got paid, he cared nothing at all about delivering reminders.

"I shall gladly wear a splint."

Finn grinned. "Wiser still to stop borrowing money with which to do your gambling."

WITH HIS SHOULDER pressed to a beam that supported the landing, Finn looked out over the gaming floor below that was enshrouded in near darkness. He'd stopped off at the Cerberus Club to transfer the collateral he'd collected to Aiden and then made his way to his own club. The Elysium.

While Aiden's was bustling with card play, drinking, and swearing as hands were lost, Finn's was already closed for the night. He had only a dozen or so members, hadn't really begun promoting the place yet because he'd been working to make it perfect. Had needed it to be perfect.

During the past three years since his release from prison, he'd worked for Aiden, learning how to manage a gaming hell. On occasion, he served as Aiden's heavy, intimidating and collecting money or collateral from those who owed Aiden more than he suspected they could eventually repay. During his spare hours, he took lessons from Gillie regarding spirits, how to properly store and serve them. Which were the best and which ladies might prefer. When Mick had built his posh hotel, Finn had spent a lot of time studying it, because unlike Aiden's shadowy and dreary place that catered to the darker side of London, Finn had wanted his club to reflect a lady's tastes because his clientele was to be of the feminine variety. He'd intended it to be a secretive place where the ladies of the nobility could engage in all manner of wickedness.

His plan had been to adopt Aiden's scheme of keeping the place elusive, so its allure was the fact that not everyone knew about it and many who did wouldn't know where to find it. Its appeal rested in its clandestineness. But he wanted it bright and fancy like Mick's hotel. He wanted to serve the finest liquors. And he wanted it done with a bit of stylishness.

He'd been creating a web of many strands, its main purpose to lure in Lady Lavinia Kent. He'd had no desire to go to her, but if he'd been able to get her to come to him . . .

After he'd gotten out of prison, recovering from the ordeal of his captivity, he'd not been in a state to confront her. In truth, he'd wanted to know nothing about her. He'd avoided the tabloids, hadn't asked his siblings what they might know of her. Hadn't wanted to know if she was betrothed or married or was mother to a horde of children already. He hadn't wanted to know if she was happy or sad or regretful. He hadn't wanted to know how she might have changed—for better or worse. He'd needed what he knew of the woman who'd betrayed him to remain unchanged in order to sustain his anger with her and his need to find some way to get back at her.

He'd created the place for her, out of vengeance, like a widow spider creating her web. He'd intended to lure her in, although he wasn't quite certain what he would have done then. Ensured she lost all her blunt, watch from the shadows, report her notorious behavior to the newspapers and gossip sheets.

Working for Aiden, helping him to manage his club and occasionally putting the Trewlove fear into someone who had run up a debt and seemed in no hurry to pay it back, Finn had slowly been saving so he could purchase a building and everything he needed to turn it into what he dreamed of. Even when Aiden called it another one of Finn's follies, he was determined not to give up on it.

Every afternoon, he took Sophie out for a ride in the park to let her stretch her legs, to keep her from going wild. A lord had spotted her and approached Finn about allowing his stallion to cover her, and the fee he'd paid had been enough to get Finn started sooner than might have happened otherwise.

Then damn it all to hell, last week he'd seen Vivi embracing three children in the wee hours and all his careful planning had seemed for naught. She wasn't the girl of eight years ago. The woman he'd encountered tonight had been nearly a stranger.

Yet still he'd been drawn to her, intrigued by her as though no years had passed. Who was this woman who now roamed the midnight streets of Whitechapel as though they belonged to her? What happened to the girl he'd once intended to marry?

Chapter 10

*F*inn waited in the shadows, his heart in his throat, worried she might not show, that in the light of day she might have been filled with regrets. He'd left her near dawn with the promise to be waiting for her at midnight. After making love to her, after holding her in his arms, he'd known he'd find it impossible to wait until Tuesday to see her. Even now, he was contemplating stealing inside—

Then the door opened, and she was slipping through the narrow gap. Before she closed the door, he was at her side, inhaling her sweet fragrance, taking pleasure from the way she beamed up at him.

"Hello," she said.

"Hello." Then because he had no resistance where she was concerned, he kissed her, loving the way she came to him with such eagerness, her arms winding around his neck, her breasts flattened against his chest, as her mouth mated enthusiastically with his. His cock hardened and strained against his trousers, and wicked wench that she was, she rose up on her toes, then lowered her heels back to the ground, again and again, rubbing her belly along his pole, driving him to distraction. It occurred to him that they could suddenly find themselves surrounded by the British army and he'd not notice.

Breaking off the kiss, he grabbed her hand and pulled her after him as he sprinted for the mews where Sophie was saddled and waiting.

"You brought her!" she exclaimed in surprise.

He'd taken the risk because their little trysts hadn't been discovered. "I didn't want to go to my brother's brickworks factory tonight, and I knew you'd miss not seeing her."

Spinning around, she placed her hands on his shoulders, held his gaze. "You know me so well."

He knew her almost as well as he knew himself.

"Where are we going?" she asked.

"It's a surprise." Then he hoisted her into the saddle. Slipping a foot into the stirrup, he swung his leg over the horse's rump and settled in behind Vivi. Taking the reins in one hand and snaking his other arm around Vivi's waist, he nudged the mare forward.

Vivi snuggled against him. "I love our riding together."

"What else do you like us doing together?"

She looked back at him. In the moonlight, he could see she'd pressed her teeth to her bottom lip. "Naughty things, things we shouldn't."

"Do you have regrets, Vivi?"

Her hand came up, and she cradled his cheek. "No. It was marvelous, Finn, and I'm a woman now. Although, to be honest, I don't feel any different. However, I did fear my parents might be able to tell that I wasn't the same as I'd been yesterday morning. It's a remarkable thing, really, that a woman can give herself to a man and no one is the wiser for it."

"I'm wiser for it."

Laughing, she turned back around and settled herself more securely against him. "In what way?"

"I know your nipples are a light pink and pucker if I blow on them."

She giggled. "What else?"

"You're a dark pink between your legs, and you glisten when you want me."

"Am I glistening now, do you think?"

Christ, he hoped so. He pressed his mouth against her ear. "I don't know. Are you?"

"Maybe."

He wanted her so badly he thought he'd burst. "Are you hurting from last night?"

"I was a little sore this morning, but not now. Oh, Finn, what are we to do? I know you can't come to my bedchamber every night."

"I can't take you to my lodgings because I share a room with Beast." Although he was fairly certain his brother would make himself scarce should he ask, but Vivi was a lady of the highest caliber, and it was imperative no one suspect what had passed between them, no one question her reputation, he bring her no shame. "And the rooms I could afford to let for the night aren't good enough for a proper lady."

"Are they good enough for you?"

"Of course."

"Then they're good enough for me."

And there was one of the reasons he loved her so fiercely. She didn't consider him beneath her. While he'd fought his entire life not to let the circumstances of his birth influence him, until Vivi, he'd never truly convinced himself they didn't matter. He tightened his hold on her, wanting to keep her near, nestled against him as long as he drew breath.

THEY LEFT THE residences and the shops and other buildings behind until eventually they crested a hill, a full moon guiding their way. Finn brought Sophie to a halt, slid off her, and closed his hands around Lavinia's waist, bringing her down to the ground as though she were delicate porcelain to be treated with extreme care. Guiding her around so her back was to his chest, he held her close, his chin resting on the top of her head. Below them, the lights of London twinkled as merrily as the stars above.

"Someday," Finn said quietly, "I want to live in a residence that will give me a view such as this. I want to be away from the crowds, the constant noise, the stench of too many people crammed into too little space. But it'll be a while before that comes to pass."

"It'll be wonderful when it does." She wanted to be there with him, sharing his home, his bed. "Will your brother build it for you?"

"I'd have to pay him for the materials and labor, but I suspect he'd give me a good price."

She turned within the circle of his arms. As lovely as it was to look out over the metropolis in the distance, she always preferred looking at him, holding his gaze. "What will you do when that day comes, when you escape the city?"

"Breed horses, train them, give lessons to folks on the proper way to care for them, to ride them"—he shrugged as though suddenly embarrassed—"I don't know the particulars, but I know I want to work with horses in some capacity. There are days, Vivi, when I leave the slaughter yard, and I'm simply sad. I despise what I do, even when I convince myself it's necessary."

She combed her fingers through the thick strands of his hair. "When all is said and done, Finn, I think you have too gentle a heart. I saw it that first day. I think that's the reason I went with you so willingly. It's not within you to cause pain."

"I hurt you last night."

Rising up on her toes, with her teeth she nipped playfully at his chin. "That wasn't you. That was Mother Nature. Did it hurt you?"

He chuckled low. "No."

While she'd not want him to experience any discomfort, it was rather irritating that only women suffered. "That's hardly fair. Why can't the world be fair?"

His lips touched her crown, her forehead, the tip of her nose. "I don't know, Vivi. But what I do know is that I want to make love to you with the moonlight shining down over us. Here, where there's no one about. Only us, the breeze, and the moon."

"And Sophie."

His laughter threaded through her. "And Sophie. But she promised me she wouldn't watch."

"You discussed the matter with her?"

"I discuss everything with her. Because you love her so, it makes me feel as though I'm almost talking with you."

"Ah, Finn." Tangling her fingers in his hair, she brought his head down until she could claim his mouth as her own, just as she wanted to claim him. She couldn't help but think it was a rare thing indeed to be so open with one person, to bare one's heart and soul with such abandon, to have no fear because the trust was absolute.

They worked quickly to divest the other of clothing until every inch of their bodies was bathed in the glow of the moon, as though it was caressing them. She thought his body, a rich tapestry of shadow and light, the most sensual, decadent image she'd ever beheld, far more artistic than any painting or sculpture.

When he carried her down to the mound of their clothes and settled himself between the juncture of her thighs, she was more than ready for him. She could not help but believe that her body had been created to cradle and shelter his and his alone. They were equally eager, hands caressing, mouths tasting, endearments echoing around them.

"So beautiful."

"So handsome."

"So soft."

"So strong."

"I love the silkiness of your skin."

"I adore the hardness of your muscles . . . and other things."

Laughter, low and deep, dark and wicked. "Say it, Vivi. Say *cock.*"

Her giggle, short and high. "I can't."

"Say it or I won't give it to you."

"I'll call that bluff."

His growl reverberated through his chest and into hers. "You're right. Why would I deny us both?"

Then the devil in her took hold. "Cock."

His snarl sounded of victory and surrender as he plunged deep and sure. She cried out at the absolute joy of his spreading her, filling her.

They rocked in tandem, a perfect rhythm quickening in pace until they were both baying at the moon as exquisite pleasure overtook them. All she could think was that she wanted this forever.

HE'D SEEN HER every night for two weeks, although when she had a ball to attend, their hours together were fewer. Yet it wasn't enough. It was never enough.

Whenever they spoke of the future, it was always in the context of his plans, what he wanted to do with his life. Never hers because they both knew what her future held: marriage to a lord, providing him with an heir. The thought of another man touching her would send such despair through him that he didn't know how he would survive it. He could not help but wonder if it would be as awful for her, if she would close her eyes and pretend that Finn was the one hovering over her, joining his body to hers, thrusting into her, spilling his seed.

He couldn't imagine having his life planned out for him from the moment he was born. If his father hadn't taken him to Ettie Trewlove's door, perhaps it would have been. In many ways, despite his humble existence, he was much freer than Vivi. He could do anything he damned well wanted. And what he damned well wanted was to ask her to do the same, to do what she damned well wanted.

That terrified the hell out of him because what he planned for tonight was going to change everything between them—for better or worse. But he couldn't go on much longer as they'd been.

As he waited for her, he was constantly wiping his sweating palms on his trousers, for the first time wishing he had a proper pair of gentlemen's gloves, but all he had were the gloves in which he worked, and he'd never touch her wearing those. So he paced and took deep breaths.

Then she was through the door, and his nervousness increased because she was so beautiful and so refined and so above him, even if she didn't see herself as such. He loved her with everything inside him and every corner of his heart. It was hers as though she'd laid her hand over it and branded it.

She eased away from the house. "Finn?"

He heard the worry and doubt echoed in her whisper and only then realized he had yet to make a move toward her, as though his feet were permanently rooted where he stood. "Here," he called out, keeping his voice low, even as he strode quickly to her, possibly reaching her before the word did.

The joy that wreathed her face created an ache in his chest. He couldn't imagine that anyone else would ever look at him as she did.

Tonight, Sophie was again their means of transport, but as there was no moon, he'd brought a lantern.

"Where are we going?" she whispered.

Every night he'd taken her somewhere different: another rise, a valley, a nearby village green.

"You'll see." The answer he always gave to that question when she asked.

The exchange had become one more ritual in an assortment they'd acquired over the past two years.

They didn't travel far before he brought Sophie to a halt in the mews behind a massive residence. He shoved himself over the horse's rump and landed smartly on the ground. Walking to the side, he settled his hands around Vivi's waist, another ritual. Of late, his life had become guided by their rituals.

"Where are we?" she asked, once her feet were firmly on the ground.

"It's not important, but it has the most beautiful garden I've ever seen." He grabbed the lantern used for thieving with its three enclosed sides from where he'd secured it to the saddle, lit the candle within, and held it aloft.

"You're not thinking of going in there, surely."

"The owner is not in residence. Only a handful of servants are about, and they're all abed at this hour. We won't be long." He'd wanted someplace special, someplace that would bring delight to a woman, that would give her a fond memory. He'd considered a park, but many were locked up after midnight and there was no guarantee they'd be undisturbed if he did manage to get them inside. Besides, he'd been able to place a few shillings in the butler's palm to ensure the gate here was left unlocked and none of the staff would become curious if they saw light in the garden.

Taking her hand, he tried to draw her near, but she resisted. "Finn—"

"Vivi, I have permission."

"Why didn't you just say?"

"I thought it would make the night more unforgettable."

She smiled. "Every night with you is unforgettable."

Tightening her hold on his hand, she allowed him to lead her into the lush and verdant gardens.

"I feel like I should know this place," she said. "Is this a lord's manor?"

"A duke's actually, but as he is unwed, I don't think he entertains. I had to put one of his horses down recently."

"You meet all manner of people in your occupation, don't you?"

"If they own a horse, eventually they'll have need of our services, but let's not discuss that tonight." Slipping his arm around her waist, he drew her up against his side and led her toward what had originally captured his attention and imagination.

"Oh, my goodness. A lovely pond with a bridge. It's beautiful."

The fragrance of so many flowers still hung on the air. He'd noticed that as well when he'd first come here. Smells like this were difficult to come by in Whitechapel.

He escorted her onto the bridge and set the lantern down near his feet. He wanted to place his arms around her, but instead he merely stood beside her because he wanted to see her face.

"Do you think there are fish in the pond?" she asked.

"I rather suspect so. Not the kind one eats though."

She chuckled softly. "No, I suspect they are not for sport."

He closed his eyes for a minute, gathering his courage. When he opened his eyes, he realized all the bravery he'd ever need was standing right there beside him. "I'll probably never own anything as fancy as all this," he said quietly.

Turning her attention away from the pond, she gave him a warm smile as she reached up and brushed the hair from his brow. "No, but you'll have your place away from the city where you can look out over London."

He swallowed hard. "The residence won't be as fancy as this manor and the gardens won't be as elaborate, but if you were there with me, no matter how small or insignificant it might be to others, to me, it would be grander than all of this."

She blinked, blinked. Her mouth formed a tiny O.

Taking her hand, he went down onto one knee. "I love you, Vivi, and I know I have no right to ask, but if you would honor me by becoming my wife, I swear to you I'd work like the very devil to make sure you never regretted it."

She pressed her free hand to her lips, and the light from the lantern reflected in the tears welling in her eyes.

"I can't go on like this any longer, sharing plans for my future when what I really want is to share plans for *our* future."

"Oh, Finn." She shook her head, and he heard the tiniest of cracks in his heart.

"I know what I'm asking, Vivi. I'm asking you to leave behind everything you know, because I don't think I'd be welcomed or accepted by the toffs. I know I'm a selfish bastard—"

"No, no, Finn."

The crack spread.

"If you're selfish, then so am I because you're all I want," she said. "Yes, I'll marry you. Yes! Yes!"

The crack healed as though it had never been as he surged to his feet, took her in his arms, and planted his mouth over hers, kissing her deeply, eagerly. He drew back. "I'll get you a ring. It'll be simple—"

"It can be a piece of string. I don't care. When?"

"I'll speak with your father on the morrow."

Her eyes contained such sadness that it nearly broke his heart. "I don't think my parents will allow it, will accept you, even if I confess to them that we've been intimate."

"Then run away with me. Tonight, now."

She cradled his face between her hands, and as he looked down into her eyes, he realized he would be gazing into them for the remainder of his life, until he drew his last breath. "I don't have anything with me."

"I'll purchase you whatever you need."

"Your coins are precious, and I have a few things I'd rather not leave behind. We must be grown up, responsible. I also need to write a letter to my parents, so they won't worry or come looking for us. Tomorrow night, at midnight. What say you to that?"

"I'll be there waiting."

Chapter 11

1871

$\mathcal{A}$rms folded across his chest, encased in midnight shadows, Finn leaned against a building across from the foundling home and watched, just as he had for three nights now, striving not to recall how familiar all this seemed, the many hours he'd waited for her when he was younger and in love. He especially fought not to remember what it had felt like to be in love, to greet each day with hopeful optimism, to believe the world was filled with promises of good things waiting around the corner, to dream she would walk by his side, that together they would conquer the world.

He didn't even know why he was here, why he felt a need to look out for her. It was folly to stand here night after night when he had no idea if she even had an arranged rendezvous with anyone. Perhaps she'd given up her quest. Perhaps she'd returned home where she belonged.

Although if she hadn't returned home in three months, why did he think she would now? If she'd come here on a lark, she had to be tired of playing about. The girl he'd known wouldn't have stayed for more than a few hours, not once she realized the harshness that awaited her. But the woman she'd become seemed intent on remaining. He was both baffled and intrigued, each sensation irritating him. Even more annoyed with himself for keeping to his post as wisps of fog began waltzing around him, bringing with it a dampness and a chill.

He was an even greater fool than he'd been eight years earlier. He should abandon this endeavor, get on with the business that awaited him, but then he heard the muffled footsteps, the clack of heels hitting stone, echoing on the other side of the wrought iron gate. His heart sped up with wild abandon as every muscle forged to fight and protect, to take and deliver blows, tightened in preparation for pouncing if the action were needed.

Then she emerged, the hood of her cloak brought up over her head in a way that kept her face hidden, but he didn't need to see it to know it was her. He recognized the outline of her body, the curves he had once caressed, although his memory recalled there being a bit more to them. She was thinner now, but still he knew that form.

With a clank, she opened the gate and walked through it. With another clank, she closed it behind her and didn't hesitate to begin marching down the street, purpose in every stride.

"Little fool," he whispered before shoving himself away from the wall and following. Her steps were as silent as his. She was aware of every sound that disturbed the night, was constantly glancing around, making careful note of her surroundings.

Why did she care about these children who weren't hers? Why was she living in near poverty? Why had she not married one of the most powerful dukes in England? Thornley could have assisted her in her quest to do good—with money, with clout, with influence. Marriage to him would have made her life so much easier. Why take the more challenging road?

She turned a corner. He quickened his pace. People were on this street, leaving taverns and public houses, staggering home. Or plying their services. Ribald laughter hung on the air. He wondered if she had any idea where she was being led.

A man grabbed her arm, and unmitigated fury swept through him, nearly causing him to stagger with its strength. She broke free of the hold, shoved the man with enough force to send him reeling backward, and carried on. The bloke righted himself, took a step to follow her—

Finn grabbed him and delivered a blow that sent the oaf to the ground. He pointed a finger at him. "Leave off."

Straightening, he began walking in the direction she'd been going, quickening into a trot, glancing around wildly, striving to catch sight of her among the thickening crowd, all the while his gut clenching tighter and tighter in danger of doubling him over.

Where was she? Where the devil was she?

Like a madman, he began shoving people out of his way, fighting to move more quickly as though that were the problem. He simply wasn't running fast enough. His stealth left him. His footsteps were no longer silent. He was hit with something he hadn't been hit with in eight years: panic.

She'd disappeared.

THERE WERE THREE of them, bulky men with faces so hideous that even the shadows avoided them. She suspected that had they lived a different life, they might have been handsome, but their ugliness, greed, and desire to hurt had shaped their features to reflect their inner souls. One had grabbed and dragged her into the alleyway between the two buildings, the others following with their laughter echoing off the brick walls. She hadn't had a chance to unsheathe her rapier, and now her arms were pinned behind her back with beefy hands at her wrists serving as the shackles.

Inwardly she cursed. Knowing Finn was trailing her—she'd caught sight of him as she'd gone through the gate—she'd become irritated, distracted, hadn't paid as much attention as she should have, and now she was in a bit of a bother, but she was far from panicked. As long as she kept her wits about her, she stood a good chance of making her way out of this mess unharmed.

"Ain't ye a pretty one," the smallest of the group sneered.

"I have money," she stated firmly.

"Ye want to pay us to take ye?" her captor asked, his foul breath a vaporous fog that nearly caused her to gag.

"I shall pay you to leave me alone."

"Ah, ye silly lass. We'll take yer money, after we've—"

Because he held her too close to effectively bring her knee up, she stomped her heel down fast and hard on his instep. With a howl of pain, he loosened his grip just enough that she was able to twist free and retrieve the knife secreted away in her boot. The smallest one reached for her, and with an upward slash she sliced into his hand. Hollering, he dropped back, and the middle-sized man began bouncing on the balls of his feet as though preparing to make a dash for her.

The growl of a savage beast echoed around them, and suddenly he was off his feet flying toward the ground with such speed that she was barely able to register that someone was on top of him.

Her original captor came at her. She held the knife at the ready, prepared to plunge it deep.

Quite suddenly he was dragged back. The resounding crack of splintering bone filled the air just before he was tossed aside like so much rubbish. Smallest ran off, leaving her gasping for breath as she realized it was over.

Then someone was standing before her, reaching out, touching her cheek. "Vivi."

That single word contained such concern she was thrown back eight years when she'd believed her days and nights would be filled with the sound of that voice. "Finn."

Without thought or care, she sagged against him as he bent over her, holding her close, so she was able to bury her nose in the soft skin at his neck, inhale the comforting scent of leather and horses, of him. He smelled the same as he had all those years before. It made her glad and angry at the same time, that something about him should remain the same.

He rubbed his jaw along her temple and she was acutely aware of the thick stubble prickling her face, catching her hair. He had a man's whiskers now, no longer soft and reminiscent of peach fuzz. During the years they'd been apart, he'd changed, and she was grateful that little of the boy he'd been remained, because it allowed her to think of the boy without seeing the man. She could separate the two, could reflect on the sweet memories, have a *before* he'd abandoned her and an *after.*

The *after* was now, even though he'd come to her aid twice now. She pushed her way out of his embrace. "Thank you, thank you for your assistance."

She made to walk by him and her knees nearly buckled, drat the weak things for suddenly turning to jam. His hand snaked out, grabbed her arm, held her aloft. How could he be so calm, so put together?

"Are you hurt?" he asked.

"No, I'm fine." Rattled, shaking like a damned leaf in the wind, but otherwise perfectly fine. Gently, she worked her way out of his grasp. "I have to go. Someone is waiting on me."

After stopping to retrieve her walking stick, she headed back to the street, grateful when she reached it, grateful as well that he had followed her. She was not going to be deterred from her task, but it was incredibly tempting to return to the foundling home.

"Vivi, this is madness, what you're doing."

"You caught me on two bad nights. I've never been bothered before."

"Yet you carry weapons because you know it's a possibility."

"Yes, it's a possibility, it's always a possibility, but I'm prepared. I know how to fight, Finn."

His sigh was so strong that if she hadn't pulled the hood of her pelisse back up, she might have felt it stirring the tendrils of her hair, sending delicious shivers down her back as it once had. She was not going to think about that. "You don't have to follow me."

"I've got nothing else to do at the moment."

Having memorized the path she needed to take, she continued along the circuitous route. She'd traversed it earlier in the day, searching for any areas that might bring danger, but she hadn't considered this time of night might fill the streets with the dregs of society. She'd never been in this section of Whitechapel before, wasn't that familiar with it, which was the reason she'd scoped it out earlier. The farther she went, the deeper she was in warrens of poverty. The rookeries. Her mother would be appalled to find her here. "Did you grow up in an area such as this?"

"Not this bad."

With a nod, she carried on until she reached the designated alleyway. Tardy in arriving, she was disappointed to not find a woman waiting for her. Beginning to pace the opening that led into darkness, she could only hope the baby farmer was late as well.

"You should have brought a lamp," he said.

"It would not only illuminate the dark corners but illuminate me. Believe it or not, I strive not to bring attention to myself. While I think it unlikely anyone from my previous life will run across me here, the men my brother hired did post some handbills with my likeness etched on them. I'd rather not risk being recognized. As you mentioned the other night, five hundred quid is a lot of blunt."

"Perhaps you should tell your brother to bugger off."

She almost smiled. "I have. Not in those words exactly, but I write him every week assuring him I am well and asking him to leave off. But as always from the moment I was born, my wishes are hardly given any credence."

Leaning against the wall, with the glow from the streetlamp limning one side of him, with one foot crossed over the other and his arms folded over his chest, he appeared incredibly masculine. "What is the purpose in all this that you're doing?"

"I told you. I can't stand the thought of these children being murdered."

"Not all baby farmers kill the children placed in their care. My mum didn't."

"But many do, and those who don't—how many of them truly love them? You saw the women the other night. Hardly sterling examples of motherhood."

"They seemed to be fighting for what was theirs."

She scoffed. "They were fighting for the coins to be made, not the children to be cared for. They measure the worth of a babe based on how many shillings it'll place in their palms, not the joy it'll bring to their lives."

"You have a cynical view."

She laughed harshly. "You taught me about the practice. And I've read a few articles about it. It's ghastly, what sometimes happens to these children."

"You can't save them all."

"I can save some, and that's preferable to none."

HE HEARD THE determination in her voice, couldn't help but admire it. Against his better judgment, he settled in and watched as she paced, three steps one way, three the other. He should leave her. He had business to see to, but it had felt so bloody good to hold her within his arms, to inhale her sweet fragrance. She might not be able to afford whatever perfume she'd worn before, but over the years, it had no doubt soaked into her skin and become such a part of her that it still lingered—or perhaps it was simply his memory of it that had caused his nostrils to flare.

In the far-off distance, he heard the pealing of a bell, twice. Two o'clock. Why was she not recognizing the reality? Why was she being so stubborn? "How long are you going to wait for your appointment to show?"

"As long as I have to. You can go on."

"You said you were late. She's probably already come and gone."

Clenching her hands into fists, she swung around, faced him, and stepped out of the shadows until the distant light fell across her lovely features. "Are you speaking from experience? Because that's the way you handle matters? You show up and then leave when the person you are to meet is a tad tardy?"

"I beg your pardon?"

As though propelled by a force over which she had no control, she marched forward with a speed that took him by surprise. "I waited! I waited for you until dawn." He could clearly see the anguish in her expression. He'd never seen such despair. "Yes, I know I was twenty minutes late. But was I not even worth a few minutes of worry, of patience, of thinking perhaps something was delaying me? How many minutes did you give me before you decided to be done with me?"

Each word she threw at him was a blow to his head, his heart, his gut. "You waited?"

"I thought perhaps the wagon broke or the horse went lame or something, but you never showed, you never sent word. You just left me there. Or did you never show up at all? Was it all some grand jest? You'd taken the one thing of mine that was of any value, and were done with me? Is that the way it was? The lowly bastard deflowering the earl's daughter. Is that what you told your mates? Did it make you a man?"

Slowly he uncoiled his body. "I was there, Vivi, at the stroke of midnight, just as I'd promised."

"Then why in God's name didn't you wait for me?"

"Because your father was expecting me and had me arrested."

Chapter 12

She'd thought her heart was naught but shattered shards, but his words broke it all over again. The pain in her chest made it difficult to breathe.

"No," she whispered in horror. "That's not possible."

"I'd barely stepped into the garden when I was accosted by constables, trussed up like a Christmas goose. Then your father emerged from the shadows. I clearly remember his words. They played in my mind a million times. 'My daughter is done with you.' I assumed you told him about me, about our plans."

Each word was a blow that threatened to drop her to her knees. She reached for him, brought her hand back, not certain he'd welcome her touch. "No, no, Finn. I told no one."

"I don't know how he knew, Vivi, but he knew. He saw to it that I went to prison."

"Oh my God." Tears burned her eyes. She no longer cared if he wanted her touch or not. She placed her palm against his cheek. "My poor Finn."

Then that was no longer enough. She slid her arms around his neck, held him close. "I'm so sorry. I didn't know. He never said a word to me."

He enfolded her in his embrace, clutching her to him as though he'd been adrift at sea and someone had finally tossed him a rope. "I thought you knew," he rasped. "Thought you were responsible."

"No, my love." The unexpected endearment, uttered on a sob, came from the depths of her soul as she suddenly needed to comfort the one who had once owned her heart. "How awful it must have been for you."

She clung to him, striving to deal with a shift in all her emotions, in the hatred she'd harbored, the disappointment she'd suffered, the crushing of her heart that she'd somehow survived. She thought she'd been alone in her anguish, yet he'd been living through torments of his own. "How long?" she dared asked, her voice raw with her grief over all he'd endured. "How long were you in prison?"

"Five years."

The words sliced into her soul as easily as a well-honed knife into butter. "No, no, no."

She could find no words strong enough to convey the depths of her despair that he had suffered so at the hands of her father, that his desire to run off with her had cost him so dearly.

Easing back, he cupped her face between his hands, holding her gaze as his thumbs gently swept at the tears raining down her cheeks. "Don't cry. It was long ago."

She shook her head. "Not so long ago, Finn. Why did you not send word to me?"

"I thought it was what you wanted. To be rid of me. That when it came down to it, you had decided you didn't want to be associated with a bastard."

"Ah, Finn." She brushed her fingers through his hair. "I wanted nothing else other than to be with you. Miriam had managed to pack so much so tightly into this carpeted satchel—"

She was struck nearly dumb as a possibility reverberated through her mind. "Oh, dear God, she knew. Could she have told my father?"

He shook his head. "I don't know, Vivi. I was careless bringing Sophie around after . . . just after." After they'd first made love. "Maybe a stable boy saw us."

"The stable boy didn't know we were running off at midnight. Miriam did. I trusted her, told her everything. And it cost you dearly."

"Cost us," he said somberly.

Dear God, but it had, and she couldn't reveal to him the true extent of what it had cost them, not now, not when she knew the truth of all he'd paid for loving her.

He glanced around. "Your woman's not going to show, and you're trembling from the cold. Let's get you somewhere warm."

He shattered her heart once more. After all he'd suffered, all he'd revealed, he was worried about her taking a chill. While she was indeed shaking, it had nothing to do with the cold surrounding her, but rather the devastation of learning what had truly happened that fateful night.

His arm came snugly around her, pressing her against his side as he led her out of the alley and down the street. Fewer people were about; the revelry had diminished. The quietness suited her mood. Her world had once been bright with promise, and now it seemed it was condemned to forever being shades of gray. How much darker it had to be for Finn.

"Oi!" he called out, releasing her hand and stepping into the street, barring a hansom's way. The driver pulled to a stop. Finn gave the man the address for the foundling home as he bundled her into the carriage and followed her inside. His hand, so warm, so strong, came around hers and placed it on his thigh, as though he needed to have some contact with her.

"I was so stupid, Finn. It had to be Miriam."

"Why would she betray your trust?"

She wanted to crawl onto his lap and hold him near, protect him from all that he had to have suffered. "If I ran off, she'd have lost her exalted position as lady's maid to the earl's daughter, who she expected to be a duchess. She'd have been simply another servant. She was looking out for herself. And because I was too stupid—"

"You weren't stupid."

"What else would you call it? I was so caught up in myself that I didn't even consider that she might see my happiness as an end to hers. And it cost you. My God. My God." The tears returned with a vengeance as she envisioned him locked in a cell, kept away from his family. "How much you must have hated me." Much more than she had despised him.

A strangled burst of laughter escaped from her. "Yet still, after all that, you've come to my aid twice." With the hand he was not holding, she cradled his jaw. "All that kindness in you, I'm glad they didn't kill it." Or at least they hadn't managed to kill all of it. She couldn't deny there was a harsher element to him now. "I'm sorry I hit you the other night."

He placed his hand over hers, turned it slightly, and pressed a kiss to the heart of her palm, all the while his eyes locked with hers. "You thought I'd abandoned you. I'd have understood if you had skewered me."

She buried her face in the curve of his shoulder, welcomed his arms coming around her in the tight confines of the conveyance. Silence eased in around them, comforting in its peacefulness. How often had they been together and not needed words? Now it was as though they each traveled through their individual memories, striving to see that last night differently as though viewing it through a kaleidoscope, turning the end so the pieces assembled themselves into something else entirely. What she'd always known, what she'd always believed, was not at all the truth of that fateful night.

Finally, they reached their destination and disembarked. With her hand nestled in his, she led him through the gate—the sisters never locked it; they were a trusting lot—and around to the back, to the kitchen where she'd left a solitary lit lamp on the table that was mainly used for preparing food. The sisters had no servants but tended to everything themselves.

When the door was closed, rather than releasing his hold on her hand, he pulled her toward him as though on the verge of leading her into a dance. His hands came to rest lightly on the small of her back, while hers folded around his upper arms. She had to tip her head back slightly to hold his gaze, to look into those brown eyes that reminded her of warm cocoa.

"I could put on a kettle," she said quietly. "Tea always makes everything better."

"So my mum says. I've found whisky usually works best though."

"Afraid you won't find any here." Reaching up with shaking fingers, she gingerly touched the bruise on his jaw, a reminder she had struck him. "I'm so sorry, Finn."

"No more apologies, Vivi. Neither of us was at fault. We were both wronged."

She wasn't quite certain she could accept that. If only she hadn't told Miriam. "I want to know, understand, everything."

Within the depths of his eyes, she saw a myriad of emotions and knew there were some things he wouldn't share. "Let's sit, shall we?" she offered.

With a nod, he released her. Without bothering to remove her pelisse, she sat at a chair on the side of the table, indicating he should take the one at its head. Once he was settled, she placed both her hands, palms up, on top, grateful when he placed his over hers. She closed her fingers over the raised veins and corded muscles that indicated his strength. She released a long, drawn-out sigh. "I can barely breathe when I think of you in prison."

"Then don't think on it. I didn't tell you so you could imagine the horrors of it. I needed you to understand where I was. Why I wasn't there."

She shook her head. "I understand the nobility has a great deal of power but to tell the authorities to send a man to prison for no reason—"

"He accused me of stealing a horse."

She thought she might be ill. "How could he do that? How could he lie?"

"Perhaps he thought he was protecting you."

"Me? No. If anything it was his reputation he was striving to keep unsullied. The shame he would have endured if it was learned his daughter ran off with a commoner." She squeezed his hands. "I saw nothing in the newspaper about your arrest."

"I think your father ensured it wasn't mentioned in the paper at all. Or perhaps my siblings saw to that. It wouldn't help any of their businesses if word got out that a Trewlove was a thief. At the time, I didn't bloody well care."

Because he'd thought it was what she'd wanted. It took everything within her not to wail at the injustice of it. Then the tears were burning her eyes again.

"No more tears, Vivi. It breaks my heart to see you weep."

"But it hurts, Finn. It hurts to know he did this to you and I didn't know. I thought you'd abandoned me, and it was I who abandoned you."

"You didn't know."

"But I feel as though somehow I should have. I was angry at you, but my anger was misplaced. It should have been directed at my father and now he's no longer here to endure my wrath." She wished she could call her father out, make him tell her everything he'd arranged, but he'd passed away a few years ago. "Prison must have been absolutely horrid for you."

"Better than what was originally planned for me: transportation."

She knew criminals were sometimes transported away from England's shores, to Australia. "How did you manage to avoid that punishment?"

"Aiden. He had a word with our father, convinced him to use his influence to see my sentence changed, reduced. I'm not exactly sure how he managed it, what he might have traded for the favor. He won't talk about it, won't tell me what price he paid, but I know it cost him dearly, simply because he won't talk about it, doesn't want me feeling beholden." He traced a finger along a line on her palm as though he'd only just discovered it. "But I feel it just the same."

And now she owed Aiden as well for what he'd done to spare his brother a worse fate, a fate that had come about because of her. "That night, my mother had come to my bedchamber, unexpectedly, shortly before midnight. She didn't seem surprised to find me still dressed, but then she hardly paid enough attention to me to notice things like that, so I thought nothing of it. She wanted to talk about"—she dug her fingertips into her forehead, trying to force herself to think more clearly, to recall exactly what was said—"my giving a recital, so Thornley could hear me perform. I played along, pretended I thought it was a splendid idea, and deep inside I was shouting with glee because I'd never have to perform again. I would never have to take on a role I didn't want."

"Were you already betrothed to him when you agreed to marry me?"

She shook her head. "No. Our fathers had signed an agreement, but he had yet to ask for my hand. Neither of us was in any hurry. I think we knew we weren't truly suited. Although earlier this year we did try to force it. We made it official and became betrothed in June. However, in the end, I couldn't see it through." She looked at him as earnestly as possible, not bothering to disguise her fury. "Mother must have been in on whatever Father was planning, must have come to my room to purposely delay my departure. How could they be so treacherous, so cruel? Then to keep it all from me.

"And then my maid, equally to blame. I'm convinced it was her. When I thought you hadn't shown, she consoled me—ah, the cheek of her. She convinced me if I gave a gentleman the milk, he wasn't likely to purchase the cow."

"Ah, Vivi. If you believe nothing else, believe this. Having tasted the milk, I damned well wanted the cow."

A burst of laughter escaped her, and she covered her mouth. She couldn't recall the last time she'd laughed, but his eyes were twinkling with merriment as though he was remembering a happier, more joyful time.

Very slowly, as though he feared she might skitter away, he

reached out and touched a finger to her lips. "I always loved your laughter."

"I've kept it locked away for a good many years now."

He stroked his thumb over her lower lip, and she nearly drew it into her mouth, remembering the saltiness of his skin and how much she'd enjoyed it, but now was not the time. They were both wounded, only now coming to realize the weapons used to inflict the damage were different than they'd thought. He placed his hand back in hers.

"Was prison terribly awful?"

"Lonely. They sent me to Pentonville. It's supposed to be a model prison, but it's just cruel. We lived in isolation. When we went for walks in the prison yard, we had to wear brown hoods and weren't allowed to speak to each other. Men went mad, Vivi. For a while, I thought I would."

"Oh my God." She brought his hand up to her lips, pressed a kiss against his knuckles, wanted to weep once again for all he'd endured. "I'm so sorry, Finn. If I could do it over, I'd have not told a soul."

"Then how would you have gotten dressed for our outing to Gillie's pub?"

He was striving to make her feel better, but how could she when she now knew what he'd suffered?

"I spent a lot of time thinking about that night and how pretty you looked."

She was relatively certain, based on the warmth penetrating her cheeks, that she was blushing. "I'd have thought you'd have preferred me in a ball gown."

"That night was more for dreams."

It had been. A magical, fantastical night. When they'd danced together. When he'd come to her bedchamber.

"I'm actually surprised your brothers didn't confront me," she said.

"I forbid it, convinced them I'd see to the matter once I was free."

"But you didn't confront me once you were free."

He shrugged. "After five years, I simply wanted to forget."

"I can't blame you."

Leaning in, he cradled her cheek. "Now I find I wasted three more years. If I'd gone to you and demanded an explanation, we'd have learned the truth so much sooner. You'd have been back in my life. We could have picked up where we'd left off."

She wasn't quite as confident of that outcome as he was. She'd gone through a lot during those five years he was in prison, things that had irrevocably changed her. If he learned of them, he might realize he no longer had a care for her at all.

"Miss Kent?"

At the sound of Sister Theresa's voice, she leaped to her feet, nearly knocking the chair over in the process, vaguely aware of Finn standing, more aware of his gaze boring into her even though she couldn't see it, but the hairs on the back of her neck prickled. He was no doubt confused by how she'd been addressed, but she'd never admitted to those here that she was of the nobility. "Oh, Sister. You startled me."

"It's a bit late for a gentleman caller."

Her heart still jumping around in her chest, she nodded frantically. "Mr. Trewlove rescued me tonight when I was attacked by some thugs. I was thanking him with some tea." Which she hoped the sister didn't notice had not been made. "A paltry offering in exchange for my life, but there you are."

"I do wish you would cease with these excursions late at night," Sister Theresa admonished.

"I'll take better care in the future. I'm going to see Mr. Trewlove out now." Turning to Finn, she indicated the door.

"Sister," he said flatly.

"Mr. Trewlove, your family is quite well known in Whitechapel. Which one precisely are you?"

"Finn."

"Have we met before? Something about you seems familiar."

"Not that I can recall, Sister."

"Well, I often mistake people for someone I've seen. We appreciate your rescuing of Miss Kent. She is quite beloved by all here. Good night, sir. Go with God."

Lavinia followed Finn out onto the stoop. "I'm sorry things came to such an abrupt end there, but I don't think she'd have left the room with you still present."

"Stop apologizing, Vivi." He grinned, the familiar grin from his youth. "Besides, I can always sneak back in."

"I share a room with one of the sisters."

"Pity."

She combed her fingers through his hair. "I'm so terribly sorry for what my family did to you. And those words seem so lacking, so inadequate."

"What do we do now, Vivi?"

"We return to our separate lives."

"You don't think we can start where we left off?"

"No. If you felt half as much anger, resentment, and . . . hatred as I felt toward you these eight years, if it festered within you as it did within me, then I don't think there's a path for us. We've changed, Finn, you know we have. The circumstances changed us. We're not the people we were. My parents, damn them both to hell, saw to that."

Bringing her hand down, she cradled his jaw. "But know this: I did love you once, with all my heart. And that night, I fully intended to leave with you."

THE CERBERUS CLUB never closed its doors, so Finn knew he'd find his brother somewhere within the walls of his gaming hell. If not in his office, then in the room where he slept. Aiden lived and breathed his club. The only time he wasn't about was when he stopped by Gillie's tavern for a pint.

As he walked through the varied rooms, he noted that business was brisk tonight, but then it always was. The club drew commoners and the less influential of the nobility—second sons, third, fourth, as well as those who were no longer given credit at the more respectable gambling hells or had lost their membership completely. Even a few women were about, matching their skills against the men surrounding them. As far as Aiden was concerned, coins were neutral. He cared nothing at all about the hand that surrendered them. He cared only that they were surrendered.

He finally caught sight of his brother standing on the upper landing, looking out over his domain, exuding the same amount of confidence and power that Zeus might have as he observed the world from Mount Olympus. Everyone knew he was not a man to be crossed. Something about him had always said he was one to be reckoned with, even when he'd been a boy, playing the pea game on the street, taking money from people who thought they could determine under which of three cups he'd placed the pea. But his hands were always too quick—not in moving the cups, but in removing the pea without his actions being spotted.

Finn made his way up some hidden stairs that only those who worked for Aiden knew about and had access to. When he reached the landing, he wandered over to where his brother stood. "Good crowd tonight, even for the wee hours of the morning."

"Tonight's take will see me bathing in whisky. How was your night?"

"Enlightening. I wondered if I might have a word."

"Certainly."

Finn glanced around. "I was thinking someplace more private."

Aiden chuckled low. "No one can hear us here."

"No, but they can see us, and you're not the best at holding on to your temper."

"I don't like the sound of that. We're not going to tussle, are we?"

More than once they'd settled their differences with their fists. "I hope not, but it depends on how reasonable you are."

Aiden grinned. "Where's the fun in being reasonable?"

Still, he led the way down a corridor to his office and took the chair behind his desk, while Finn took the one in front. It was leather, thickly padded, extremely comfortable. Aiden did like his creature comforts.

"You've never answered before when I asked, but tonight I have a need to know. What bargain did you make with our father to ensure I wasn't transported?"

His brother's brow knitted even as he waved his hand over his desk as though shooing away a pesky fly. "Don't worry yourself over it. I've told you before I paid it gladly."

"Aiden, some information has come to light about the night I was arrested, and I feel a sudden need to know everything about that time. I didn't press on a lot of it because it was unpleasant to face—or I thought it would be. I've discovered that letting things lie has proven to be a great disservice to a good many. Please. What was the bargain you struck?"

Aiden leaned back in his chair, dropped his head back, and stared at the ceiling. Finally, he released a great gust of air, lowered his head, and met Finn's gaze head-on. "Sixty percent share of my profits from the Cerberus Club."

"You're not serious. You can't have been daft enough—"

Aiden shot out of the chair. "He wasn't going to do a bloody thing to help you, not lift so much as a goddamned finger. You're his son! I don't give a fig that we were born on the wrong side of the blanket. He shouldn't care that we're not legitimate. He fucked our mothers, and then thought to be done with us by placing a few quid in Ettie Trewlove's hand? It doesn't work like that. His blood is in our veins." He was breathing heavily, harshly. This was one area where they'd never agreed—Aiden resented their father with every bone in his body while Finn couldn't have cared less about the scapegrace. "The authorities were going to send you to the far side of the world. I couldn't let them do that." He dropped back into the chair. "I knew his finances were in dire straits, so I used his difficulties to get what I wanted, what I needed."

"But sixty percent—"

He shrugged. "I offered fifty. He's a hard bargainer, our damned sire, more of a bastard than either of us. But it was worth it, Finn. I'd have gone as high as ninety."

"And you call me a fool."

"I love you, brother."

Seemingly embarrassed by his last declaration, Aiden busied himself pouring whisky into two glasses. "You're all I have."

"You have Mick and Beast and—"

"It's not the same." He shoved a glass across the desk to Finn. "Their blood is not my blood. Don't misunderstand. I love them, I'd die for them. But you and I have a bond that goes far deeper than anything I share with them."

After swallowing some whisky, Aiden set down the glass, ran his finger along the rim. Finn could fairly see the wheels turning in his mind. "Why the curiosity tonight?" he finally asked. "You asked when you got out of prison, were content with me not saying. Why insist tonight? What's this information that came to light?"

"She didn't betray me, Aiden."

"Ah, God. Are we talking Finn's Folly here? You've seen her, spoken with her? What good will come from that? Besides, the cunning bitch would lie—"

"She wouldn't, not to me. And don't call her anything disparaging. I won't have it."

He rolled his eyes. "If she didn't betray you, then who did?"

"She believes it might have been her maid. She was the only other person who knew we planned to run off together."

"The maid." He scoffed. "Toffs always blame the workers."

It was an odd thing that they both had such a low opinion of the aristocracy when two of their siblings had married into it and Finn had once fallen for a girl of it. "Maybe I was just careless."

"Not you, brother."

"I was younger then, Aiden. Not as cautious."

"You've always been cautious."

Finn wasn't in the mood to argue. Taking a sip of whisky, he tried to recall how he'd been back then, how in his excitement to see Vivi, he'd often thrown caution to the wind. But Aiden was correct. He'd never been that reckless. He was no longer quite certain he could say the same of his brother. He took a slow swallow of the whisky, waited as it burned its way down. "So how long do you have to give our bastard of a sire sixty percent?"

"Into infinity."

"Christ, Aiden."

He laughed. "Do you know I've actually considered hiring some dealers who are skilled with sleight of hand, who could ensure the house loses? To lose everything, to deny him anything more?"

"But you love this place."

"I do, that."

"Perhaps we could transfer your debt to him over to me."

"You're not giving him a penny. Avoid him, Finn. He'll find a way to make you pay what you don't owe. He's good at that."

He nodded. "Life's not fair. Our mum's husband appeared to be a good man, and he died young. The earl is a scapegrace of the first order and still draws in breath."

"I'll get even with him eventually. Don't concern yourself over it. Simply leave it to me. Are you gonna marry the girl now?"

Shaking his head, Finn took another swallow, welcomed the burn, waited for the haze it might bring. "She feels responsible for what happened to me. She says we've both changed too much, aren't who we once were. She's right about that. I loved the girl she was. I'm not sure how I feel about the woman she's become. She's different. There's a hardness to her, and yet a generosity. I can't figure her out. I don't understand why she's chosen this path."

"You *sound* like a man smitten."

"Intrigued, more like. You'd have to see her again, Aiden, to know what I'm talking about."

"I have no desire to come within a hundred miles of her."

"Yes, well, that desire's been dashed. She's living at a Sisters of Mercy foundling home not so far from here."

"She can't be happy there."

"Oddly, she seems at peace there."

"Smitten," Aiden grumbled disgustedly.

"I'm not." He wasn't, but couldn't deny there had been something comforting about sitting at the wooden table in the warm kitchen, holding hands, talking with her. He'd once imagined them together in a house, her preparing his meals. It had never occurred to him that a lady of the nobility might know nothing at all about how food was prepared. How young and innocent he'd been. If they'd married, they'd have no doubt starved to death. What had he been thinking to believe she'd have been content to live in the squalor he'd had to offer her?

But he'd believed he'd have been content, that together they'd have found happiness. Knowing now she'd not betrayed him, he couldn't help but mourn the loss of what they might have had. He wondered if any portion of the girl she'd been remained. If, together, they could again find what they'd lost.

Chapter 13

With her hands clasped before her, striving to appear as contrite and repentant as possible, Lavinia stood before the desk where Sister Theresa sat, studying her through dark eyes, a raven's eyes. She'd never particularly cared for the birds. While she thought highly of Sister Theresa, she wasn't enamored of the way she made her want to squirm. She was a grown woman now, not a seventeen-year-old girl who'd sought to run off with a commoner.

"I have to admit, Miss Kent, to being somewhat concerned at finding a gentleman in the kitchen in the wee hours of the morning."

"As I explained, he'd done me a great service, and I'd thought a cup of tea was in order, as a thank-you, you see." And because they'd needed to discuss matters, a past that had turned out not to be what they'd both thought it was.

"So by the time I arrived, he'd either been there long enough to finish off the tea and for you to clear things away or it had yet to be served."

She pressed her lips together. "I discovered he preferred whisky to tea and so we just chatted."

"I see. I know you feel you have a calling, but these late-in-the-night assignations are not only dangerous to your person, but I fear might be posing a threat to your soul."

Her soul was already damned, not that she was going to confess that to the sister. "I assure you nothing untoward occurred between Mr. Trewlove and myself last night."

"Still, you must not allow him, or any man for that matter, inside this residence again, not at night, not at any hour, without chaperone."

"We shan't be seeing each other again. That was part of the reason for our discussion, to put past matters to rest."

"I see. And you came to an understanding, then?"

"Indeed."

Sister Theresa studied her, and Lavinia had the unsettling notion the woman could burrow beneath the surface and uncover all her lies and secrets, secrets she hadn't shared with Finn, secrets that were her burden to carry.

"He is a rather handsome devil."

Lavinia couldn't help it. She stared openly at the woman who sat so primly and judgmentally behind the desk.

"Do close your mouth, Miss Kent. It's hardly flattering to look like a fish tossed onto the riverbank."

Unaware her jaw had dropped as though suddenly unhinged, she snapped her mouth shut. "Apologies, Sister. I just—"

"I might be a Sister of Mercy, but I'm also a woman. I daresay, Mr. Trewlove has led a good many of our gender into temptation."

She wasn't quite certain he'd led her, but she'd managed to find the path by herself, running headlong down it and into his arms. "I have no interest in him in that manner. I have but one focus now, and that's the children."

"A worthy endeavor. However, I do wonder if you aren't hiding from something."

"From my family. I told you that when I came here."

"I fear you are hiding from something more . . . personal. Something deeper within you. Perhaps you need to return home and settle matters there."

"My mother is an incredibly forceful woman." More than once she had locked Lavinia away until she "regained her senses."

"Most are. But you can't hide out forever. Gather your courage, and when you are ready, know that you go with God."

She gave a little curtsy, a quick bending of her knees. "Thank you, Sister."

Leaving the room, she retreated to the small desk in the cramped office that the sisters allowed her to use when she was working on her calling. The one saving grace of the tiny room was that its window looked out on the back gardens where the older children and toddlers frolicked. Their laughter filled her soul.

With the newspapers spread out before her, she combed the advertisements for widows seeking to take in children of poor health. "Poor health" was one of the phrases that was used to identify a baby farmer. The healthiest of babes could be brought to them, but in time, they would perish because of poor health. Seldom could it be proven that the death was a result of neglect. Babies died, far too many from natural causes.

Usually she was quicker with her scouring and circling of the adverts that caught her attention, the ones she would respond to with a letter of inquiry that hopefully would result in a meeting, but her mind kept drifting to the night before, to the revelations uncovered.

She'd been unable to sleep, all the memories of Finn assaulting her whenever she closed her eyes. She'd seen him as he'd been, tender and sweet. Then the man he was now wiggled his way into the memory, and he was no longer the boy she'd loved but a grown man she didn't know. She'd been correct in discouraging anything between them. Yet, suddenly, she missed him, wanted to know everything about him. So many regrets, so many missed moments.

With a shake of her head, she refocused her attention on the task at hand and located an advert that appeared promising. She slammed her eyes closed. Promising was for something wonderful, not horrific. She wished there were no adverts, no need for women to take in by-blows. Because many orphanages turned illegitimate children away, as though they were responsible for their condition, she understood the need, but surely there were better ways to address it. She'd been interviewing women who'd given birth out of wedlock, as well as a few of the farmers she met, hoping to write a series of articles that would awaken Parliament to the desperate need for reform when it came to caring for the most innocent among them.

As she reached for a piece of foolscap in order to respond to the advertiser, she became aware of louder laughter and joy coming from beyond the window. It filled her heart with such gladness, replenished her soul, and made the awful tasks that awaited her not quite so awful. There was a purpose, a goodness, to them that might not erase all her sins but would certainly make them easier to live with.

The patter of small feet echoed down the hallway, growing louder, until a tiny sprite named Daisy burst into the office. "Miss Kent! He brung a horse!"

She furrowed her brow. "I beg your pardon?"

"The gent. He brung a horse, the cleanest one you've ever seen. It's all white."

Her heart slammed hard against her ribs. "A horse?" she repeated as though she didn't even know what one was.

Daisy bobbed her head with such force that her blond braids slapped against her shoulders. "We can ride it in the garden!"

Shoving back her chair, she was surprised when her knees nearly buckled as she stood. It could not be the horse she was thinking of. It could not be the man. But when she arrived at the window, she discovered it was both. Sophie and Finn. Beautiful Sophie and handsome Finn. His attire was casual, his hat the flatcap she remembered from her youth, his jacket a plain brown but the lines of it shaped to his broad shoulders.

He was leading the mare around with three children—a girl and two boys—sitting on her back, their smiles so bright it caused her heart to ache. What a simple thing to do to bring such joy.

She didn't particularly like the shot of pleasure that swept through her with the knowledge he'd returned. She'd expected to never see him again, had thought she'd made her position on the matter clear, but perhaps he'd detected the lie in her voice. Because the truth was that for the first time in years, sitting in the kitchen last night, she'd known a spark of happiness. He hadn't abandoned her. The wounded girl she'd been had wept with the knowledge, while the woman she now was recognized they'd both changed too much to return to what they'd been.

Tiny fingers curled around hers. "Come on, Miss Kent. He'll let you ride it, too."

No, no, she couldn't go out there, couldn't give him the freedom to begin melting her heart all over again. Couldn't risk causing him even more pain.

Another tug. "Miss Kent?"

She smiled down at the precious child. "You go on. I need a minute."

A minute to erect a shield around her heart.

He didn't know what had prodded him to come. No, it had been more than a prod. It had been an obsession, gnawing at his gut, threading through his soul—the thought he could finally see her as he'd always dreamed of viewing her: in the daytime, bathed in sunlight. As he'd planned to see her on the day following the night when they were to have run away.

This morning when he'd awoken after a restless night and watched the fog curling in on itself and growing smaller, fainter, as the sun worked its magic, he'd known it was going to be a glorious day, one for walks in the parks and boat rides along the Thames. A rare day when autumn was determined to burst forth in brightness before giving way to the gloomier days of winter. There was a crispness to the air that made it easier to breathe—

Until she strolled into the garden.

It was as though the moon had descended and woven itself through her hair, taking shelter there until the night when it would again return to the sky. Her skin was alabaster, but not pale. It had a healthy glow to it. Her cheeks were flushed. As she neared he saw the delight shining in the green of her eyes, a shade that wasn't as dark as he'd always assumed. The sun's brightness shrunk the pupils, leaving an abundance of green to hold him captive. A black line circled the outer edge of the iris. He'd not noticed it before, not even when she'd been tucked beneath him, her eyes wide with wonder as they'd moved in tandem creating sparks, the memory of which even now put him in danger of growing hard.

The children were bouncing around him, eager to grab his attention, wanting to have their turn on the mare. But he seemed incapable of tearing his gaze from *her*.

She stopped several inches away, close enough that he could see the fraying edges of her collar and cuffs. He didn't want to think of her scrounging through someone else's discards, seeking something serviceable that would keep her warm when the cold winds of winter arrived.

Her gaze locked with his, the way it had when he'd first eased her onto her back and covered her body with his, when he had cupped her delicate face between his large roughened hands and told her that he loved her. Would always love her.

"You still have her," she said quietly, reverently, as though he'd been the deliverer of some miracle.

Knowing how much his actions pleased her seemed to rob him of words.

"Once I went to your brother's brickyard to see her, but she was no longer there." And he could well imagine she felt he'd taken the mare from her as well, stolen something else from her.

"May I?" She pointed toward the horse.

Something was lodged in his throat, making it difficult to swallow, to speak, so he merely gave a brisk nod, then watched as she walked around him, grabbed the halter, and rubbed her other hand along the horse's forehead beneath her forelock. "Hello, sweet girl. Oh, I have missed you."

And he couldn't help but hope she'd missed him a bit as well. "Did you want to ride her?"

She glanced around at the children. "I don't want to spoil their fun. I wouldn't mind walking along beside her though."

He placed three different children on Sophie's back and slowly began leading her around the edge of the garden, Vivi falling into step on the other side of the horse so the mare's head provided a barrier between them and he couldn't see her clearly. No doubt she'd taken up her position in her effort to keep distance between them.

"Miss Kent! Miss Kent!" an imp of a girl cried out, running up to her. "I want to pet him."

Without hesitating, she lifted the girl into her arms. "It's a her."

"How do you know?"

"Yes, *Miss Kent*," he said, stepping ahead of the horse so he could at least look back at her. "Explain *that* to her."

She blushed, and he realized he'd never seen her cheeks so rosy. No hat shaded her face, and he wondered if she even possessed one. No gloves protected her hands, nor had there been any during the nights when he'd seen her. Had she given up all her worldly possessions?

"Because she once told me she's a girl horse," she said simply to the blond-haired lass in her arms who couldn't have been older than four, thin as a rail, with huge blue eyes. He imagined Vivi with a daughter, similar in appearance. She should have had her own children by now, should have been married. Accepting her explanation, the girl reached out and patted Sophie on the nose. Vivi tipped her own nose up haughtily, and for the first time in years he chuckled with the sheer appreciation of being bested.

"I noticed last night they refer to you as 'Miss Kent.'"

"I thought it best to be discreet concerning the status of my family."

He glanced around at the modest surroundings. "Are you on your way to taking vows, to becoming a nun?"

"No. I'm not worthy of such a life."

"That's crock—but I'm glad to hear it. There's too much sensuality in you to have it wasted on celibacy."

"That's not appropriate talk around the children."

"These children you . . . collect. They provide for them here?"

"Yes. Although we're running out of room. There are so many children, Finn."

"Creating them is a good deal of fun." She appeared stricken by his words. "My apologies. I don't mean to make light of it. I know firsthand it's a problem. But people aren't going to go against their nature."

"They need to be educated. I should write pamphlets."

"Many who need those pamphlets can't read."

"Makes it rather a continuous circle, doesn't it?"

He brought the horse to a halt where children were lined up. He lifted the three children off, put three more on, and began walking again, glad when Vivi continued along beside him. He decided a change of topic was in order. "Why did you come to Whitechapel?"

"Because it was very unlikely I'd run into anyone here whom I knew. It's not as though duchesses and countesses stroll about the streets."

"And the foundling home?"

"Two reasons. I knew my brother would never look for me among nuns. And I wanted a place where children would be welcomed."

"You came here with a specific purpose, knew what you wanted to do."

"What I've wanted to do for some time now, but it took me a while to work up the courage to do it. It's complicated. So much has transpired since I last saw you."

He wanted to know all of it, just as he'd once wanted to know everything she'd done while she was away from him at the country. "You've quite deliberately taken up the cause of children."

She met his gaze, sadness in the depths of her eyes. "You're responsible for that. What you told me that night in the garden touched me deeply. I never forgot how embarrassed you sounded for something in which you were not the least bit responsible."

The circumstances of his birth had tainted his life. She'd made him feel scrubbed clean and imagined she did the same for all the children here. "Do you have an appointment with a baby farmer tonight?"

"Not tonight."

"Then go on an outing with me."

He could see the desire to say yes warring with the need to say no. Slowly she shook her head. "If those men my brother hired—"

He brought Sophie to a halt. "You can't live your life hiding away. I've been a prisoner, Vivi. It's no way to live. Take a chance that nothing bad will happen, that no one will figure out you're a quick five hundred quid."

"Not so quick or easy. I'll fight."

"That's my girl. Now come on. Let's go have a pleasant evening at a reasonable hour, something denied us before. What say you?"

"It won't be the same. We're not the people we were."

"I'm not expecting anything of you, Vivi. We'll just enjoy each other's company. I'd say we're two people in need of a bit of fun."

Her brow furrowed; the lips that always curled up so easily formed a straight line. "As a result of all that's happened, I'm damaged, Finn. I'm not certain you'd like the person I've become."

"Someone who fights for children when so many view them as expendable? I like what I'm seeing so far."

"We can't go back, Finn."

"I'm not expecting us to. We'll have a little outing, a few laughs. Then say goodbye."

"Where would we be going?"

"It's a surprise."

"Finn—"

"You trusted me once, Vivi. Trust me now."

IN THE CORNER of the garden, Sister Theresa stood beside Mother Margaret and watched the tableau taking place not too far away while children raced around the couple who had stopped the horse and seemed to be in serious discussion. Something about Finn Trewlove was familiar. The cut of his jaw, she finally decided. She had once cradled a jaw very much like it as she whispered words of love.

"You spoke to her?" Mother Margaret asked.

"I did." Mother Margaret often assigned the most unpleasant tasks to the sisters, her belief being that adversity would strengthen their faith. "I cannot help but believe she is hiding from something."

"She is running from something, Sister. Perhaps with this young man suddenly appearing in her life, she will finally begin running *toward* something."

Sister Theresa knew all about running. Sometimes a person had to run in the wrong direction before she could run in the correct one.

Chapter 14

They were having an outing simply as a means to put the past completely behind them. Although she wouldn't read more into his request than that, she did wish she had a fancier frock, but she possessed only two, one a dark blue, the other black. So this evening it would be the dark blue because at least the corners of the collar weren't too badly frayed. She thought she'd cast aside her vanity in want of a simpler life. What a disappointment to discover it had only been in hiding and that the attentions of a young man could bring it forth so easily.

She did hope Finn had spoken true about having no expectations regarding tonight. He had to know the roads they'd each traveled had taken them in different directions, would never converge.

Stepping back from the oval mirror that hung above the washbasin, she tried to get a better look at herself. No cheval glass in this residence. The sisters never had a need to see themselves in their entirety, to know if they were put together properly. Their clothing was as it was and there wasn't a lot they could do with it.

"What do you plan to do with your hair?"

Only then did she notice Sister Theresa reflected at the edge of the mirror as she stood in the doorway. With a laugh, self-consciously, she touched the braid she'd wound around her head and pinned into place. "I've already done it."

She turned to face the sister. "Does it not look right?"

"If I were going to spend the evening with a gentleman caller, I might want something a bit more . . . elaborate. Would you like me to have a go at it?"

She couldn't help it. She stared.

"You really must learn to hide your shock a bit better as that stunned fish look is terribly unflattering. I didn't always wear a habit, you know." She walked into the room. "Sit."

Lavinia did as she was ordered, easing onto the wooden straight-backed chair. There was no dressing table, merely the small square table where the washbasin was kept. Seated, she couldn't see herself in the mirror.

With a great deal of efficiency, Sister Theresa removed the pins and unplaited her hair. She almost groaned from the pleasure of having someone else drag a brush through the long tresses.

"This young man is from your past," the sister said quietly.

"Yes."

"Do you love him?"

That was the question, wasn't it? "I did once, but we are hardly the same people any longer."

"Do you not believe yourself worthy of love?"

She rather wished she'd declined the offer for help as she wasn't really in the mood for an inquisition, and yet she'd held so much in for so long. "We were to marry, and when that didn't happen, I found myself in situations where I proved myself weak and cowardly. I did some things, Sister, of which I'm not proud."

"You fear he will find fault with you?"

"I would if the situation were reversed."

"Will you tell him about them?"

"I want to, but no good would come of it. I suspect tonight will simply be an opportunity to say a proper goodbye."

She felt a tug, a pull, an upward yank of her hair.

"I wouldn't be so certain, Miss Kent. When I was younger, before I ever even considered taking the veil, I sold my soul to have a man look at me the way Mr. Trewlove looks at you."

The fervor of the sister's words astounded her, and she started to twist—

"Be still now," Sister Theresa ordered. "Almost done." And then her voice softened. "We all make mistakes, Miss Kent. The secret is not to let them hold sway over us. There you are. I hope you like it."

Slowly, Lavinia rose to her feet until she could see her reflection in the mirror. Her hair was piled on her head in an elegant coiffure, with curling tendrils dangling down to tease her face and neck. "It's quite lovely."

"It would look nicer with pearl combs, but those have not been provided to us."

Lavinia swung around. "Were you once a lady's maid?"

"No, Miss Kent." Sister Theresa smiled wistfully. "I was once a lady."

"Of the nobility?"

The sister gave a short burst of laughter. "Is there any other kind? I daresay, I should think not. The door knocker just sounded. I believe your young gentleman is here. Don't close yourself off to the possibilities, Miss Kent."

Before she could question the sister regarding what she thought those possibilities would be, she was left alone with nothing but her nerves. Loving her had cost Finn five years of his life. Loving him had cost her—

She refused to think about that. She was simply going to enjoy the evening. Perhaps with a bit of prodding he would tell her everything he'd done with his life during the past three years, after he was released.

When she stepped into the entryway and saw him standing there, she realized she wanted to know that more than anything. What was his life truly like now? How did he spend his days and nights—other than skulking about following her?

He was nicely decked out in a jacket, waistcoat, shirt, and cravat. Not as fancy as what a gentleman might wear in the evening, but rather something he'd wear for a stroll through the park. In his hand, he held a beaver hat. "Don't you look lovely?" he said.

Why did her heart have to misbehave by flipping in her chest? "Shall we be off?"

He arched a brow. "No chaperone?"

"I hardly require one these days." She wasn't a young debutante in need of having her innocence protected. "Although the sisters did offer to accompany me, but I trust you not to get up to no good."

"Ah, Vivi, when will you learn?" He gave her a smile that threatened to send her hurtling back eight years. "Once a scoundrel always a scoundrel."

"YOUR CARRIAGE?" SHE asked as he handed her up into the conveyance he'd had waiting in the street for them.

"Mick's." He settled against the squabs opposite her.

"Your brother has done very well for himself."

"He's earned it. He's worked long and hard for every ha'penny that now lines his pockets." He was tearing down and rebuilding a poorer section of London, had built a massive hotel that was becoming quite the talk of the town, and had married into the nobility—even if he himself remained without a title.

"What do you do, Finn? Are you still a slaughterer?"

"Going to prison for horse theft put an end to that."

She squeezed her eyes shut. "God, I'm so sorry."

Leaning across, he took her hand, wished he'd brought her a pair of gloves, was glad he hadn't, and squeezed her fingers. "You weren't to blame. I don't want us thinking about that tonight."

She opened her eyes, and the sadness within them would have brought him to his knees had he been standing. "What do you want?"

Hell if he knew. To go back eight years. To start anew. But that would mean forgetting all the wonderful moments they'd had together. To begin where they'd left off? That would require facing the pain. "A bit of conversation. A few laughs, some beer. Something to eat. A lovely lady on my arm."

She gave him half a smile. "No flirting."

He grinned crookedly. "We'll see."

She sighed, and in the sound he thought he heard her surrender.

"If you're not a slaughterer, what do you do?"

"A little of this, a little of that."

"Such a man of mystery."

He supposed if he wanted her to tell him everything, he couldn't hold his own story back. "I earn coins working for Aiden."

"In his gambling hell?"

"I do the odd job there, but mostly I put the fear of God into those who owe him money and don't seem to be on the verge of paying him. I visited Dearwood the other night. Collected some collateral from him and threatened to break his arm if he didn't wear a splint."

"Is that what you do? Break arms?"

She didn't sound horrified, but rather sad that his life had come to such an uninviting place. "I've had to punch a fellow now and again, but only because he came at me. Or didn't take me seriously. A bloody nose usually teaches a fellow I'm not there as a lark. They owe my brother. They will pay my brother. And from time to time, if a bloke gives me a particularly hard time, I threaten to break his arm if he doesn't wear a splint for six weeks and inform people I'm the one responsible for it. Enhances my reputation as a bad bloke to deal with."

"So Dearwood gave you a difficult time."

He shrugged. "Not really. But I recalled not much liking him when I met him years ago"—his dancing with her playing a major role in his attitude toward the man—"and felt a need to make sport of him."

She smiled, only a small smile, but it was a start. "I've never fancied Dearwood. Something about him isn't quite . . . nice."

"He's a bit of an arse."

Her lips spread more fully, more beautifully, and he felt somewhat victorious, grateful he still had the ability to coax joy from her, grateful she still had it within her to experience gladness. "How do you earn your keep, Vivi?"

"In exchange for my room and board, I give lessons to the children in the morning. Reading, writing, ciphering. The remainder of the day I scrub floors and make beds and am very much a maid-of-all-work. I'm not complaining, mind you, but I am searching for an occupation that will provide me with a bit more than that. Coins, for example, as I want to create more shelters for children. There are so many unwanted children, Finn."

The smile was gone now, the sadness had returned. "I know."

She'd made them her cause, and he couldn't help but wonder if the same would have happened had they married all those years ago. Doubtful, as she'd have had a brood of children of her own to care for by now.

She glanced back out the window. "It looks as though we've left London. Where are we going?"

"Not far. I heard of a nearby village having a little fete. It's unlikely anyone will recognize us." Certainly no lords or ladies would be in attendance to spot or question her. Most were away at their country estates by now, save for the young bucks who found more adventure in town, many at his brother's gambling establishment.

She studied her hands, knotted in her lap. "Is there anyone special in your life?"

"I have a good many special people in my life."

Lifting her head, she moved her lips into something that wasn't quite a smile. "I'm glad." And turned her attention back to the passing scenery.

Fear of chasing her away because things between them were too fragile kept him from admitting, *I'm looking at one of them right now.*

THE MERRIMENT STRUCK her as soon as they exited from the coach, and it only grew after he tucked her hand in the crook of his elbow and led her into the center of things. She hadn't realized how badly she'd needed to be surrounded by joy and happiness. Even the brisk coolness of the evening couldn't dampen her spirits.

"I haven't been to a festival . . . my word. I suppose it was the last time I was at the country estate before our fateful summer." After she thought he'd abandoned her, she'd begun referring to it as her *fateful summer* or her *fateful night,* but now she knew the terms belonged to both her and Finn.

"When you told me how you spent your time in the country, you never mentioned festivals."

"I didn't want you to think I was enjoying myself without you about."

"Vivi, I didn't want you to be miserable when we weren't together. I'm glad you had fun at them."

"I didn't say that. I always felt as though something was missing, that they'd have been so much more pleasurable if you were there. Did you come to fetes while I was away?"

"Sometimes."

With a grin, she nudged her head against his shoulder. "Yet you didn't tell me about them."

"I'd come with my brothers. Aiden always managed to find a saucy wench to go off with him."

"And you?"

His eyes warmed as he glanced over at her. "I was only ever interested in you, Vivi. I told you that. Although if I'd followed Aiden's lead, perhaps our first time would have been more pleasant for you."

"I found no fault with it, although I wouldn't imagine you've been celibate since me."

Slowly he shook his head, before turning his attention back to the crowd. "No."

"I'm relieved to hear that, Finn. I wouldn't have liked for you to have been alone all these years. I suspect you really craved the company once you got out of prison."

"There were a lot of things I craved. Not all of it nice."

She suspected he was referring to retribution, but rather than hurt her, he'd stayed away.

A man suddenly leaped in front of them and began juggling balls in the air. Finn tossed him a coin. The man snatched it on its descent to the ground, without dropping a single ball. "Thanks, guv."

With a nod of his head, and the spheres going around and around, he strutted away, gaining the attention of children, making them laugh.

"Wouldn't the orphans of the foundling home love this?" she asked as he led her deeper into the fray of activity where two men tumbled, one stepping into the locked palms of another who would then toss him in the air, where he'd do a somersault before landing on his feet, only to repeat the process. They wandered by another man swallowing flames.

"Why would anyone desire to do such a thing?" she asked.

"Puts coins in his pockets."

"Still, the danger of it . . ."

"I suspect there's a trick to it."

"I can't even imagine the first person sitting around and suddenly thinking, *It would be jolly good fun to put fire in my mouth.*"

"As baffled as you are by him, I daresay he would be equally baffled by a lady of the nobility deciding it would be a grand idea to wander the streets at night rescuing children." There was no censure in his voice, but his raised eyebrow did give her pause. But even it wasn't mocking. Rather she thought perhaps he admired her efforts. Although she wasn't doing it to be admired, she did have to admit to finding gratification in his approval.

A dancing monkey caught her attention, its owner playing the accordion. Suddenly the little fellow darted over to her, gave her skirt a tug, then doffed his hat. Finn handed her a shilling, and she dropped it into the waiting hat, where it was promptly retrieved and studied. Then the monkey raced to the accordion player and climbed up him as though he were a tree, finding a perch on his shoulder.

"I could do with some food and beer," Finn said. "Join me?"

He purchased meat pies from a lady at one stall, two tankards of beer from a gent at another, and leased a blanket for three-pence from a young girl who sat near a small knoll, a stack of coverings beside her. Once they were settled, she looked out over the gathering, torches striving to hold the darkness at bay. She felt almost carefree, without worries, without concerns.

"Would have been nice to have been able to do this when we were younger," he said quietly.

Shaking her head, she took a nibble from the meat pie. "I'd have had at least one chaperone in tow."

"I could have pitched balls at bottles and won you something."

She looked over at him. So masculine and bold, sitting there with one leg raised, his wrist draped over his knee, the tankard gripped in his strong hand. Lifting it, he took a long, slow swallow and she was rather tempted to remove his cravat, so she could watch the muscles of his throat working to quench his thirst. "You gave me Sophie. That was the gift of a lifetime. I needed nothing more."

"But I wanted to give you more anyway."

He'd given her so much more than he'd ever know. "I don't know that it's wise to traverse back into the past. We were so frightfully young, naïve. I'd have never imagined something as glorious as what we shared could have brought such pain. I can't stop thinking about how awful it all turned out for you."

"Could have been worse." He said it as though loving her hadn't cost him everything.

They sat in silence for long moments, eating their meat pies, sipping their beer. He'd had to pay extra for the loan of the tankards. The money would be given back to him once the pewter was returned. She'd never given any thought to how affairs such as this were managed. She'd simply enjoyed them.

"Why don't you return home?" he asked. "You'd have a better life there."

How to make him understand? He'd shared his horrors with her. Could she share hers with him?

"I know you're concerned your mother will make you marry someone you don't want as a husband, but you're no longer a child."

"It's more than that, Finn. My mother is an incredibly forceful woman. I didn't realize how forceful—" She squeezed her eyes shut, fought back the stinging tears. Her chest tightened, her stomach knotted. Opening her eyes, she took a large, unladylike gulp of the beer, wondering if she could find solace in the brew, if it could help her relax, open up. "If I tell you something, you have to give me your word that you will not confront my mother."

He narrowed his eyes. "Why would I want to?"

"Just promise me. Not you, not your brothers, not your sisters. None of your family goes near my mother." She was not willing to risk his going to prison again, and she feared he might be angry enough to do something stupid.

"I give you my word."

"I will hold you to it."

He gave a brusque nod.

Taking another deep swallow of beer, she formed her thoughts. "About a year after you and I had planned to run off, I found myself in a position where I could no longer remain in residence. Mother and I had been having rows, you see. One night I lost control and slapped her, quite forcefully. I began packing to leave and she called for some footmen to take me in hand. My parents decided I had become too unruly, too wild. I needed to be brought to task, to be taught a lesson that they would not tolerate misbehavior. I was delivered to a madhouse."

THE RAGE THAT swept through him robbed him of breath, of words. He was barely aware of the tankard he'd been holding tumbling to the ground as he enfolded her in his arms, held her close as though he could protect her when it was far too late for that. "My God, Vivi."

He rubbed his cheek along hers, aware of the slightest trembling in her body as she clutched the sides of his coat.

"It's all right, Finn," she whispered softly. "Like your time in prison, it was long ago."

"But it never leaves you, not completely. Jesus, Vivi." It seemed taking the Lord's name in vain was all he was capable of at the moment. Then something occurred to him and he leaned back, studying her features. "What about Thornley? What the devil was he doing during all this? Why didn't he stop it?" He was going to have a quiet word with his brother-by-marriage. A quiet word and a hard punch.

"He didn't know. No one knew. Not even my brother. Mother told them I was traveling the continent with an old aunt. It wouldn't do at all for it to be known their daughter had gone mad. Thorne wasn't responsible for me yet, Finn. You can't blame him."

"How long?"

"Three years."

Three years. Dear God. He knew exactly how long three years were when they were lived with no freedom. If her father weren't already dead, he'd meet with him tonight and put him in the ground. "Thornley didn't find it odd that you were away for three years?"

"He was in no hurry to marry, was sowing his oats. I think he rather found it a relief that no serious courtship was yet called for."

"If I'd known—"

"What could you have done, Finn? From prison?"

He'd have found a way to escape, to save her. Having never felt so impotent in his entire life, he skimmed his knuckles along her soft cheek, searching for solace for them both. "How did you even survive something like that?"

"It wasn't quite as bad as it could have been. Oh, there were the occasional ice baths and restraints. But as long as I was quiet and calm, I seemed merely to baffle the alienists. They couldn't quite determine what was wrong with me. And I learned to fight, because while I might have tried to remain docile, not everyone did."

He couldn't imagine it, the terror she must have felt, the horrors she must have experienced.

"It's an odd world, Finn. There was one girl in particular who took an immediate dislike to me. She would attack for no reason. Yank on my hair or punch me in the stomach. Yell that I was a beast. I don't know. Maybe in her mind she saw monsters.

"Then there was this man, called himself d'Artagnan—I never learned his real name. Anyway, he started my lessons on using the rapier. Only we used broom handles. And he taught me how to use my fists, how to fight dirty. Other than believing himself to be captain of the musketeers I never saw any madness in him. After I returned home, I went back to see him, once, but they told me his family had come for him. They wouldn't tell me who he was. Sometimes I like to imagine that perhaps he was needed in France."

Those brave words uttered tore into his heart—that she would strive to make it sound as though it were all normal. He cupped her cheek. "I want to commit murder."

She gave him an understanding smile. "I know. That's the reason I made you give me a promise not to harm my mother." Gently, she placed her hand over his heart. "Every now and then, I see bits of the boy you were, the one I loved so desperately. I knew that part of you would not take well to this news."

"Do you think if you go home, she'll send you back there?"

"To be honest, I don't know what she will do. But I am tired of fighting her. I want to live my own life on my own terms. That's what I've been doing for the past three months, since I left poor Thornley standing at the altar. He's madly in love with your sister, you know."

"As well he should be. She's a catch, our Gillie."

She smiled, and he wished he could keep that smile on her face forever. "But are you happy, Vivi?"

"As happy as I can be based on all that's happened the past eight years. Yes, I wear someone else's discarded clothing. Some of it is a bit frayed and tattered and has been mended countless times. I have to dress and bathe myself. My comforts are fewer. Nonexistent, really, if I'm honest. But no one tells me what I can or can't do. All the decisions are mine. It's going to sound silly, Finn, but what I feel is . . . free." She rolled her eyes. "To a degree. I haven't yet determined how to convince my brother to stop searching for me. And I need to find some sort of employment that will allow me to do more than I'm doing now. But it'll all come in time." She placed her hand over his where it still rested against her face. "Tell me you're happy."

He didn't want to lie to her. How could he be happy when all he'd ever wanted was her, and all she now wanted was the freedom to do as she pleased? He'd been imprisoned only five years, but was beginning to understand that she'd been imprisoned her entire life. Drawing her in, he pressed a kiss to her forehead. "I'm getting there."

Chapter 15

*I*t was the hand covering the Earl of Collinsworth's mouth that brought him out of a deep sleep, the tiny prick of pain at the underside of his jaw that kept him still as he slowly opened his eyes. The man staring down at him lifted the dagger from where it poked Collinsworth, pressed a finger of the hand holding the weapon to his pursed lips as his head bent slightly in the direction where the countess slept peacefully, completely unaware of the drama playing out beside her.

The intruder's message was clear: cooperate or she will suffer.

Collinsworth gave a barely perceptible nod of understanding, fairly certain his tormentor could feel the hard thudding of his heart causing a reverberation through his body. The intruder slowly lifted his hand from the earl's mouth and stepped back. With his fingers, he indicated Collinsworth should leave the bed.

He did wish he'd slipped back into his nightshirt after making love to his wife, but he much preferred the feel of his naked flesh against hers as they slept. On the other hand, he knew himself to be an impressive specimen of manhood. Perhaps he could intimidate after all. Carefully, he slipped out from beneath the covers, striving desperately not to awaken the love of his life. Once his feet hit the carpeted floor, he straightened to his full height.

The intruder seemed far from impressed, his gaze barely dipping to that in which the earl took such pride. Instead he grabbed the dressing gown from the foot of the bed where it lay in wait and tossed it to Collinsworth, before signaling that the earl should precede him out the door.

Once in the hallway and adequately covered, with the door closed, Collinsworth turned on him. "What is the meaning of this?"

"I want a word," the scapegrace said in a tone he might use when asking for someone to pass the salt. "The library."

Collinsworth had taken as much ordering about as he intended. "This room will suffice." He opened the door to a bedchamber opposite his, turned on the gaslights, and stood in the center of the room with his arms across his chest, waiting as the intruder followed him in and closed the door. He narrowed his gaze. "You're a Trewlove, aren't you? I saw you at your sister's wedding, but I don't believe we've ever been properly introduced."

"Finn."

Hardly a proper introduction, but his heartbeat had returned to a calmer pumping. He couldn't imagine a family striving for acceptance among the nobility was going to risk it by killing a member of said nobility. "What is your purpose in breaking into my residence, into my bedchamber?"

"I want you to call off your hounds."

"My hounds?" The man was making no sense. "I don't keep my hounds in London."

Finn sighed, rolled his eyes. "The dogs you hired to find Lady Lavinia."

Collinsworth swept a hand through the air as though shooing away an irritating fly. "I called them off weeks ago at Thornley's urging." The duke had seen his sister and assured him she was well, living a life she desired. It made no sense whatsoever to Collinsworth, but he'd dismissed the men he'd hired to find her.

"Did you inform her of that?" The anger in Finn's tone was palpable enough to cause Collinsworth to take a step back in fear he was on the verge of becoming intimate with the fellow's fist.

"I have no idea where to find her in order to get a missive to her." He narrowed his eyes as a possibility dawned. "It's you. You're the one from her youth."

He'd known only that when she was seventeen, during her first Season, she'd become involved with someone entirely inappropriate. His father had taken some sort of action to ensure the scoundrel—as the previous earl repeatedly referred to the person—never again bothered Lavinia or the family. Collinsworth had known none of the details, only that his father had arranged transportation for the fellow. His sire had then sent Collinsworth to a remote estate for a year to test his mettle at managing it. When he'd finally returned to London, it was to find that his sister was off touring the continent. His parents had hoped the time away would make her forget about the young man and more amiable to seeing to her duty of marrying Thorne upon her return. Only she didn't return for three years, not until their father passed. Thorne, naturally, had never been told about the young man. But as he'd still been enjoying his own pursuits, in no hurry to wed, all had worked out. Or so they'd all believed, until Lavinia left him standing at the altar.

Rather than acknowledge the obvious, Finn said, "You're going to write her a letter and I'll deliver it."

"You know where she is?" Trewlove simply stared. Collinsworth sighed. "Of course you do. Is she well? At least tell me that."

"Well enough. She'll do better once she knows no one is looking for her."

"Tell her to come home. All will be forgiven."

His expression was one of disgust and fury. "She's done naught for which she needs forgiveness."

Ah, yes, he was definitely the chap from her youth—or perhaps he was a recent conquest—but it was obvious he cared deeply for her. For some reason, Collinsworth felt a measure of relief to know this man was watching out for her. "We're not going to the country until she is back within the bosom of the family. We keep thinking she'll come to her senses—"

"There's nothing wrong with her senses. Now get that damn letter written."

AN HOUR LATER, Finn stood in Vivi's bedchamber, watching as she slept. Unlike her companion in the room whose snoring reminded him of the arrival of a train, she was silent. In sleep, she looked almost as young and innocent as she had when he'd first met her—only now the tiniest of furrows creased her brow as though even in dreams she worried about the children or was reliving her time in a madhouse. He wished he could wipe away every moment of pain she'd ever experienced.

He glanced around at the sparse furnishings. Two beds that looked more like cots, small, narrow with plain wooden bedsteads and thin mattresses. A small plain pine table beside each bed. A washbasin, mirror, and one straight-backed wooden chair. Drab curtains at the window. Christ, the room was depressing.

As he set the letter her brother had written on the bedside table, he had little doubt she'd find employment elsewhere, that she could soon move into more comfortable lodgings now that she was free to move about as she desired without fear of being hauled off to her mother, who had treated her daughter so unconscionably cruelly. If she hadn't extracted a vow from him earlier in the evening, he'd have paid a little visit to her mother as well. As he turned to leave, she whimpered. He froze, waited.

She made another sound, this one more desperate, more alarming. He glanced back at her. Her head had begun thrashing, her hands were fisted in the sheets. Small strangled whimpers escaped. He was familiar with those noises. He'd made them enough times in prison when locked in a nightmare where danger lurked. Within the gossamer shadows of the dream, he'd be striving to scream for help but it was as though his vocal cords were frozen, couldn't function properly, and no one would ever be alerted to his distress.

He folded his hand over her shoulder, gave her the gentlest of shakes, leaned near, and whispered in her ear, "Shh, now. You're safe. No one will ever harm you again."

She quieted, stilled, and he left his hand where it was until her breathing slowed and deepened. He pressed his thumb to the pleats between her brows, rubbing them until they disappeared. With one last look at her, lost in peaceful slumber again, he crept on silent feet from the room, wondering how he could ensure the words he'd just spoken were a promise.

LAVINIA AWOKE ON a sigh. She couldn't recall the last time she'd slept so well or felt so rested upon first opening her eyes. Perhaps she should attend a fete every night. It was still dark, but she knew dawn would be arriving soon because Sister Bernadette had lit the lamp and was going about her morning ablutions at the washbowl.

She remained beneath the covers, preparing herself for the briskness of the chill that would greet her, dreading the moment she placed her feet on the cold floor. If she ever had any extra coins, she was going to purchase rag rugs for each of the sisters so they could ease into the day. So much she had taken for granted— never having cold feet, for one.

Taking a deep breath, she prepared herself and pushed her way up—stopped. Stared at the letter resting on the bedside table, a letter with her name on it. She recognized the handwriting as her brother's, and her breath caught. "Did Sister Theresa deliver this?" she asked, picking it up with care as though it were a hideous spider that would suddenly leap free and skitter over her.

"I don't think so," Sister Bernadette said. "It was there when I lit the lamp. Good morning, by the way."

"Good morning." She settled back against her pillow and studied the letter, a small smile beginning to form. She had a strong suspicion she might know how it had come to be where she'd found it. Finn was still ever so skilled at breaking into bedchambers.

Turning it over, she slipped her thumb beneath the wax that

bore the family crest and worked it free. She unfolded the paper and read the words.

> *My dear Lavinia,*
>
> *I have called off the hounds—the two gentlemen I hired to find you. Actually, I did it weeks ago, but I didn't know how to get word to you until your friend made his presence known and offered to deliver a message to you. So you are now free to go about your pursuits without worry that you will be snatched from the streets.*
>
> *However, I do hope you will consider returning home. Mother worries terribly, as do I. I don't know what objection you had to Thornley—I've always found his company to be top-notch—but be that as it may, I am certain we can find someone else more agreeable for you to marry. We will remain in the city until you are again in residence.*
>
> *Your loving brother,*
> *Neville*

Clutching the letter to her chest, she felt as though a great weight had been lifted, as though she could float to the ceiling if she so desired. Bless Finn. What a glorious gift he'd given her, almost as grand as Sophie. She was free at last.

LATER THAT MORNING, after finishing with the daily lessons, she was tapping the letter she'd written Finn on the desk, wondering how to get it to him. She had no idea where to find him. She supposed she could take it to his sister at the Mermaid and Unicorn and ask her to deliver it to him. Only she didn't really want to send him a letter expressing her gratitude to him for what he'd done. She wanted to tell him in person. Which the letter she'd written indicated. *I need to see you. —V.*

Simple and sweet.

She did wish she'd asked him where he laid his head at night. The patter of tiny footsteps sounded just before Daisy charged into her office. She came to an abrupt stop, hopping from foot to foot, as though she needed to be taken to the loo. Her eyes brightened, her impish grin filling most of her face. "He brung the horse back, Miss Kent! 'N' this time, it's gots a saddle!"

She shouldn't have felt such immense joy and yet she did. She wondered if he might like to have another outing. This time in Whitechapel. Yet even as she had the thought, she knew they needed to end their association. But it was so difficult when they were once again friends, in spite of the past.

She followed Daisy out into the garden to discover he'd not only brought Sophie but another horse, a fine chestnut specimen. She wasn't surprised someone who'd once spent a good deal of his day calming horses would be the owner of good horseflesh.

In a grand gesture, he swept his flat-cap from his head. "Miss Kent."

"Mr. Trewlove." She couldn't stop herself from moving up to Sophie and greeting her with a rub of her neck and a kiss on her forelock. "You brought her back, delighting the children once again."

"Did my actions delight you?"

"You know I'm always delighted to see Sophie," she said, giving him a teasing little smile. "However, with a saddle on her, it's going to take most of the morning to give these children a ride."

"The saddle is for you. I was hoping you'd accompany me somewhere."

"Going about during the day is a bit risky. Or at least it was. I received a letter from my brother, so now I'm given to understand that no one is searching for me."

"How fortunate for you."

She angled her head thoughtfully. "You gave me your word you wouldn't bother my family."

"I vowed not to bother your mother. You'll never know how hard that vow was to keep."

She narrowed her eyes. "What did you do to my brother to prompt him into writing his letter?"

"Merely woke him from his slumber."

"Is he now gallivanting about town wearing a splint?"

He grinned. She did so love his grins. "No. As he was an innocent in all this."

"Yes, he was. Did he look well?"

"He looked put out to be disturbed. But I do think he is worried about you. I assured him you were where you wanted to be, doing what you wanted." He tipped his head to the side. "Now, I'm hoping you'll want to take a ride on Sophie."

She did. Desperately. "She is my weakness."

THE AIR SEEMED a bit clearer today, the sun a bit brighter, as she rode Sophie slowly through the streets of London. It felt marvelous to have her beneath her.

"The manner in which the sisters were watching me, I think they believe me to be up to no good," Finn said.

"Are you?" she asked.

He hitched up a corner of his mouth. She'd never seen him ride a horse. He rode one well, with confidence, but then he'd never been lacking in that regard. "Would you be disappointed if I were?"

She was disappointed in herself because she wouldn't be. But she held her silence on that matter. No point in confirming what he no doubt already suspected. "How did you manage to keep Sophie all these years, while you were in prison?" she asked.

"When I was arrested, Aiden came to see me. Actually, all my brothers did, but Aiden was the first, so I asked him to take Sophie from Mick's pen and see to her for me. I was afraid your father knew she was alive, might discern where I was keeping her."

She furrowed her brow. "I wonder where my father came up with the notion you'd stolen her. I never told Miriam—I never told anyone—she was alive."

"I'm not certain he did know. He just claimed I stole his horse, didn't give specifics. He didn't need any proof. He was an earl. They took him at his word."

She was horrified by the notion that her father would wield such power so unjustly. "His actions disgust me. I know you don't want me to continue to apologize, but my family owes you so much. My father treated you shabbily, and I had no idea. If he were still alive, I'd not be able to bear looking at him."

"Let's talk about something more pleasant."

She couldn't blame him for wanting to move on. "I'll be rescuing more children tonight if the woman comes through on her promise to meet me. Although as I mentioned last night, I must find a source of income rather quickly. I've been using the money I received from selling my wedding gown and jewelry to purchase children. It's almost gone."

"You might do better to place the ads yourself, to be a baby farmer. Then you'd acquire the children right off. Or at least some of them."

She looked over at him, not at all surprised to find his gaze focused on her. "That's brilliant, Finn. I hadn't thought of that. An advert would no doubt be less costly than what I've been paying these women, and the children would be brought to me directly."

He shrugged. "I was a thief in my youth, for a while anyway. Considering all the angles is one of my strong suits. Although you're likely to discover some of these children belong to people you know. How would you feel about that?"

"I won't judge them. I can assure them their children will be well cared for. Hopefully they'll find some comfort in that."

"And when the sisters run out of beds?"

With a sigh, she rolled her eyes. "I'm working on it." With the freedom that she'd gained this morning, opportunities opened. She just needed to sit down and explore all the possibilities. Perhaps she could find people—some among the nobility—willing to support her cause.

"Here we are," he said suddenly. He brought them to a halt in front of a large brick building that had three rows of windows. She'd paid very little attention to the path they'd taken, wasn't quite certain where they were. He dismounted, walked over to her, and placed his large hands on her small waist, and she fought against welcoming the familiarity of it as he lowered her to the ground. Afterward he tethered both horses to a post and flipped a coin to an eager lad. "Keep watch on them."

"Aye, guv."

Then he led her toward the steps. "What is this place?" she asked.

"The Elysium Club." He said it as though the name explained it all.

"I'm afraid I must beg ignorance as I've never heard of it. Is it a gaming hell?"

"It is." He leaned toward her, a mischievous glint in his eyes. "For women."

INSERTING A KEY into the lock, he led Vivi inside. The mornings were the quietest and his favorite time of the day, when possibilities loomed before him. In the hush of inactivity, all dreams appeared obtainable.

They entered a small lobby where people could leave their cloaks and coats with a young woman who would hang them in the tiny room behind her until the guests were ready to leave. Then they walked into the main room. All the gas lamps were alight, bathing the room in a golden glow. She gasped, which delighted him beyond all measure.

"So this is what a gaming hell looks like," she said in awe. "Is this your brother's?"

"It's mine."

She spun around, surprise and awe momentarily returning the lost years to her features, reminding him of the girl she'd once been. "But I thought you worked at Aiden's club."

"I do, although not as often since I've begun managing this place."

Slowly she took in the surroundings, and he wondered if she saw the same potential he did. "It's incredible, Finn. What's the purpose of the various tables?"

"We have faro, roulette, dice games, and naturally card games. We even have a book over here similar to the one at White's where ladies can wager on anything they choose."

She flipped through the pages. "They're blank. Have you not yet opened?"

"We have." He shrugged. "We just don't have many customers yet."

"Did you announce it in the *Times*?" She picked up a pair of dice and rolled them along the table.

"No, I want to keep the club more exclusive. And that's where you come in."

She swung around and stared at him. "I beg your pardon?"

"You can't get into a gentlemen's club without someone vouching for you." He bobbed his head to the side. "Except for Aiden's, of course. Show enough blunt and he welcomes you with open arms. I want you to help me determine who to invite. I'll pay you for the service."

"This club is for the ladies of the nobility?"

"It is. As well as some commoners whose husbands are well-off. What do you ladies do when your gents are out for the evening?"

"We embroider." Turning on her heel, she began wending her way between tables. "Why call it the Elysium Club?"

"Aiden named his club for the three-headed hound that guards Hades. I thought to name mine for the heavens where the gods lived. I want the ladies to feel like goddesses."

She ran her fingers over the green baize of a card table, and he remembered how it had felt to have her fingers running over his chest, thought about how badly he wanted them skimming over his skin now.

"There are two sorts who might seek refuge here." She faced him. "Have no doubt about it, they are seeking refuge. One sort will be the outgoing girls, the bold ones, the ones gentlemen tend to discount as being unbiddable. The other will be the shy girls. Both groups sit at the balls, bored beyond reason, feeling . . . less than. Judged, although for entirely opposite reasons."

"You say that as though you understand them, as though you've experienced it. I've seen you at a ball—you're not a wallflower and you certainly never gave the impression of being unbiddable."

"I changed a bit after that masquerade ball. I had to force myself to be enthusiastic about things and found myself not really being part of either group. I'd ridiculed them before, came to know them better afterward."

After she'd thought he'd abandoned her. Pity her father was dead. Finn had changed as well. The earl no longer would have had the power to intimidate him, which he'd have learned when Finn planted his fist in his face.

"But those are the ladies you'll want to invite. At least in the beginning." Looking up, she released a sigh of wonder. "You had clouds painted on the ceiling. It's beautiful. That must have cost you a fortune."

"I'm giving the painter's wife a lifetime membership in the club. He'll appreciate a few nights of peace or going out with his mates to their club."

"A clever way to keep your funds on hand."

"I had a lot of time to determine how best to go about making this place what I envisioned it could be." He'd begun his planning while in prison and had been forced to keep it all in his head, because they wouldn't provide him with paper to work it out. "I have a dining room, a taproom, but it's still missing something."

"A ballroom," she replied without hesitation.

"Women like to dance with themselves, do they?"

"Remember, you'll begin by having wallflowers as members, and they seldom get to dance, which is a mainstay of being a wall-flower. But if you were to hire men whose job it was to dance with them—"

"That sounds terribly wicked, Miss Kent."

"Women have fantasies, too. They want to be desired. Very few are, really. They're courted for what they'll bring to the marriage."

"What were you bringing to Thornley?" He hated that he'd asked, that although he knew the man was madly in love with

Gillie, he couldn't seem to move past the notion that at one time he'd planned to marry Vivi.

"Land." Her answer was sharp and succinct. "It was lunacy, Finn. When I was born, our fathers agreed we'd marry because there is a small patch of land his father wanted. And it was much less bother for my father to sign a contract than to go through the process of interviewing young swains and ensuring I had a good match."

"You didn't love him at all?"

"I cared for him. He was a friend. But I never loved him as I once loved you."

He didn't miss the fact she was specifically stating she'd loved him in the past, not now. "What do you feel for me now?"

"Sadness because so very much was stolen from us, so much that we can never regain. Guilt. Because of me your life was ruined."

He was hardly aware of taking the strides that brought him to her. He cupped her cheek, not quite as round as it had been the last time he'd held it. She was thinner, not scrawny, but not as robust as she'd been at seventeen. He looked deeply into those green eyes that had haunted him for so long. "Not because of you. Never because of you."

Then he lowered his mouth to hers, and it felt as though after eight long years he'd finally come home.

IT WAS MADNESS to welcome the kiss but welcome his kiss she did. She'd gone years without feeling anything, without truly feeling at all, until she'd run from the church and embraced her mission of rescuing children. As fraught with risk as the endeavor was turning out to be, she felt a measure of excitement and anticipation bursting through her chest each time she received a letter from a woman stating she was willing to meet. The exhilaration would grow as she wandered the streets toward the designated meeting place; the satisfaction was immense when she finally had the children in hand. But everything she felt during all of those moments paled when compared with the elation rushing through her now, causing her heart to beat with wild abandon, her skin to tingle, her toes to curl.

She didn't want to care for this man, wanted to leave the past behind, wanted to leave *him* behind because the guilt she felt where he was concerned was overwhelming. And yet as she tasted him again after a long fast, as he wrapped his arms around her and drew her in close to his body until she was pressed flat against him, she felt nearly whole when for so long she'd been shattered and broken.

She wanted to weep for the joy of it . . . and the terror. To risk seeing the disgust on his face if he learned all of the truth—

He wouldn't continue to sweep his tongue over hers, to groan low, to hold her tighter. He would fling her away, condemn her to the life of isolation she deserved. He would discover that at her core she was a coward. When it had mattered most, she'd retreated in fear and shame. When the courage had finally begun to leak back into her, she'd been punished mercilessly until the cowardice returned. Unlike him, she still struggled to remain strong, to not retreat. With him, she was on shaky ground, contemplating that perhaps sins could be forgiven, that she deserved happiness.

A part of her, a wicked part of her, could not help but think that of all the places in England she could have gone, she'd come here because there had been a chance she might see him again—in passing, if nothing else. She'd longed to simply catch a glimpse of him, to know he was well. Now, that didn't seem enough. Suddenly she wanted more, wanted what she could not have, what she did not deserve.

Drawing back, he trailed his fingers along the inside seam of her cheek. "You taste the same."

"You taste darker, richer." More masculine, more mature, more man. Simply more. How did she explain that without sounding like a complete ninny? Eight years ago, she'd thought them grown up. Only now did she realize they'd truly been just children. She didn't know if they'd have been able to survive all the challenges that would have awaited them. She stepped back, needing the distance between them, and watched with regret as he slowly lowered his hand, as a sadness plunged into the depths of his eyes. "Yes, well." Needing to get herself on firmer emotional ground, she glanced around. "It's truly remarkable. I think you're going to do very well here."

"I want you to be my partner."

SHE STARED AT him as though he were mad. Perhaps he was. She had knowledge he needed, but it was more than that. He wanted the opportunity to get to know her again and following her around on her midnight excursions wasn't conducive to that happening. And he wasn't confident he could convince her to go on a series of outings with him.

Finally, she blinked, shook her head, and released a quick burst of laughter. "You jest, surely."

"I've never been more serious. You know who I should invite. You know how to get word to them. You know what would bring them pleasure, what would cause them to return. I want to show you something else." He took her hand, grateful she didn't fling his aside, but she was probably in too much of a shock to do so. He escorted her back into the foyer and toward a small alcove. Inside was a set of stairs. He led the way up and into a long corridor. Along one side of it were several doors. The other side was adorned with a railing and looked out over the gaming floor. "The offices," he explained, before directing her to one in the center and pushing the door open. "Mine."

He stepped inside, not surprised that she followed. The room was huge with an enormous desk set before the windows. Since he'd been released from prison, he'd been unable to abide small, cramped quarters of any sort. "There's room here for another desk, so you would have a place to work."

She wandered over to the bookshelf that lined one wall. He had an assortment of books. Some on management, most simply to serve as an escape. Soon, he expected to store his ledgers there. Presently, the first of what he hoped would be many sat on his desk.

"I'll be issuing invitations to people you know. If you have concerns, don't want them to know you're involved in the enterprise, there is a way in from the rear of the building, from the alley. No one would ever see you or know you were here. You'd never have to go out on the floor unless you wanted to."

Shaking her head, she faced him. "I can give you a list of names—"

"I want more than that. I want your expertise. If something isn't working, I'll need you to tell me why, what the ladies find objectionable. I'll make you an equal partner. Fifty percent of the profits."

"Finn, no. I'm not deserving of that."

"You told me you needed employment. I'm offering it to you. And something else." He indicated they were going back into the hallway. She stepped out of the room, and he followed. "There are living quarters at each end of the hallway."

She tagged along behind him as he walked to the last door, opened it, and allowed her to go in first. The room opened into a large parlor, presently scantily furnished with only a sofa and low table. "It still needs some furnishings."

He leaned against the wall and watched as she walked to the windows and glanced out on the street in front of the building. The other quarters looked out over the mews.

She wandered into the bedchamber, but he kept himself rooted where he was. There was a large bed in that room, and he imagined her spread out over it, her eyes and body inviting him to join her. His cock reacted with a vengeance, and he began doing sums, anticipating profits.

Finally, she appeared and approached him, her head angled as though she were giving serious thought to something. "These are your lodgings. They smell of you. Leather, horses, earth. Rich and dark."

"Presently they are mine, but they would become yours. They have a more pleasing view, certainly better than the one you presently have. And you wouldn't be sharing these quarters with a steam engine. I've no idea how you manage to sleep through her racket. You could still teach the children in the mornings, if you wished, but you wouldn't have to scrub floors for lodgings or meals. Here, you'd have that freedom you craved. You could do whatever you wanted."

"You're being awfully generous, Finn. Why?"

"Your Sophie played a large part in my acquiring this place." He told her about the lord who'd made him an offer. "It wouldn't have happened if you hadn't begged me to save her. So you see, Vivi, you are *entitled* to a part of this place."

"I'm glad something good came of your taking care of Sophie, but I fear you're giving me too much credit."

He also wanted a chance to get to know her again. "Four of my siblings have successful businesses. I'm a bit behind. I want to get things up to snuff and quickly. I think you can help me do that. Working here won't interfere with your personal desire to help children. As a partner, you would tend to business whenever it pleases you to do so. Although since your income will be based on profit, I can't imagine you slacking off."

She nodded, glanced around, brought her gaze back to his. "Thirty percent."

He stared at her. "I beg your pardon?"

"My portion. Thirty percent."

He laughed. "I've never known anyone to bargain for less favorable terms."

"I don't deserve fifty percent. It was your idea and you've already invested a good bit in it. We'll set up a payment schedule until I've reimbursed you half of what you've already put into the place. And I'll take the other rooms."

He considered arguing but could tell she'd made up her mind. It was her terms or nothing. "You strike a hard bargain," he said wryly. "But I accept your terms. I'll have my solicitor draw up an agreement."

"Is that really necessary?"

"To protect you from my taking advantage of the situation, yes."

"All right, then. I have an appointment tonight. I could begin working for you tomorrow."

"You're not working for me, Vivi. We're working together. We're *partners*." He emphasized the last word because he needed her to understand she owed him nothing. They were coming into this arrangement as equals. Not an earl's daughter and an earl's bastard, but two people working to make a success of this place.

"Partners," she repeated, and held out her hand.

He wanted to press a kiss to those knuckles, turn her hand over and place a kiss in the center of her palm. Instead he folded his fingers around her offering and gave a light squeeze. "Partners."

Chapter 16

*L*ater that night when she stepped through the gate at the foundling home, she wasn't at all surprised to find Finn waiting for her. On the way back that morning, he'd casually asked what time her appointment was, and without thought she'd told him. It seemed they were going to become partners in all their enterprises.

But tonight, it wasn't only him waiting, it was his brother's carriage.

"I thought it would save us having to deal with any footpads," he told her.

She gave the address to the driver, who was standing beside the two horses, then allowed Finn to hand her up into the carriage. She settled onto the squabs facing forward while the conveyance rocked as Finn climbed in and took his place opposite her.

"I attended your brother's wedding. I saw you there." She glanced out the window. While she'd been furious and hurt when she'd seen him, she saw no point in mentioning it now that she knew the truth of things. "Perhaps if I hadn't, I could have married Thornley. But seeing you caused memories to crash in on me, and suddenly I felt as though I'd somehow stumbled onto the wrong path." She'd feared she'd have been miserable married to Thornley, regardless of how good a man he was.

"Gillie's rather glad you didn't."

She looked at his silhouette within the dark confines, glad no lamp burned inside to cast light over them. It was always easier to speak when encased in shadows. "Is she happy?"

"Extremely so. We'll have to grab a pint sometime at her tavern."

"I doubt she'd welcome me as gladly as she did before."

"She will if you're with me."

She wasn't certain she deserved a welcome.

"How did the sisters take your leaving?" he asked.

"They were rather surprised, I think, at the haste with which I'll be making my departure. Although Sister Theresa remarked that God provides. They'll continue to take in the children until they have no more beds. Sister Bernadette will assume my teaching duties." Hopefully, before long, she could purchase a residence with an abundance of rooms, so she could provide the shelter herself. She'd hire people to look after the children, see to their needs. She'd ensure they were all educated, that they had better lives than they might have had otherwise. The possibilities were suddenly endless, all the various ways she could make a difference filling her with a hope she'd not felt since that night when she and Finn had agreed to run off together.

"It'll be hard to say goodbye to the children," she confessed. "But I'll visit them often. It's not as though you're locking me away."

"I never would, Vivi. You're free to come and go as you please. The horses are kept in a small stable near the club. You can have Sophie saddled for you anytime you want to have a jaunt."

"You're being awfully good to me, Finn. I'm not deserving of it."

"I've told you. I don't blame you for what your father did."

"The kiss this morning . . . before I sign any agreement with you, we must come to an understanding that what will be between us is business only. We can't recapture what we had."

"I know that, Vivi."

She experienced a measure of relief and disappointment. He wasn't the boy she'd loved. He was a man to be reckoned with, and if the stirrings for him she felt in her heart were any indication, what she might eventually feel for him had the possibility of being downright terrifying.

"But that doesn't mean," he stated slowly, "that we can't find something even better than what we had."

IN THE DARKNESS he heard her small gasp. Ah, yes, she was once again Finn's Folly because he did believe there was a chance more could exist between them than discussing who should receive an invitation to their club and what to do with the varied rooms that currently remained empty. He thought working in close proximity might spur the need for additional kisses, touches, whispers.

He had an advantage because now they would be living in close quarters, and she would be in his life every day and every night. In their youth, the time they'd had together had been rare, a treat, something special to be anticipated. Perhaps the rarity of their time together had influenced them into believing what they felt would never dwindle. But he was of a mind to test the waters, not to reclaim, but to build anew. She intrigued him in ways she never had. He liked knowing what she cared about, what she thought. Watching her as she'd considered the characteristics of the ladies who would frequent their club had created a titillating sensation. But then everything about her titillated and aroused him. It always had. Even when she'd been young, and he'd first met her and every fantasy of kissing her had been inappropriate. Christ, he'd never thought she'd be old enough so he could lower the walls he'd erected to protect her from him and what he wanted to do with her.

Then she *had* been old enough—no, he'd considered her old enough, but looking back he acknowledged that they'd both been too young and inexperienced. Yet the yearning had been so strong as to block out any common sense. He longed for the nights when he'd been unable to sleep because of his want of her.

"If you seek to take advantage of this partnership—"

"I was willing to give you fifty percent," he cut in. "I'd hardly call that taking advantage."

"I'm not referring to the financial aspects. I'm referring to the physical."

He was surprised she'd put it so bluntly, but then he was discovering she was bolder with the confrontations. Before where she might have thrown an upset, now she kept her tone even yet somehow deadlier, more effective at getting her point across.

"I noticed several doors," she said. "Perhaps behind one of those is a room I could use as my own office."

"So I have to get up from my desk and go searching for you whenever I have a question? It'll be more convenient if we share an office, so we can discuss matters that arise."

"Finn, I don't have it within me to love again."

"That's not true, Vivi. You love those children."

"That's different. They're different. I'm speaking of passion—"

"You didn't stop me from kissing you earlier. What are you afraid of? Of discovering something even better than what we had? Or perhaps you fear discovering we paid an ungodly price for something that wasn't worth paying anything at all for."

She released a great gust of air. "Maybe. I don't know. I just want to make sure we're being realistic going into this arrangement. I'm not certain we were before, and I think it's imperative we are now to avoid any further hurt."

"If you never experience pain, Vivi, how can you ever truly appreciate the joy that arrives when you don't?"

His words seemed simple when in truth she found his sentiment profound. She'd once never gone without, and during the past three months she'd struggled with her dwindling finances and what she felt now, knowing the struggle was behind her, was sweet indeed. She'd always taken for granted what she'd had. No longer.

But it was more than that. Before, everything had been given to her, and now, with Finn's help, she would be earning her coins, she would be gaining independence in a way she hadn't before. Since leaving her family, all her decisions had been her own, but many of her actions had been tempered by her lack of funds. His offer was opening up an entirely different world for her. She would be able to see to her own needs, care for herself. There was power to be found in not relying on anyone—even though she had to acknowledge she was reliant on his generosity. But once the papers were signed, once they became partners, she would earn her way, make herself invaluable. He'd given her an opportunity to make something of herself that she had no intention of squandering.

She'd always followed the path set before her, but now she had the means to forge her own route, could determine her own destination. She wanted to glory in it.

He had no idea how broken she'd been, and if she had her way, he'd never learn the entire truth of it. Finally, she was on the mend, stronger than she'd been. A shattered teacup, pieced back together, might not be as lovely to look at as one that had never been dropped, but if both were dropped again, the shattered one was less likely to break because it was reinforced with glue. She drew comfort from that.

She didn't respond to him. The point of his question had been to make her think, not to obtain an answer. And he didn't press. He sat there with no tension whatsoever radiating off him. She marveled at the calm of him. She'd noted it that first night in the alleyway when the women had threatened her. He didn't fear the dark or any of the miscreants who crept through it. He was capable of caring for himself, had learned to put all his faith in his abilities.

It was something about herself she was only just coming to comprehend: she had the power to stand on her own. Any victory or defeat came about because of her own actions, her own decisions, her own resolve.

The carriage came to a halt. Immediately he opened the door and leaped out before reaching back for her.

"Keep driving along these streets," he called up to the driver. "Periodically make your way back here. This is where we'll meet you when we've completed our task."

As the carriage carried on, he turned to her. "Lead the way."

It wasn't very far, and they were a bit early. She was grateful he'd had the foresight to bring the carriage. A brisk wind whipped through the air, bringing a chill with it that caused her to shiver. She brought her pelisse in more snugly against her as she stepped over rubbish and recalled the path she was to follow from this point. They seemed to walk through a maze of warrens before she reached the darkened building with a long sash tied around the handle. She wasn't to go in. The meeting wouldn't happen there. The sash merely marked the spot.

"How many?" he asked.

Widening her eyes, looking in the direction from which his voice had come, she realized he was lost in the shadows. "Pardon?"

"How many children tonight?"

"Three."

Only when a woman finally approached, barely limned by the light of a distant streetlamp, three children were clinging to her skirt, fairly tripping over their feet in their effort to keep up with her pace, and one babe was nestled in her arms. "Ye be the one wot wants to pay me for this brood?"

Lavinia stepped forward, already reaching for the smallest. "Yes, I am."

"That'll be ten quid."

She stopped as though the carriage had returned and now separated her from them. "You said five."

The woman bounced the infant. "That was afore I got this one handed over to me last night. Fresh from the womb, I'd say. Ye want 'er, it'll be ten quid for the lot of them."

The other three blinked up at her through large, round eyes, eyes too large for their thin faces. She looked back to the shadows. "Have you any money on you?"

"I have." He stepped forward into the light. "But you won't be needing it."

The baby farmer squeaked like a rat pounced on by a cat. "Who ye be?"

"Trewlove. Perhaps you've heard of my family."

The woman took another step back. "I've 'erd of ye."

"Then you'll know we tend not to tolerate those who seek to take advantage of others," Finn said. "You've only just acquired the infant. I doubt you've paid a single penny for its care, so what was handed to you last night is pure profit. Be content with that. Otherwise you might find me stealing into your residence some night." He gave the beastly woman a smile that sent a chill racing down Lavinia's back.

"'Ere." She thrust the babe into Lavinia's arms, then worked to free her skirts of the fisted hands that clung to them, transferring the children to Lavinia's pelisse.

She was in the process of cradling the babe in one arm when she noticed Finn holding a banknote out to the woman, who snatched it and raced off. The children, who'd been eerily silent until that moment, began bawling.

"Here now," Finn said. "Who wants to ride on my back?"

"Me," the tallest, a boy, proclaimed. The others went quiet as Finn grabbed him and swung him around as though he were a little monkey. Perhaps he was, because he scrambled up the man's back and wound his arms about his neck and his legs around his stomach.

Finn knelt and patted his thighs. "All right, you two. Up here. Into my arms. I'd wager you've never seen the world from up here."

She'd wager that as well as they rushed into his arms and he uncoiled that long lengthy body of his. Her insides did funny little twirls at the sight of him waiting patiently as the children clambered into position. She didn't want to contemplate what a wonderful father he might have been had they married, how he might have played with his own children.

Her father had certainly never played with her. He'd always been someone to obey without question. She had no memory of ever laughing with him. She couldn't help but believe Finn would tickle his children until he heard their laughter, his joining in with theirs.

"Let's go," Finn said. "Everyone, hang on tight."

And she had this ridiculous urge to hang on to him as well. They began trekking back along the path they'd traversed earlier. The streets were quiet, dark, abandoned. She supposed the baby farmer wanted no witnesses to what she was doing. Eventually they reached the spot where the carriage was to meet them. It arrived less than a minute after they did. They settled into the carriage with the girls sitting on either side of her, the boy beside Finn. Based on their size, none of them could have been any older than four, although it was also possible their growth had been stunted with insufficient food and care.

"You were planning to handle this lot on your own?" Finn asked.

"It would have been a challenge, but I'd have managed."

"And when she asked for more blunt?"

"I'd have arranged to meet her tomorrow or perhaps I'd have tried to bluff my way through."

The girls were curled against her sides. She was aware of their bodies relaxing and assumed the swaying of the coach was putting them to sleep.

"From now on, Vivi, I go with you on these excursions."

It was pointless to argue, because she knew he'd tag along even if she objected. Besides, she liked knowing he was near if something unexpected turned up. Although she was a little cautious in asking, "It seems the work you do for your brother has given you quite the reputation."

"It's more than me, it's all of us. My brothers, Gillie. We've often helped people out of one scrape or another."

"Well, you've certainly helped me, not only with the children, but with your generous offer. Here, I thought I was special," she teased.

"You are." His tone carried no teasing whatsoever, embarrassed her a bit with the earnestness of it. She felt as though she'd been fishing for some sort of reassurance, even though all he'd done for her already proved his statement true.

The carriage came to a halt in front of the foundling home. The path was short, so the children walked through the gate, Finn following along behind them as she led them to the back of the residence. After ushering the children inside, she turned back to Finn. "I'll awaken one of the sisters to help me. They're not comfortable with a man in the residence."

"Will you need help moving tomorrow?"

She shook her head. "I have very little to bundle up."

"Take a hansom. If you haven't the means, I'll pay him once you get there."

"I do wish you wouldn't be so generous, Finn."

He grinned. "You complain about the oddest things." Then he leaped off the step and disappeared into the darkness.

Turning, she came up short at the sight of Sister Theresa standing there, wondered if Finn had seen her and that was the reason he hadn't lingered.

"Your gentleman seems most persistent," the sister said as she retreated inside where the children were patiently waiting.

Clutching the infant close, Lavinia followed. "He's not really *my* man." She wasn't pleased that her words seemed to lack utter conviction.

Sister Theresa merely gave her an indulgent smile before asking, "What do we do first? Bathe them or feed them?"

"Feed them, I should think."

Chapter 17

The following morning, with all her meager belongings stuffed into a burlap potato sack, she clambered into a hansom cab and headed to the club. Saying farewell to the children had been remarkably hard, but she'd promised to return on the morrow for a short visit. The ones she'd acquired the night before had settled in well. She knew the sisters would take good care of them.

When next she visited, she'd bring all the children sweets. After that, shoes. As her finances allowed, she'd provide them with clothing, something new and special to wear to church on Sundays. Eventually she'd purchase a multiroom residence so she could care for more children. She would live there with them and travel to the club each day. Her partnership with Finn would provide her with the means to do the things she wanted, but it wouldn't be her main focus. No, that would always remain the children who were in need of love and care.

Her excitement was far greater than what she'd experienced when she'd managed to successfully escape the church in search of a life with more meaning. The future potential for fulfillment was extraordinary. Her imagination wasn't keen enough to envision all the possibilities, but she would be an independent woman, free to do as she pleased. She'd experienced a measure of freedom during the past three months, but it hadn't been complete because of her limited circumstances, but now because of Finn's kindness she'd soon have financial freedom and found the notion exhilarating. She would repay him by working diligently to help ensure his business became the success he envisioned. His dream was allowing her to realize hers.

She had to wonder—if her parents hadn't interfered on that fateful night, would she and Finn have been working together to achieve their dreams . . . or would they have merely settled into a life where she learned to darn his stockings while he continued being in the employ of a horse slaughterer? Her desires then now seemed so small. Content merely to be with him, she'd truly given no thought to what would have come after they married, how they might have survived, carried on. In truth, she'd been rather naïve, a realization brought home after spending three months away from the aristocracy. She'd truly not known what to expect. Would the girl she'd been back then have been disappointed by the reality? She preferred to think not, preferred believing she'd have embraced her life and made the best of it, but a small part of her wasn't convinced she'd have possessed the maturity to handle what life would have expected of her.

When the cab came to a halt outside the club, she was surprised to see Finn standing on the steps, dressed as any gentleman, particularly a successful one, would be in a black jacket and gray waistcoat, with his white neck cloth perfected knotted. For an insane minute, fear ratcheted through her, and she nearly told the driver to carry on. Finn had been handsome enough as a young man, but as a mature one he was devastatingly so. She feared she might find herself falling for him all over again, and that was bound to bring up an ugliness in her past she didn't wish to revisit.

If she were wise, she'd seek another means for making her own way. Now that her brother was no longer searching for her, she could possibly find a position as a teacher, a governess, or a companion to a woman of means, but she had to admit to being caught up in his excitement regarding what this place could become—and what it would mean for the ladies of her acquaintance to have a venue that could offer them entertainments, even if they had no beaux to escort them around.

So she waited, while he approached, tossed money up to the driver, opened her door, and offered his hand.

"I was beginning to think you'd changed your mind," he said as he helped her down.

"It took me longer to say goodbye to the children than I'd expected."

"You can see them anytime."

"I know, but they've been a major part of my days for a few months now, and I theirs. I have no doubt, however, we'll all adjust."

He relieved her of her pitiful little sack. She strove for a witty comeback should he comment on it, but instead he merely led her up the steps and into the club. His club. Her club. Their club.

"My solicitor's here, in our office, with the papers you're to sign."

Our office. Our. Business arrangement. It would be nothing more than that.

The solicitor was a kindly looking gent. He was sitting behind Finn's desk—or at least she assumed it was Finn's; a second one rested in the room now, placed before the other window, hers possibly. As she entered, he stood.

"Mr. Charles Beckwith," Finn said by way of introduction. "Miss Lavinia Kent."

She hoped her eyes expressed her gratitude that he'd not referred to her as *Lady*. They'd not discussed how she was to be addressed, but she was discovering Finn was a keen observer and didn't need everything explained to him. She wondered what else about her that he might notice had changed.

"Miss Kent," Mr. Beckwith said with a polite bowing of his head, his blue eyes peering at her through spectacles that made him seem incredibly knowledgeable, before sweeping his hand over the papers scattered on the desk. "Shall we get to work?"

If he knew her true identity, who her family might be, he gave no indication, but simply began explaining the terms of the agreement. "Thirty percent of all profits go to you. Upon your death, any future earnings that would have come your way, instead of being reverted back to Mr. Trewlove here, will be placed in a trust for use by the Sisters of Mercy Foundling Home, located at . . ."

She stopped paying attention to his words, but instead stared at Finn. "You can't mean to continue this arrangement beyond my death, to give them money, surely."

He was leaning with his hip against his desk, one foot crossed in front of the other, his arms folded over his chest. He shrugged. "I took a guess. You can name a different benefactor at any time."

"And if you die?"

Looking at Beckwith, he arched a brow.

"Twenty-one percent of the business will be transferred into your name, giving you a total of fifty-one percent ownership," Mr. Beckwith explained. "Forty-nine percent of all future profits will go into a trust for the Trewlove Foundling Home."

The Trewlove Foundling Home? She had questions about that, but they could wait. She was struck by something that seemed much more important. "Why are you giving part of the business to me?"

"Because by the time I go toes-up, which I'm planning to be a goodly number of years from now, you will have poured a great deal of yourself into the business. I want you to be able to manage it without any interference from my siblings. They'd be well-meaning, but they can be a pushy lot. The Elysium Club will become whatever you and I envisioned it to be, worked hard to make it be. I want you to be able to carry on with it. There's also a provision that, should you marry, your portion goes into a trust, so your husband can't get his hands on it."

"I've no plans to ever marry."

"Better to have and not need, Miss Kent," Mr. Beckwith said, "than to need and not have."

"I'm not comfortable with so much coming to me," she said.

"And I'm not comfortable with it going into a trust that will be overseen by someone who won't give two figs about the place," Finn said. "Just sign the papers. We can work out any particulars later and have it amended. For the moment, I want you to know I'm going into this with full faith in you."

"You may regret that when you discover you're a fool, Finn Trewlove."

"I have a lot of regrets, Vivi, but none of them revolve around anything you've done."

Oh, but they should. It was madness to have him back in her life, but she didn't want to walk away from the possibilities, no matter how much they frightened her. She'd run too many times. This time, she intended to stay put and see this through to the end.

She dipped a pen into the inkwell and scrawled her name where Mr. Beckwith indicated, watched as Finn did the same. The solicitor then signed the document as a witness. He placed the agreement in his satchel. "I'll keep these in my offices," he said.

With a nod to each of them, he walked out.

And it was done. She was a partner in a gambling hell.

HER EXCITEMENT AS she'd stepped out of the hansom had been palpable, infectious. As much as he'd anticipated running his club, perhaps even competing with Aiden's for a bit more success, suddenly there was a joyous aspect to it that had been missing before. His family had always been supportive of his efforts, but now that she was part and parcel of what he hoped to achieve, the possibilities suddenly seemed not only infinite but reachable. If it were late afternoon, he'd pour them drinks. Ah, hell, it was late afternoon somewhere. "Let's celebrate," he said, grabbing two glasses and a bottle of whisky off the credenza.

"It's not even noon," she said, clearly shocked by his suggestion.

"Which will make it even more special." He put just a splash in each glass, handed her one, and lifted his. "To our success."

Hitching up a hip, he settled on the edge of his desk, took a sip, and watched as she did the same. She blinked; her eyes widened. "I'd forgotten how tart it was."

"Have you not had any since that night?" The night when he'd first made love to her.

She shook her head, then glanced over at the other desk. "Is that mine?"

"It is."

After wandering over to it, she trailed her finger along its edge. "You certainly managed to obtain it in short order. How did you accomplish it?"

"I have my ways." It had been in the office next door, waiting for the day when he hired someone to assist him, so late last night with some help from one of the dealers, he'd moved it in here.

"Are you going to continue to be mysterious now that we're partners?" she asked.

"When it serves." He didn't want her to decide she should have her own office. Already this one was more to his liking with her in it.

She settled back against her desk, and he suspected she regretted not being tall enough at that moment to sit on the edge of it as he was. "Tell me about the Trewlove Foundling Home."

"Not much to say. It is what it says—"

A knock on the doorjamb stopped him, and he caught sight of a young woman standing there, one he'd been expecting. "Pardon my interruption, Mr. Trewlove. Your man downstairs told me to come on up."

Setting his glass aside, he slid off the desk, aware of Vivi straightening. "Your timing is perfect. Miss Kent, meet Beth. Gillie's seamstress. She's here to take your measurements for a couple of frocks."

"I'm not in need of frocks."

"Of course you are."

"What I have will suffice. You don't need to purchase me clothing."

"I'll add it to your tally." Which was a lie. These were going to be gifts from him because he couldn't stand to see her in rags. It took him only three steps to reach her, three seconds to touch his fingers to her chin. "You're a partner now. While you might not go onto the gaming floor, you'll be dealing with employees in here and the back rooms. It won't do for you to look less than polished. Mick had a lover once who told him if he didn't dress like a successful businessman before he was one, he would never be one." He dropped his hand to her collar, ran his thumb along the tattered edge. "It won't do for you to be dressed in worn clothing."

He could see she wasn't happy but also had no rebuttal to his argument.

"Yes, all right. But two, only two for now."

It was going to be three. He had something special in mind for the third, but it was to be a surprise. Hopefully just as much of one as she was to him. He'd expected her to jump at the chance of having a new frock. Lady Lavinia would have been mortified to wear anything that had so much as a single frayed thread. But this woman was a mystery he wanted to unravel.

"Let's get you set up in your rooms so Beth can get to work. I'm certain she has customers and stitching awaiting her back at her shop." He lifted the burlap sack that, based on its weight, contained hardly anything at all. He recalled all the frocks she'd worn on their outings. He didn't think he'd ever seen the same one a second time. Then there was that froth of a ball gown, which he suspected had depleted China of all its silk. Beneath every fancy garment had been layers of petticoats. It would have taken trunks to haul her clothing anywhere, trunks and an extra carriage or two to transport them. Yet here was this small bundle. How far she'd fallen.

No, not fallen. She'd gone willingly, with purpose, had made the choice to leave the other life behind, had kept the vow she'd made to run off with him—only she'd had to do it without him. He intended to prove to her that the vow they'd made in their youth was still worth honoring.

SHE COULDN'T BELIEVE the amount of pleasure it brought her to know she would be getting a new frock, even if she didn't feel it was necessary. Although Finn was correct: she needed to project a certain image. She'd been brought up to understand the importance of the face one showed the world. A person could be dying inside, but still had to give the impression that nothing was amiss, that happiness abounded within.

However, she would be grateful to replace her clothing with something new, something that had never been infested. Her current attire often made her itch as though fleas resided within the woven fabric. Even though she knew they didn't, she couldn't help but believe the very possibility existed that they might have once.

She followed Finn and Beth into the hallway and came to an abrupt halt as Finn turned left. "My quarters are in the other direction," she announced.

He faced her. "Those rooms are not yet furnished."

"Then I shall make do."

"We're just temporarily putting you in the rooms overlooking the street."

"Where will you sleep?"

He released an impatient sigh. "*I'll* make do."

"Finn, I don't want my presence here to inconvenience you. I can return to the sisters until the other room is ready."

"That'll prove to be an inconvenience to us both."

"But—"

"Vivi, if you continue to argue with me on every matter, our partnership is likely to become unpleasant for us both."

He had a point. "Very well. But only until the other room is furnished."

It was really a rather nice room, but when they walked into it, she noted on a table beside the sofa a vase of petunias that hadn't been there before and was touched by his thoughtfulness.

He went into the bedroom, no doubt to place her sack in there, and returned empty-handed. "I'll be in the office if you need me."

With that he was gone, and the room suddenly seemed lonely.

Beth placed her satchel on a small square table where Lavinia thought she might take her meals, although she had no means for preparing them. Although there was probably a kitchen downstairs since he planned to have a dining room. The seamstress removed her tape and smiled brightly. "Let's get some measurements, shall we?"

While the young woman worked—measuring and making notes in a little book—Lavinia couldn't help but study the masculinity of the room with its dark fabrics and even darker wood. Everything within these walls suited Finn, everything except her. "It was nice of you to go to the bother of coming to me," she said to Beth. "I suppose I could have gone to your shop."

"I didn't mind coming here." The girl knelt, stretching the tape from Lavinia's waist to the floor. "I'd do anything a Trewlove asked. Wouldn't have my shop without them."

Her curiosity was piqued. "Why is that?"

"My landlord was a brutish man. Come Black Mondays—"

"Black Mondays?"

"Aye. Rent for my shop came due every Monday. I didn't always have what was owed, and when I didn't, he'd want payment in other ways."

"What ways?" she asked hesitantly, hoping she might not have the right of it.

The girl didn't look at her. Simply continued to work. "He expected me to be his lightskirt, took what he wanted. One time when I objected, he smacked me. Bruised my cheek. Gillie came in the next day, in want of a new skirt. Noticed it. Asked me what happened." She shrugged. "I told her. She has a way about her that'll have you unburdening yourself without even thinking about it." Unfolding her body, she began tucking her things into her satchel. "Apparently, a few nights later, my landlord ran across the Trewlove brothers in an alley. He didn't fare so well but offered to sell me the shop. Mick Trewlove helped me get a loan." She smiled at Lavinia. "So no trouble at all to come here. I'll return in a few days, so you can try on the frocks and I can make any last-minute adjustments to make sure they fit properly."

"Thank you, Beth. I look forward to it."

After showing the woman to the door, she leaned with her back against it, admiring the young woman who life had dealt an unfair hand but who had managed in spite of dark days to bring such a sunny disposition with her. An abundance of unfortunate circumstances, and she'd been blind to a host of them. But not Finn, not his family. They cared for a good many beyond themselves. Perhaps she'd have not found herself darning stockings, but instead working to secure others' rights.

As she meandered through the rooms that smelled of Finn, she imagined him looking out for a little dressmaker, looking out for her. Looking out for Sophie. He had such a protective nature about him. If her father hadn't seen him sent to prison, everything would have turned out so very differently. But she wasn't convinced she'd have appreciated him as much as she should have. She certainly wouldn't have appreciated acquiring a new frock. She'd have considered it her due. What a selfish girl she'd been, thinking of herself, while he and his family tended to think of others. Resisting him was going to be incredibly difficult.

But resist him she would because she had more important matters than falling in love all over again with which to contend. There was no better time to test her mettle than the present. With a quick glance in the looking glass that hung on the wall above the washstand where he had possibly shaved that morning—she was not going to think about that intimate task or how satisfying it would be to do it for him—she ensured every strand of hair she'd pinned up earlier was still in place. She patted her cheeks to bring some color to them before heading out of the rooms and down the hall to his—their—office.

Sitting behind the desk, he was studying some papers. They seemed so fragile in his large hands; the room seemed so much smaller with his presence. Even relaxed, he possessed an alertness, an awareness, that shimmered off him in an extremely masculine manner. She imagined him striding through the gaming floor and realized she wanted to do more than imagine it. She wanted to see it. She thought of him waltzing with one of the wallflowers and knew a spark of jealousy. Perhaps he'd leave that task to those they hired, although she knew there might come a time when she'd see him with a lover or a wife. A man such as he was not without needs. She wanted him to find happiness, to have someone better suited to him than she was, someone more courageous than she'd been.

He lifted his gaze and pinned her to the spot as effectively as Neville had fastened dead butterflies he'd found to a small board for his collection when he was much younger. She'd always found the practice morbid, and whenever he went away to school for a few months, she'd free the colorful creatures and give them a proper burial.

At the moment, however, she feared she was in danger of expiring because it was a challenge to draw breath into her lungs with his dark, penetrating eyes focused so intently on her. Slowly he came to his feet, and she had the unsettling thought that she'd made a terrible mistake in coming here, in agreeing to be his partner. Certainly, she could find safer means for earning money—climbing on to rooftops and cleaning chimneys, for example.

"Are you ready to get to work?" he asked.

With those few words, he broke the spell and she could breathe again. She'd applied her signature to an agreement, which she would honor to the best of her ability. He needed her knowledge, what she knew in her head, not her body. If only he hadn't kissed her the day before, if only he hadn't reminded her of what he was capable of making her feel. She swallowed hard, inhaled deeply. "Yes, quite."

She was rather pleased she managed to stroll to her desk without giving the impression her legs were somewhat weakened by his nearness. She sat in the comfy leather chair and began taking stock of the items on her desk: parchment, pen, inkwell, his backside.

He'd wandered over and taken up his position as though he

were completely unaware of the inappropriateness of his putting that portion of his anatomy within easy reach, as though he were oblivious to the way the cloth of his trousers pulled taut against his backside, outlined his hard thigh. He'd removed his jacket so nothing shielded her eyes from the scandalous sight, and she remembered how lovely it had felt to dig her fingers into that firm flesh and muscle.

Leaning forward, he planted his forearm on that enticing thigh. "We have a cook."

She feared he detected a hunger in her eyes and was misinterpreting it. "So we have kitchens?" Inane question. If they didn't, why would they need a cook?

"Down below. So if you fancy a cup of tea or some lemonade or anything else for that matter, she can prepare it for you. We have"—he furrowed his brow—"they're not exactly servants, but they see to the place, tidying it up, running errands, fetching things. We'll get you a little bell, so you can call for them when you're in need of something."

"I don't need them waiting on me."

"There's a time when you would have."

"Yes, well, that time has passed. Truly, Finn, I've left that life behind. I enjoy seeing to my own needs."

"All of them?" His voice was low, sensual, flavored with decadence.

She knew to what he was referring, the naughty scamp. The pleasuring of herself. Angling her chin haughtily, she strove to look down on him even though he towered over her. "The ones that need seeing to."

"I'm always available if any require assistance."

She sighed. "Finn, if you continue to persist in this unacceptable manner, our partnership is likely to become unpleasant for us both."

He grinned. "You're using some of my earlier argument against me."

"We are business partners. We can be nothing more."

"In spite of how things ended, it was good between us, Vivi."

"We were young and foolish."

"Now, we're older and wiser. It should be even better."

She was prepared to argue further, but he shoved himself off the desk, taking that lovely backside with him.

"Come along," he said, grabbing his jacket from where it rested on the back of his chair and working his way into it. "Let's introduce you to the staff we presently have on hand."

There was the cook, who looked to be too thin to do much sampling of her own work, a man referred to as "The Boss," who was charged with keeping order on the gaming floor, the dealers and croupiers, a barman, young lads who saw to the guests' needs, bringing drinks when requested, two footmen who served the meals in the dining room, two girls who swept, mopped, dusted, and set the fires.

"Why can't women serve as dealers?" she asked, once she was again seated behind her desk and he was behind his.

He scooted his chair back, and she feared he was going to bring that backside within reach. Instead he simply twisted around, placed his elbow on his desk and his chin in his palm, and studied her. "Because it's a man's job."

"Why?"

He blinked, his brow furrowed.

"A woman can deal cards. I've often dealt when I played whist."

"These aren't afternoon pastimes. The games are designed to bring us money."

"Why not have men doing the dusting?"

"Men don't dust."

"Neither do I."

"We're not going to turn things upside down."

"I'm not asking you to, but, Finn, if you want women coming here, joining your club, playing your games, you need them to see that you view them as equal as men doing the same thing."

"You suggested we hire men to dance with them. Wouldn't they prefer to have a handsome bloke flirting with them as he dealt the cards or handed them the dice?"

He might have a point there. "Just consider the possibility of hiring women for positions other than tidying up."

He shrugged. "You'll be part of the selection process in the future. You can weigh in on whom we should hire."

The thought of it sent a thrill and a shiver of dread through her. Her mother had taught her what to look for in a servant, a footman specifically since they were so visible in the household. She suspected the employees here needed more than matching heights and fetching calves. Still, she wasn't going to divulge any trepidation on her part. "Very good. How many ladies should I invite?"

"Every single one you know."

In retrospect, it was a silly question. "Most families are in the country now. Some will be returning for the Little Season. Perhaps we should have . . . not a ball exactly since this is for women only, but some sort of affair. A social evening where they can get a flavoring of what we offer. Maybe they could play at the tables for free that night."

"We're not a charity."

"No, of course not. But a night where we dangle the fun to be had—like bait, when fishing. Then once they're on the hook, they are ours."

"When have you ever been fishing?"

"My father took me a time or two on the estate." One of her more pleasant memories of him, when he'd been loving and gentle with her. Now all she could imagine when she thought of him was his role in seeing Finn hauled away.

"Do you miss it? The life you had?"

She heard true interest and sympathy in his tone. He wouldn't fault her if she did. But she had no desire to travel that path at the moment. With determination, she picked up the pen he'd laid out for her and dipped it in the inkwell. "I shall invite them to an evening at the club three weeks hence, so if they aren't in the city, they will have time to get to town should they decide to come." She looked askance at him. "Does that meet with your approval?"

"You're in charge of getting them here. I leave it to you to determine the best way to do that."

She was surprised by the pleasure his words brought her. Having been on her own for three months now, she'd grown accustomed to making her own decisions, but no one had ever expressed a belief she would make the correct ones, that her opinions had merit. Even the sisters had occasionally questioned the wisdom of her actions, expressing their concerns. Although she'd appreciated that they cared enough to worry over her, it was somewhat reassuring now to have his support.

But incredibly dangerous to wonder how much nicer it would be to have so much more than that—to once again have his heart.

$\mathcal{F}$inn sat sprawled in a large plush chair in his living quarters—he'd lied to her about these rooms not being furnished because he'd wanted her to have the room that carried his scent. After she'd mentioned it yesterday, he'd thought if she went to sleep in that room, she might dream of him—and fought not to think about how close she was, within reach, at the other end of a lengthy hallway. Having her here was a mistake because he'd gotten very little of his own work done having spent more time than was wise surreptitiously peering over to watch her. The way her brow pleated when she concentrated, the way she would touch the un-inked end of the pen against her lower lip, the way her mouth would curl up whenever she was pleased with whatever decision she made and began writing.

She enjoyed making lists apparently. She'd created one of the ladies she would invite to the club, the tunes the orchestra would be asked to play, the types of refreshments they would have on hand, little foods that could be enjoyed while wandering around. From what he could gather, their club would very much resemble the festive atmosphere of a ball, not the dark, wicked place he'd envisioned, but he could see now the wisdom in not going that route.

So while it was a mistake to have her so near because she served as a distraction, having her on hand to provide her expertise regarding what women of her caliber would fancy had been a wise move on his part, ensured his—their—club met with a measure of success.

Shoving himself to his feet, he began pacing the room like a caged animal, desperate for freedom. He'd done that for five years in his small cell, thinking about gaining vengeance on her and her family, her father especially. But when he'd finally been released, he'd simply wanted to be done with it all. Especially as her father had died while he'd been locked away.

But since the final time he'd heard the clank of the key going into the lock of his cell door, he'd been unable to stay in a room for long. He certainly wasn't going to remain in his quarters simply because she was inhabiting hers. He needed to get out for a bit. He needed a drink.

He stepped out of his rooms and onto the landing that circled the upper floor and looked down on the gaming area. A dozen or so ladies—the wives or daughters or sisters of wealthy merchants he'd met through their association with Mick—were testing their luck at a couple of the card tables. They were desperately in need of more patrons, not only to give their employees something to do but to refill their coffers. Vivi's timeline of three weeks seemed far too long. He needed the elite ladies she could bring in to make a difference as soon as possible.

Heading for the front stairway, he noted that light was spilling out of the office. Stopping, he glanced inside. She was working, even though they'd both decided not more than an hour ago when the clock struck eight to be done for the day. Leaning against the doorjamb, he watched her, making note of the fact that she appeared . . . at ease, content. Years ago, she'd seemed happy to be with him, but he'd always had the impression she saw gladness as a fleeting thing, only to be had when she was in his company. He wondered now if she'd agreed to marry him because she'd thought he'd bring her happiness, had been placing the burden of that responsibility on him. He'd been willing to take it, to do anything to make her smile. He'd liked feeling needed, wanted, desired. But there was something much more powerful about desiring this woman who had found her own happiness—not in nice clothing or a comfortable dwelling or myriad items, but in herself. "Don't you think—"

Releasing a little screech, she flung herself back in the chair, nearly tipping it over. Breathing heavily, staring at him with wide eyes, she pressed a hand to her chest. "My God, Finn, you startled me."

It took everything within him to bite back the laughter he was fairly certain she wouldn't appreciate. "Terrified, more like."

"I was lost in my efforts here."

"Thought we'd decided to call it a day."

"This is personal." She gathered up several sheaves of paper, opened a drawer, and placed everything inside.

He narrowed his eyes. "I was hoping we were past keeping secrets from each other."

She clasped her hands together on top of the desk. He could see her knuckles turning white as she studied them. He was struck hard with the disappointment that after all they'd discovered, after they'd become partners in the club, she didn't trust him, wouldn't share with him. "I'm going to Gillie's for a pint."

He turned on his heel—

"Finn?"

He stopped, waited three heartbeats, needing the time to turn his expression into an unreadable mask. He swung back around, wishing she didn't look so bloody vulnerable.

"I'm writing an article about my experiences in the streets. It is my hope to have it published in a newspaper, to bring attention to the reforms that are needed when it comes to the treatment of our most vulnerable."

Even from this distance he could see her cheeks turning red as though she were embarrassed by the admission.

"I suspect it's not good enough to be published—"

"If you pour half your passion into it, Vivi, it'll be good enough."

"You're kind to say so, but you were always a voracious reader so you know it takes more than a desire to form a well-turned phrase. It takes a certain skill, which I fear I might lack. I'm trying to be incredibly honest with the words I use, about what I've seen, the women I've met. It's terribly hard. It's like baring one's soul. Sometimes what I write makes me feel as though I'm in the process of discarding my clothes in preparation of walking through the streets naked."

Quietly, he ambled into the room until he was standing before her. "I should think that is what honest writing requires."

She looked incredibly nervous, biting into her lip, a furrow between her brows. "Will you read it?"

The joy that hit him—that she would trust him with her words—was unlike anything he'd ever experienced before. It also humbled him, greatly. "I'd be honored."

With a quick nod, she opened the drawer, pulled out the papers she'd placed in there earlier, and held them out to him.

"Now?" he asked.

"If you've the time."

For her, he always had the time, but thought if he spoke the words out loud, she'd dismiss them and merely accuse him of being flirtatious. Taking the sheaves of paper, he walked over to his desk and sat. After turning up the flame in the lamp, he began reading.

"I want an honest opinion on whether what I've written is ridiculous."

"I would give you nothing less."

"I won't take offense if you don't like it."

He gave her a wry smile. "Vivi, let me read it."

"Yes, all right. Carry on."

Out of the corner of his eye, he saw her lean forward and clasp her hands in her lap, her gaze on him similar to that of a cat waiting to pounce. The tension in her was palpable, radiating out, causing the hairs on the nape of his neck to rise.

He concentrated on what she'd written—

And then suddenly he was no longer aware of her, the room, the flickering flame. He was walking through alleyways, he was comforting frightened children, he was holding a babe too weak to survive no matter how much milk or encouragement he offered. He felt the pain of women being forced to give their babes into another's keeping because society's censure would prevent them from being able to provide for the children. He read of heartbreak, grief, pain, ugliness. When he was finished, he could do little more than strive to regain a sense of himself.

"It's very raw," he finally said.

"I know." She hopped out of the chair and began to pace. "I haven't a way with words. I feared I'd embarrass myself if I sent this to a newspaper." She came to a halt. "I should no doubt just tear it up."

"No, Vivi. The words are perfect. The writing itself is raw in a way that is completely honest. You've held nothing back here. You've put me in the alleyways and mews. You've given me a window into baby farming that even I had never peered through. Only the most callous will be able to read this and not be moved. It needs to be published."

"Do you think so? Truly?"

"Truly. It needs to be read."

With a tender smile, she took it from him. "I'll send it out tomorrow."

"Meanwhile, come with me to Gillie's."

As THE HANSOM cab came to a stop in front of the Mermaid and Unicorn, Lavinia refused to let the sight of the building throw her back eight years—when she'd thought she was being so brave and bold to sneak out of the residence to come here with him. How she hadn't known she'd be called upon to be even braver and bolder or how she would eventually fail in that endeavor.

He climbed out of the cab, then helped her down. His hand landed on the small of her back, guiding her forward, and she rather regretted she'd donned her cloak to ward off the chill of the night. A few people were hurrying along the street, some going into the tavern, others departing it. So much activity, so much life.

He opened the door, propelling her over the threshold as though aware she was having second thoughts, and followed her in. The smoky haze brought on by patrons puffing on their pipes or cigars burned her eyes. The mixture of fragrances assaulted her memories. Her father had smoked a pipe, and she'd loved the aroma. Her brother enjoyed an occasional cheroot. She fought so hard not to think of her family, not to recall more pleasant times when she'd thought herself happy.

But she didn't know if she'd ever been as happy as the people here, talking and laughing, their din a cacophony of various tones to the ears. It was difficult to distinguish them all, not that it mattered. The only voice she truly wanted to hear belonged to the man standing next to her.

He began guiding her between tables toward the wooden counter, behind which kegs lined the shelves. She easily spotted Gillie, who was nearly as tall as Finn. Her red hair was cropped short. Lavinia had been appalled by her rebelliousness when she'd first met her, but now she had the fleeting thought it was a style that wouldn't require nearly as much work to maintain. Perhaps she would shear her own hair.

Then she spied the Duke of Thornley and staggered to a stop. He was behind the counter, without a jacket, his sleeves rolled up, as he filled a glass with beer. Smiling brightly, he handed it off to a customer, turned, and bussed a quick kiss over Gillie's cheek before turning his attention back to another patron. He was working as a barman, and she'd never seen him happier or more appealing. The last remnants of the guilt she'd been harboring over leaving him at the altar dissipated. Certainly, she couldn't deny she'd handled the matter poorly, but he'd never have been as at ease if married to her.

Finn's arm came around her back, his hand settling on the side of her waist. "Come on," he urged. "They'll welcome you."

She wasn't as confident as he was, but she did want to let Thornley know she was gratified to see him looking so joyous. Finn deftly worked their way between customers until they were both standing at the counter. Although for the first time since she'd begun this new life, she was very much aware of her tattered clothing, wished they'd waited until the seamstress had finished her work—then chastised herself for caring about appearances.

Gillie smiled at Finn, her grin momentarily faltering when she realized her brother wasn't alone. She touched Thorne's arm, jerked her head toward them. He turned. His eyes grew warm, his mouth curled up. With his duchess at his side, he approached. "Lady Lavinia."

"Lavinia will do. I've cast off that aspect of my life. It seems you might be doing the same."

He chuckled. "No, I just enjoy helping out from time to time. Gillie, have you met—"

"Yes, years ago. Finn, this is a surprise."

"Vivi is my new partner," he said without preamble.

Gillie's hazel eyes widened. "What? In your club?"

"Indeed. We signed the papers today. Thought we'd come celebrate."

"That's an interesting turn of events."

"What club?" Thornley asked.

"My brother has the notion that women are in need of a gambling hell."

"It's more than a notion," Lavinia said, feeling a need to defend Finn against anyone who didn't think he was going to make a success of himself. His siblings were successes in their own rights, but then they hadn't been delayed from their pursuits by her father. "He's making it happen, and I think the ladies are going to love it."

He gently squeezed her waist, and her body instinctually moved nearer to him as though it had suddenly become metal shavings and he was a magnet. He'd always provided her with a protective shelter; only now she wanted to provide him with one.

His sister's eyes seemed to be twinkling with approval, which was much preferred to the suspicion that had lurked there when she'd first caught sight of Lavinia. "Why don't you find a table and we'll bring you drinks." She angled her head toward Lavinia. "Red wine, as I recall."

She was impressed by her memory but was in the mood for something a bit stronger. "I'd prefer brandy if you have it."

"What respectable tavern owner wouldn't have brandy?" Gillie asked with a smile.

With the pressure of his hand, Finn guided her toward a square table near the rear of the room, where the din of others' conversation was softer, less intrusive. He pulled out the chair for her, then settled into the one beside it. She started to tug off her gloves before remembering she wasn't wearing any. She placed a hand on the table. He quickly covered it with his own.

"Were you defending me, Vivi?" he asked low, seductively.

"Defending your dream and your right to have it. To reach for it. Even if you fall, I think it's better to have reached. Not that I think you'll fail. Truly, Finn, the ladies will enjoy having their own establishment where they can be a bit naughty."

He leaned nearer. "What's your dream?"

To be free of the guilt, to be at peace, to know—

She glanced up with a start at the arrival of both Gillie and Thornley. The duke set a snifter in front of her, and a tumbler of what appeared to be whisky beside her, while the duchess set a similar glass at the empty chair beside her brother and a tankard in front of him. Thornley pulled out a chair for his wife, who, upon further and closer inspection, Lavinia thought might already be carrying his heir.

After taking a seat, Thornley raised his glass. "To the success of your enterprise."

Everyone else lifted their glasses and sipped, although she couldn't miss that Gillie hardly dampened her lips with her drink. Apparently, she'd brought the glass over simply to blend in, to make them feel comfortable.

"Does Collinsworth know about this venture of yours?" Thornley asked.

She shook her head. "No, and I'd rather you not tell him."

"He's worried, you know."

"It's more family pride than love, I suspect. He shouldn't be worried. I write him weekly to let him know how well I'm faring."

"I have to admit to being curious about how all this came to pass, you two teaming up for a venture."

"It's a rather long and frightfully boring story," she admitted.

"While you tell him about it, I need to have a private word with my brother," Gillie said. "Finn?"

He released a long, drawn-out sigh. "Whatever you have to say, Gillie, you can say here."

"No, this really is very personal. Step outside with me for a moment. Please."

She could see his hesitation as he looked at her, thought worry for her was his reason for denying his sister. "I'll be fine," she assured him.

Shoving back his chair, he stood and pointed a finger at Thornley. "Don't upset her."

She couldn't imagine the duke had ever been ordered about by anyone. It seemed, however, that the Trewloves didn't give much credence to rank. She watched as Finn followed his sister out into the night, trying not to remember another time when she'd watched him leave and he'd failed to return.

Thornley's hand covering hers catapulted her back to the present. "I want to let your brother know that I've seen you and you are well."

"Just don't tell him where to find me. I'm not yet ready to face him or my mother. There's a good deal about our family that you don't know. Be glad things turned out as they did. You seem happy, much happier than you'd have been with me."

"I wish you would tell me everything," he said.

But to do that would destroy her.

"WHAT ARE YOU thinking, Finn?"

Gillie's question came as soon as they turned into the alleyway between the brick building that housed her tavern and one that housed an apothecary. Folding his arms over his chest, he leaned against the wall, grateful she hadn't begun her inquisition on the street. "I need information she possesses."

"Then pay her for it. Don't make her a partner."

"Too late."

She shook her head forcefully and began pacing. "I shouldn't have told you she was here."

"She's changed, Gillie. She's different. She's not the girl I once loved."

She brought her pacing to an abrupt halt. "So you feel nothing for her?"

"I didn't say that." Lowering his gaze, he scuffed his boot against the ground, then lifted his head so he could meet her eyes. "She didn't betray me, Gillie. And while I realize there is a great deal of pain in our past, I'm not willing to give her up without at least exploring the possibility of a future with her." He produced a self-mocking smile. "She's not as receptive to the notion, but I think I can win her over."

He saw the stubbornness in the set of her mouth. "If she hurts you, I'll yank every strand of hair from her head."

He laughed deeply, the sound filled with love. "You're so fierce." He sobered. "She is, too. More so than she was. I wasn't the only one who suffered during the time we were apart. They broke her, too, and now she's putting herself back together."

"Broken things can break again."

"Or they can become stronger, impenetrable."

THE DUKE OF Thornley shook his head. "I'd have never thought to look for you among Sisters of Mercy. To take shelter among them was a stroke of genius."

Desperation, more like. She'd feared her brother might think to look for her in a shelter, and she hadn't wanted to sleep on the streets. "I really am sorry, Thorne, for any embarrassment I might have caused you."

"You've apologized before, and I told you then that I hold no ill will." He grinned. "Besides, it all turned out in my favor."

"Your mother must have been appalled by the notion of you marrying a tavern owner."

"Gillie won her over, and in time, every member of the aristocracy will adore her as I do."

"I have no—"

"Are ye a fairy?" A very sweet voice interrupted her.

Glancing over, she saw a young lad of seven or eight, and her heart gave a little lurch. His clothing appeared relatively new, his dark hair straight, his eyes even darker.

"Robin, you don't interrupt when someone is speaking," Thornley said. "If you must interrupt, then you beg their pardon."

The boy scowled at the duke before turning his attention back to her. "Beggin' yer pardon, miss. But are ye a fairy?"

She laughed lightly. "No. Why would you think that?"

"Because ye're so pretty and . . ." He furrowed his brow. "Can't explain it, but ye stand out, like ye're glowing or somethink. 'N' ye're so very pretty."

He seemed to be focused on her prettiness, although it had been a good long while since she'd felt pretty—inside or out. "So your name is Robin?"

He nodded with such force that his dark locks flapped against his forehead. "I lives here. I protects it. Until my mum comes. She's a fairy."

"Is she now?"

A quick bob of his head, and she wondered if he had expected her to know his mother. "And who is she?"

He shrugged. "Dunno. The duke here give me a book on animals. I like animals. Do ye?"

"I do. I once had a cat. It slept on my bed."

"I feed the cats milk, but not too much. Don't want 'em so full they won't eat the rats."

Her stomach roiled at that image. "That's awfully sweet of you to care for them so much."

"Hello, young Robin," Finn said as he pulled out his chair and sat. He looked over at Thorne. "Gillie's back at the bar, working."

"I'd best join her, make sure she doesn't overdo it," Thornley said as he stood. "It was good to see you, Lavinia."

"You, too."

As he walked off, Robin sidled up next to Finn. "Ye got anythink for me, guv?"

"In two days, I should think, I'll have some errands for you to run." He ruffled the lad's hair. "Now, off to bed with you."

Robin glanced slyly over at her, then back at Finn. "Ye kissed her?"

"You're a nosy one."

"She's pretty. Ye ought to kiss her."

Finn grinned broadly. "I'll keep that in mind. Now off with you."

Robin gave her a little salute. "Night, miss."

"Good night, Robin."

He dashed off.

"He's quite articulate. Seems to have mastered his *h*s." She knew some of the lower class tended to lose them when speaking.

"That's Gillie's doing. She thinks it's important for people to talk properly. I suspect next she'll start working on his pronunciation of *you*."

"Does he live here?" she asked Finn.

"In the kitchen."

Horror swept through her. "That's awful."

He shrugged. "It's where he wants to be. He's convinced his mum will find him here. We took him to our children's home, but he made his way back here, so Gillie keeps an eye on him and he runs errands for us."

"Tell me about your children's home. Would there be room there for any other children I might find?"

"There's some room."

"Do you think we'll make enough and that my share will be such that I could purchase a home someday?"

"If things go as I hope they will, you can purchase several."

Smiling, she lifted her brandy. "Then here's to our outstanding success."

THORNE LENT THEM his carriage to return them home. Apparently, he kept it on hand to take him and his duchess to their London residence when the tavern closed up for the night, which wouldn't be for a couple of more hours.

Home. The word echoed through her mind, bringing with it a hollowness. Not exactly the destination to which she was traveling. She was going to a business where she had rooms, and yet she couldn't deny she felt more comfortable within those walls that smelled of Finn than she had ever felt at any of her family's grand residences—whether in the country or in London. The furniture was certainly more comfortable than what the sisters had provided, but then they were more interested in comforting the soul. Yet in spite of their best efforts, hers still remained ragged and torn. But then perhaps it always would; perhaps there weren't enough children in all of England to make a difference, to absolve her of the guilt.

"Do you ever think of your mother?" she asked quietly.

Although Finn had been sitting across from her, unmoving, she was aware of him going even more still. "Sometimes."

"You still don't know who she is?"

"No."

"She no doubt thinks of you." She looked out the window. "As word of your club—"

"Our club."

He was as obstinate as he'd been in his youth, but still she couldn't help the warmth that swept through her at his insistence it was theirs. "*Our* club spreads—and it will spread as there is nothing ladies like more than telling tales that enhance their reputation, and receiving an invitation to an exclusive secretive club will certainly be something to boast about—"

She laughed lightly. "It will appear innocent, of course. A whispered, 'I didn't see you at the Elysium Club,' or 'What are you going to wear to the club?' Followed by, 'Oh, did you not receive an invitation? Perhaps I can put in a word.' And on and around it'll go. Until there are more whispers about this elusive club. Even the men will hear about it. They might ask their mistresses if they know about the club where their wives are going." She turned her attention back to him. "Your mother might hear of it, regardless of her station. She might even make an appearance, ask for a membership."

"I very much doubt she knows who I am or anything at all about what became of me. For surely if she did, during all these years, I'd have had some word from her."

Unless she'd died in childbirth. Or after. Perhaps she went mad with her child being taken from her. "Will you still not tell me who your father is?"

"He's unimportant."

"I wonder if he knew my father."

"I suspect he did."

"I wonder if they were friends."

"Possibly."

"I have a thousand questions I'd ask my father if he were still alive."

"That would mean facing him."

"Yes." She looked back out the window. "I enjoyed going out tonight. I should like to do it again."

"Then we shall."

He made it seem so easy, as though there would be no consequences. She wondered how her mother had felt when her brother told her he'd called off the hounds. She didn't trust her mother not to hire her own. "Will you teach me to pick a lock?"

"If you have fears that they'll lock you away again, know this, Vivi. If they do, I'll come for you." There was a vow, a promise, a determination in his voice that should have brought her comfort, peace, reassurance.

"But if they also lock you away? They've done that before as well."

"Now my allies are stronger. My brothers have more wealth and influence. Mick has the support of the Duke of Hedley and married an earl's daughter. My sister is a duchess, married to a powerful duke. And a few lords owe me for not breaking their bones when I came to collect monies owed. I'm not afraid of your family."

She smiled softly. "I should have your confidence."

"I think you do. You just don't recognize it. My God, Vivi, you've risked your life on more than one occasion, traipsing about in the middle of the night."

"My purpose outweighed my fear."

The carriage came to a halt and a footman opened the door. Finn climbed out, then handed her down.

"We should still have some patrons being entertained," he said. "Let's go around to the back. I'm not in the mood to have the night ruined by any problems that might have arisen while we were gone."

As they made their way inside and up the stairs at the rear of the building, she loved the way he kept his hand splayed firmly over the small of her back. The way he remained a half step behind her, providing her with a protective shelter. The manner in which he seemed in no hurry to escort her to her rooms.

"Where are you sleeping?"

"Where would you like me to sleep?" he asked, his voice low and seductive, his warm breath skimming over her ear as they reached the landing.

She didn't know whether to laugh or smack him for ruining the spell under which he'd been placing her. "You said the rooms at this end weren't furnished."

"I lied."

Coming to an abrupt halt, she faced him. "Why?"

"Because there was a time when I dreamed of you sleeping in my bed. Now you are—even if I'm not there."

"But you want to be."

He flashed a grin. "Indeed." Taking her hand, he led her over to the edge of the landing where they could look down on the gaming floor. Perhaps a dozen women were scattered at various tables. "Imagine it, Vivi. A hundred women, laughing, having fun. Any chance we can move the date up? Make it happen next week?"

"There is a proper amount of time that must pass between when an invitation is dispatched and when the event is to occur."

"But this place isn't proper. It's all about being improper. Shouldn't our actions reflect that standard as much as our words?"

"I suppose you have a point."

"We'll stride through the gaming floor—"

"No, I won't do that. I'm a secret partner in this endeavor."

"Ashamed of it? Or ashamed of being seen with me?"

She was horrified by his conclusion. "Neither. But while no one at the tavern might have known who I was, the ladies I'll be inviting certainly will. I don't want to be part of that life any longer. I'm not well suited to it." She sighed. "I'm tired. I think I shall retire."

She began walking sedately toward her rooms, not at all surprised when he followed.

"Promise me you won't be going out to meet with anyone."

"I've already told you I have no appointments."

"That doesn't mean you won't be going out."

Stopping at her door, she faced him. "I plan to do nothing more than curl up in bed and sleep soundly." Possibly better than she had during the three months since she'd run off.

He slowly skimmed his fingers along her cheek. "I've been thinking about something Robin said. You're very pretty."

She doubted it, as she was rather certain her skin was turning blotchy with the blush that was creeping over it—if the warmth she suddenly felt was any indication.

"And I should kiss you," he said quietly, his fingers ceasing their stroking and burrowing their way into her hair as his palm cradled her chin, her cheek.

"Finn." She'd intended to voice an objection, but his name on her lips was little more than a breathy sigh, an invitation, a welcoming.

When his mouth touched hers, she gave in to all the desires and yearnings she'd been holding at bay and returned his kiss with an enthusiasm that mirrored his. His tongue stroked hers, then swirled about leaving no corner, no hollow, untouched. He was skilled at causing her body to react, to grow lethargic and warm, to tingle and curl in on itself. He sent nerve endings rioting and pleasure cascading. With so little effort.

It had always been thus between them, kindling waiting for the strike of a match. But somehow, now, everything seemed to burn hotter and brighter, threatened to consume until nothing remained except ash. And in the ash perhaps she would be reborn to love again, perhaps her heart would heal, perhaps the wounds would cease to fester, perhaps she would find the courage to confess everything.

Drawing away, he pressed his lips to the underside of her chin, to that lovely spot near her ear where his heated mouth, when laid against it, always turned her knees to jam. She seemed incapable of stopping the sigh of surrender from escaping.

"I want you, Vivi," he whispered.

"You want the girl I was, and she no longer resides within me."

Lifting his head, he met her gaze. "You're wrong. It's the woman I want, the woman you are now."

She forced herself to flatten her hands against his chest and push him back until the air she breathed no longer carried his dark fragrance. "If all this, the partnership, was in hopes of getting into my bed, we should cancel it before we go any further."

"It's what you can offer my business not what you can offer *me* that spurred me toward offering you a stake in this place—but that doesn't mean there can't be more between us."

Reaching up, she brushed the hair off his brow. "You wouldn't find me attractive in the least if you knew everything that transpired since the night we were to run off together."

"Then tell me."

Rising up on her toes, she planted a kiss on the corner of that lovely mouth of his. "Good night, Finn."

Turning, she opened the door, crossed the threshold, and closed the door behind her. She took three steps forward and waited, waited to see if he'd follow her in. She didn't know if she'd find the strength to resist him if he did.

After several long minutes, still alone, she walked to the window and gazed out on the street, determined to remain strong against the allure that was Finn Trewlove.

Chapter 19

$\mathcal{S}$he'd nearly finished writing out the invitations when the seamstress arrived two days later, a couple of servants in tow carrying several boxes. She didn't bother tamping down her excitement as she stood and—out of the corner of her eye—caught Finn's smug expression. It seemed in the matter of clothing, he understood her better than she understood herself. She thought she'd resigned herself to wearing worn frocks, but now the prospect of wearing something that was hers again brought with it unexpected delight. Perhaps she hadn't left her previous life behind as much as she'd hoped.

She led Beth and her girls into the living quarters, nearly bouncing on the balls of her feet as she waited for them to unpack the boxes, tossing aside the thin paper and carefully displaying her new wardrobe over various pieces of furniture.

A navy-blue frock with buttons up to the collar and at the cuffs. Smart. Sharp. Something perfect for a business owner. A gray frock with blue piping and a flounce here and there, something else a woman of business or one with a purpose would wear. Undergarments, corset, silk, lace, ribbons, and bows—

And lastly an evening gown, a froth of dark rose satin and taffeta with a low bodice and straps that would fall off her shoulders, leaving them bare for wandering lips to savor. It was the most beautiful thing she'd seen in ages. She had to clutch her fingers at her waist to stop herself from reaching for it. "I'm not in need of a ball gown."

"You might be," a deep voice said with authority and conviction.

Spinning around, she wasn't surprised to find Finn leaning negligently in the doorway. She couldn't remember if she'd closed the door in her excitement, not that it would have mattered. He had a way about him of moving stealthily and silently.

"You could change your mind about attending our soiree the night when all the ladies will be arriving to see what we're offering," he said, not giving her a chance to offer any sort of excuse for why the gown was unnecessary. "Besides, it's been made now. I doubt Beth would find any of her other clients in want or need of it. It wouldn't be fair to her to refuse it."

"But the cost—"

"It's a gift."

"You've given me so many already." Rescued her from women who would do her harm, men who would do worse. Lodgings, an occupation, a return of some dignity.

He shrugged. "Then what's a small bit more?"

She didn't know how she would repay him for all his kindnesses. "Yes, all right."

At least he had the good graces not to gloat, but she could see that her response pleased him. And pleasing him seemed to please her as well. She made a shooing motion with her hand. "Off with you. I need to try everything on to see how well it fits."

"I could stay and offer a second opinion on how well everything fits."

She nearly burst out laughing at his innocent expression. "Don't," she whispered instead. *Don't make me fall in love with you all over again.*

They'd changed once, and they would change again, and she didn't know how one remained in love when people constantly changed. Success would change them, failure would change them more. All the trials, tribulations, and challenges that life would throw at them—even without her family to muck things up—would eventually alter them.

He seemed to know what she was asking, what she was referring to, because he did little more than bow his head slightly, step into the hallway, and pull the door closed behind him.

"You'll need to hire a maid to help you dress," he told her an hour later after the dressmaker left and Vivi returned to his office wearing the light gray frock. He'd spent that time imagining her climbing in and out of each piece of lace and silk, envisioned helping her with the process, his cock becoming so stiff he'd feared he might have to take himself in hand just to get it under control—the inconsiderate bugger. Not that she was aware of his unconscionable state since the front of his desk provided a barrier from prying eyes, or any eyes for that matter.

"I suppose I shall," she said as she took her place at the desk beside his. At present, his favorite place for her to be if he couldn't have her in his arms. "Beth and her girls assisted me with getting into this. Very little additional sewing was needed on any of the clothing, merely a tuck here and a tuck there. She's very skilled." She twisted around, facing him, placing her elbow on her desk, her chin in her palm, very much resembling his pose, he realized. "She told me what you and your family did for her."

"We've little tolerance for men taking advantage of their positions."

"I've always felt safe with you. You won't press me on what I'm not willing or ready to give."

"There's no pleasure in taking what isn't freely given." He grinned wolfishly. "Doesn't mean I won't test you to see where the boundaries are."

"You're a stubborn scoundrel." She studied him for a minute, and he thought she might get up, come sit on his lap, and show him she was willing to stretch those boundaries, perhaps break them completely. "So you're going to hire Robin to deliver these invitations?" She patted the stack on her desk.

"I am. He can start tomorrow."

"He's a bit young to be traipsing all over London."

"I'll borrow Mick's carriage again. The driver can make certain Robin gets all the addresses correct. He likes to feel important, and he'll deliver them with a great deal of earnestness."

"How did he come to live in the tavern?"

"Gillie found him sleeping on the stoop one morning and took him in. He's an independent bugger though, convinced his mum will come for him at the tavern."

"Did you ever think your mother—the woman who gave birth to you—would come for you?"

He shook his head. "I had my mum. Ettie Trewlove. The woman who took me in. She loved me. I wanted for nothing more."

"I wonder if most children are curious about their mothers."

"I suspect it depends on whether or not they're content where they are. It's funny. Gillie and I never gave much thought to the people who were responsible for delivering us to Ettie Trewlove's door. Mick and Aiden, however, care a tad too much. It worked out for Mick. I don't know if Aiden will be as lucky." And that bothered him, knowing his brother was striving to forge a relationship with their . . . *father* wasn't the correct word. The man who had spilled his seed into their mothers.

"You have another brother—Beast. How does he feel about it?"

"Not really sure. He keeps his thoughts to himself for the most part."

"I suppose he knows about your venture. I suppose they all do."

"We don't keep secrets from each other."

"You're fortunate in that regard, Finn. You're accepted for who you are. My family has always strived to shape me into something I'm not." Turning away from him, she placed a sheaf of parchment before her and dipped her pen into the inkwell. "Perhaps after our grand soiree I shall go have a word with them. I shouldn't like to miss it should matters go awry."

He wanted to reassure her, but fate had worked like a bloody devil in the past to prove to them that they weren't meant to be together. Even knowing neither was to blame, she seemed hesitant to accept they could have a future. He needed to show her that they could. "Have dinner with me this evening," he said. "In the dining room. We'll close it off. It'll only be us. We'll sample the fare we'll be offering, make certain it meets with your approval."

She glanced over at him. "That's a smashing idea, to make certain that aspect of the business is fit for ladies of quality."

"Wear the rose gown."

THE GRAY WAS serviceable and as the dinner was more about business than pleasure, it would suffice. She told herself that for the remainder of the afternoon as she finished up the last of the invitations and divided them into the ones Robin could deliver in London and those that would need to be dispatched to the country. In spite of her leaving Society behind, she'd kept up with the gossip sheets and knew who was in Town and who wasn't. The amount of ink given to covering the aristocracy was quite telling. It would have been better spent writing about the impoverished, the orphaned children who roamed the streets, the practice of baby farming.

With that thought in mind, she pulled out the article she'd written. For it to carry any weight, she would need to claim her heritage, sign it as Lady Lavinia Kent, use her family name to do good in the world. She was beginning to feel she no longer needed to hide who she was. Being separated from her family these many months had allowed her to become her own woman. Perhaps very soon she would confront them, allow them to see that they no longer had any sway over her.

By early evening, as she was leaving the office, she was feeling quite buoyant regarding her prospects for the future, and when she walked into her chambers, the froth of rose silk beckoned like an errant lover who had returned after being away for too many years. It was silly to dress up for Finn, and yet he'd asked it of her when he'd asked for little else. And he'd given her so much.

She enlisted the assistance of two of the women she spotted walking around with feather dusters. They prepared a bath for her. She might have lingered in the warm water longer if she weren't suddenly anxious to see the pleasure on Finn's face when he caught sight of her in the rose. One of the girls, Meg, turned out to be rather skilled with hair, sweeping Lavinia's tresses back from her face but securing them so they dangled in waves down her back. It was a simple style, requiring few pins, but she found herself wishing she hadn't sold her combs, the ones she'd worn in her hair on the day she was to wed. But she'd kept nothing, determined to leave her old life and any reminders of it behind.

"I was wondering, Meg, if you'd care to be my personal maid?" Lavinia asked the young woman now.

"If it please you, Miss Kent." Her eyes were wide as she bobbed a quick curtsy.

"Yes, it would, thank you. I'll let Mr. Trewlove know your duties will be changing."

"Thank you, miss."

After the servants left, she studied her reflection in the mirror for several long minutes. It had been a good long while since she'd truly given herself a thorough looking over. She was all of twenty-five and yet she couldn't deny that she appeared considerably older. Worry, grief, and sadness had taken a toll. Yet Finn still kissed her, wanted her.

With one last lingering gaze at the reflection, she walked out of her rooms, wondering at the gladness that swept through her at the sight of Finn, partly bent with his forearms resting on the railing, looking out over his domain. He'd changed his clothing as well, his jacket a dark blue, his trousers black, his boots polished to a shine. While only his profile was visible to her, she could make out the flow of a perfectly knotted cravat.

Turning his head, seeing her, he smiled, pleasure darkening his eyes, and every womanly aspect of her reacted as though he'd just skimmed his hands up the entire length of her person. She'd seen him not less than two hours earlier. How could it be that gladness swept through her as though she'd not seen him in ages?

"I knew the color would suit you," he said, straightening and facing her completely. He'd taken a razor to his face, which made him appear more civilized, more polished. Yet she couldn't deny she rather fancied the rough and dangerous way he looked when his whiskers began making themselves known. He was more handsome than he'd been in his youth, in a rugged sort of way. There was strength and character in his features.

"You went to a lot of bother to dress up for the evening," she said.

"Thought we'd celebrate."

"We celebrated last night at the Mermaid."

His grin spread, and she could see he was well aware she was striving to ensure tonight's dinner was nothing special. "We can celebrate more than once."

He offered his arm, and against all her better judgments, she placed her hand in the crook of his elbow. He guided her toward the rear stairs and down into a small warren of hallways that eventually led into the dining room. The dark dining room.

She knew chandeliers were in this room, but they weren't glowing. Instead the only light was provided by the three tapered candles burning on one of the cloth-covered tables. "Finn—"

"It's just a bit of atmosphere, to determine if we want the ambiance of candles or gaslights."

"Ambiance? I've always been impressed with your vocabulary."

He pulled out a chair for her. "Amazing what you can learn from reading. Although I sometimes have to ask the fellow at the lending library how to pronounce the word or exactly what it means." He took the seat next to hers. "My siblings and I used to compete, tossing words out at each other, having to identify what each meant. Gillie was always the best at stumping us, but I came in a close second, throwing her off her game on occasion."

She could hear the pride and the love in his voice as he spoke about that time. It had been a friendly competition. She had no memory of ever playing any sort of game with her brother. However, she didn't blame Neville; it was simply the way it was.

A footman came over and poured a burgundy into their glasses. Finn lifted his. "To an evening of discovering what works best."

She had a feeling he might not be referring to what worked best for the club, but what worked best when it came to seduction.

SHE WAS BEAUTIFUL, but then he'd always found that to be true about her. Whether she'd been angry at him for carting away her beloved horse, grief-stricken for the same reason, overjoyed at the sight of Sophie, standing toe-to-toe against women who wished her harm, gathering children about her like a mother hen with her chicks, defending his dream to his sister—

The beauty wasn't so much in the shape of her mouth, the curve of her chin, the slope of her nose, the green of her eyes. It came from something that flowed from deep within her, something that sometimes brought a glow to her skin or a blush at other times. Something fierce, strong, and undeterred by any obstacles that might have been placed in her way.

"That gown needs a necklace to set it off," he told her now.

Her hand—so small, so delicate, when compared to his—came up, her fingers landing in the hollow at her throat. "I'd have once thought so as well, but I have no interest in jewels any longer. I wore a pearl necklace on the day I was to wed. I sold it, so I'd have funds for purchasing children." She shook her head. "That's a ghastly thing to say, an awful way to word it."

"You're not really purchasing children, making slaves of them."

"I suppose not. It's just a sad state of affairs that we live in a world where something like that happens."

"I thought things like jewelry were passed down through generations. Did the pieces you wore on your wedding day have no sentimental value?"

She took a slow sip of her wine, licked her lips. "My father gave the pieces to me on the day I was presented to the queen, not so much out of love but obligation. It was expected. He didn't

present them to me directly. As I recall, my maid brought them
to me in his stead. If I'd married Thornley, I might have passed
them down to my daughter, although I suspect he'd have purchased pearls for her. I don't mean to pry, but Gillie looked to be
in the family way."

"She is."

"They've only been married a few weeks so . . . I'm glad he did
right by her."

"He didn't marry her because she was with child. He didn't
even know when he proposed."

"Would she have kept it, do you think? If they hadn't married?"

"Without a doubt."

"She's a strong woman, your sister."

"Stubborn, more like. She knows what she wants, and you'll
have no luck convincing her otherwise. And unlike a lot of women
who find themselves in her situation, she has the means to make
her own way. She has a very successful business, and she's put
money aside. Before long, you'll be as successful."

She laughed lightly, a sound that wound its way through his
chest, tightening it. "I can't imagine it. Women of my station don't
work. They get pin money but it's not enough to make a difference. We marry. We go from the care of our fathers to the care of
our husbands. It terrified me, running from the church. I hadn't
thought it through completely. To be honest, I don't know that I
thought being your partner through completely either."

"You can always walk away."

"I'm not that foolish."

He bent toward her, wanting the conversation to move on. "So
tell me. Do you prefer the candles or the chandeliers?"

She glanced around as though giving it serious thought, before
returning her attention to him and leaning toward him until he
could see the reflection of the flames flickering in the dark center
of her eyes. "Since only ladies will be dining in here, I should
think the chandeliers alone would suffice. I suppose you could
open the dining room to men."

"I suspect most would never get this far once they spotted the gaming tables."

"Perhaps the ladies could use the gaming room as a gauntlet to test their lovers' devotion."

Settling back in his chair, he studied her for a long moment. "Put temptation before him, and see if he can ignore it in order to be with the lady to whom he recites sonnets?"

Her lips curled up into a wicked but enticing grin. "Something like that."

"Perhaps he would pass through the gauntlet without making a single wager because he was hungry, starving, in fact. How would she know?"

Her laughter was like bells tinkling, sprites dancing on petals, real and magical at the same time. "And which are you? Devoted or hungry?"

"If you have to ask, then I'm making a rather poor effort at it."

SHE MEANT FOR it to be a joke, something to laugh about, to tease each other over later—but the look he gave her was indeed that of a man who was hungry, ravenous, in fact, but it wasn't food he sought or a belly that was in need of sustenance. His intense stare was that of a hunter who had sighted his quarry, a predator who was accustomed to capturing what he sought, to holding on to it, to claiming it.

She had an insane urge to run—but that had always been her answer. Planning to run off with him because she hated her life with the family, the future they'd mapped out for her. Running away from Thornley for the same reasons. Afraid, always afraid to stand her ground. But here was this man who had lost five years of his life because of her, looking at her as though no time had passed at all. No, that wasn't true. He'd never looked at her like this, as though he could devour her and make her grateful he had, as though everything he'd ever wanted was within reach, if she would just stand her ground.

Nearly jumping out of her skin as a footman set a bowl of soup in front of her, she was grateful his intrusion forced her to break eye contact with Finn. The hold he had on her was such that she wasn't certain she'd have had the strength to look away. "My, this looks delicious." Reaching for her glass, she was dismayed to find her hand trembling.

He chuckled low, darkly, as though he'd followed her thoughts down the errant path they'd traveled, as though he knew she didn't want to be drawn to him. "The cook will be glad to hear that."

"We should probably call her a chef, start some rumors that perhaps she's from France."

"That rumor would die the moment anyone heard her speak."

"I could teach her a few words."

"We might be a house of vice, Vivi, but I want us to be an honest one."

His expression was earnest, no teasing, no seduction. When discussing the business, he was serious. "You're right, of course." She tasted the soup, pleased with the flavor. "This is rather good."

The conversation turned to other good things. Funny moments from his youth, teasing his brothers and sisters, being teased in return. Happier times from hers when she'd been given Sophie and taught to ride. They avoided talking about their own past, the past they'd shared. And she couldn't help but think that if they hadn't met before, if they were only starting to know each other tonight, she would have been charmed by him. If there was no past, perhaps she would feel comfortable charming him.

Although old habits, ingrained since birth, were difficult to ignore, and she found herself being a bit more flirtatious than she should have been, smiling secretly, lowering her lashes provocatively. Especially when the wine—as fine a vintage as anything served at a lord's table—was urging her to lower her resistance, to reveal her interest in every word he uttered, and she was interested. She always had been. He was the first not of her class to speak to her as though she were an equal, to show her a nongilded world. He'd been brawn and muscle, strength and tenderness, and the years had only added to his allure. He filled her with hope for a better world, a more meaningful life. He was the reason she no longer cared about pearls or diamonds. Although she did very much enjoy wearing the silk gown for him, especially when his gaze would dip to the swells barely contained within the cloth. She did wish she'd stop imagining his lips dotting her flesh with kisses.

She told herself it was the wine, but two glasses were hardly enough to make her lose her head. It was him and the candles and the fine dinner. They finished their meal with a snifter of warm brandy, the heat making it taste all the smoother.

"The ladies will enjoy dining here. The cook outdid herself." She wasn't surprised. She'd tasted other offerings when food was brought to the office midday, brought to her rooms in the early evening. But tonight's fare had been special, designed to seduce the taste buds. Everything tonight had been designed to seduce, from the caress of silk over her skin to the tantalizing spirits on her tongue, to the shadows, the flickering flames, the low voice of the man sitting with her.

"I studied the dining room at Mick's hotel," he said. He lifted his snifter. "And naturally, Gillie shared her knowledge of liquors. Thornley took her to wineries in France after they were married, not that she did much sampling from what I understand. But she'd always wanted to see them. Her excitement—after their return—at telling us about everything she experienced"—he made a sound that could have been a laugh or a scoff, but either way there was affection in it—"you'd have thought he laid gold at her feet."

"I should think for a tavern owner his gift was better than gold."

"Do you regret not marrying him?"

"No, we weren't well suited. We never really talked. We simply went through the motions. My entire life has been going through the motions. I think I have lived more in the months since August than I did my entire life before." She shook her head. "That's not true. I was always more alive when I was with you. I always felt more myself. Perhaps the fairies switched me out at birth, and I don't have noble blood coursing through my veins after all."

"You have noble blood, Vivi. There was a time when I'd have faulted you for that."

"It seems we are all too quick to judge, based upon what we see of a person rather than what we know or are willing to learn about the person."

"Maybe we'll change a few minds when our patrons are mingling."

"I shall hope so. That would be a wonderful contribution from our establishment."

He set aside his empty snifter. "Are you finished?"

She'd savored the last drop of the brandy, wished their time together would continue, but it was getting late and they had a lot of work remaining to be done on the morrow. "Yes, I suppose I am."

Shoving back his chair, he stood, assisted her in standing, and offered his arm. Certainly, she could wander back to her rooms of her own accord, but she welcomed the opportunity to again touch him. However, instead of heading toward the door through which they'd entered, he began leading her toward one in the opposite direction.

"You're going the wrong way," she told him.

"No, I'm not. I have something else to show you."

He opened the door, and she stepped through into a salon where the gas-lit chandeliers glowed, filling the room with warm lighting that barely held the shadows at bay, giving the area she'd designated as a ballroom an intimate feel. Then the lilting strains of an orchestra began to fill the silence, and pleasure flowed through her as though she were comprised of strings that were being plucked.

Without words, without urging, with nothing more than his hands to guide her, he swept her across the polished parquet floor. This, she realized, not dinner, was the reason he'd wanted her to wear the gown. The meal was merely a prelude to his seduction. It was here with her in his arms that he would pursue her in earnest.

Where she would welcome him doing so.

She was weary of fighting the attraction, of ignoring what she felt for him. They moved in tandem, complementing each other. Always it had been thus between them, an understanding that required no voice. Holding his gaze, she realized that with him she was always falling, falling in love, always would be, going deeper and further. That was the reason she'd been unable to marry Thornley. Because she hadn't wanted a life without this, without a connection that spoke volumes without speaking at all.

Finn never tried to shape her or mold her into what he thought she should be. From the beginning, he'd merely accepted her as she was, foibles and all. From the beginning he had made her happy.

No one had ever looked at her as he did—as though he would die if he couldn't have her, as though he would die if he did. His failure to show had hurt so desperately, because he'd meant so much to her. And she'd allowed that hurt to create a fog that was only now beginning to lift. He hadn't abandoned her. He'd been taken from her.

And now he was back. Different, altered. But impossibly very much the same, but not the same at all. He exuded sensuality. She could sense the need for her shimmering off him in waves. His brown eyes had grown darker, smoldering with banked desire.

The orchestra players skillfully moved from one tune to the next, Finn's steps never faltering. He'd been a fine dancer before, but now there was a confidence in his movements. "You've been practicing," she said, surprised how breathless she sounded, as though she'd just come unglued with him in her bed.

"No, just watching. Too many weddings of late where dancing was called for."

She was well aware his brother Mick had married that summer, Gillie in the fall.

"Are you going to dance with the ladies who come to the club?" She wasn't particularly pleased with the spark of jealously that thought brought, imagining him as one of the men making each woman feel special, treasured. Touching a lady, holding her as close as he held Lavinia. She wouldn't claim him as hers, and yet she didn't want anyone else to either.

"It depends," he said.

"On what?"

"On whether there's a chance in hell that I would feel for one of them so much as an ounce of what I feel for you."

Every speck of air seemed to have fled the room, leaving her struggling to draw in a breath. Halting, he cupped her face between his hands. "I know you're afraid to feel anything for me again because of how much it hurt when you thought I'd tossed you aside like so much rubbish. Do you think I didn't experience, too, the agony of thinking you'd betrayed me? I was a wreck, Vivi. I walled off my heart, built a moat around it, made it impenetrable, or so I thought. Until I saw you again, until I watched you lead children—clinging to your tattered skirt—away from a woman who didn't have it within her to care for them properly. You're a sorceress, with a magic about you that renders all my barriers ineffectual. Do I fear I'll experience that pain again? I know I will—if you walk away or fate takes you from me. But I'm willing to risk it for just one more night with you."

It wasn't fair that he could spout such beautiful words that weakened her resolve. Had he taken to reading poetry or romantic novels of late? He was baring his heart to her, and she could no more allow it to be wounded again than she could return to her previous life. He must have seen her answer in her eyes, or heard it in her sigh, or felt it in her body melting against his, because when she wound her arm about his neck and lifted her mouth, his was already there, waiting and ready, taking what she was offering as though it was nectar from the gods.

It did not escape her that they were behaving entirely inappropriately in front of an audience of musicians who didn't miss a single note as they played on, a realization that would have mortified Lady Lavinia but merely amused Vivi. With him she was different, saw shades to herself she hadn't even known existed. He was good for her, unfurled her like a tightly wrapped bud that feared opening and revealing itself to the sun.

He loved what she'd become, what she was now, what she was doing. He hadn't used the word specifically, but she felt it in the way his hands roamed over her back and pressed her ever nearer. Then they were no longer roaming, but lifting, lifting her into his arms, cradling her as though he could keep harm at bay, as he might have held her on the night after they wed, as though no one had ever hurt them or torn them asunder.

As the music continued to play, the notes rising in crescendo as though foreshadowing the arrival of the climax to a tale, Finn began striding from the room, a definite purpose echoing with each step, he who could move about so silently, no longer taking any care to do so. She pressed her knowing smile against the underside of his jaw, where the skin was soft and warm, fragrant from the heat there, releasing the scent of sandalwood. He'd bathed for the evening as well. The short whiskers along his jaw tickled her forehead, delighting her with the pure masculinity of the bristles.

He barely paused as they reached the backstairs, ascending them like a man who found no weight too much of a burden. His breathing remained even and calm while hers occasionally hitched as they grew nearer to her rooms.

He passed the corridor that would have taken them to his, continuing along the hallway that looked out over the gaming floor, keeping to the wall that housed offices so they weren't visible from below, striving to protect a sterling reputation she no longer possessed, but then it wouldn't do for the servants and staff to know they were up to no good.

As they approached her door, he said, "Do I leave you here or go on through?"

He was giving her a choice in case he had misread her acquiescence, the way she burrowed against him, and she loved him all the more for it. For not assuming their wants were the same, their needs mirrored in the other. She took his earlobe between her teeth. He groaned. "Carry on," she whispered as seductively as she could.

She moved about this building with locks not used, with nothing worth pilfering, but when he closed the door behind them, he lowered her to the floor, reached back, and turned the lock. Then he looked at her and waited, just waited.

"It's a shame the orchestra didn't follow us," she said, not doubting the path they were on but not quite certain how to follow it. "I rather enjoyed the music."

"We'll make our own." Lifting the lit lamp from the table where she'd left it, so she wouldn't return to darkness, he took her hand.

"No." He stilled. "Leave the lamp here, lower the flame. We'll make our way through the shadows."

"I want to see you."

As much as she wanted to see him as well, still she shook her head. "I want only moonlight."

He gave her a tender smile. "I've seen you before, Vivi. Why the shyness now?"

"I'm older. You might not find my body as . . . fetching."

"Twenty-five is hardly an old crone."

"Please, Finn. I don't want to argue about this or ruin what we've begun. I want you in my bed, but it must be on my terms with the romance of shadows and moonlight."

He set the lamp back on the table and lowered the flame, and she loved him for that. Again, he took her hand. He began leading her toward the bedchamber. She heard a crash, flesh and bone against wood.

"Damn," he muttered.

"What happened?"

"I ran into one of the low tables. You've moved the furniture."

"Only a little." Squeezing his hand, she walked around him. "I'll lead."

He followed closely on her heels, his other hand coming to rest on her waist. "You'll have to kiss my shin, make it better," he said near her ear, his breath stirring tendrils of her hair.

"Oh, I intend to kiss a lot of things."

Chapter 20

He couldn't stop his breath from hitching at her provocative words, words that mirrored his intentions as well. He'd been an untried lad when they'd come together before. He had a bit more experience now, had learned a few things, things he intended to share with her.

She came to a stop beside the bed and turned to face him. He had to admit there was something seductive about seeing her cast in naught but shadows and moonlight. She was a sensual silhouette, moving gracefully through the faint, shimmering light, reaching out for his neck cloth and tugging the knot loose. Her confidence had increased over the years.

"Have you been with anyone since me?" Knowing Thornley had gotten his sister with child before they married, he couldn't help but wonder if the man had known Vivi as well. He'd hate to make his sister a widow in short order, but if the man had been intimate with Vivi—

"No." Her voice was low, soft, the volume just above a whisper. His neck cloth sailed under his chin as she tossed it aside. Her hands came under the lapels of his jacket, gliding up until she was shoving it off his shoulders. "You have. You admitted as much."

"Yes."

Her hands stilled for only a fraction of a second before carrying on to divest him of the coat.

"But none of them meant anything, Vivi. It was need."

"Don't you need me?"

He felt the loosening of the buttons on his waistcoat. "With everything that is within me. With the others it was simply physical. With you, it's more, it's always been more." After shrugging off his waistcoat, he cradled her face between his hands and took what she'd granted permission for him to have, to taste, to explore. Nothing had ever pleased his mouth more than the flavor of her. There was a sweetness to it, mellowed by the brandy. He savored it, knowing it could intoxicate him as effectively as any liquor.

With a sigh, not moving her mouth from his, she pressed up against him, scraping her fingers up along his scalp. He deepened the kiss, relishing her mewling, welcoming the increasing of her enthusiasm as her tongue parried with his. It was as though for the briefest of moments, she'd been holding back, had been afraid of giving freedom to her desires. But the moment had passed and now she was untethered, unfettered.

She was his and he would have her.

DEAR LORD, IT had taken little more than his kiss to drive her into a frenzy. No slow arousing this time. It was as though the tension had been building beyond bearing, like the string of a bow that suddenly snapped from the strain. She wanted him desperately.

It hurt to know he'd had others, but he was a virile man. She couldn't have expected him to remain celibate. As much as it had pained her though, his reassurances so quickly, so unwaveringly, had comforted her. His tone hadn't indicated a boasting, but merely a desire to be honest with her.

He'd always been up front and straightforward with her. No teasing games for him. It was one of the reasons she loved him. After all this time, it had taken so little for her to fall back under his spell, but how could she not adore him when he was such a good man?

Spinning her around, he went to work on the lacing of her gown. She didn't admonish him to take care, not to tear it, because if he ripped it in his eagerness, she would have it mended. And any time her fingers skimmed over the additional stitching, she would recall this night, the fevered pitch of it.

After the gown pooled at her feet, she began helping with the undergarments until she was standing bare in the moonlight, staring at the shadowy bed that would soon welcome them.

Her back was still to him, and he planted his mouth between her shoulder blades. "You are as silky as ever," he rasped as he slid his tongue along her spine.

Dropping her head back, she concentrated on the trail he followed, down to her bum where he nipped at one cheek, then the other. His hands closed around her knees, and he skimmed them up her thighs, over her hips, along her sides to cup her breasts. Her moan was one of pure delight as he kneaded the pliant orbs, his thumbs and forefingers rolling her nipples into tightened buds.

"I love the way you feel," he growled low, near her ear.

"Being in the darkness makes all the other sensations clearer, more pronounced."

"Climb onto the bed."

"Your clothing."

"I'll see to them."

She clambered onto the bed and had barely rolled onto her back before he was joining her, and she wondered if he'd torn his clothes from his person. His body half covered hers as he nuzzled her neck, nibbling on the tender flesh there. "You smell so good," he said.

"So do you." She caressed his shoulders, his back.

"Did you go without this for eight years?"

"I told you I had."

"No. You said you'd been with no man. That doesn't mean you didn't know pleasure." He trailed his mouth along her collarbone until he reached the other side of her throat. "Did you pleasure yourself?"

"Finn—"

"Did you?"

Licking her lips, she felt a coiling in her nether regions between her thighs. Rolling slightly, she pressed the sensitive area against his hard thigh. "Sometimes," she confessed, her voice sounding raw as though she'd just spent hours screaming his name in rapture.

"Did you think of me when you did it?"

Even though he was little more than shadows, she slammed her eyes closed and shook her head in denial of the truth, not intending to answer but the word came out just the same, proving her actions false. "Yes."

In spite of everything, he'd always been the one she took with her into her dreams.

He glided his mouth down and began peppering her breast with kisses. "When the rapture came, did you cry out? Did you scream my name?"

"I whispered it."

"I thought of you. I thought of doing this to you." He closed his mouth over her nipple, circled it with his tongue, until she released the tiniest of squeals. "Your name was a curse on my lips every time I spilled my seed in my hand. I tried thinking of other women, the ones I saw at penny gaffs showing their legs, or the girls serving at Gillie's tavern with their breasts nearly spilling from their bodices, but thoughts of them brought me no relief, no surcease." He shifted until he was nestled between her thighs. "Only you, Vivi. I'd think about your tight, hot channel and how it felt to be inside you."

"I would think about how full I felt with you inside me, how complete."

"It might hurt again tonight."

"I don't care."

He eased down, pressing kisses to her stomach, dipping his tongue into her navel. "But I'll ensure you're wet and juicy and ready for me."

Pushing himself farther down, he placed his hand beneath her hips, tilted them upward. "Tell me if you ever fantasized about me doing this."

He lowered his head, and she felt the stroke of his rough tongue against the silk of her core.

"Oh my God, Finn." She tried to sit up, fell back down, down into heaven or hell, she knew not which. She knew only that his tongue swirled with maddening accuracy, his mouth suckled, his fingers spread her farther so he could feast. She'd never felt anything so sublime, so erotic, so intoxicating. She threaded her fingers through his hair, glided her soles along his thighs, pressed them to his buttocks—encouraging him to stay where he was, to have his fill of her. Her breaths came in short gasps. She couldn't stop herself from making little mewling cries.

If there could never be more between them than this, this would be enough. Only she couldn't envision having him here in her bed if she didn't love him. And she did love him. Every wonderful glorious inch of him. Every adventurous part of him.

Her body began to coil as though it were a spring in a clock, being wound tighter and tighter. She rolled her head from side to side, cursed the darkness that she'd insisted upon that now prevented her from seeing him, from looking into his eyes, from discovering if he knew precisely what he was making her feel. Oh, it had been good before, but nothing like this.

At that moment he was filling her with pleasure, taking her to new heights—

And suddenly she couldn't go any higher. She simply flung herself off the ledge into the cataclysm of sensations that rocked her to her core. She screamed his name, a benediction and a curse. In gratitude and in wonder that he could make her feel so much.

Pushing himself up, he took her mouth and she tasted him and herself on his lips. She lifted her hips. He shifted his weight, and she felt him nudging at her entrance.

"Take me," she rasped.

And he did. Sliding into her, stretching her, filling her with the glorious length and the beautiful weight of him. His thrusts were shallow at first, testing her readiness, and then they lengthened, nearly leaving her, then shoving back in. Over and over while he rained kisses on her eyelids, her cheeks, her mouth. While he whispered her name like a litany that would deliver salvation.

Within her the sensations began to build again until they peaked, and when he fell over the edge, she followed.

FINN AWOKE LETHARGIC and well-sated, the sunlight hitting his closed eyelids, alerting him they'd slept the night away. She was still in his arms, snuggled against him, the covers gathered below her hips. There was a chill in the air, and she was going to feel it when he moved away from her to begin his day. Reaching down, he knotted a hand around the sheet, dragging it up, his gaze landing on her stomach, a belly not quite as flat as it had been when he'd first made love to her. Pausing, he studied the strange markings. In her youth, her skin had been flawless. Now it was marred here and there with a slight bluish discoloration, thin ragged lines. Releasing his hold on the sheet, he touched his fingers to a shallow indentation, was aware of her stiffening and realized she had awakened.

It was so shallow in fact that he couldn't really feel it, certainly hadn't felt it last night. Was this the reason she'd wanted the darkness? "What happened here?"

"It's nothing."

She started to sit up, but he stayed her with a press of his hand, a splaying of his fingers. "It can't be nothing, Vivi. There are several scars—"

"They're not scars, not really, I don't think."

His brow furrowed, he traced some of the other marks. "How did you come to have them?"

"It's not important."

He lifted his gaze to hers, and within the green depths he could see a fear, a shame. He should let it go, let her have her secrets, but the thought of someone hurting her had him wanting to commit murder. "Vivi, how did you come to have them?"

Tears welled in her eyes and he feared hearing the answer as much as he feared not knowing what it might be. He watched the delicate muscles of her throat work as she swallowed, the sudden trembling of the lips he'd devoured last night. His own trepidation increased as though he were suddenly facing a hundred men wielding knives, because suspicion of how they'd come to be was beginning to lurk. "Vivi, tell me."

"They happened when my belly increased . . . to accommodate your child growing within me."

Chapter 21

Tears stung her eyes and she struggled to hold them back, knowing if she gave in to them, they'd flow until they drowned her. She fought to shove him aside, to scramble out of the bed, but with one powerful arm, he snagged her about the waist, pulled her back down, and covered half her body with his.

"You had my child?"

The wonder in his voice was a punch to her chest that gave freedom to the tears, that prevented her from keeping them dammed. She was devoid of words, could merely nod.

With one hand, he gently cradled her jaw, stroked his thumb over her cheek, gathering the wetness that showed her to be weak. "Where is it?"

"I don't know. They took it from me." The tears gushed forth as the sobs burst free. "Oh, Finn. I never got to hold it. I don't even know if it was a boy or a girl."

The years of wondering and worrying and grieving crashed in on her, caused her to want to curl into a ball, to hide away from him, to hide her shame. But he wasn't having it. He combed his fingers through her hair, over and over, while she bawled, her tears raining down her cheeks and over his chest. Then he moved away from her, and she didn't cry out in protest or call him back. She deserved his rebuff. She hadn't fought hard enough for it, hadn't protected it, hadn't been able to stop them from taking it away.

She was vaguely aware of the sheet and blanket being wrapped around her, barely realizing she was being lifted, carried away, cradled within his arms, her cheek pressed to his bare chest as he lowered himself into a chair, until she found herself curled on his lap. He wore trousers now, and she realized he'd left her in order to partially clothe himself, wondered if without clothing he'd felt as vulnerable as she did.

"Tell me everything," he urged, his voice raw and raspy as though he'd screamed as much as she had when the midwife had swathed the babe and handed it over to her mother.

"I wanted it. Even believing you'd abandoned me, I wanted it." She pulled back until she could hold his wounded gaze. "You must believe that. I was happy when I realized I was with child. Frightened, yes. Terrified, certainly, but happy."

He skimmed the back of his hand along her cheek. "What seventeen-year-old lass wouldn't have been terrified at the prospect of facing so much alone? Ah, Vivi." He closed his eyes. "What a scapegrace I was to never once consider I might have burdened you with a child. Never once in all the time we were apart did it occur to me that I might have given you a bastard. The irony is not lost on me. You would have been forced to give it away—"

"I was going to keep it. I didn't see it as a burden." She pressed her lips to his brow until she felt the fluttering of his lashes against her skin as he opened his eyes, and she could once again hold them, find strength in them. "My parents were furious, of course. Mother wanted to take me to Europe, so no one would notice me increasing, to have me deliver the child there. But I refused to go. It's the one time I won out against them—and I was so smug in my victory. Yet I knew I couldn't leave London. I held out hope, against all odds, that you'd return for me. I didn't know you were in prison." She combed his hair back from his brow. The dark golden locks were a mess from sleep, smashed on one side of his head, the strands sticking out at odd angles on the other, and yet his rumpled state was such a balm to her heart.

"I'd have broken down the iron door, smashed through the wall, had I known you were with child," he said.

It was a nice fantasy, but she knew the truth of it. He'd have not been able to break free, but instead would have simply been tormented more by his incarceration. "I came to Whitechapel, tried to find you, to give you a good piece of my mind for leaving me. Only I didn't know where to look for you. I went to your sister's tavern, but I couldn't bring myself to go inside. I feared her judgment or having her tell me that you'd run off with someone or your whereabouts were none of my business. So I came and I went and I decided I was on my own in this."

"You wouldn't have been alone, Vivi. My family would have stood by you."

"I saw the way they looked at me, Finn, that night at the Mermaid. They didn't like me or trust me. Knowing more about their pasts now, I don't blame them. But I knew I couldn't rely on them. As I began increasing, I stayed in residence."

"What of Thornley? What was he doing during all this time?"

"The duke is much older than me, you see. He wasn't yet ready for marriage, and he wasn't truly courting me. Mother told him I'd returned to the country because I found the Season too overwhelming, wasn't prepared for it. There isn't a particular age when a girl must have her Season. It's whenever her parents deem her ready, so she told him I wasn't. Urged him to give me time. I'm rather certain he merely saw it as an understandable delay, and he was willing to grant me whatever time I required. He didn't pursue me. Instead he engaged in the pursuits of all young men his age, sowing his wild oats—only he could do it guilt free, thinking I wasn't yet ready to wear the mantle of duchess."

She fought not to recall how lonely she'd been, with no friends about, not daring to call on anyone who might discern the truth of her condition. Her only company was Miriam, who tended her. She had the occasional visit from her mother, who simply glared at her and sighed her disappointment. Her days and evenings were spent singing lullabies to the child, reading to it, and taking joy from its movements within her.

"Winter came, and everyone retired to the country, except for Mother and I. Even Father went. He was so angry with me, couldn't stand the sight of me, would always turn away if we crossed paths. I fought so hard not to let it hurt, not to let him know it pained me to be treated so unkindly."

The blanket slipped down from her shoulder, and he lifted it back into place as though he needed any small action to demonstrate he would protect her.

"When did the baby come?" he asked.

"The first of spring. There was still a brisk chill in the air. It was raining, I remember. It was my birthday, although there was no celebration, of course. I've not celebrated it since actually. It was a day wrought with sadness." The tears came again, burning her eyes. "Mother just took it. I tried to stop her, but I was too weak. Through you, I'd learned of the fate that awaits a child born of an unwed mother. I knew how she would rid our family of my shame."

IT WAS AS though she'd taken her rapier to his heart.

Finn needed to hit something, someone. Hard. Over and over, until his knuckles bled, and his bones cracked, and the physical anguish would drown out the pain crushing his heart, the sorrow he heard reflected in her voice, felt in her slight trembling. He wasn't even certain she was aware she was shaking, like a leaf struggling to remain tethered to a branch when the wind was determined to see a different outcome. He fought to keep his body from coiling with the need to strike out, so she wouldn't be aware of the struggle within him. If her father weren't dead, he'd have found a visitor in his rooms later that night.

Placing his hand against her cheek, he tucked her face into the hollow of his shoulder, his throat tightening as he felt the cool dampness left by her tears. "It wasn't your shame, Vivi." He bit down on his back teeth to keep himself from howling at the unfairness of it all. "Why didn't you tell me? That night when we first crossed paths or when we spoke in the nuns' kitchen?"

"I was ashamed. I didn't want you to know how weak I'd been. Although that first night, I was still angry with you, thinking you'd left me. Later when you were no longer looking at me with hate, I couldn't bear the thought of you doing so again."

He hated now, hated himself for not being there for her, even if others had been responsible for keeping him away.

"I couldn't stop her from taking it, and afterward I fell into such despair. I was in a lot of pain after the birthing. A midwife was on hand, but they had to send for a doctor. He gave me laudanum. It not only eased the aches in my body, but in my heart and my soul. So even after I healed physically, I continued to take it. For a year, more, I lived in a fog. Then one day Mother came into my bedchamber and told me she'd had quite enough. It was time for me to stop moping about and get on with my life. I asked her where my child was.

"'If God is merciful, it's dead,' she said. And I went mad and slapped her. So hard, Finn, but it wasn't enough to stop the terrible grief and the anger. That's when I started packing to leave, but instead I was hauled off to the madhouse."

"My God, Vivi." He held her tighter, wanting to block out that for which he'd been responsible, in which he'd had a hand. He'd thought he could have her without consequences. He'd been a young man so full of himself, unwilling to recognize the differences between her place in the world and his.

"I thought I would go truly mad there. I told you what it was like. Then Father died, and she came for me because eyebrows would be raised if I wasn't there to mourn. Mother blamed me for his passing, said my sins were responsible, laid his death at my feet. And I let her. So when I might have left, I stayed, striving to make up for the wickedness, determined to bring honor back to myself and my family. To uphold the contract my father had made, to marry Thornley. But as you're well aware, I wasn't strong enough to do that either."

"Leaving took more courage than staying." He turned her face up until he could look into her eyes. "My brave, brave girl."

He kissed her temple, the corner of her eye, the tip of her nose.

Tears again welled. "Not a day goes by that I don't think of him . . . or her. The shade of his eyes. The color of her hair." She shook her head slightly. "It never occurred to me they'd be so cruel as to take it, and then to hold their silence on the matter as though none of it had ever happened. Between the laudanum and the madhouse, so much time passed that I knew I would never find it, so all I could do was carry on."

He didn't know how she had survived any of it because the ache in his chest was such that he could barely draw in breath.

A knock on the door had them both giving a startled jump.

"Miss Kent?"

Vivi gave a huff of nervous laughter. "Meg. No doubt come to help me prepare for the day."

"Tell her to come back. We're not done here."

With a little nod, she slid off his lap, adjusted the covers around her, and padded from the room. He almost followed. He didn't want to lose sight of her ever again. Instead he shoved himself out of the chair and walked to the window, surprised to discover she wasn't the only one who'd been trembling. So many emotions— anger, grief, hatred for what they'd done to her, to them, might have done to their child. Their child.

Looking out on the street, busy with wagons rolling by, carts being pushed, people strolling, children running, he seemed incapable of focusing on a single thing other than the fact that he had a child. A son or a daughter somewhere. It would be seven by now, if it still lived. How could he care so much for someone he had never met? And yet he did.

He heard the patter of feet, was aware of her coming to stand just behind him, felt the warmth from her skin radiating toward his. "Do you take children from baby farmers because you're searching for ours?" he asked quietly.

"In a way, although I know it's unrealistic to think I'd even recognize the child as ours. So if I saved him or her from an un-happy life, I probably wouldn't even know, although it brings me comfort to think I might. However, all the children I've managed to rescue so far have been younger. Three or four in age. But even then, if the child is blond, like either of us, I think . . . perhaps he or she is ours."

He caught sight of Robin strutting up the walk with a walking stick the Duke of Thornley had given him, decked out in the fine attire the same man had purchased for him, his dark hair flow-ing out from beneath his pint-sized beaver top hat. "My hair was darker when I was younger."

Turning he faced her. "You know I'm going to confront your family."

She nodded. "It'll only increase your frustration. The person who knows the most, my father, is dead. I don't think my brother even knows I gave birth. He was a young buck off gallivanting, sowing his wild oats, and they'd sent him to one of the distant estates to manage it for a while. My mother keeps her lips tightly sealed, knowing her silence is a punishment to me. So what will you do? Strike them? Threaten them? With what? Bodily harm?" She skimmed her hand down his arm. "That's not you."

"I have to do something, Vivi."

"Then help me find more children who are in need of a better home."

He DIDN'T WANT to find more children. He wanted to find *his* child.

He'd left her then because he hadn't known where to put all her revelations, how to categorize them, how to deal with them. Plus there was still much to see to in planning for the evening when they would introduce their club to the ladies of the *ton*. Although at that particular moment, he couldn't seem to work up any enthu-siasm regarding the future of the establishment. He could barely work up any enthusiasm for properly dressing himself.

How had Vivi managed it all these years?

That hurt the most, imagining her going through it all alone. She'd been so young, had barely crossed over the threshold into womanhood, and she'd had to face so much responsibility, so much worry, so much unkindness from her family. What she would have endured from Society would have been much worse had anyone discovered her state. She'd had to set aside all she knew, her friends and acquaintances—

And then to have been locked away in an asylum. Even though she'd told him that part of her story the night they went to the festival, now that he knew the full extent of the agony she'd endured . . . it was all too bloody much!

It didn't even register that he had plowed his hand into the oak wardrobe until the jolting pain of it traveled up his arm. Slamming his eyes closed, he fought for control.

Her father might be dead, her mother silent, her brother ignorant, but by God that didn't mean he wouldn't confront the ones who remained, wouldn't find a way to bring her peace, to bring them both peace.

By the time Meg had finished assisting her in dressing for the day, Lavinia was surprised not to find Finn waiting for her in the office. Instead she found Robin, looking quite dapper, a small replica of a lord if she'd ever seen one.

"Morning, miss. I'm here to run yer errands."

Her gaze shifted over to the invitations stacked on the desk. She couldn't quite find the energy to hand them over to him, to explain where they needed to be delivered.

"Have you seen Mr. Trewlove?"

He shook his head quite forcefully, and she couldn't help but believe that Finn was in his rooms striving to disseminate all she'd confessed that morning. She'd never meant for him to learn the truth, to know how she had failed him and their child. She'd never wanted him to experience the devastating grief of it. She'd had seven years to come to terms with the sorrow, and yet still it lingered. For him, it was fresh and raw. And she didn't know how to lessen the hurt of it.

She looked over at the lad who was waiting so expectantly for her to give him a chore, and suddenly all the running, all the avoiding of her family, seemed unbecoming and cowardly. She was no longer a girl of eighteen, young and naïve. She was perfectly capable of standing up for herself. Hadn't her nightly excursions taught her that? Hadn't her time with Finn shown her that she was different than she'd once been?

She'd told him everything and felt stronger for it. She knew what she needed to do, what she must do. "Tell me, young Robin, would you welcome earning five hundred pounds?"

His dark eyes widened, his mouth dropped open. "Five hundred quid? It'd make me bloody rich, the richest in all of London!"

"Not quite that rich. You'd have to put it away in the bank. You can't spend it all at once."

He scrunched up his face. "I could hide it under me mattress."

"No, it must go in the bank. It'll still be yours, but they'll protect it for you."

He didn't seem to like that notion but eventually he nodded. "Good lad."

She penned a quick note for Finn and left it on his desk. Then she set out to do what she should have done long ago.

Chapter 22

"*L*avinia, are you seriously insisting that this lad found you, brought you here, and is deserving of the reward?" her brother asked incredulously after she'd walked into his library and explained he owed Robin five hundred pounds for bringing her to him as indicated in the handbills.

"Did I not just say that?" It was a little lie. The lad hadn't actually *brought* her, but he had accompanied her in the hansom.

Neville stood behind his desk, appearing somewhat flummoxed. "He can't be more than eight or nine."

"Old enough to git a bird to come with me for some fun," Robin piped up.

Her brother scowled. "What does that even mean? This is ludicrous."

"Simply pay him, Neville, so we can get on with this." If she was going to return to the residence, she wanted someone to benefit from it. She was wearing the navy frock. It made her feel powerful, in control, even if her stomach was trying to tie itself into an assortment of knots.

"But I called off the hounds. I wrote you a letter telling you so. Trewlove was supposed to deliver it to you."

"He did. You let the men go. You didn't cancel the reward."

"They are one and the same."

"No, Neville, they are not. The idiots you hired passed out

handbills, so I was **not** completely free as anyone could have hauled me over here **for the** blunt. And young Robin did."

With a put-upon sigh, Neville sat, opened a drawer, withdrew a leather-bound book, opened it, and began writing.

"Ye're not s'pose to write in books," Robin announced. "The duke says so."

Her brother paused, his pen lifted from the parchment. "You hang about with dukes, do you?"

"Yes, as a matter of fact he does," she said. "Thornley, to be precise."

Neville narrowed his eyes. He was the Earl of Collinsworth now, and everyone referred to him by his title, but she simply couldn't. It reminded her too much of her father. "Have you been hiding out in Whitechapel, then? That's where Thorne believed you to be. I was inclined to believe you asked my driver to take you there to simply throw us off the scent."

"It doesn't matter where I've been. It only matters that I'm here now." To settle her affairs, and if she found herself trapped, Robin knew to scurry back to the Elysium Club and alert Finn as to her whereabouts. She knew nothing would stop him from coming for her, not this time. She jerked her chin toward her brother. "Get it written."

He completed his task, tore the note from the book—

Robin gasped as though he'd just witnessed someone committing murder.

"It's all right," she reassured him. "It's a special book for writing in and tearing paper from."

Neville shoved back his chair none too gently, marched up to Robin, and extended the paper.

Robin, holding his hat and walking stick in one hand as any gentleman might, merely looked up at him and blinked. "Wot ye take me fer? A dimwit? That ain't five hundred quid, guv."

"It's a banknote," Neville said impatiently. "It's worth five hundred quid."

Snatching it from Neville's fingers, she presented it to Robin. "You take it to a bank, and they'll give you the money. We'll do it once I'm done here. Now go find the kitchens and tell the cook that Lady Lavinia said you were to be given some biscuits and milk." She had little doubt he was resourceful enough to make his way through the house, and since the butler had seen the lad arrive with her, she knew they wouldn't toss him out.

With a nod, Robin took the paper from her, placed his hat on his head, and tapped the tip of his walking stick—a lion's head—against the brim. "Thanks, guv. Ye ever need anythink, any errands run, ye let me know."

Then he strutted out.

"Thorne has a walking stick like that, with a lion's head," Neville said, sounding somewhat perplexed by the notion.

"Yes. Robin told me Thorne had given the miniature one to him as a gift." The lad had told her a good deal as they'd journeyed through London. He was quite the magpie once he got going. "I need to have a word with the dowager countess. Do you know where I'll find her?"

"Just like that? You just come in here, demand I pay the lad, and don't offer any explanation as to where you've been or why? We've been worried sick." His tone reflected true concern.

"I wrote you every week to let you know I was well."

"For all I knew, someone could have been forcing you to write the letters."

She gave him a small smile. "Really, you must stop reading those ghastly stories about murders and such." Her brother enjoyed the more gruesome tales.

"We're not going to discuss my reading habits. I've spent more than three months telling people you were ill. I have no doubt most of London believes you to be on your deathbed. If it's any consolation, I've received an abundance of condolences on your poor health. I want an explanation regarding what the devil is going on."

"I'm sorry, Neville, but I told you I had doubts regarding my marrying Thornley. You wouldn't listen. Mother locked me in my room on the night before I was to wed."

Looking down at his polished shoes, he seemed contrite. "Yes, I learned of that later." He lifted his gaze. "What you told that boy about the bank—you're not leaving with him, surely."

"I can't stay. There's so much you don't know, Neville, but I wasn't happy here. This isn't the life I want."

"It is the life to which you were born."

"But that doesn't mean it is the life I must live."

"I don't understand, Lavinia. What the deuce do you want?"

With a long sigh, she held his gaze. "To let go of the past. Now where will I find Mother?"

"In the morning room."

Spinning on her heel, she headed out of the shelf-lined library, keenly aware of her brother following closely behind her, his faint sputtering reaching her ears. There was too much to explain, too much he wouldn't be able to comprehend. He strongly resembled their father and every earl who had come before him and lived by their creed. Honor, duty, and respectability ruled. There was no room within their world for a girl's tender feelings or a woman's determined plans if they didn't involve marrying a lord.

The wide French doors to the morning room were open and she swept through them in the same manner that her mother had once swept out of her bedchamber, a tiny bundle cradled in her arms—with vengeance and righteousness shimmering off her. Her mother sat on the bright yellow brocade sofa, sipping her tea. She did little more than arch an eyebrow at Lavinia.

"Where is my child?" she asked, coming to a halt in front of the low table that provided a barrier between her and the woman who'd given birth to her.

Neville, who had moved past her to be nearer to their mother as though he feared he might need to serve as her protector, staggered to a stop and stared at Lavinia. "Pardon?"

Her mother simply looked at her, her expression passive and

unchanging. Lavinia might have received more of a reaction if she'd asked her if she were expecting it to rain.

"Which baby farmer did you give it to?" she asked determinedly. "What were her initials? M. K. or D. B. or X. X. or some other combination?"

"What the devil are you talking about?" Neville asked, his gaze roaming over her from head to toe as though he were searching for the evidence that a babe had once grown inside her. "What child?"

Slowly, carefully, her mother set her teacup on the saucer, the bone china making only a hint of noise, and set the saucer on the table. "You are ranting, dear, but I am grateful to see you finally have had the good sense to return home."

She took a step forward, her skirt touching the edge of the table. "I want to know to whom you gave it."

"Do you need to spend some more time in the madhouse until these delusions go away?"

"You no longer have any control over me, Mother."

"Don't be absurd. You are five and twenty, not yet wed, with no means to support yourself. Of course I retain control."

"I do have means." The words empowered her, made her feel stronger. "Did you not notice my new frock? You certainly didn't purchase it for me."

"I daresay, it is rather obvious it did not come from Paris."

"Wait, wait," Neville said, stepping nearer to their mother in order to meet Lavinia's gaze more squarely. "Lavinia, are you implying here that you gave birth—"

"Yes, Neville. When I was eighteen."

"How did I not know of this circumstance?"

"Because your father kept you occupied," the countess said with a sniff. "We didn't need you blabbing to Thornley that your sister had gotten herself into such an unconscionable situation, with a commoner of all people."

Her brother dropped down onto the edge of the sofa cushion near where their mother sat, his mouth agape, and she recalled

Sister Theresa's words about looking like a fish. She found strength in that as well, remembering that she had someplace else she could go if need be. Neville blinked, blinked, looked around the room as though struggling to recall how he had come to be there. "You had a child?" he repeated. "You were going to marry Thornley, but you weren't . . ."

He seemed at a loss for words. She, however, was not. "A virgin? Untouched? No, I was not."

"And as Thornley had the poor judgment to marry someone with questionable origins, we shall now have to find someone else for you to wed. Perhaps the Duke of—"

She interrupted the countess. "I'm not here for marriage. I want to know about my child. Was it a boy or a girl?"

"I don't recall."

"How could you forget something like that, Mother?" Neville asked, giving Lavinia a glimmer of hope that perhaps her brother would side with her on this.

"A boy or a girl?" she repeated.

Her mother merely glared.

"To whom did you give it?"

"A servant. However, he is no longer employed here."

"What was his name?"

"I don't recall."

"Was he to take it to a baby farmer?"

"He was. For putting away."

She slammed her eyes closed as the reality and the pain she'd been holding at bay ripped through her. She'd learned that *putting away* was code for killing. Opening her eyes, she stared at the horrid woman sitting on the sofa as though she were innocent of heinous actions. "It was your grandchild."

"It was not. It was a bastard. Born in shame, born in sin. A nonperson."

"How could you have it killed?"

"Killed?" Neville came up off the couch as though it had suddenly caught fire and backed away. "You had it killed?"

"It was necessary in order to protect her and *you*, your position, to ensure it did not return to haunt us. Look at the Duke of Hedley. His bastard lived and is now married to his ward, of all people. The scandal of it. If people learned of what Lavinia had done, the trouble she'd gotten herself into, it could have ruined your prospects for a good marriage as well. I did what needed to be done for your heritage and legacy. Your father not only agreed but wholeheartedly approved."

Shaking his head, Neville looked at Lavinia. "I feel like such a fool. I had no earthly idea you'd gone through all this. What a wretched brother I've been."

She had been a fool as well for holding out hope her mother was not the monster she'd come to suspect she was.

"I'm glad," her mother said. "I'm glad we are rid of it."

Lavinia was barely aware of launching herself at the hideous crone. The slap she'd delivered to her mother years earlier was nothing compared to the one she now delivered with such force it sent the woman flying off the sofa.

HAVING SPENT HIS early years on the streets, Robin had a keen sense when it came to trouble being afoot, so as he neared the kitchens in anticipation of enjoying a warm biscuit, he was acutely aware of the weight of unnatural silence in the hallways leading to his destination. Slowing his step, rising up on his toes, he crept toward the doorway where the aromas of beef juices and oranges wafted out.

Peering inside, he barely made out a dining hall—for the servants, he supposed—those within standing at the table or against the wall, none of them moving, not even appearing to be breathing, their eyes wide and unblinking, their mouths slightly agape. Not that he blamed them. He was familiar with the sight of barely leashed retribution waiting to pounce, and Finn Trewlove wore it as easily as any other man might trousers.

"I find it difficult to believe that not a single one of you knows anything about a child born in this residence and taken out into the night seven years ago. I know damned well the countess herself didn't deliver the babe to a baby farmer, so to which of you did she hand it off in order to see the deed done without getting her own hands dirty?"

If at all possible, the silence increased. Robin thought if one of them whispered it would sound like a shout in the deafening hush.

"Sir, if I might so bold," began a man he recognized as the butler who had greeted him and Miss Kent when they'd first arrived, "the ladies of this residence are above reproach. I believe you're barking up the wrong tree, sir."

"Servants know everything that happens above the stairs, even if they pretend to be ignorant of it. Which one of you is Miriam?" Finn asked, not deeming to even acknowledge the older man.

A young woman with red hair hesitantly raised her hand, wiggling her trembling fingers. "I am, sir."

"The lady's maid? The one who betrayed her?"

"No, sir. I would never—"

"Yet you did. What became of the child?"

The woman glanced around. "Please, sir, not here, not in front of everyone."

"The rest of you, out!" he bellowed.

The remainder of the servants scrambled hastily out of the doorway as though fleeing a fire, causing Robin to have to press himself against the wall to avoid being trampled. While he considered traipsing after them to ensure his own safety and to nick a biscuit, his curiosity was too great, and so he stayed.

FINN HAD COME in through the servants' entrance and immediately taken control of the situation, the staff, and the area below the stairs. After gathering the servants into the room where they shared meals, he demanded to know what they knew of Lady Lavinia's child. Perhaps he should have done more to protect her reputation, but he was beyond caring about that and suspected she was as well. Something greater was at stake.

Yet the servants had remained mute, and he didn't know if it was out of ignorance or loyalty to the family, to the girl who had once lived here.

He would put the maid who now stood before him as being close in age to Vivi. "You told the earl that his daughter planned to run off."

She gave a brisk nod. "She was deserving of better than a commoner."

Although he wondered if it was her own position she'd been more concerned with. Certainly, Vivi would have taken her maidservant with her to the duke's residence, elevating her status among the help. Lady's maid to a duchess was a much loftier title than maid to a commoner's wife. Not that he'd have been able to afford her at the time.

"What do you know of the child's fate?"

"Nothing at all. Her ladyship's mother took it from the bedchamber, and that is the last I saw of it."

"You don't know to whom she gave it?"

The woman shook her head. "But you're quite right. She would have given it to someone, a footman most likely. I haven't a clue regarding which one. Is Lady Lavinia safe? Is my lady well?"

"Crikey, she's here," a young voice said.

Finn swung around to find Robin standing in the doorway. "What the devil are you doing lurking about?"

"The lady brung me. I can show you where she is."

The thought of Vivi in this house without him, how they might hurt her or try to lock her away again, had him trembling. "Take me to her."

Only when they got to the library, it was empty.

"They were here," Robin said. "Her and her brother. He paid me five hundred quid."

He slammed his eyes closed. Of course Vivi would ensure someone benefitted from that scandalous reward. "Help me find her," he ordered, and Robin didn't hesitate to rush out of the room with him and begin peering in others.

Finally, they found her in a bright yellow room, standing over a woman sprawled on the floor, a hand pressed to her jaw, looking up in fear. He assumed it was her mother. Her brother stood nearby, staring at the tableau as though he were lost, trying to discern what action he should take. Finn placed his hand on Robin's shoulder. "Wait for us on the front steps."

With a nod, the lad dashed off, and Lavinia swung around, whether because she'd heard his words or the boy's footsteps, he didn't know, didn't care. The sorrow woven into her features nearly brought him to his knees.

"She had it killed."

The rage and fury that swept through him carried him to her, would have carried him beyond her to the self-righteous bitch who lay there glaring—if his first concern wasn't Vivi. He took her in his arms, pressed her face against his chest.

"Come along," Finn said, his voice low, surprised he was able to make it sound tender when he spoke to Vivi as grief and torment swirled through him. For the loss of a child he'd never known, to the suffering brought upon the woman he loved. "Let's go."

Straightening, dashing the tears from her cheeks, she gave him a tremulous smile and a nod.

The countess pushed herself to her feet then and stood there with fury blazing in her eyes. "You will not take my daughter anywhere."

"Take?" he repeated. "As though she is a possession to be carried about in my pocket? No, I will not *take* her, but if she chooses to come with me, not you, not a horde of servants or constables or the dogs from hell will be enough to stop me from allowing her to leave with me."

"Lavinia, think hard on this because if you leave with this scoundrel, I will never again welcome you back into this residence."

"You heartless bitch, I don't want to be welcomed back into your residence. You took my child. You sent me to a madhouse. You made me feel ashamed when all I did was fall in love. Then when I was still vulnerable, you laid Father's death on me, in an attempt to bend me to your will. And I bent. But no longer. Father didn't die because of my sins. But our child died because of yours. You saw to it that it was murdered. An innocent babe who had done you no harm. You're a horrid, hateful woman. I am done with you."

She separated herself from Finn, and with her spine straight, her shoulders squared, she walked from the room with grace and dignity. He'd never loved her more.

He glanced back at the hideous creature. "May you rot in hell."

"My daughter will join me there for her sins."

"It is not a sin to love." And with that, he strode from the room, quickening his pace once he entered the hallway, until he caught up with Vivi, slipped his arm around her waist, and brought her up protectively against his side. "I'm so sorry, my love."

"I never want to see her again."

"You shall never have to."

"I'd have never believed her to be so cruel."

"Wealth, power, and prestige are not indications of kindness."

Tilting her head up to hold his gaze, she furrowed her brow. "How did you know I was here? My note didn't tell you where I was going."

"I didn't know you were here. Nor did I see your note. I came to speak with the servants, to see if I could learn anything from them before confronting your mother and brother."

"Poor Neville. I fear this morning was a rather unfortunate revelation for him. Somehow they managed to keep everything from him."

They had just reached the foyer when he heard, "Lavinia?"

Stopping, they turned and faced her brother as he scurried from the hallway. "Lavinia, I hardly know what to say," he said as he halted before them.

"I think the countess said it all."

He looked at Finn, gave a slight nod. "Trewlove. We don't seem to meet under the best of circumstances." He turned his attention back to Vivi. "I knew there had been a boy in your youth. It was he, I assume."

"Yes. It's a long story."

"Perhaps you'll share it sometime. Meanwhile, I want you to know I cannot condone what Mother did. I shall be moving her into the dower house posthaste as I cannot inflict her upon my wife, my heir, or any future children."

"Your relationship with her is your business, not mine."

He nodded, darting a glance between Finn and Vivi. "I need you to be aware of the status of your dowry."

"Neville, that dowry will pass on to your daughter as I'm not going to marry some duke—"

"Hear me out."

She gave him an acquiescing nod.

"As you are well aware, the property of Wood's End was placed in a trust to be used as a dowry for the first daughter of an Earl of Collinsworth who married. I've spent considerable time reviewing the terms of the trust and speaking with my solicitor because I had hoped to find a way to sell it to Thornley. It buttresses up against his ancestral estate, and you know how desperately he wanted it."

"Enough to marry a woman he didn't love."

"I think he'd have come to love you eventually." He waved his hand. "But that is neither here nor there now. What is important is that the dowry remains in a trust as it was intended. In spite of everything, and I don't blame you in the least for hating us all at this moment—"

Reaching out, she touched his arm. "I don't hate you."

"I am still struggling with my ignorance on the matter. Had I paid more attention—"

"It wouldn't have made any difference."

"You're kind to say so, but it will be a while before I can accept that. However, I digress. Should you marry, the trust dissolves and the land passes over to your husband. At which point, you—he—could sell it. I know for a fact that Thornley will pay a princely sum for it. It might be enough to see you nicely situated in whatever life you choose. I wish I could offer you more, but I will help where I can."

"I told the countess true. I can make my own way."

"I completely understand your wish to never see her again, but I do hope you will consider not making yourself too scarce when it comes to me and my family."

Finn watched as she hugged her brother. "Thank you, Neville."

When she stepped out of his embrace, the earl looked at Finn. "You will take care of her."

"It will be my pleasure to do so."

"I'm sorry there was not more welcome news."

"Goodbye," she said quietly, and he knew she wasn't yet ready to contemplate all of the unwelcomed news.

They turned for the door.

"Oh, wait," Collinsworth called out. "How did you get here?"

Vivi looked at Finn, then the earl. "A hansom."

"I rode my horse," Finn told him.

"Let me have a carriage brought around. It's the least I can do."

"Thank you," Finn said, thinking her brother wasn't such a bad fellow after all as he escorted Vivi out of the manor.

Robin popped up from where he'd been sitting on the steps and dusted some crumbs from his jacket.

"The cook gave you your biscuit, did she?" Vivi asked, and Finn heard the slight lifting of her mood in her voice. He also realized that's what had brought Robin to the kitchens when he'd been speaking with the servants.

"It was jolly good, miss. Should I fetch us a hansom?"

"No, the earl is sending his carriage around for us."

They waited in silence, there on the portico, with Finn's arm around her holding her close. It seemed there was too much to say, and yet not a single word was adequate for what either of them was feeling. He couldn't help but believe that her grief ran deeper than his. She'd had nine months with the child, feeling it growing inside her, seven years of hoping it was alive, while he'd only just come to know of its existence.

And then had it snatched away.

It wasn't until they were in the carriage, his horse tethered at the back following along, with Robin across from them, and Finn sitting beside her, his arm around her, tucking her in close, that she burrowed against his chest, clutching his lapel with one hand, and let the sorrow have its way with her.

"I'm sorry," she rasped, and he didn't know if she was apologizing for all that had happened or that she no longer had the strength to hold the grief at bay.

"Shh. It's all right." He skimmed his hand over her soft hair, knowing that inside she was so much softer, even as she fought to appear harder. But there was strength in softness, tenderness.

"Why ye be sad, miss?" Robin asked.

"We had a bit of unhappy news," Finn told the lad, making light of the devastating news because he didn't want to upset her more or cause the lad to worry.

"I should have shared half me biscuit with her."

Her laugh was a strangled sound. "Yes, that might have helped," she said.

But it wouldn't have. Only time and distance would ease the ache.

With a sniff, she straightened. He was reaching into his pocket for his handkerchief when Robin produced a piece of linen and held it out to her. "Thank you," she said, wiping the tears from her cheeks.

She glanced at Finn. "Neville gave Robin a banknote, so we need to take him to the bank."

"We'll do it tomorrow."

"I'm rich, guv," the lad crowed.

"Five hundred quid is a lot of blunt. Don't go boasting about it. You don't want someone trying to steal it."

"Right-o. Won't breathe a word of it to a soul."

Still, Finn held out his hand. "Why don't you let me have it for safekeeping?"

He could see the boy thinking about it, but finally he brought it out of his jacket pocket, slightly wrinkled and a little worse for wear, and gave it to him. He winked at the lad. "You come see me tomorrow, and we'll get this matter sorted out."

With a nod, Robin turned his attention to the passing scenery, and Finn wondered if he was contemplating all the things he could do with his newfound wealth. Or if he simply wasn't comfortable staring at a saddened Vivi.

They had the driver stop at the Mermaid and Unicorn first, where young Robin disembarked. Then they carried on. Vivi slumped against him.

"Just a bit longer," he assured her.

She nodded. "It's hard."

"I know, love."

SOMEHOW, SHE MANAGED to keep herself together until they entered her rooms, and then she lost her way, sinking down onto the floor, no strength left to her. "I didn't think I'd ever see it or find it, but I'd always thought that at least it lived."

Great, gulping sobs broke free of her, bringing with her such pain that she didn't know how she'd survive it.

She was aware of him lifting her into his arms and carrying her across the room into the bedchamber. Gently, he placed her on the bed, and she curled into a ball of anguish.

"I hate her. I hate what she did. How could she be so uncaring?"

He didn't answer. She didn't expect him to, because there was no answer that would suffice. Instead he removed her shoes, rubbed his hands over her feet, then moved up to the head of the bed and began removing the pins from her hair. When the strands were combed out over her pillow, he stretched out on the bed and cocooned her within the warmth of his embrace, holding her tightly while she wept, all the while knowing that he had to be hurting as well.

"Horrid woman," she blurted. "I don't know a strong enough word to describe the ugliness of her."

"*Bitch* comes to mind."

Rolling over, she faced him and gazed into those brown eyes. "I should have stopped her. I should have fought harder."

"Vivi, you were a young woman, nearly a child yourself. You'd just gone through childbirth." Tenderly he combed his fingers through her hair. "Do not take responsibility for what she did. You are not to blame. If I'd kept my cock in my trousers—"

"No." She pressed her fingers to his lips. "You can't take the blame either. I just wonder if it will always hurt like this."

"I don't know. I've never hurt like this."

The sobs broke free again, and she wept for dreams lost and a life unlived. She cried for a child she'd never held, never rocked to sleep. A child to whom she'd never whispered, *I love you.*

She cried until there were no tears left, no strength remaining. Then against all odds, she drifted off to sleep.

WHEN SHE AWOKE, he was still holding her close, his gaze on her face, his hand roaming over her hair. The room was not as bright as it had been. The late-afternoon sun was allowing the shadows to creep from the corners.

"You need to eat something," Finn said.

"I'm not hungry."

"Try, for me, lest I worry about you all the more."

A knock sounded on the door, and she rolled her eyes. "Seems you already sent for supper."

"No, wait here. I'll see who it is."

He rolled into a sitting position. She placed her hand on his broad back. "No, I will. What will people think to find you here?"

As she clambered out of bed, she nearly laughed at the thought of worrying over her reputation now. What did it matter when she'd never return to Society? She was done with it for good.

He didn't object, but he did follow her as though he expected her to collapse on the floor again. So much for worrying what the staff might think to find him in her chambers.

She opened the door to find Meg standing there. She bobbed

a quick curtsy. "Sorry to bother you, miss, but there's a gent here looking for a Lady Lavinia. I don't know who that could be, and I can't find Mr. Trewlove to ask him about it, but he's rather insistent that this is where she lives. Mayhaps he's mad."

Finn stepped up behind her. "Have him brought to our office."

Meg's eyes widened, but she had the good sense not to comment on his being there while Lavinia's hair was cascading down her back and her feet were bare. "Yes, sir."

She bobbed another quick curtsy and hurried down the hallway.

Closing the door, Lavinia sighed and faced Finn. "Maybe it's someone who saw the handbill."

He furrowed his brow. "Perhaps, although I'd have thought he'd have just snatched you when you stepped out. Whoever it is, I'll dispatch him quickly enough."

In no mood for visitors, she merely nodded. Tucking his finger beneath her chin, he lifted her mouth to his and placed a gentle kiss there. "Think about what you'd like to eat while I'm gone. Perhaps I'll even cook it for you myself."

"Will it be edible?"

"No promises."

She could hardly fathom that her lips sought to create a smile. As he closed the door behind him, she pressed a hand to the wood. Perhaps he was right, and she would feel better after she ate. Perhaps they both would.

Returning to the bedchamber, she grabbed a brush and began sliding it through her hair. She would wear it loose tonight. She wanted to feel young and free. She wanted—

She heard the door open, and Finn call out, "Vivi!"

She dashed into the front room to find him standing beside a man who looked to be in his mid-thirties.

"He says he serves as a footman in your family's residence and needs to have a word with you."

Cautiously, she approached, trying to remember. Ah, yes, setting plates before her during dinner, carrying packages, stirring a fire. A footman. Tall and dark, matching each one who served within the Collinsworth household. It would not do at all not to be perfect. "James, isn't it?"

He gave her a sad smile. "Yes, m'lady."

"How can I help you?"

"I'm the one to whom your mum gave the babe."

Chapter 23

*S*he staggered back two steps as though a blow had been delivered, might have crumpled to the floor if Finn hadn't immediately reached her, taking her in his arms and steadying her. Her heart was pounding so ferociously that she feared the footman might hear it. But then what did she care what he heard, what he thought of her?

"The one who was tasked with delivering it to a baby farmer?" she asked.

He gave a quick nod and clutched his hat in his hands. "Yes, m'lady."

She wanted to rail at him, to call him all manner of unkind names, but he was a servant who'd merely been following orders. "Do you know if it was a girl or a boy?" she heard herself ask through a roaring in her ears.

"A girl. The prettiest thing you'll ever see."

Only she wouldn't see her—ever. And she wanted to scream with the reality of that.

"Do you remember exactly where you took her?" Finn asked, and for a moment she felt pity for the woman she was fairly certain he intended to confront. The baby farmer who had murdered an innocent.

"Yes, sir. That's why I came." He looked down at the floor, sighed, lifted his gaze to them. "My sister, you see, she tried for nearly a decade to get with child, wanted a bairn of her own so badly. When the duchess put that wee one in my arms, handed me the five quid, told me where I was to deliver her and what I was to say . . . I thought of my sister and all the times I saw her crying . . . and I said to myself, 'Where's the harm? Who will ever know?'"

She felt Finn's arms close more tightly around her. "Are you telling us that you gave the babe to your sister?" she asked, striving not to let the joy take hold until she fully understood all the ramifications of his confession.

He nodded. "Aye." He slid his gaze to Finn, back to her. "I held my silence in the kitchens because I thought no good would come from speaking, and if the duchess discovered what I'd done, I'd lose my post. Then I saw you waiting on the steps—I've seen women at wakes who didn't look as sad as you, m'lady."

She took in a shaky breath as a spark of hope flared. "She's alive."

"Yes. Before I came here, I went to Watford to visit my sister, talk things over with her. Let her know you'd probably be coming, once you knew the truth."

An earl's daughter did not show weakness or tears or any emotion at all in front of staff—ever. But a sob, hideously loud and ugly, broke free and she burrowed her face against Finn's chest.

"I can take you to her," James said. "I thought tomorrow. Give my sister and her husband tonight to get used to the notion of you coming for her daughter."

Her daughter. The words crashed into Lavinia. For seven years the woman had rocked her, sung to her, held her, loved her. Possibly. Likely. Most certainly. Nodding, she was beyond words, beyond speaking as every emotion imaginable rioted through her.

"Can you give us a moment of privacy?" Finn asked.

"Yes, sir. I'll wait in the hallway."

"Go downstairs. Have someone bring you a whisky, on the house."

Out of the corner of her eye, she saw him nod, take a step back toward the door, pause, turn the hat in his hands. "I'm sorry, m'lady, that I didn't say something to you long ago, when you were still living in residence. But I truly thought you didn't want her. Her being born on the wrong side of the blanket and all."

"I don't blame you, James," she said.

Giving her another nod, he quit the room, and she sank onto the sofa. Kneeling before her, Finn took her hands. "She's alive, Finn. We'll get her back. She'll be ours."

"She doesn't know us, Vivi."

"Not now, of course, but tomorrow, tomorrow she will."

"She's been with these people for seven years."

"But she's mine. Ours. She should have never been taken from me."

"Stop and think about this, Vivi. She's their daughter. She calls them 'Mum' and 'Dad.' They love her, and she loves them."

"They don't love her as much as I will! And she doesn't love them as much as she'll love me, love us."

He squeezed her hands. "We can't regain what we've lost."

"You don't understand, Finn. You can't understand because you weren't there." Shoving him aside, she stood and began to pace. "You didn't carry her for nine months. You didn't feel her moving within you. You didn't talk to her because there was no one else to talk with. You didn't share your hopes and dreams."

The memories were cascading through her like a rushing waterfall after heavy rains.

"I was prepared to keep her with me, was planning to do so. I was willing to face being ostracized, gossiped about. I knew no man would have me with an illegitimate child hanging on to my skirts, but I didn't care." She swung around, faced him, her breathing harsh and heavy, her fists balled, while he stood there looking at her as though he didn't know her. "You cannot feel the love I feel for her. You cannot want her as I want her. She doesn't mean to you what she does to me. I've had seven years of thinking about her, wondering—"

"And they've had seven years of loving her," he repeated.

She wanted to beat her fists against his chest, wanted him to know how much she despised him at that moment. She shook her head fiercely. "You simply don't understand."

"That's where you're wrong, Vivi. I was once just like that little girl."

IF THE DAGGERS she'd been shooting at him with her glares had been real, he'd be dead. But his final words seemed to take some of the fight out of her.

"I doubt they've told her that she wasn't born to them," he said.

"We'll explain it kindly and gently."

"No matter what words you use, it will be neither kind nor gentle. We were eight, Gillie seven, when we found out that Ettie Trewlove hadn't given birth to us, that we were brought to her door by someone who didn't want us."

She stepped forward, her hand reaching out imploringly. "But I *want* her. That's the difference, don't you see? I've always wanted her."

"Maybe my mother wanted me. I don't know. My father was the one who delivered me. But my point is that for eight years Ettie Trewlove was my mum. I loved her as my mum. When I learned she didn't give birth to me, my first thought wasn't that I wanted to be with the woman who had. My first thought was that it didn't make a difference. Ettie Trewlove was still my mum. I couldn't love her more if she had brought me into this world. And I'm standing here trying to imagine how I would have felt if someone had knocked on the door and taken me away from her."

"You *can't* know, Finn. You can assume or speculate or imagine, but you can't *know*."

"But I can know, Vivi, because I was taken from her. I was twenty-three, old enough to comprehend I was being taken and why I was being taken, but it didn't ease the hurt. It didn't ease my missing of her. I was a young man, capable of dealing with the loss, to understand, yet still it was difficult and saddening and devastating. I wasn't a child who had to learn how to cope with life's harshness. Robin can't be much older than her, and he still believes in fairies."

"And he still wants his mother to come for him."

"Our daughter doesn't know her mother isn't there."

This beautiful, brave woman looked as though she wanted to scratch out his eyes. "Fine. On this matter we will disagree. I'm going to get my daughter tomorrow. I shall take her to the Sisters of Mercy, and we shall reside there until I can make arrangements for other accommodations. This partnership between us has come to an end. I shall meet with Beckwith and see that the contracts are voided."

"This isn't what I want."

"We don't always get what we want. Now if you'll excuse me, I need to let James know when to be here tomorrow, so we can depart."

With her feet bare and her hair a tangled mess, she walked out, and he let her go because his love could not compete with a dream he feared she'd soon discover was not to be had.

Finn sat at a back table in a shadowed corner at Gillie's pub drinking his beer. He hadn't been in the mood to remain at his club, to chance running into Vivi. Indeed, his mood was foul, as foul as it had ever been. His disappointment great.

He'd thought she'd changed, but tonight she'd been the spoiled daughter of an earl who always got what she wanted—no matter who was hurt in the process. He found himself glad they'd not married years ago, because he wasn't certain they'd have managed to keep each other happy for long.

Aiden was correct. It was folly to love her, but even knowing that, he seemed incapable of shedding her from his heart completely.

"You look like someone kicked your dog."

Glancing up, he couldn't find the strength to work up a smile for his brother Beast. He was the tallest and broadest among them, someone Finn wanted on his side in a fight. Not that he'd be doing any fighting tonight. Or maybe he would. Throwing a few good punches might make him feel better. "I don't have a dog."

Beast nodded toward the chair opposite Finn. Unlike Aiden, he wasn't one to assume his company would be welcome. Finn considered shaking his head, knowing his brother wouldn't take offense. Instead he waved his hand, palm up, over the table in invitation.

Beast dropped into the chair. "Want to talk about it?"

Finn shook his head, then heard himself say, "I just learned today that I have a daughter."

"Christ. You're a father," Beast said slowly as though the words made no sense. "Mum know?"

"You're the first. Keep it to yourself for now."

"I'm not one to blab." Then he grinned. "I'm an uncle. Imagine that. Never thought you'd be the first though. You weren't one for going around poking your stick in the honey pot."

He sighed. "The irony is not lost on me."

"Who's the mum?"

"Vivi."

Beast nodded as though it all made sense, then shook his head as though it didn't. "Aiden told me she was back in your life. But that's only recent." His eyes widened. "Are you telling me this little one is from before?"

Finn took a long swallow of his beer, draining the mug. Didn't object when Beast signaled for two more to be brought over. "Yeah. She's seven, being raised by a family in Watford. I'm to meet her tomorrow." He would go with Vivi because he did want to see the little one.

"That's gotta be hard."

Placing his elbows on the table, he leaned toward his brother.

"I've got all these feelings, Beast, and I don't know what to do with them. Like you said, I'm a father. I have a little girl. I haven't even met her yet, but my heart has expanded to fill my entire chest. I love her that much already. And I'm terrified. I don't know how to ensure I do right by her. How to be the father she needs me to be. God knows none of us had a good example."

"You're a fine man, Finn. You'll know what to do."

"But that's the thing. I don't know. Vivi wants to take her. We had a row about it. She's convinced it's the best thing for her. We don't even know her name, and she's going to take her."

"You don't think she should?"

"This couple—they've loved her for seven years, Beast. They're all she's known. How would you have felt if someone had taken you from Mum when you were seven?"

"I'd have run back to her."

He gave a slow nod, acknowledging he'd have done the same. "Vivi won't listen to me. She wants nothing to do with me anymore actually. I'd begun to think there was a chance for us, but every time I do, something steals her away."

"Fell in love with her again, did you?"

"I never fell out of love with her, but what I was feeling now was stronger, more settled. I can't explain it. The depths of it should have terrified me and instead it brought me peace. Makes no sense, I know. Too much beer already."

"You once loved her as a boy would—when joy was found in fleeting moments of chasing after things, where the chasing was more fun and the capturing disappointing. Now you love her as a man would—when the joy is found in the holding, in finding the permanence, in no longer chasing the happiness because what you've captured at last is the best of all, and you know it'll never be better."

Beast had always had a knack for figuring out people, what they were feeling, the truth behind their lies. Although he didn't usually put his thoughts into so many words.

"Yes, well, apparently I didn't capture what I thought I had, which is the reason that I'm sitting here getting foxed and con-templating doing something truly stupid."

Beast's brow furrowed. "How stupid? What are you going to do precisely?"

"Visit the bugger who fucked my mother."

"Now WHICH ONE are you?" the Earl of Elverton asked, lounging indolently in a large purple velveteen chair in his study, holding an etched tumbler aloft, paying far more attention to the way the light from the flames dancing on the hearth were captured in the amber liquid than to Finn, who stood before him.

He'd not bothered to offer his bastard a drink, not that Finn would have accepted if he had. He wasn't here to socialize. He was here for answers.

However, taking in his surroundings, he couldn't help but wonder if the lord's fine threads had been purchased with Aiden's profits, along with the thick gold rings that adorned three fingers of his left hand, the gold letter opener lying on the desk, the gold statuettes of naked nymphs in various poses of play, and the strumpet who'd been on his arm when he'd walked into the residence. Finn had been in the foyer, standing in the shadows, awaiting his return.

"I'm Finn Trewlove, your bastard, and I'll have a word," he'd announced as he'd stepped out into the light, causing the lightskirt to squeak and the man responsible for his existence to merely scowl.

The earl had instructed the girl to wait for him in his bedchamber and not to disturb the countess while making her way there. His words had made Finn ill. If he was that disrespectful of his wife—to bring his dove here—how badly did he treat his mistresses? Badly enough to take their children from them.

"The second lad you delivered to Ettie Trewlove's door," Finn said.

The older man shook his head. "I don't recall."

He almost identified himself as Aiden's brother but each of the earl's by-blows could fit that description. "The one who was to be transported to Australia. You made an arrangement with Aiden Trewlove. In exchange for using your influence to keep me here you would share in his profits from the Cerberus Club."

"Ah, yes." Finally, he took his gaze from his scotch and focused it on Finn. "Got yourself in trouble with some earl's daughter as I recall. He was not at all pleased with my interference. Lucky for you, he was someone I didn't much fancy, so I took pleasure in proving my power exceeded his. Have you gotten yourself in trouble again? It'll cost more. The whole point in dispatching with my bastards was to avoid the irritation of having to deal with them."

He'd never before met the man or spoken with him, but he was coming to loathe him more than he had. To think of Aiden humbling himself before this maggot to ask a favor of him on Finn's behalf caused his stomach to roil. "Who is my mother?"

Elverton laughed, an ugly, hideous sound, the sort Finn had once heard lads making as they pulled wings off flies. "How the hell should I know? Boy, do you have any idea how many bastards have come into this world because my impressive cock plowed into a woman?"

Fury erupted within Finn, swift and hard, and it was all he could do not to attack the creature sitting there all smug.

"I keep a drawer filled with adverts from baby farmers promoting their services. When a wagtail comes to me in tears, blubbering that she's carrying my child, I hand her a clipping and a pouch of coins and tell her to see to it herself."

He was sickened to know this man had sired him, that he showed such unkindness to promiscuous women who found themselves in trouble. Still he shook his head. "No. *You* delivered me to Ettie Trewlove's door."

Shrugging, he took a sip of scotch, licked his lips. Finn could see none of himself in this toad. "Then perhaps she died so it was left to me to handle what remained. Or perhaps I cared for her a bit and wanted to spare her the humiliation. There were a few I saw to, especially if I didn't think the woman would rid herself of it."

"So you might have taken me from her."

"If it was the only way to ensure I wasn't bothered by the brat."

Finn was barely aware of launching himself across the space separating him from the vile insect. The glass of scotch went flying. Pressing his knee to the man's chest, his shin to his belly, holding him in place, he closed his hands around the man's throat until Elverton was gasping for air and his eyes were bulging from their sockets. They were equal in height, but the earl lived a slovenly life of vice and laziness. He didn't possess Finn's muscles or strength. "Look closely at me, you swine. Do you see no woman from your past in my features?"

The loathsome pig frantically shook his head, and Finn accepted that he was never going to learn anything at all about his mother. What did it matter? Ettie Trewlove was his mum. Perhaps he was simply striving to understand what his daughter might feel when she learned the truth of her parentage.

He gave the earl a shake, watching as his face began to take on a purple hue. "Listen well. You are done taking any more money from Aiden. If I hear differently, I shall take those rings from your fingers after I've separated the pudgy things from your hand."

A gurgling came from the gent who had sired him as he struggled to say something. Finn loosened his hold and bent his ear toward the earl. "Pardon?"

"I'll see . . . you hanged."

Finn gave him a wolfish grin. "Think you that your influence or power is greater than that of either the Dukes of Hedley or Thornley or Mick Trewlove or the entire Trewlove clan? Facing them together, you'd find yourself little more than a gnat against lions."

Shoving hard on the man, Finn released him, straightened, and stepped back. "Your bastards are no longer youths of the streets with no recourse. We can stand on our own, but when family stands with us, we are unstoppable."

Spinning on his heel, Finn began striding from the room, stopped, and glanced back. "Which arm do you favor?"

FINN BROUGHT HIS horse to a halt outside a rather ramshackle house and tethered the gelding to a post, knowing no one in this run-down area of London would dare steal from a Trewlove. He strode up to the door, didn't bother to knock, but simply walked into the residence that had been gutted and rebuilt for the woman who lived here.

"Finn, love," Ettie Trewlove said as she got up from the cozy chair before the fire and approached him.

He bent his head to make it easier for her to press a kiss to his cheek, the way she always greeted him. After visiting with his vile sire, he was in need of a good deal of comfort, of a visit *home*.

"Mum." His voice sounding scratchy and raw, he enfolded her in his embrace, hugging her tightly, welcoming the comforting feel of her arms cocooning him in love.

He held her securely for several long moments before easing back. She patted his cheek affectionately.

"I'd put on the kettle, but you look to be in need of something a bit more bracing. Gillie brought me a fine cognac. I'll pour us each a drop."

Standing there, he watched as she efficiently went to a sideboard and poured more than a drop into two snifters, stirring to life the warm memories of all the times she'd done for him, never expecting anything in return.

He took the glass she offered and sat in the chair opposite the one she took. She lifted her snifter. "Cheers."

They both sipped, studied the amber liquid, waited.

"What troubles you?" she finally asked.

Leaning forward he dug his elbows into his thighs, clasped

the snifter between his hands. "When I was seven, if the woman who'd given birth to me had come for me, had taken me from you, how would you have felt?"

"My heart would have broken, love. Just as it did when you were twenty-three and taken from me."

"But you had other children." Children the footman's sister didn't have.

"Dear Finn. No child replaces another. You're all so different, you see. From the beginning, you were each unique. Mick, he was stubborn, determined to have his way, whether it was the way I held him or fed him—he'd let me know if he didn't like it. And Aiden, there was always the devil in him. But you, the first time I held you, you burrowed against me and I knew you had a tender heart, a protective nature. So the taking of you, even when you were a wee one, would have broken my heart."

"Would you have fought to keep me?"

"That's a question, isn't it? Having given birth to my own children, and having illness snatch three away from me—well, I know that side of things as well, don't I? I'd understand a mother's need to come for her bairn. As long as she loved you proper, I don't know that I'd have the right not to let her take you."

"I have a daughter, Mum."

"Ah, my lovely boy."

He barely had time to stand before her arms were around him, holding him close, as tears burned his eyes. "She was born while I was in prison. I didn't know, Mum. I didn't know I put a babe in Vivi. I thought I knew the price I paid for loving her, and now I'm learning it was so much more costly."

His mum eased him back into the chair, pulled her footstool over, sat on it, and took his hand in her frail one. But still he felt the strength and love in her touch. He took a shuddering breath. "Vivi's back in my life. Our little girl lives with another couple. Vivi wants to take her away from them. I'm trying to understand what she's feeling because it seems so unbelievably cruel to take her from what she's known. I'm afraid it's going to tarnish my love for her."

She rubbed his upper arm. "I don't know the right answer, pet. Sometimes there isn't a right answer. But know this. Had you been taken from me I'd have never stopped loving you, never stopped wondering about what you were up to, never stopped worrying over you."

Chapter 24

*L*avinia had been unable to sleep, too many emotions toying with her through the night keeping her awake. The excitement of being able, at long last, to hold her daughter in her arms was beyond bearing. She had spent hours considering all the various frocks she would have sewn for her, the bonnets she would wear, the toys with which she'd play, the books that would be read to her as she was rocked in her mother's lap. Then like a kaleidoscope pointed toward the sun, the glass turned, and another image came to mind: the sorrow and disappointment easing over Finn's beloved face like shadows covering the land as night fell.

Dressed in the gray, she left her chambers, striving not to fret about the possibility of encountering Finn. She'd cloistered herself in her rooms after their row. She hadn't packed up her remaining frock and gown because she would leave them here, taking nothing with her except for the clothes on her back, once again determined to start over—only this time with her daughter by her side.

She would have simply gone down the stairs but caught sight of Robin sitting with his legs crossed beneath him on the landing outside the office door. She needed to take him to the bank and then there were the errands he was to run for them, delivering the invitations, which she didn't want to think about. She wouldn't be here when all the ladies arrived, wouldn't see the success of the place. Perhaps she would read about it.

"Hello, Robin," she said, heading for the office.

His face brightened, and he nimbly jumped to his feet. "Morning, Miss Kent."

Ruffling his hair, she walked by him and into the office, surprised Finn wasn't yet there. "We'll have to search Mr. Trewlove's desk to see if we can find your bank draft."

"That's not why I'm here."

Turning, she noticed there seemed to be movement in his jacket. He reached inside and pulled out a tiny kitten.

"Ye was so sad yesterdee, I thought this would help." He held the ball of white fur toward her. "He's so small I don't think he'll make a good mouser, but I think he'll be a good snuggler. I tested him last night, sleeping with him and all, and he snuggled right fine."

"Oh." Tears stinging her eyes at his thoughtfulness, she took the offering, smiling as the kitten mewled. "Where did you get him?"

"One of the cats I cares for that keeps the mice away—she had a bunch of babies. She made a loud *meow* when I took the kitten, but Gillie says she'll forget I took it after a while, cuz animals don't keep their babies with them."

"No, I don't suppose they do." Not like people, not like her, who had never been able to forget the infant she'd brought into the world. "I think you might be wrong, though, about his mousing capabilities. He just needs to grow a bit."

"You like him, then?"

"I do indeed, very much."

The lad puffed out his chest, rocked back on his heels, clearly delighted at the notion of pleasing her. She was going to miss him when she left here, although perhaps when she was properly situated she could find errands for him to run.

"What have we here?" Finn asked, standing in the doorway, looking a bit like death warmed over.

"Are you unwell?" she asked.

"Head hurts. Got foxed last night, did something stupid, which caused me to get foxed some more. A kitten?"

She held up the little lad. "Robin thought I was in need of cheering. We must take him to the bank and then"—she waved her hand toward the stack of invitations on her desk—"we have the errands for him to run."

"We'll do the errands tomorrow. What are the arrangements for today?"

She knew he was referring to her going to get their daughter. "I sent a missive to Neville with James yesterday evening instructing my brother to lend him a carriage today. He'll be arriving at eleven."

"All right. I'm going to run young Robin to the bank, see him safely to Gillie's. Don't leave before I return."

His words surprised her. "Are you going with me?"

"If you have no objection."

She shook her head. "You have as much right to be with her as I do."

"All right, then. Come on, Robin, let's go make you a rich lad."

"I'll find a box for the kitten while you're away," she said, feeling a strong need to say something, to convey that she was glad he was coming with her without actually telling him how relieved she was.

He gave a little nod while he ushered Robin from the room. As he disappeared from sight, her heart gave a little lurch. How was it that in acquiring what she'd longed to have for seven years, she felt she was losing so much more?

NOT A WORD was spoken as her brother's carriage carried them to Watford, which only caused her nerves to tauten. Finn and James sat opposite her, both looking as though they were on their way to a funeral. It should be a day of rejoicing, a journey toward happiness, yet worry began to take hold. She wanted to ask James a hundred questions.

What was her daughter's name? What did she look like? What did she like to do? What made her laugh? Did she eat her vegetables?

She'd almost brought the kitten with her, to bring her comfort, to remind her that while Finn might be put out with her, Robin still very much liked her. She rather regretted having not gone to the bank with them. She imagined he'd been quite the young gentleman opening up his account. It would have been placed under Finn's care, Robin being so young, but she knew it was safe with him and he'd guide the lad in how best to make the funds work for him.

The carriage came to a stop in front of a small quaint cottage on the outskirts of the town.

"What does your brother-by-marriage do, James?" Lavinia asked.

"He's a cabinetmaker. Makes a good living at it. Fanny has never had to do without."

"Fanny?"

"My sister."

"Of course." She hadn't thought to ask for any of their names, perhaps because she was hesitant to make them real.

James alighted, then handed her down. Finn followed them out.

She clasped her hands in front of her, suddenly not certain she really wanted to be here, as James opened the gate of the white picket fence.

Finn placed his hand on the small of her back. "I'm here."

She looked up at him, holding his brown gaze, so grateful he was. "I didn't expect to be so nervous."

"She'll adore you."

But did he any longer? She knew she was going against his wishes, but she had little doubt that once he saw their daughter, met her, he'd understand the wisdom of her plans.

With a gentle nudge, he guided her through the gate and up the path. A woman, neither tall nor short, stepped out onto the porch, wringing her hands in front of her. Her brown hair was brought back into a sensible bun. Her dark blue dress showed no wear. Her brown eyes were sad, but her smile was warm. She bobbed a quick curtsy. "Welcome, my lady."

"Miss Kent will do."

"This is m'sister, Fanny Baker," James said, the introductions all out of order. "Fanny, this gent is Mr. Trewlove."

She nodded toward Finn. "Mr. Trewlove."

"You're kind to have us, Mrs. Baker."

The woman merely nodded. "Please, do come in. Angela is playing in the back with her fa—with Mr. Baker."

The front room was as warm and welcoming as the woman, with a fire burning on the hearth and comfortable-looking furniture scattered throughout. Lavinia didn't want to think about the woman holding her daughter on her lap, with a quilt wrapped around her as she read or sang to her on a cold evening.

"Would you care for a cuppa tea?" Mrs. Baker asked.

"No thank you." Her stomach was such a coiled mess she feared she wouldn't be able to hold down the simplest of brews.

"Of course not," the woman said, seemingly embarrassed now that she'd made the offer. "You'll be wanting to meet . . . *her*."

"I'll just wait here," James said, lowering himself into a chair, leaning forward with his forearms on his thighs, his hands clasped, his head bent. A man not too pleased with his role in all this.

Fanny Baker led them through a room with a table that would seat six and on into a kitchen that smelled of fragrant spices. Through a door and into a garden where pansies still bloomed in spite of the colder weather.

And there at the far end, standing beside a man at what appeared to be a makeshift workbench, was a little girl, her blond ringlets blowing in the breeze. Reaching out blindly, Lavinia found Finn's hand, squeezed it. The joy and love that swept through her nearly took her to her knees.

The girl turned, her eyes brightened, and she began running toward them, holding something. "Mam! Mam!"

Lavinia nearly lowered herself to the ground and spread her arms wide, but out of the corner of her eye, she saw Fanny Baker doing the same and had to acknowledge that she wasn't the one to whom the girl was running, wasn't the one she was calling out to. But soon, she would be. Soon they would have moments like this.

The lass was taller than she'd expected her to be, slender, but when she flung herself at the woman greeting her, she nearly caused her to tumble. "Look, Mam! Da taught me to use the hammer." She showed her mother a block of wood with one small nail protruding from it. "I didn't hit my thumb when I wielded it. He taught me a new word, too. *Wield.* That's what you do with a hammer."

Her smile was bright, with a gap in the front where a tooth should have been, her face filled with such joy that Lavinia's chest tightened into a sweet ache.

"Well done, I say," Fanny Baker said. "But we have company. This is Miss Kent and Mr. Trewlove."

The girl looked up at them through huge green eyes. "Hello."

Releasing her hold on Finn, Lavinia knelt. "And you're Angela. What a pretty name."

"I'm named for the angels what brung me."

Aware of Mrs. Baker backing away, Lavinia reached out and skimmed her fingers over the child's hair. "I like your ringlets."

"Mam fixed them special this morning." She scrunched up her face. "But I like my braids better."

How many other things did she prefer—preferences Lavinia would learn with time.

Finn knelt beside her, placing a forearm on his raised thigh, clutching his hands together, and she wondered if he did that to stop himself from reaching for the child, for hugging her close. "You did a smashing job with the nail."

"I'm practicing." Her eyes sparkled. "We're going to build a cottage in the tree."

She pointed toward a huge oak at the back of the garden, and Lavinia wondered when the plans had been made, how many other plans her actions would interrupt. Her daughter grabbed her father's arm—not realizing, of course, that it was her father's arm she held. "Come on, I'll show you," she exclaimed excitedly, as though they couldn't see the tree perfectly fine from here.

Finn glanced over at Lavinia, and she gave a small nod. He unfolded his body, reached down, and drew her to her feet. Then he swung Angela up into his arms and her delighted screech echoed around them. He strode to the tree where Mr. Baker met him and shook his hand, while his daughter began pointing at various branches.

"They've been planning to build the hideaway in the tree for some time now. Joe promised her they'd do it in the spring for her birthday. She likes climbing, is fearless when it comes to heights. That's why she squealed when your man lifted her up. She's happiest up high. Is he her father?"

"Yes. We were very young, not married. I wanted to keep her, but my mother took her from me while I was too weak to stop her."

"She's been a blessing to us. Smart as a whip. Already knows her letters. She likes flowers. Helped me plant the pansies. Occasionally she'll hold a funeral for the blossoms that die. Don't know where she got the notion to do that."

Lavinia thought of the funerals she'd held for her brother's butterfly collection. Were they so very much alike? What other things might they have in common?

"I'm trying to think what else I should tell you, but I suppose you'll figure it all out," Fanny said, her voice trembling slightly. "I'll go pack up—"

There was a catch in her throat. She gave Lavinia her back, and using the hem of her apron, dabbed at her eyes. When she circled back around, she offered a tremulous smile. "Forgive me. The breeze always causes my eyes to water."

This woman was being so brave, striving not to let Lavinia see that she was dying inside, and suddenly she knew that's exactly what the woman was doing—because she had died when she'd begged her mother not to take the baby from her. All the sorrow and grief—a lifetime's worth—had been smashed into those few minutes when she'd watched her child being taken beyond her reach.

"I'll go pack up her things, shall I?" Fanny Baker continued. "I didn't want to do it before you got here. She's a curious one, would have been asking questions, and I don't know that I have the right words. Hopefully you do." She turned—

"No." Lavinia had pushed the word up from the depths of her soul. She met the gaze of the woman staring at her. "We won't be taking her."

Fanny Baker released a great sob, sounded as though she was strangling on the next one trying to keep it from bursting forth, pressed a trembling hand to her mouth as tears welled in her eyes and flowed over onto her cheeks. "I'm sorry. I'm sorry. Forgive me for crying."

Shaking her head, Lavinia drew her daughter's mother into her arms. "It's all right. For seven years, I lived with the guilt of not protecting her. All I wanted was for her to be loved and happy. I can see that she is, more than I ever hoped for."

Fanny eased back, swiped at her damp cheeks. "Thank you, m'lady. Thank you for not taking her."

"Vivi, please. Perhaps you wouldn't mind if I were to be her auntie and came to visit from time to time."

"You'd be most welcomed."

"Thank you." She glanced over to where the child was still nattering, and Finn was smiling. She hoped he'd agree with her decision. Based on his stance the evening before, she was rather certain he would. "I think I need to take a closer look at that tree."

She wandered toward the group, feeling a sense of peace she'd not experienced in eight years, not since the night when she'd made plans to run off with a boy she'd desperately loved. As she neared, Finn turned his attention from their daughter to her, the smile that had been so bright for the lass dwindling, his gaze sobering. She stopped beneath the wide boughs of the tree. "It's time for us to leave. Just you and I."

Warmth seeped into his dark eyes, one corner of his mouth eased up slightly as he threaded his fingers through hers.

"Thank you," Joe Baker said, his voice hoarse with emotions.

"No," she said. "Thank you, Mr. Baker. Thank you for loving her."

He placed his large roughened hand on Angela's small delicate shoulder. "You need to give the nice lady a hug goodbye."

Without any hesitation at all, her daughter raced toward her. Lavinia dropped to her knees as the slender arms were flung around her neck with enthusiasm. Closing her own arms around the slight body, she held her precious child close, inhaling her fragrance of grass and woods, her cheek pressed against a smaller one, not caring one whit that her eyes were filling with tears, rolling down her face, remembering how she had screamed for her mother to let her hold the babe just once . . . just once.

Now at long last, after all these years, she had the embrace she'd longed for.

Angela began to squirm, and Lavinia released her hold, not surprised to find Finn's hands cradling her waist, providing support as she rose to her feet. With gratitude, she took the handkerchief he offered and wiped the lingering tears from her cheeks.

"Did I hurt you?" Angela asked.

"No, sweetheart, you made me all better."

Joe Baker lifted his daughter into his arms. "Say goodbye now."

"Bye."

"Perhaps we can come back to visit sometime," Lavinia told her.

"You can play in my cottage with me," she said, pointing up.

"I'd like that very much."

With her hand clinging to Finn's, she walked away with her heart at once joyous and breaking.

SITTING ACROSS FROM Vivi in the carriage, Finn watched her carefully, striving to get a sense of what she was feeling. He'd asked James to ride atop with the driver because he was rather certain Vivi was in need of some time alone, would not want any witnesses should she fall apart. Instead she merely glanced out the window as if the graying scenery was the most fascinating thing in the world. Rain began pattering on the roof, adding to the somber atmosphere. He'd have to give James a few quid for the inconvenience of being rained on.

"She looks like you," he finally said.

She released a light laugh and glanced over at him. "Funny. I thought she looked like you."

"She has your green eyes."

Her smile was whimsical, as though she couldn't decide whether to be happy or sad. "She does that, but I think she got your height. I was surprised by how tall she is already. For some reason, I expected her to be smaller." She looked down at her gloved hands, clasped so tightly that he suspected the knuckles were turning white within the leather. "I couldn't take her, Finn."

Leaning forward, he placed his hands over hers. "I know. I'm glad."

"Perhaps if she was still a baby who didn't know she was being taken." Tears pooled in her eyes. "But she isn't. She has plans. To build a cottage in a tree. She loves Fanny and Joe Baker, and they love her. That was so obvious. She has roots there. If I had pulled her up, she might have withered."

She shook her head, the tears spilling over onto her cheeks. "I worried for so long that she was with someone who wouldn't care for her or love her as I would, that she was mistreated and miserable, but she has a good life, I think." More tears. She covered her mouth. "But still it was hard to walk away from her, probably the hardest thing I've ever done."

Crossing over, he took her into his arms, held her tight, hated the trembling he felt coming from her. "I know."

"Was it hard for you?"

"It nearly killed me, even knowing you'd made the correct decision, that it was the right thing to do. I didn't expect to love her so much, so quickly." The moment she'd turned and he'd seen her smile, he'd been lost. "I don't know where you found the strength to walk away, but I admire you for it."

"I do want to see her again, often, but not enough to interfere. Although maybe when we've met with success, we can establish a trust for her, help provide for her. If I'm still your partner, that is."

Drawing back, he cupped her cheek, damp and cold with her tears, and stroked his thumb over it. "You are, in all things."

"I'm sorry for everything I said to you last night."

"We've survived worse than ugly words, Vivi." He wanted to kiss her but didn't think now was the time. She was too heartsore, and his emotions were raw as well. "Will you have dinner with me this evening?"

"I'd like that very much."

He tucked her face back into the crook of his shoulder and held her near as they journeyed toward a destination he was beginning to doubt was right for them.

Chapter 25

*H*aving not slept the night before and enduring all the emotional upheaval of the morning, she retired exhausted to her bedchamber after they returned to the club. With Meg's assistance, she removed her clothes, climbed into bed, and rested her head on the pillow. Within a few minutes, the rain pattering on the panes lulled her into sleep.

When she awoke, the room was cast in shadows, night had fallen, and her heart was not as heavy as it might have been. It helped immensely to know her child was well cared for. Hearing the mewling, she got out of bed and lifted the kitten from its box.

"I shall have to give you a name. Mouser, I think. No, that's not right. I shall consult with Robin on the morrow. I'm certain he knows the perfect name for you."

Setting the kitten back into its box, she pulled the sash that rang the bell downstairs. Soon after, Meg joined her and began to help her prepare for dinner. When she was finished, she had the servant carry the cat down to the kitchens to be fed, while she took a few more minutes of quiet to settle herself. She needed to stop looking back, and to begin looking forward. She needed to stop blaming the young girl she'd been for things that had not been her fault, matters that could not be changed. She needed to forgive herself.

With a sigh, she headed for the door. Perhaps the forgiveness would come on the morrow.

Stepping out of her rooms, she saw Finn once again at the landing, arms folded over the railing, glancing out over his domain. She thought she'd never cease to take pleasure from the sight of him. When he glanced over at her, that sensual smile taking possession of his mouth, she thought her chest would forever tighten as her heart swelled with the love she felt for him. She would forever remember the sight of him swinging his daughter into his arms, the moment of bittersweet realization that she couldn't give him his child forever, that he had understood and accepted long before she did that it was an impossibility.

He straightened. "You wore the gown."

Taking the skirt in her hands, she swished it around and gave him a saucy smile. "I thought you might take me waltzing as well."

"I don't have the orchestra on hand tonight, but I can hum."

"That will work."

He tenderly touched his fingers to her cheek. "Are you all right?"

"I will be. Sleeping for a bit helped. How are you?"

"Thinking I might help with the building of a cottage in a tree in the spring."

"You might have to have Angela teach you how to pound a nail into wood."

"We'll see her often, Vivi, I promise."

Of course, she could go see her daughter without him, but it would be more pleasant to have him about. And it was time to turn their attention to other things. "I've thought of a couple of more ladies we can offer memberships to. I'll write out invitations to them before Robin arrives tomorrow to dispatch them."

His smile dwindled, his brow furrowed. "Is it what you really want? To manage this place?"

"It'll provide me with an income, so I can establish homes for children who might otherwise go to baby farmers. And I want to write my articles."

"What if there was another way for you to have an income?"

She shook her head. "I don't understand."

"This business"—he waved his hand through the air as though to encompass all the space between the walls—"this club for ladies was never a dream of mine. I had the notion of it because I thought it might bring you into my world where I could wreak my revenge on you."

She arched a brow. "I see. You wished me ill."

"I did." He didn't appear the least bit contrite. "Although I suspect not as much as you wished ill upon me."

"I cursed your name every night before I went to bed."

"Perhaps you'll curse it tonight as well, but as more of a benediction, in gratitude rather than disappointment, as I pleasure you. But I digress. As I was saying, this was not what I dreamed of before I went to prison, it wasn't what brought me excitement, what spurred me on to work so hard."

"I remember you wanted to have a horse farm. You wanted a place that looked out over London."

He grinned, no doubt pleased she remembered that long ago outing. "I've been thinking about your dream of providing a good home for children. Yes, the success of this place could, in time, make that happen. But there is a more expedient way to bring about your dream and mine."

"What would that be?"

"I've been considering what your brother said before we left him. If you marry, your husband gains land." He wrinkled his brow. "What was it?"

"Wood's End."

"Right. Thornley will purchase it from you at a good price, from what I'm given to understand. You could buy some land outside of London, build a residence with a hundred bedchambers. I'm sure I could talk Mick into giving you a bargain on building it. When it's full, you'll build another. And another. You let women know that their children, born out of wedlock, do not need to be handed over to a baby farmer. You'll have all the children you can love, and you'll be there with them."

"Where will you be?"

"Well, I was hoping you'd be amenable to my raising horses there. You would share in the profits, of course, and with them, you will have funds for the foundling home."

"How are we going to manage this club and a foundling home and breed horses?"

"I have another idea for the club—and it won't require that we be here at all. We'll live in the country."

As though pondering his words, finding it difficult to comprehend, she rubbed her chin. "There's only one little problem with this plan of yours. I would have to find a gent to marry, one who wanted to marry me, a fallen woman."

"Close your eyes."

She did as he bade.

"Open them."

When she did, all she could see was his beloved face, his eyes searching hers.

"You need look no further than this, Vivi. I have loved you from the moment you punched my arm in the stables. I thought I could love you no more than I did, until today when you sacrificed your heart for our little girl." Taking her hand, he lowered himself to one knee. "I don't know if the Fates will be kind enough to let me give you another, but I'll certainly try. Marry me, Vivi."

With her free hand, she brushed the hair back from his brow. "I promised to marry you long ago, Finn. I'm still bound to that vow. You've held my heart since you promised to sing a sweet lullaby to my horse. All you have to do is take me to the church."

Chapter 26

*T*hree weeks later, they married on a Tuesday in a small church with far less pomp and circumstance than she was accustomed, but one far better suited to her new station in life, with only those they considered family gathered around them. Mick and Lady Aslyn, Gillie and Thornley, Aiden, Beast, Fancy, and their mum, Ettie Trewlove. Her brother and his wife joined them. She didn't send word to her mother. She planned to never contact the hateful woman again.

Although Neville did report to her that when her article ran in the *London Gazette* the previous week, their mother had a near apoplectic fit because the piece had reflected Lady Lavinia Kent, sister to the Earl of Collinsworth, as the author. That the *ton* now knew her daughter was intimate with the worst areas of London brought her shame. Neville, however, had applauded her efforts and had assured her that he would be representing her cause in Parliament. In addition, she'd been paid a modest sum for the article and the editor had indicated he'd be receptive to receiving more of her work.

After the wedding ceremony, once she and Finn signed the wedding registry, they traveled in a caravan of fine coaches to Coventry House—the London home to the Duke and Duchess of Thornley—where the solicitor, Mr. Beckwith, awaited them in the duke's library, with a small stack of papers before him.

"The papers for the trust that holds Wood's End to serve as

a dowry," he announced, separating them from the others and turning to a page at the back. "Lord Collinsworth, if you will sign here that the terms have been met . . ."

Neville did so with a great deal of flourish.

"Mr. Trewlove, if you will be so kind to serve as witness."

Mick scrawled his name in the proper place.

After taking back the papers, Mr. Beckwith signed them, set them aside, and picked up others. "The deed to the land, Mr. Trewlove."

Finn took it and promptly passed it off to Thornley.

"Thorne is working on legislation so women won't have to give up their property when they marry," Gillie announced. "It is not at all fair that we are treated as though we are too frail to handle such matters."

Lavinia couldn't help but smile. Her newly acquired sister-by-marriage was anything but frail.

"I'm afraid it's not going to happen as soon as my wife would like," Thorne said. "But I shall not rest until it does happen."

Gillie gave him a quick peck on the cheek.

"I will need you gentlemen to place your signatures here and here to indicate the land now belongs to the Duke of Thornley."

More signing, more witnessing. Then Thornley handed a bank draft over to Finn.

"The agreed-upon amount," the duke said.

With a smile and a wink, Finn showed it to her, then tucked it into his jacket pocket. "We appreciate it, Your Grace."

Beckwith stood and began stuffing everything into his satchel. "I believe that does it, gentlemen." He inclined his head toward her. "And, ladies. It has been a pleasure to sort this all out to your satisfaction. Do call upon me if I can be of further assistance."

"Do stay for breakfast, Beckwith," Thorne said.

"Thank you, Your Grace, but I have another matter to which I must attend."

He shook hands all around before taking his leave.

"I know it's early," Thornley said, "but before we meet up with the others in the dining room, let's have a small celebration, shall we?"

He poured a splash of brandy into six snifters and passed them around. He held his aloft. "To family and friends and everything turning out spectacularly well in the end."

"Hear! Hear!"

Taking a sip of brandy, Lavinia nestled against Finn's side, more content and happy than she'd been in her entire life. What a circuitous route it had been, and yet somehow, in spite of the odds, they'd found their way back to each other.

"Let's go eat," Mick announced. "I'm starving."

As everyone headed for the doors, Finn held her back, holding her gaze. "Are you happy, Vivi?"

"As a lad I know once similarly remarked, 'I'm bloody rich, the richest in all of London.' And it's not because of the draft in your pocket. It's because of you, Finn. I love you so much."

Lifting up on her toes, she kissed him, this man who would forever be the center of her heart.

Breakfast had been a loud boisterous affair, nothing at all like the quiet and sedate meals held in the household in which she'd grown up. The Trewlove siblings teased each other, spoke around, over, and under each other. Only a look or clearing of the throat from Ettie Trewlove would put them in their place. It was obvious they worshipped the woman who had taken them in. Family wasn't about blood, it was about hearts and where they belonged.

"Finn introduced me to a cabinetmaker. A Joe Baker. And he is making the most beautiful shelves for my bookshop," Fancy Trewlove said. Lavinia was only coming to know her. She was so much younger than the others, only seventeen, but she had a dream of owning a bookshop and Mick was giving her one. "I can't wait for you to see them."

"You can't wait for us to help you put the books on them," Aiden said.

"Well, that, too, of course. It goes without saying. I can hardly wait until everything is ready so I can open."

The conversation was carrying on, but Lavinia barely listened. Beneath the table, she squeezed Finn's thigh. "I didn't know you'd done that."

He shrugged. "Figure he could use the extra work. Building a cottage in a tree is not going to be cheap."

"Perhaps Mick will donate the lumber."

He winked at her. "We'll see that he does."

"And if he doesn't, there is bound to be lots of scraps from the building of our house that will suffice."

They'd found some land near Watford. Thornley's payment to them earlier would see it become theirs.

Leaning in, Finn pressed his lips to hers. Suddenly there was a burst of laughter and cheers. She turned away, her face growing warm with embarrassment.

"Knock it off, you lot," Finn called out. "A man should be able to kiss his wife when he wants."

The sound of silver tapping glass had them all quieting, and she looked over to see Thornley standing at the head of the table. "As I'm of the highest rank here, I believe it falls to me to make the toast." He lifted his coupe of champagne, and everyone followed suit. "I once saw marriage as a duty. A ghastly way to view it. I have learned of late that it is a privilege, and that love can make it the closest thing to heaven we might know upon this earth." He looked at his wife and smiled before turning his attention back to those gathered at his table. "Lavinia and Finn, I wish you a long life to enjoy what you have found in each other, troubles that are easily dealt with, and a love that grows ever deeper every day. To your happiness."

"Hear! Hear!"

She brought the coupe to her lips—

"Oh, one last thing."

Stopping, she looked at Thorne, and he lifted his glass a bit higher. "Thank you, my dear Lavinia, for leaving me standing quite alone at the altar."

She laughed. "It was my pleasure, Thorne."

WHEN THE BREAKFAST was over and people retired to the parlor to visit for a bit more, Lavinia made her way down to the kitchens where she found Robin sharing some biscuits and milk with Mouser. She'd wanted the lad here, to feel part of the festivities, even if he was too young to participate in them fully.

She wished it was warmer, so they could go out in the gardens, but winter had arrived, and the winds were blowing fierce and cold. Pulling out a chair, she sat. "I want to thank you for being willing to watch Mouser for me today."

"Ye married now?" Robin asked.

"I am. You may call me Mrs. Trewlove instead of Miss Kent."

"Ye happy about it?"

"Very much so. Finn and I, probably shortly after Christmas, are going to be moving to the country. We're going to have stables and barns. As mice like stables and barns, we're going to need a lot of cats. As you're so very good at taking care of cats, I wondered if you might like to come live with us and see after ours."

He scrunched up his face. "You mean leave Gillie's?"

She'd spoken with both Finn and Gillie about her desire to have Robin live with them, to be the first of the many children they'd welcome into their home. "Yes. You could also help Finn with the horses."

"Will ye have dogs?"

"I suspect so. We're going to have a lot of land, so I imagine we'll have a good many animals. Chickens, ducks, and geese. You could be master of the animals. You'd have your own bedchamber and dine with us."

Biting his lower lip, he shook his head. "Can't. My mum won't know where to find me."

"But you see, Robin, that's the thing about mothers. If they are able, they always know where to find their children. And if they're not, say if they've gone to heaven already, then they can look down on them and they always know where they are. And if your mum goes to Gillie's, well, Gillie can tell her where to find you. And until she does, well, I would be your mother."

"But ye're not a fairy."

"Here's the thing. I still have magic. It's called love. And it can make such a wonderful difference in a life. I love you so very much. We think you'd be happy with us, but you don't have to decide right now. You can think about it. You can wait until you see it, decide then if it's a place where you'd like to live."

He nodded. "I'll think on it."

"Splendid." She smiled at him. "Now, come upstairs. We're going to have some cake."

AIDEN HAD NEVER been one for sweets, so Finn wasn't surprised to find him standing on the terrace after cake was passed out to everyone.

"Bloody cold out here," he said as he went to stand beside his brother.

Aiden held up a glass. "Why do you think I brought whisky with me?"

"Is it helping?"

"No."

He moved nearer, hoping for a bit of warmth. "I appreciate the kindness you've shown Vivi." The kindness being a lack of animosity.

"She's family now. Can't believe you married Finn's Folly."

"She's all I ever wanted, Aiden."

"Well, she doesn't look to be a bad sort."

"High praise indeed."

"And she's definitely a looker."

He grinned. "She is that. I have something for you, from both of us." Reaching into his pocket, he pulled out a leather encased packet and handed it to his brother.

"What's this?"

"The deed to the Elysium Club. We've transferred ownership to you."

Aiden swung around. "Are you bloody mad? I can't take this."

"Nothing for you to take. It's done."

Aiden shoved it toward him. "Undo it."

"If not for you, I'd be on the far side of the world. Even after I finished my sentence, I doubt I'd have ever gotten back here. How many people have you heard about returning? I wouldn't be looking forward to a life with Vivi. She wouldn't be anticipating one with me. We owe you. Take it and be gracious about it."

With a sigh, Aiden tapped the leather against his thigh. "Only if you'll take twenty percent of the profits."

"Twenty? I expected you to offer forty."

Aiden scowled. "I've visited the place. You've got less than a dozen patrons. It's going to require a lot of work on my part. I'll give you thirty."

"We'll take ten."

His brother laughed. "You are the worst bargainer."

"Learned it from my wife."

"Lord help you. Twenty and that's final. Your heart was never really in it."

"No, it wasn't. You're not obligated to make it what I envisioned. Make it a gambling hell for men if you want or for both. Burn it to the ground. It's yours to do with as you will."

Aiden nodded. "What I'm going to do is make it a success. By the way, funny thing. Out of nowhere, our bastard of a sire sent word, through his solicitor, that my debt to him is paid in full, that the terms of our agreement are at an end."

"Maybe his conscience got the better of him."

"I doubt it. Saw him walking about with a splint on his arm. You wouldn't have had anything to do with that, would you?"

"The bone in his forearm snapped like a twig and he squealed like a pig whose tail was tugged on."

Aiden lifted his brows. "It really is broken?"

Finn couldn't help but smile as he nodded. "I took great plea-sure in delivering the blow. He is vile, our sire."

"So you had a word with him?"

"I did. Don't know how you did it before. The man is sickening scum. Knows nothing at all about my mother."

"Probably for the best. I prefer to think he had his way with mine once and then was done with her. Better than thinking she had to put up with him on more than one occasion."

"Guess we'll never know for sure. The one thing I am glad of is that he delivered us both to Ettie Trewlove."

SISTER THERESA WAS surprised when she saw Miss Kent walk into the rear gardens that afternoon wearing white silk and satin. She'd known the marriage was to take place that day; she just hadn't expected to see the bride—and the groom, who was equally as stylishly decked out in black.

"Miss Kent, the last time you came to us wearing a wedding gown you looked much less joyous. I assume I'll not to be taking this gown to sell."

"No, Sister. And now I'm officially Mrs. Trewlove."

"Congratulations to you both. My best wishes on your future happiness."

"We have something for you, Sister," Mr. Trewlove said, and handed her a small package.

Inside were several pound notes.

"We'll be making periodic donations to the home," he told her.

"You're most generous. We appreciate it."

She watched as Mrs. Trewlove tenderly touched her husband's arm. "I'm going to visit with the children for a few minutes before we leave."

"Take as long as you want."

Lifting her skirts, the new wife raced to the area where chil-dren played and dropped to her knees, apparently not caring one whit that she was going to get grass stains on her gown as the little urchins whooped and gathered around her.

Sister Theresa turned back to the man whose hair, like hers when she was younger, was an assorted shade of blond unruly curls. "You are good for her."

"She is even better for me."

"I can't help but believe that we have met before, Mr. Trewlove."

"I don't think so, Sister."

"I doubt there is a person in Whitechapel who hasn't heard of the Trewlove family, who doesn't know that Ettie Trewlove's children are all by-blows."

He arched a brow.

"I find no fault with children born under those circumstances," she rushed to assure him. "I do wonder, however, if you know who sired you."

"I'm not in the habit of speaking his name. To be honest I find him quite vile."

"It wouldn't be the Earl of Elverton, would it?"

He stared at her as though she'd uttered Beelzebub, although for him they might be one in the same.

"You know him?" he asked.

"Our paths crossed some thirty-odd years ago. He could be quite charming when he put his mind to it."

"I can't speak to his charm. I only met him once. It didn't go well for him. I broke his arm."

A godly woman of her position shouldn't take delight in hearing that, but then the earl had once broken her heart. "I hear no remorse in your voice, Mr. Trewlove."

"Because I have none where he is concerned." Then he smiled, and it was that smile that hit her in the solar plexus and confirmed what she'd begun to suspect as she saw more and more of herself reflected in him as they spoke. He was the child taken from her when she had succumbed to sin. Perhaps if she was not now devoted to the church, she'd have told him. But she knew another woman had taken her place as mother within his heart. She would not, could not, compete with Ettie Trewlove.

She looked to where his wife was now standing, saying good-bye to the children. "I think she no longer has a need to run."

"Only into my arms."

She chuckled softly at that. "I have no doubt, Mr. Trewlove, that your mother is incredibly proud of the man you are."

And for the first time in a little over thirty-one years, she knew a true measure of peace.

HE TOOK HER to the Trewlove Hotel. Since he had family connections, he was able to get them a rather lavishly appointed room, with lacy white curtains flowing down from the canopy. As she stepped over the threshold, Lavinia thought perhaps this room had been decorated with newly married couples in mind. It was rather romantic with a low fire burning on the hearth and flickering candles positioned strategically to relegate shadows to the corners while illuminating the large four-poster bed.

She thought she should be nervous on her wedding night. But she was with Finn and had always been comfortable with him, so she merely was anticipating the night—anticipating the remainder of their days and nights together.

"Are you pleased with the room?" her husband asked as he came up behind her and wound his arms around her.

"Extremely so." Spinning around within his embrace, she faced him, lifted her heels off the floor, and nipped at his chin. "Much more pleased to be your wife."

"Eight years ago, I wouldn't have been able to bring you here. While I regret and oft resent the years we were apart, we'd have had a lot more challenges awaiting us. While we will still face challenges, I don't think they'll be as difficult to overcome."

"I'm letting go of the night we were to run away together, Finn. I'm not going to allow my father to haunt me. I'll have naught to do with my mother any longer. I fear she is a toxic woman and I refuse to be poisoned by her. We have your family. We have my brother and his family. We have each other. That's all that matters."

"Too many times to count I have thought of having you as my wife." He pressed a kiss to one corner of her mouth, then to the other. "Lady Lavinia Trewlove."

"I don't want to be addressed as 'lady,' Finn." Except as the moniker she would use in articles and publications. "Mrs. Trewlove will suffice."

"But you are a lady, Vivi. You shouldn't give up what is yours by birth and by right. Our children will benefit from your place in Society."

"Our place. I shan't move about in circles that won't include you. I shall set an example and perhaps there will come a time when even the royals will dare to marry commoners. When someone will be judged by neither the origins or the legitimacy of his birth."

"We're probably a long way off from that happening, sweetheart."

"Perhaps not after they see how happy my commoner has made me." Once more, rising up on her toes, she claimed his mouth as hers. Before the night was done, she intended to claim every aspect of him as hers. She would touch, mark, and brand. Never again would he be taken from her.

He returned her kiss with fervor and a low groan as though he'd never before had the taste of her, could never get enough of tasting her. She savored the dark flavor of his mouth, noting the champagne they'd enjoyed during the wedding breakfast, the whisky with which they'd toasted all their plans finally coming to fruition. The brandy he'd shared with his brothers later as they wished him well before she and Finn had taken their leave.

Tonight was about making a fresh start, of fulfilling a dream they'd both held for years. Of holding and cherishing, of loving and caring for, of building a life that suited them and brought them joy.

With the greatest of care and small steps, he backed her up until her legs hit the bed. All the while she never released the hold she had on his shoulders. Broad shoulders she'd always admired.

Sliding her hands beneath the lapels, she coaxed off his jacket and let it fall to the floor. It was as though she'd fired a gun to signal the start of a race, because their clothes came off hurriedly until they were both standing there with no cloth to separate their skin. When she would have moved to press the length of her body against his, he stalled her with a hand on her ribs, before lowering himself to his knees. He pressed his lips to her navel, then circled it with a series of kisses like a stone being thrown into a pond creating ever widening circles.

"One of our children has grown here." His tone was at once melancholy but awed. "Hopefully another will, and I'll be able to watch you increasing. And you'll have an easier time of it because you won't be forced into hiding to prevent the world from seeing your shame."

"I was never ashamed, Finn. Perhaps a bit embarrassed at having gotten caught doing something I shouldn't have. But I wanted the child, because it was yours. I never considered giving her away. I do worry that I might not be able to give you more children. The birth was hard."

"Vivi, if we have other children, it will be a blessing. And if not, we'll still have hundreds to take care of. We will have children in our lives." After unfolding his body, he cradled her face between his hands. "As I learned growing up, it is not blood that creates a family. It's love. And I do love you. I have for a good bit of my adult life and that will never change. You are what makes me whole."

"Oh, Finn. I love you so much."

As his mouth reclaimed hers, he tumbled her down onto the bed, covering her body with his. She would never tire of the glorious sensations that fluttered through her when they were touching skin to skin, head to toe. She loved every aspect of his fine, honed body. The way his muscles bunched and flowed as he caressed her. The entire length of him. So warm and inviting. Moving beneath her fingertips with incredible purpose. To claim, to hold dear, to pleasure and treasure.

She'd waited a lifetime to become his wife, to be taken fully and completely, with her conscience no longer whispering, *This is a sin.*

She'd wanted him, always wanted him, in her bed, nestled between her thighs. No matter how right it felt, her conscience had never left her alone in order to feel no guilt. But now it was pure bliss. To have and to hold from this day forward.

It was imperative he understand she was free at last to love him, to make love with him. No guilt nagged at her. All the little voices that had always questioned her were now silent.

Because this man was finally hers—heart, body, and soul.

With her hands gliding over his firm muscles, his taut buttocks, his broad shoulders, relishing the outlining of the dips, curves, and flat expanses. Claiming his body as hers.

With words of love and endearments whispered into his ear, she claimed his heart.

Opening herself up to him freely and enthusiastically, she claimed his soul.

This time was different from the ones that had come before because this time was marking a beginning. The beginning of a new life together with no one to interfere. She was relaxed and joyous as she accepted her role in their lives: equal partner. No matter what challenges the future brought, they would face them together.

She was more than ready for him when he slid inside her, filling her with the wonder of him. The gentleness he managed even though she could feel the tenseness in his muscles, his need to conquer and possess. "I love you," she said on a sigh.

He groaned low, his arms quivering as he held himself over her but buried his face against her neck. "I'll never tire of hearing that, Vivi. Or saying it back. I love you more than life."

He withdrew, then thrust forward, once again filling her. Over and over, withdraw, thrust. And each time her muscles closed around him, needing, wanting, to keep him near, within her, where he belonged.

Pressing on his shoulders, she urged him to roll off her. When he did, she immediately straddled him, positioned his cock, and slid down over it, not stopping until he was enveloped to the hilt, taking him deeper than he'd ever been before. His growl reverberated around them, filling her with such joy.

While he kneaded her breasts, she began moving against him, up and down, up and down, never leaving him completely free of her. She watched his face, the increasing hunger in his eyes, as though this journey was what he wanted, what he feared. Losing sight of himself.

But he'd never lose sight of himself as long as he could view himself through her eyes.

Continuing to slide up and down the length of him, she lowered herself enough to press her mouth to his, to be greeted with such welcome that her heart soared. A lifetime spent with this man would never be enough. He moved his hands to her hips, cradling them, guiding her movements, his hips thrusting upward whenever hers dropped down. They were moving in tandem, each enhancing the other's pleasure.

The sensations began spiraling, taking her to the edge, their breathing growing harsher, their movements more frenzied. She teetered at the ledge, and when she jumped from it into the abyss of ecstasy, he followed, their cries mingling, their names on each other's lips a benediction, an affirmation of their love.

And a heart that had once been shattered found itself whole once again.

While the laughter of children echoed from the back gardens, Lavinia walked down the front steps to greet their latest visitors as the carriage came to a halt. A footman opened the door and Angela scrambled out, followed by her mother.

"Auntie Vivi," her daughter cried as she rushed forward and wrapped her arms around her waist. Or tried to. Lavinia had been increasing for several months now.

She skimmed her hands over the child's head, taking care not to mess the two braids that fell on either side of her head and were secured together with a ribbon at the back. "Hello, sweetheart. Are you ready for your lesson?"

Finn had begun teaching her how to ride.

Releasing her hold, she bobbed her head enthusiastically.

"Go on over to the paddock, then." They had more than a dozen horses now. "Your uncle Finn is waiting for you."

As she scampered off, Lavinia greeted Angela's mother by entwining their arms and following the lass they both loved. "Fanny."

"It looks like that little one is going to be coming any day now."

"Not for two more months." She pressed her shoulder to her dearest friend's. "He's doing an awful lot of kicking though, so he might come early."

"What a wonderful thing that must be to feel."

"Perhaps he'll get active while you're here." Fanny had been so joyful when she'd learned that Lavinia was with child. She shared the experience with her as much as possible.

"Good progress being made on the new house," Fanny said.

Lavinia looked toward the framed structure that was being built within the shadow of the residence that had been erected for them two years earlier. It had the hundred bedchambers Finn had promised, as would the second. They'd hired an extensive staff to see after the children. "We're overflowing, so we'll move all the boys into it when we're finished. We'll have a residence for the boys and one for the girls. And over there"—she pointed to vacant land where a few horses grazed—"we're going to build a school. The local children can attend as well."

"What a fine thing that will be. I read your latest article on the merits of not ostracizing women who give birth out of wedlock. You made some persuasive arguments."

"I have a publication coming out next month addressing the inadequate laws when it comes to children." Then she would be speaking to Parliament. She was becoming known for her work as a social reformer.

They came to a stop near Angela, who was standing on a fence railing, her hand slipping up beneath Sophie's forelock as she petted the horse.

Finn wandered over, his stride loose and relaxed. He never failed to take Lavinia's breath. He belonged out here with the horses. They responded to his voice, his touch, as she'd never seen any other equine respond to a person. "How's my favorite girl?" he asked, coming to stand beside Sophie and tweaking Angela's nose.

She giggled. "You always say that."

"Because it's true." He leaned down and winked. "Well, I have two favorite girls. You and Auntie Vivi."

Her green eyes widened. "What if her baby is a girl?"

"Then I'll have three favorite lasses, won't I?"

"And if it's a boy?"

"Two favorite lads."

She wrinkled her nose. "Where's Robin?"

As though her mentioning him summoned him, he came out of the barn, saw her, and raced over. "Angela! Come on! You gotta come see what Uncle Thorne brought us. The biggest tortoise you'll ever see. You can even ride it."

With a squeal, she rushed off, following Robin. The lad had moved in with them, become part of their family. His love of animals astounded her.

"Where did Thorne get a tortoise?" Fanny asked.

"I don't know. The Galapagos or somewhere. Robin can tell you all about it. We have quite a menagerie out behind the barn. We've added an ostrich since you were here. Robin is insisting we need to have a giraffe, but I don't know about that. You should go see them, then come to the garden for some tea."

As Fanny wandered away, Finn climbed over the fence, dropped to the ground, and took Lavinia into his arms.

"You smell like horses, hay, and leather," she said.

"You love it."

Turning in his arms, she wound her arms around his neck. "I love you."

"That's only fair. Because I love you as well."

Lowering his head, he kissed her soundly and deeply. She would never tire of this, tire of the way he made her feel appreciated and loved. While she returned his kiss with equal fervor, horses neighed, children squealed with delight in the distance, and their baby moved within her.

Author's Note

$\mathcal{M}$y dear reader:

I hope you enjoyed Finn and Vivi's story. I will admit I struggled a bit at first with their falling in love so young, with Finn being drawn to Vivi when she was only fifteen. In 1861, the age of consent was thirteen, so I hope his waiting until she was seventeen to kiss her, to declare his feelings, showed his true devotion to her. I made them so young because I've always been fascinated by couples who fall in love at an early age and their love endures through all the years that follow. I also wanted them to be young enough that they had no power to wield and were at the mercy of their elders, who thought they knew what was best.

As for Finn being a horse slaughterer in his youth—it wasn't a romantic occupation, but it was one that was desperately needed in a city that had millions of horses residing within it. King George III was responsible for seeing the practice licensed. *The Horse-World in Victorian London* by W. J. Gordon provided much of my insight into this mysterious, yet fascinating, world.

I am always amazed by the things that draw me in when I'm researching, and how they linger, becoming tiny seeds that find their way into my stories. I look forward to sharing more with you as Ettie Trewlove's remaining bastards journey toward love.

Warmest regards,
Lorraine

Coming next

Aiden's story

A duke's young and above-reproach widow decides she wants to toss off the mantle of respectability to pursue wickedness, and who better to serve as her guide than a man who is an authority on vice and pleasure?

The Duchess in His Bed

Coming September 2019